DREAM MAGIC

Also by Joshua Khan
Shadow Magic
Burning Magic

DREAM MAGIC

JOSHUA KHAN

with illustrations by Ben Hibon

Disney • HYPERION
LOS ANGELES   NEW YORK

Text copyright © 2017 by Joshua Khan

Illustrations copyright © 2017 by Ben Hibon

All rights reserved. Published by Disney • Hyperion, an imprint of Disney Book Group. No part of this book may be reproduced or transmitted in any form or by any means, electronic or mechanical, including photocopying, recording, or by any information storage and retrieval system, without written permission from the publisher. For information address Disney • Hyperion, 125 West End Avenue, New York, New York 10023.

First Hardcover Edition, April 2017

First Paperback Edition, April 2018

1 3 5 7 9 10 8 6 4 2

FAC-025438-18054

Printed in the United States of America

This book is set in Adobe Caslon Pro, Caslon Antique Pro, Charcuterie Ornaments, Cartographer Regular/Fontspring; Solid Antique Roman/Monotype.

Designed by Marci Senders

Library of Congress Cataloging-in-Publication Control Number for Hardcover Edition: 2016013966

ISBN 978-1-4847-3798-9

Visit www.DisneyBooks.com

To my wife and daughters

This thing of darkness I acknowledge mine.

—From *The Tempest,*

by William Shakespeare

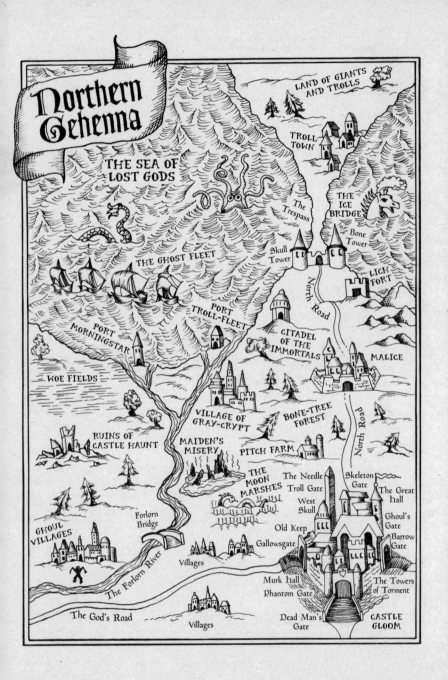

CASTLE GLOOM

Lilith Shadow, the young ruler of Gehenna and a
   necromancer

Ying, the Eagle Knight and member of the Feathered
   Council, a suitor to Lilith

Baron Sable, a nobleman and adviser to Lilith

Tyburn, the executioner

Old Colm, the weapons master

Dr. Byle, a physician

Ongar, the stable master

Lynch Tenebrae, a squire

Wade, a squire

Thorn, a squire

Dott, a servant

Kath, a widow

BONE-TREE FOREST AND MALICE

Pitch, a farmer

Milly, his wife

Alfie and Sam, their sons

Mary, a townswoman

Jared, a village headman

MERRICK'S TRAVELING PLAYERS

Merrick, owner of Merrick's Traveling Players,
  a minstrel of little talent
Weaver, a conjuror
Hurricane and Firestarter, his companions
Gabriel Solar, a refugee from Lumina, fiancé to
  Lilith
Mr. Funny, his fool

THE UNDEAD

Iblis Shadow, once ruler of Gehenna, father of
  Lilith
Old Man Husk, a zombie
Custard, a ghost puppy
Tom, a zombie
Gart and Mal Shade, two ghost brothers

BEASTS AND MONSTERS

Thunder, a warhorse
Zephyr, a gift from Sultan Djinn
Hades, a giant bat
Jewel spiders, a plague . . .

CASTLE GLOOM

ONE

"Trolls did this," said Wade. "Anyone can see that."

"Can they?" Stepping lightly on the snow, Thorn picked his way over the rubble that had once been a farmhouse, his bow ready with an arrow nocked. He breathed slowly and deeply, ignoring the white mist emerging from between his lips, scanning ahead for any troll-sized trouble.

But the closer he got, the more he realized they were too late.

The morning's snowfall sprinkled the broken wooden fence and the trampled chicken coop. A feeble thread of smoke still rose out of the chimney, but there were two other big, fresh holes in the thatched roof.

The rest of the patrol, all squires like him and Wade, were cautiously spreading out across Pitch Farm. Twenty boys, with hands tight around spear shafts and bows, and thickly wrapped in their black wool cloaks and whatever armor that fit. A few searched the shed at the edge of the trees; another was poking his head into an empty dog kennel.

Wade pointed to the roof. "Give me a leg up."

"Get up yourself. It ain't high."

Wade gave a long, theatrical sigh. "I'm not a forest-born sprite like you, Thorn. And how long have you been a squire, exactly?"

Thorn knew where this conversation was going. "Three months."

Wade grinned. "I've been a squire three years, and I was a page for the three before that. Remind me, how old are you?"

"Twelve," Thorn replied sullenly.

"A mere twelve?" Wade stroked the few strands of hair on his chin, which he proudly referred to as his "beard." "I, on the other hand, am thirteen. Face it, *young* Thorn, I'm superior to you in all things, ways, and matters. So you have to do what I say."

"Is that right?"

"Sadly, it is. I don't write the rules. And even if I did, you couldn't read them, could you?"

Thorn glared at his roommate. His lack of progress in learning his letters was a sore point. "You know I'm gonna snip those chin hairs off when you're asleep, don't you?"

Wade laughed. "Anyway, you've got that brutish strength all peasants are famous for, and a flat head for me to rest my foot on as I climb."

"My head is not flat!"

Wade waited. "Well?"

Thorn scowled, then leaned against the wall and cupped his hands. "Just get up there."

Wade grabbed the edge of the low roof and pulled himself up, using Thorn's shoulder—not his head—as an extra step. He grunted with the last push and knocked a slab of snow right onto Thorn. "Oops."

Thorn gritted his teeth and tried to ignore the freezing snow now sliding down his back. "No problem. We peasants are famous not just for our brutish strength but also our hardiness."

Anyway, Wade had no right acting all high-and-mighty. His mom was a fisherwoman, making him just as common as Thorn.

Still, Wade *had* been a squire a long time. He could use a knife and fork properly, vault onto a horse while wearing armor, and read and write more than just his name.

And Wade could *dance*. Really well. Thorn danced like he was trampling spiders. The dancing master had burst into tears and sworn to kill himself if Thorn dared to attend another lesson ever again.

None of this stuff—the jousting, the dancing, the reading and writing—mattered back in his home by Herne's Forest. What mattered there was being able to shoot a bow and trap a rabbit and knowing the difference between wolf tracks and those left by sheep.

But this was Gehenna.

Gehenna. A country of nightmares. How many nights had his parents told him stories about the ghosts and ghouls that walked the bleak moors of the land of darkness?

Stories that turned out to be truer than he could have possibly imagined.

Sometimes Thorn felt really useless and far from home.

Maybe I should have gone back.

He'd had his chance to sail all the way to the village of Stour, with its pond and apple trees and the endless Herne's Forest beyond.

Best you forget about it.

He wasn't going back. He'd run away, and his dad was a wanted man there. Thorn's future—his whole family's future—lay in Gehenna and in service to House Shadow. His parents and five siblings would be here by spring, and like him, they would swap the earthy hues of Herne's Forest for the black of Castle Gloom.

A snowball thwacked his ear.

Wade stood at the ridge of the roof, another ball in his hand. "It wasn't me."

"You're an idiot."

"Quit daydreaming," said Wade, "and get busy."

Thorn inspected the farmhouse. Made of moss-clad stone and with a log pile stacked against it, the building sat half-sunk into the earth. The thick oak door lay shattered at the doorway, its iron hinges torn out of the frame.

Yeah, it does look like trolls.

Thorn ducked under the icicles dangling from the lintel and entered.

He immediately recognized the lingering, moist smell of earth, people, and animals mixed with the bitter bite of smoke. It stung Thorn's nostrils and reddened his eyes. Herbs hanging from the roof beams scented the air with thyme, parsley, and sage. His mom dried hers the same way, and the thought made him homesick.

It took a moment for his eyes to adjust to the gloom. Winter sunlight, pale and watery this early in the morning, lit the interior through the pair of big holes that had been smashed through the roof. Snow drifted in, forming two white patches on the floor.

His family lived in a place a lot like this—crowded, smelly, and full of heart.

The blankets had been tossed off the straw-stuffed mattresses. At the foot of one bed was a rough bundle of old clothes, covered in gray hairs and saturated with the friendly stink of dog. Clay shards from a broken jug crunched under his boots; its spilled water was now a sheet of ice. A crusty loaf sat on the chopping board and, lined up alongside, a row of jars. Thorn picked one up and inspected the dark red sludge within.

Strawberry jam, his favorite. He and his siblings would spend long summer days collecting the berries. They'd be out till dusk and come back only when every basket was overflowing and each face smeared with juice. He put the jar down. It wasn't right, handling other people's stuff. This was someone's home.

He'd met the family on a market day at Castle Gloom. Farmer Pitch; his wife, Milly; and their two boys, Alfie and Sam. They'd brought their scraggy wolfhound, Devil. Thorn remembered showing the boys how to trim its nails, and swapping a jar of flea powder for a basket of apples.

They were just everyday folk who'd lived their lives in accordance with the seasons, like generations before them, probably in this very farmhouse. And now this. He doubted anyone would live here after today.

A bulbous cauldron hung over the smoke-blackened stone fireplace, a ladle dangling from a hook beside it. Thorn laid his hands on the iron.

"Still warm," he muttered, enjoying the heat entering his frozen fingers.

"What did you say?" Wade leaned down through one of the holes in the roof.

Thorn scanned the room one last time. He'd seen all there was to see. "Make room. I'm coming up." He jumped onto the trestle table and clambered out.

The solidly built roof held them and the six-inch snow cover without a problem. Yet something, or someone, had smashed through it as easily as Thorn cracked his morning egg.

"Trolls," said Wade. "Knocked the roof in, reached down, and grabbed them right out of their beds. They'll be in the stew pot by now, poor sods."

"But why didn't they take the animals, too?" asked Thorn. A pig was snuffling at the tree roots. Chickens flapped about as squires tried to catch them.

"They're trolls. Who knows?"

Thorn drilled the last of the snow from his ear. "I thought there was peace between the trolls and Gehenna. Ever since—"

"The Battle of Ice Bridge," finished Wade. "That was years ago, and you're right, we've had no trouble ever since Lord Shadow killed the last troll king."

Thorn, like all squires, knew the story. "They say he summoned a black cloud of howling spirits. It blew over the troll army, and when it moved on, there was nothing but a pile of bones."

Wade sighed. "I'd have given anything to see it. Lord Shadow was the greatest sorcerer in all the New Kingdoms. With him gone, the trolls have regained their courage. They're not scared of his thirteen-year-old daughter."

Thorn smiled to himself. "That's 'cause they don't know Lily."

"What does that mean?" asked Wade suspiciously.

"Nothing." Thorn changed the subject: "What's bringing trolls so deep into Gehenna?"

Wade kicked at some snow. "The ones from the Troll-Teeth Mountains must be getting hungry. They came down here for easier pickings."

Maybe Wade was right; there *had* been reports of attacks on villages at the base of the mountains. Most of the Black Guard was now stationed there, all the way up to Ice Bridge, which left the local patrolling of Gehenna to the squires.

But something bothered him. "These trolls are big, right?"

Wade stared at him. "What sort of dumb question is that? They're huge!"

"So how'd they get all the way down here without anyone seeing them? The Troll-Teeth are hundreds of miles north."

Wade shrugged. "Made their way down through Bone-Tree Forest. Easy enough to sneak down, even if you're the size of a troll."

Thorn gazed at the trees on the other side of the farm. "Maybe in the summer, when the trees are covered in leaves. But look at 'em. All bare now."

"Someone made these holes, and someone took the farmer and his family. And I'll bet you a week of stable cleaning it was trolls."

Snow clouds stretched across the sky, heavy, gray, and promising a blizzard. The wind stung; its freshness scratched Thorn's throat, and he rewrapped his scarf. "It don't make no sense."

Wade fished out a wrinkly apple. He bit out a chunk and handed it over. "You know what your problem is?"

"Having you for a roommate?" Thorn took a bite and handed it back. That was their deal when it came to snacks.

"Ha-ha. How my sides ache with laughter." Wade tapped his brow. "You think too much. Think and think and think. It's not healthy. It leads to a muddled head."

"A muddled head?"

Wade chucked the apple core at one of the squires. "Leave the thinking to those above you, Thorn. Which, in your case, is everyone except the privy cleaner. Just do what you're told, and life will become much easier."

Thorn glowered. "That's how a sheep lives."

"Have you ever seen an unhappy sheep?" Wade spread out his arms. "And isn't this better than slaving away in the stables?"

Thorn nodded. "Them new horses are hard work. Never met animals that need so much pampering."

"That's because they're not just any old horses, but fire breeds," said Wade, his eyes shining. "The stallion, Zephyr—made out of desert wind, he is. Lady Shadow's been receiving some fine gifts these last few months."

Thorn scowled. "Sultan Djinn gave her them horses because she helped save his son, K'leef. Do you know who else helped save him?"

"Oh, here we go again . . ." muttered Wade, eyes rolling.

"Me. Right here," said Thorn. "And what did I get? A box of mangoes."

"Anyway . . ." Wade continued, clearly not bothered by the injustice Thorn had suffered. "Have you seen the clockwork aviary the Eagle Knight gave her? Not a single spell required! All mechanical, they tell me. You wind the birds up with a golden key."

"Yeah, I've seen it, and heard it," said Thorn sourly. "And Captain Moray sent her a chest of black pearls."

Wade jabbed Thorn in the ribs. "And how do you know what's in Lady Shadow's jewelry box?"

"Dott told me."

"You've got one of Lady Shadow's maids spying for you?" Wade tutted. "You have to aim lower, Thorn. Way lower. Lady Shadow's not for the likes of us."

"It's not like that!" Thorn snapped.

Wade just didn't get it. How could he? Wade wasn't the one who'd helped Lily back when her uncle had tried to overthrow her. Wade hadn't been there when she'd—

"Thorn, look at this," said Wade from behind him.

"I'm not interested."

"Thorn, *look*."

Reluctantly, Thorn turned around and looked.

Wade had his hands wrapped around a sword hilt. Its blade was half-buried in the roof. "It's stuck." He braced his legs on either side and *pulled*.

It did not budge.

"How did it get up here?" asked Wade.

"Let me try and use some of my brutish strength." Thorn gripped it with two hands and pushed it forward. Then pulled it back. Inch by inch he worked it loose, then looser still. "Just a bit more . . ."

There was a sharp *crack*, and the sword tore free.

Wade stared at the sword, then the hole in the roof. "Maybe Pitch had it for protection? Grabbed it as he was pulled up?"

Thorn hefted the weapon in front of him. The blade was bright and the edge razor sharp. "Too good a sword for a farmer. Would have cost him a year's labor, at least."

"What are you two trolls playing at? Get down here!"

The shout shook more snow off the roof, and Old Colm stood below them, glaring. "Are you deaf as well as stupid? I said get down! Now!"

The one-legged weapons master wore a grimace. His heavy crossbow, Heartbreaker, rested on his broad shoulders. "What have you got? Show me."

Thorn and Wade slid down the slope and handed him the sword. "Found this, Master Colm. Sticking in the roof."

Old Colm inspected the blade. "This is from the forge of Castle Gloom."

"Really?" asked Thorn.

Old Colm scowled at him. "Four eyes between the pair of you, and not one of them works. Look at the maker's mark. The hammer and crescent."

Thorn saw it, just where the blade joined the hilt. Every sword and piece of armor from Castle Gloom had that mark. How could he have missed it?

Old Colm tucked the weapon into his belt. "Got the same mark on my pewter. Not that the likes of you eat off anything but clay."

Wade winked at Thorn. Everyone knew how proud Old Colm was of his pewter dining set, a gift from the previous Lord Shadow. A squire polished it every evening, and Thorn's turn had come last Sunday. Eight spoons, four knives, and four forks, along with ten plates, six cups, and a mug deep enough to hold two pints of ale. By the time he'd finished, every piece had shone brighter than silver.

Old Colm scratched his wooden leg, something he did when he was thinking. "Troll, go help catch the chickens."

"Me, Master?" asked Wade.

"Of course you! That's what I said, wasn't it? Now go grab some feathers before they all run off into the forest!" He turned to Thorn. "You, follow me."

Old Colm taught the squires how to shoot, how to wrestle, and how to fight with sword, ax, staff, and anything else that came to hand. He was as mean as a wounded boar. But right now he just looked like an old, tired man as they crossed the farmyard. His eyes were on the horizon, his thoughts roaming even further. "A bad business."

"What do you think happened?" Thorn asked.

"What else? Trolls."

That was Old Colm, through and through. If it was too wet, trolls. If it was too dry, trolls. Too windy, too calm, too deep, too shallow, too much of this and too little of that, all the fault of trolls.

Still, I suppose having your leg torn off by one might make you a little bitter.

"Then where are their footprints?" said Thorn.

"It's snowing. It's covered their tracks."

"No. We have ogres in Herne's Forest, smaller than your trolls but just as heavy. Their prints go in deep; it takes more snowfall than this to cover them."

"How do you know? The trolls could have been here days ago."

"Hearth fire's still warm. Someone was tending it not twelve hours ago," said Thorn. "They attacked last night, and whoever they are, they ain't trolls."

"You ever met a troll, troll?"

Thorn met Old Colm's hard stare. "Yeah, I know the one who—"

"I don't mean *her*," Old Colm interrupted. "A *real* troll, one taller than that hovel over there, with teeth made of stone, and fists that could flatten a bull. I've seen one rip a tree out of the ground, roots and all. I've seen them, fought them, killed them for more years than you can count, and I don't need a troll like you telling me about trolls."

Thorn couldn't keep his mouth shut. "But something ain't right. Where's the dog?"

"Dog?"

Thorn nodded toward the empty kennel. "Devil. Their wolfhound."

"Your point?"

"If it *was* trolls, Devil would have heard them coming. It was sleeping in the farmhouse; our dog does the same when it's cold out. A squirrel steps on our roof, and he's up, barking. No way a canny old mutt like Devil would sleep through a troll attack. It would have warned Pitch and his family way in advance."

Thorn snapped his fingers. He knew what else was wrong. "And their ax is missing, too. There's a log pile, so Pitch must have one. If he's like any farmer I know, he would have his ax resting up against the door. My dad does. First thing you grab when there's trouble. If it's not here, he's still got it with him."

"You found any human footprints?"

Thorn gestured at the squires spread across the farm. "After they've been all over? Forget it."

Old Colm peered out into the forest. "So you think the family is still out there? That they made a run for it?"

"Let me look."

"They could be anywhere. Bone-Tree Forest's a big place."

"I'll have help."

Thorn whistled and summoned a monster.

TWO

A hellish shriek pierced the quiet dawn air, driving terrified birds from their roosts. The sky darkened as massive black wings spread across the sky. They beat slowly and steadily, whipping up swirling clouds of snow as the creature descended. Sword-long ivory fangs shone wetly in his maw, and his claws flexed as the beast settled himself on a nearby boulder. The thick fur covering him glistened with ice drops, as though he'd been coated with diamonds. He spread out his wings, spanning over fifty feet in width, before refolding them around his body. It was a thing straight out of nightmare, a giant vampire bat. A monster.

Thorn's monster.

"Is Hades getting bigger?" asked Old Colm.

Thorn stroked the beast's fur, brushing off the worst of the ice. He smiled as he gazed upon Hades. He wasn't actually his pet. Monsters couldn't be owned.

Hades burped. Thorn put his hand against Hades's belly. It rumbled, and Hades twisted uncomfortably. "Bellyache?" asked Thorn.

Hades bristled and didn't meet Thorn's gaze.

"Open your mouth."

Hades didn't.

"Open up."

Hades burped again. This time it was a deep, long, throat-shaking belch exhaling the foulest smell this side of the grave.

Thorn tugged a bloody strand of gunk from between Hades's teeth.

"This is wool." He shook the gory thread in front of the bat's beady black eyes. "Like what you find on sheep. Makes me wonder where the rest of that sheep might be."

Hades's growling stomach answered *that* question.

"That's gonna come out of my pay, Hades!" said Thorn. "And that's the third one this week!"

Hades leaned down so they were eye to eye, or eye to jaw. He opened his mouth wide and slowly, making sure Thorn got a good look at the lethal fangs.

"Oh, am I supposed to be scared?" Thorn folded his arms across his chest. "Why would anyone be scared of a fat bat like you?"

Hades snapped his jaws shut.

"Yeah, I said fat. What with all those extra snacks you've been having, it's a miracle you can get your toes off the ground."

Hades spread out his wings and jerked them once. The wind blast knocked Thorn down.

Thorn got up and brushed the snow off him like it didn't matter. "I'm selling you to the next zoo that comes trundling past. Just wait and see if I don't."

Hades snorted skeptically.

Thorn grinned. How could he live without this bat?

Old Colm scratched Hades under the chin. "Where's the saddle?"

"He doesn't like it." Thorn grabbed one ear to pull Hades down and himself up. "So it's his job to make sure I don't fall off."

Bat and boy worked together. Hades rolled his shoulders to make things more comfortable for Thorn, and in return, Thorn let Hades take the lead. The bat knew what Thorn wanted, so there was no need for him to pull him this way or that.

But Thorn had to be careful. If Hades didn't like something he did, the old monster wouldn't hesitate to fling him off, even if they were five hundred feet aboveground.

Thorn rubbed the frosty bristles between Hades's big ears. Was there anything better in the world than this?

But even up here, he wasn't free of his thoughts about Lily.

Wade didn't understand; none of them did. To them, she was *Lady Lilith Shadow*, as high from them as the moon was from the earth.

Thorn had first met her when she was a lonely nobody, like him. It wasn't right to wish for those days back, but he missed the old Lily.

He hardly ever saw her now. She was too busy ruling Gehenna, and he was usually too busy fetching oats for the horses. So he'd made her something, something that would remind her he was still around. Thorn had taken a piece of oak—twisted, knotted, and beautiful—and spent every evening over the last two months carving her a brooch. He'd worked hard at sculpting the Shadow family seal, a pair of entwined crescent moons, and decorating it with vines and oak leaves, motifs from his old home.

Then he'd seen the gift that the Eagle Knight, Ying, had brought Lily: a mechanical aviary. Thorn had stood at the back with the other squires, behind the nobles and knights and important guests, when Lily had taken the golden key and wound the device. How could such a tiny key work a whole tree? The tree was so tall it almost reached the gargoyles perched on top of the Great Hall, and its ivory branches fanned out all the way across the courtyard. The feathers on the clockwork birds were made of beaten gold, and their eyes were precious gems. In the torchlight, the whole tree seemed sprinkled with stars.

Then the birds had sung, their songs rising together in perfect harmony that no living choir could match. Even Tyburn had smiled. Thorn hadn't thought there was a spell in all the world that could make the executioner smile.

Why would Lily look at Thorn's stupid carving when she had such a marvel? How could a simple piece of wood compete with beautiful fire horses?

Thorn had chucked the brooch into the fireplace.

Wade wanted him to aim lower in his choice of friends, but how could he? As someone who could fly among the clouds, how could Thorn aim for anything lower than the moon?

Hades growled. He could sense Thorn's moods. This moping wasn't going to help them find Pitch and his family.

A pale sun balanced on the horizon, casting a dull, shadowless light over the landscape.

Which way had they run? Did they have a shelter out here? Or had they fled blindly, stumbling through the night with no idea of direction?

The Caves of the Hag lay eastward. Plenty of hiding places there.

Hades shook his head.

"Not the caves? Why not?"

Hades didn't explain. He merely glided away to the west. Each wingbeat was slow and easy as Hades skimmed the treetops.

"There," said Thorn. He nudged the bat with his right knee. "I saw something."

Hades wheeled around. For such a huge beast, he moved almost as sharply as a sparrow.

The birch trees bent in the wind Hades created as he settled himself in a small clearing. Thorn slid off his back and sank shin deep into the snow. He plowed through it, heading to where he'd seen it. He wasn't even sure what *it* was, just that it had been wrong.

Thorn clambered over a frost-painted boulder. And found Farmer Pitch and his wife, Milly.

It looked as if they were lying on a red rug, but it was bloodied snow. The farmer still held his ax. Wounds covered their backs—long gashes that had gone through flesh and bone.

It was a woeful sight, but it didn't sicken Thorn. He'd hunted and killed animals for food since the day he could draw a bowstring. Growing up in Herne's Forest made you familiar with all the ways a creature can die. Poisonous berries. A fall that splits a skull. A wound that goes bad. He'd seen sheep torn apart by wolves. He'd twisted a few chicken necks, shot deer, and trapped squirrels and rabbits. Were dead people much different? They bruised. They bled. They broke. All in the same ways.

But where were the boys?

He heard something to his left.

There, a thicket. A perfect hiding place for a couple of small children.

Thorn dropped to his hands and knees and crawled into the foliage. "Hello? Sam? Alfie? You in there?"

He was answered by a growl.

"Devil?"

The big, shaggy wolfhound faced him, his ears flat and his lips peeled back in a snarl. His haunches quivered, either to flee or attack, Thorn wasn't sure which.

Thorn, already crouching, held out his palm. "Easy, boy. You know me."

The dog's bloodshot eyes glared and spittle dangled from his jaw.

"It's all right, Devil," said Thorn, speaking as calmly as he could, despite his heart hammering against his ribs.

Devil took a step forward, grinding his teeth.

He's gone rabid.

It wasn't disease but fear. Something had thrown the dog into madness.

Devil launched himself at Thorn. He hit hard, and both tumbled back. Thorn threw his arm across his own neck just as Devil bit down. The fangs sank through the stiff leather of Thorn's sleeve and pricked the arm beneath.

Hades shrieked and tore at the dense lattice of branches, snapping furiously at Devil but unable to reach.

Thorn tried to push the dog off, but Devil clamped his jaws tighter into the flesh. Thorn cried out as blood ran down his arm. He fumbled for his dagger.

A bowstring thrummed. Devil yelped and collapsed. The fearful fire in his eyes died with a hissing breath.

Thorn lay under the big dog, feeling the animal's blood pour out of a puncture wound in his ribs. His fingers touched the shaft of a quarrel buried more than halfway in.

Old Colm crouched at the edge of the thicket, Heartbreaker resting on his good knee and a second quarrel already loaded. "You'd better not be dead, boy. I'm not crawling in there to get you."

Thorn shoved Devil off. Then, wearily, he dragged himself back out the mass of twigs. "Thanks. You got here quick."

"You've a talent for getting into trouble, so I had to keep an eye on you." Old Colm tapped the snow off his peg leg. "And I can move on this if I have to." He looked over at the dead dog. "I thought you Herne folk had a way with animals."

Thorn grimaced. The pain was really kicking in. "We do. Usually."

"So we've got the parents." Old Colm gestured at the two dead bodies. "What about the boys?"

"Vanished." Thorn stood up and regretted it instantly, as a spell of dizziness struck him. He sucked in the fresh air and tried to clear his head. Blood dripped down his sleeve and decorated the snow with small crimson petals.

He stared at the farmer and his wife. What had happened here? There was a way of finding out secrets even from the dead. "Lily will want to see these two."

"Will she?" asked Old Colm suspiciously. He inspected the pair. "And why's that? Seems to me we should bury them here, by their homes."

Thorn bit his lip. He knew Old Colm had heard the rumors regarding Lily.

She was his friend, and while only thirteen, she *was* the ruler of Gehenna. She was also a Shadow, descended from the lord of darkness himself, the greatest necromancer the world had ever known.

And death itself could not stop a Shadow. . . .

THREE

"**W**elcome to Castle Gloom," said Lily.

"*Huurugg muur.*"

Lily frowned. "I'm sorry, I didn't quite get that."

Matilda Husk stepped closer and curtseyed. "My father-in-law said, 'Thank you,' m'lady."

"Ah. Good."

Lily looked at the zombie.

The zombie looked at Lily. Sort of.

One eye had rolled into the back of his skull. The other was so loose he had to jerk his head constantly to get it to stare in the right direction.

The flagstones glistened with frost in the Great Hall, which was empty but for the four of them—Lily, the zombie, Matilda, and Baron Sable. Not enough to bother lighting the fires for. Still, Lily wished she'd arranged a brazier. She huddled deeper into her Mantle of Sorrows, wishing the cloak were made of fur instead of the collected miseries of her ancestors. The memories made it heavy, but they didn't make it warm. She sighed and watched a cloud of breath rise up and float toward the pair before her.

Matilda Husk wore a homemade wool shawl over her shoulders and was awestruck, eyes wide enough to fall from their sockets.

Lily knew the look well. Everyone bore it the first time they entered the Great Hall. The room was immense in all directions, raised not by masons and craftsmen but by magic.

No breath emerged from the zombie as he waited patiently in nothing but a pair of patchy pants and a threadbare shroud. Ice sparkled on his skin, and icicles dangled from his gray beard. They tinkled whenever he moved his head.

Baron Sable shuffled his feet, bored. He stood beside her high-backed chair, and his gaze drifted to the small table with the wine jug.

Lily leaned forward. "I'm sorry, Mrs. Husk, but what is it your father-in-law wants?"

"*Rhhurr. Rhurrr. Urrgh,*" said the zombie.

Matilda Husk elbowed him. "Where's your respect, Dad? It's 'm'lady.'"

The zombie, Old Man Husk, bowed. His spine creaked like dry twigs, and Lily feared something would snap and leave him stuck doubled over.

"*Rrruur. Mrrruuy,*" said the zombie.

The woman curtseyed. "He wants his old room back, m'lady." She glanced sideways, her eyes narrowed. "I've told him Henry and his new wife have that room now. After all, he's been dead eight months."

"*Rrurrh! Rrrhur! Mhhuur rruhh!*" said the zombie, waving his hands about.

"It's no use complaining, Dad!" snapped Matilda. "And we built you such a lovely tomb, too, one you know we couldn't really afford! Marble all the way from the quarries of Sparklestone. Cost us half our herd."

"*Rrurr. Huur.*"

The country was suffering a plague of undead. On Halloween, the dead had come out of their graves, no one knew how many. First the people had been happy, overjoyed at seeing loved ones they'd lost and missed. Families had thrown resurrection parties.

Now, three months later, things were different. The undead had come home to roost and would not leave. There was no place for them here alongside the living.

And not just zombies, but also ghosts and even the odd vampire. One bloodsucker had caused a lot of trouble in Witch Glade, draining livestock and attacking villagers until he'd been captured and reburied, this time with an iron stake through his chest. The price of garlic had tripled.

Lily gazed at the hour candle, wishing it would burn faster. She wanted this over and done with so she could get down to the castle library. A shiver of excitement went through her at the thought. Her studies were going well, learning what it really meant to belong to House Shadow. . . .

Bats flitted overhead. As they crept out of the cracks and vents within the high walls and roamed in search of dinner, their shadows decorated the ceiling with living patterns. They were all wild, and free to come and go as they pleased.

Unlike Lily.

She should have gone with Thorn and the other squires. Off on some adventure in Bone-Tree Forest. Troll hunting, wasn't it?

Not for the first time, Lily's thoughts drifted on bat wings to Thorn. She never got to see him anymore. He was always running off on some errand for Old Colm or Tyburn. She could order him to attend her, but that might make him think . . .

What? That she liked him? A lot? Maybe too much?

He'd forgotten her. That was it. She'd seen him, out in the courtyard of Dead Man's Gate, with his bow and his friends. She'd watched him tend to Hades—magnificent, beautiful, and deadly Hades—taking him off for evening flights and brushing his fur and picking bits of sheep from his fangs. Did he know she paid for extra livestock for the bat?

You are Lady Shadow. You should not concern yourself with commoners.

Why had it fallen quiet?

They were all waiting. Old Man Husk had even gotten both of his eyes to face her.

"Er . . . carry on," said Lily.

"We can't look after him at home, m'lady." Matilda leaned closer. "And have you smelled him? Dad always had a problem with his bowels, but now? The chickens won't lay eggs. They're that upset."

"Hhhurr murr duurh, muurr murr murr drrur."

"What did he say?" asked Lily.

Matilda scowled. "He said he may be dead, but he's not deaf." She turned sharply to face her father. "You'd know how much you stank if your nose hadn't fallen off!"

"Enough. I have made my decision." Lily stood up. "Mrs. Husk, your father-in-law is family, alive or dead . . . or undead. He deserves a home."

"But, m'lady, we've no room. Henry and his missus are—"

Lily raised her hand and Matilda Husk fell silent. "I have not finished. You say the tomb is marble?"

"As black as night, m'lady. We even sold our prize bull."

"Castle Gloom is in need of black marble. I shall send my masons to dismantle your tomb now that you have no use for it. We shall settle on a fair price, Mrs. Husk. Use that money to build a room for your father-in-law."

"But when, m'lady?"

"In the spring. Until then Mr. Husk will be a guest of Castle Gloom. Go see Dr. Byle. He will take your father to Old Keep." Lily paused and reached into her pocket. "Oh, and when you see the doctor, please give him these. Perhaps he'll know who they belong to." She handed over two squishy balls.

Matilda frowned. "What are these? Dumplings?"

"Eyes. I found them in the Tower of Torment this morning. They must have fallen out of one of the servants."

Mrs. Husk and her father-in-law left, and Lily sank back into her chair. "Is that it for today?"

Baron Sable smoothed down his immense mustache before he helped himself to a drink. "You still haven't replied to the Eagle Knight. And he'll be off soon. He did give you that clockwork tree."

"That's four marriage proposals, isn't it?" said Lily. "It's nice to think I'm so popular."

"Five. Your engagement to Gabriel Solar was never officially annulled."

Gabriel Solar. The pompous, arrogant, bullying, and entirely moronic heir apparent to the kingdom of Lumina. To think she'd come *that* close to marrying one of the lords of light.

Lily remembered the Solars' visit. All dressed in white and strutting about Castle Gloom as though they owned the place. It made her skin crawl, thinking how they'd planned to put windows into the Great Hall. Windows! What would her ancestors have thought of her if she'd ever let sunlight into Castle Gloom?

Ying was nothing like the loathsome Gabriel. He was dashing, handsome, and by all accounts a brave and well-renowned warrior, despite being only sixteen. He was a prince of the Feathered Council, and she knew he was a good match; their marriage would join Gehenna with the kingdom of Lu Feng, far to the east. But still . . .

"I will not marry Ying for a tree. Draft a polite letter. When will these proposals cease?"

"When you *do* marry," said the baron. "And you'll not want to marry into the wind clans. Children there are born with feathers, so I hear. No, you'll want someone closer to home. I have four sons, by the way."

"*Four*, Baron?"

He tapped his head. "Ah, did I say four? I meant three, of course. All handsome lads, thanks to their mother."

He wasn't wrong. His sons were much admired by the ladies in the court. Dark-skinned with almond, sultry eyes, and thick, curly black locks, all inherited from their desert-born mother. "Baroness Suriya is very beautiful," Lily said.

"She's given me fine sons, no mistake." He held up three fingers. "Asmodeus, the eldest, and a charming idiot. Then there's Baal. A brave idiot and owner of the second-best mustache in Gehenna." The baron brightened. "And finally, I've got Caliban. Sweet-natured, and as loyal as a pup. Also an idiot. Take whichever one you want."

"That's meant to be an offer? A choice of three idiots?"

"You don't want a clever husband, m'lady. You are the ruler of Gehenna, and thrones rarely fit two backsides, if you don't mind me being so bold. Clever men have ambitions. You want someone who looks good on a horse and spends his days hunting and out of your hair. My boys will do you right, or I'll be having words with them."

"I'll ponder your kind offer, Baron." Lily blew a stray ribbon of hair out from her eyes. "Can I go now?"

"It's your country, m'lady," answered the baron wryly. "But there is the business of the trolls."

"You sure they're back?"

"And bolder than ever. I've got the Black Guard spread out across the north, but I need more men. I'll have to take the older squires, too, with your permission?"

"Of course, but are you sure that's really necessary?"

"It's not just small raiding parties—those we can handle," continued the baron. "But we've lost two patrols, and villages near Ice Bridge have been ransacked. It's bad. And there's word that the trolls have a new king, and that's the worst news of all."

"Why?"

"The troll clans hate one another. You've got the Stonehammers fighting the Rockheads, the Flintfists against the Longtusks. Most of their time is spent battling each other. But a troll king will be bigger and meaner than all the rest, and he'll force them to join up. I saw a troll army on the march once. I have no wish to see it again." Baron sighed. "They know we're weak."

"Weak?"

"There's no other way to put it. We've never had a big army. Our fleet's just a collection of fishing boats. Gehenna's strength has always been in its magic. Lord Iblis, your noble father, kept the trolls in check because they were terrified of his sorcery. Without such magic to protect our borders, the next few years will be . . . challenging."

Magic. The solution was always magic.

But it was the problem, too.

"How about the zombies?" asked Lily. "We have hundreds of them now. Gehenna used to have a zombie battalion once."

"The Immortals?" Sable shook his head. "Have you had a look at what we've got? Most of them just shuffle about, moaning. Their brains have rotted all the way through. You just wait and see: Old Man Husk will be the same in a few months. The only thing we could use them for is target practice."

Lily tried to speak with as nonchalant an air as she could manage. "Other sorcerers could protect Gehenna just as well as my father. Then no one would dare call me . . . I mean, *us*, weak."

Baron Sable twisted the tips of his mustache tightly. He was angry but trying hard to control it. "There are no other sorcerers," he declared, daring her to contradict him. "All we have are rumors. Rumors that are best ignored."

Lily sank a little deeper. "Yes, quite. Rumors best ignored."

But the rumors were rising faster than the dead.

Rumors of new, powerful magic.

Of sorcery greater than that of her father, Lord Iblis Shadow.

The baron broke the uncomfortable silence with a clap of his hands. "A troupe of players arrived this morning. With your leave, we could have them perform tonight, during the Eagle Knight's farewell feast."

"They're touring this late in the year?" Travel through Gehenna was hard work during the winter. "Do what you think best. I have other business to attend to."

"In the Shadow Library, I suppose?"

Lily stopped. "What of it?"

"People talk. You shouldn't go down there. It's not right."

"You forget your place, Baron. It is not your position to tell me what I should or should not do."

"It's my position to protect Gehenna," said the baron, eyes cold and hard. "From threats both without and within. You could bring ruin—"

"Enough, Baron. I understand your concern."

"But, m'lady, you need to—"

"Enough!" Lily shouted.

The shadows around Lily lurched forward. Their mangled forms twisted across the cold floor, stretching out long, throttling fingers toward the terrified baron—

"Enough," Lily repeated, quietly this time. The shadows retreated, reluctantly, to haunt the hall beyond the flickering light.

She'd lost her temper. She mustn't allow that to happen. It could be dangerous.

More than dangerous.

Lily smiled at the baron, pretending nothing had happened. "Just the wind upsetting the candle flame," she said. "A sudden breeze. You get them in the hall. Lots of gaps in the old walls."

The baron, ashen-faced, wiped his brow. "A breeze, as you say."

She shouldn't have frightened him like that. The Sables were the most loyal family she had. "I know you mean well."

"Your welfare, and Gehenna's, is always my greatest concern." He wrapped his hand around his sword hilt. That didn't stop it from shaking.

There's that look again.

Sable knew what she was doing in the library. And others in Castle Gloom were wondering about it.

The answer was simple. And obvious.

Lily was learning magic.

FOUR

L ily pushed the Skeleton Key into the lock and gave it a firm twist.
The vast doors before her rumbled as they *unpeeled*. Demons,
frozen into the iron, twisted away into the cracks within the walls. Lily
knew that if she tried to open the door without the key, they would leap
out from their metal prison and devour her. She put the key safely back
into her pocket.

Lily clapped. Balls of soft moonlight floated out of the darkness and
unveiled the Shadow Library.

Oh, yes.

The glowing orbs bobbed around her as she walked into the heart of
the chamber, stopping in the circle of Princes, like she always did.

The gigantic statues still terrified her a little. Each stood seventy feet
tall, their heads wreathed in the darkness of the unlit ceiling vault. The six
legendary princes who'd brought magic into the world and founded the
great houses of magic. Her ancestors.

Djinn, the master of fire.

Coral, lord of the seas.

Typhoon, ruler of the endless winds.

Herne, the antler-headed sorcerer who commanded the earth and the beasts.

Solar, the great shining one.

And Solar's twin, Prince Shadow. The first and greatest of the lords of darkness, and the founder of her family. Phantoms, ghosts, and skeletons lurked in the folds of his black marble robes. Lily touched the prince's big toe for good luck. The toe shone from centuries of other sorcerers following the same superstitious tradition.

She had a few hours before tonight's feast and didn't want to waste them. She removed the Mantle of Sorrows and hung it over a chair.

A series of short, high-pitched yaps echoed from down one of the countless rows of shelves. A small figure came bouncing over, wagging its stubby tail.

"Custard!" Lily knelt down and patted her lap. "So this is where you've been hiding."

The black-and-white puppy scampered up and dove straight at her. And straight *through* her. He tumbled, catching his ears with his little legs, then sprang up again, none the worse for wear.

"Silly dog." Lily grinned. He still didn't understand what he was.

"I'd expected you earlier, Lily." The voice radiated out of a patch of mist near a table.

"I'm sorry, Father. There've been some . . . unforeseen events."

The haze condensed to create a face, a body, limbs, and flowing robes, and the ghost of Lord Iblis Shadow formed into a defined shape. But there was no color, no life; it was a person made of memories and wishes. Like all ghosts.

But when the ghost smiled, with the corners of his lips only slightly raised and his head tilted as if he was being ironic, Lily saw her father again: real, whole, alive.

"Zombies?" he asked.

"Isn't it always?"

"You did tear open the Veil, Lily," said Iblis. "There were going to be consequences."

The Veil. Lily had spent weeks studying it, the barrier between the land of the living and the realm of restless spirits, the Twilight.

"It's not like I did it on purpose," she replied. "I did it to escape . . . you know."

"Pan," said Iblis. "My brother and my murderer."

The chill in his voice made the temperature drop. Lily wrapped her arms around her, a little cold and a little afraid. "I don't want to talk about it."

About how her uncle, Pandemonium Shadow, the man who'd practically raised her because her parents had always been busy ruling, turned out to be a traitor and assassin. He'd used stolen magic to kill her parents and her brother in a plot to take over Gehenna. He had almost killed Lily, too, during the Halloween Ball. But she'd defeated him with her own magic and the timely help of Thorn.

Lily knew that Baron Sable and the other nobles thought she should have executed Pan and stuck his head on a spike up on Lamentation Hill. In a last-minute act of mercy, she had stayed Tyburn's ax, deciding instead to banish her uncle forever.

Lily shook herself back to the present. It really was cold in here. "But I read that the Veil heals itself."

Iblis nodded. "Eventually. But many hundreds of spirits fled back into the living world that night." He drifted closer. "Myself included."

"Why not Mother and Dante? I want to see them, too, Father."

"The Twilight is a place for *restless* spirits, Lily. Salome and Dante are at peace, in a realm far beyond one even I can reach. Would you deny them that?"

No, but that didn't mean she didn't still ache inside. Lily wiped her eyes. "And now we have all these undead on the loose. Mainly zombies, though."

"The spirits of recently dead people cross the Veil more easily, and most of those will still have bodies, hence the overabundance of zombies," Iblis explained. "But the decaying body and brain offer the spirit a poor home. It may be familiar, but it is damaged. My . . . physical body was destroyed, so I could only return as a ghost." He paused thoughtfully. Was he remembering his violent death? Lily hoped that moment was a faint memory. Iblis smiled at her, and it was both glad and sad. "We ghosts maintain our memories and identities better, but we're more limited in other ways. For instance, we're trapped in one location."

"It's not just people, Father," added Lily. "The butcher at Deepgrave wants compensation. His sheep carcasses climbed down from the counter and wandered off. He says half the village has turned vegetarian."

"Interesting. Animals rarely have strong enough spirits to linger after death."

Custard yapped.

Iblis scratched the ghost puppy's ears. "Oh, you have spirit in abundance. It's no surprise you came back." He turned to Lily. "Powerful magic was unleashed that night, by you."

"Me?"

"You are a necromancer. The dead are yours to command. You just need to learn how."

Lily looked down at Custard. "Roll over."

Custard stuck his tongue out and stayed on all four paws.

"Roll over," she repeated more firmly.

Custard didn't.

"Obviously it'll take practice," said Iblis. "Your specialty may lie elsewhere. The magic of darkness is not just limited to the undead. You can already manipulate shadows, and there are the realms of sleep and dreaming, as well as control over the moon and the creatures of the night. You have a lifetime of study ahead, Lily." He gestured to a pile of scrolls. "But since you have a pressing issue, let us start with the undead. Lucifer Shadow commanded hundreds of zombies and skeletons. Those are his spells. We shall read them together."

Lily gestured toward her cloak. "The Mantle could help. It makes my magic stronger."

Iblis scowled. "And how do you feel after you've used it?"

Lily paused. She'd first used its powers when fighting her uncle. Afterward, she had felt . . . "Tired. It weighed me down, as if it were made of lead."

"The weight of the Mantle did not change. It sapped your strength, as sorrows do." He approached the strange cloak.

The Mantle of Sorrows fluttered, and tendrils spilled out to wrap themselves around him. "Be wary of this treasure, Lily. Every ruler of House Shadow has worn it, and the cloth has absorbed some of the wearer's power, as a shirt takes on the scent of its owner. In times of need, the Mantle will augment the power you already have, but it will steal much more in return. Then you are more vulnerable to any . . . aftereffects caused by excessive magic use."

"You used it in the Battle of Ice Bridge, didn't you?"

"We would never have won otherwise. But afterward I developed a terrible thirst, and not for wine." He ran his tongue across his teeth. "It was hard to rid myself of the craving, and I never wore the Mantle after that."

Lily changed the subject. "Let's get back to the zombies." She picked up a scroll. It was in Old Gehennish, and the ink had faded. "We have over five hundred here now. They're living in Old Keep, but we're running out of room. I have no idea what to do with them."

Iblis tapped his forehead. "What you need is brains."

"I'm studying every night, Father. Learning magic isn't easy."

"No. Fresh brains. Feed the zombies some, and they'll be able to handle more."

Lily shook her head. "We tried that on an earlier batch. Fed them some sheep brains. They started eating grass and bleating. It was odd."

"Human brains, not sheep," said the ghost. "I know a man in Gallowsgate who can supply them. No questions asked."

Was that a joke? It was hard to tell with ghosts.

"My reputation is bad enough without getting involved with brain robbery, Father."

Custard yapped and jumped up onto the table. He ran up and down, scurrying through the piles of scrolls and open spell books, not stirring a single page.

"No one takes me seriously. They just see a girl playing at being a grown-up." She stopped by a marble bust of old Lord Malfeus Shadow and picked a cobweb from between his fangs. "My own nobles think I'm a joke. Count Tenebrae is late with his taxes, *again*. He owes Castle Gloom over fifty sacks of flour and a herd of cows. You know what he sent me instead? Dolls." Lily flushed with shame as she remembered the package arriving. "Baron Sable wanted to go and burn his castle down. Maybe I should send Tyburn? When he's back?" Her executioner had ways of keeping rebellious nobles in line.

"Send him flowers. A dozen black roses from the Night Garden," suggested her father.

"Flowers? How will that get him to cough up what he owes?"

"Lazarus Shadow planted the roses. He used his victims for compost. And most of his victims were—"

Lily grinned wickedly. "From House Tenebrae."

Iblis touched her hand. Lily felt a cold breeze, but that was all. "I never wanted this for you, Lily. Rulership was meant to be your brother's burden."

"It would be easier if you could be with me, in the Great Hall."

The ghost sighed. "I'm stuck down here. You know that."

"There has to be a way. Custard's a ghost—"

Custard growled.

"You *are*," said Lily, giving him her sternest look, "whether you like it or not." She shook her head. Silly dog. "Custard's a . . . the same as you, and he roams all over the castle."

Iblis picked up the puppy. "Custard was at home in every nook and cranny. I was most at home here. I spent too many hours among these scrolls and books when I should have been with you, Dante, and your mother. I've been given another chance, and the irony is not lost to me that this place is now the whole of my kingdom. One of paper and dust. It's something I deeply regret, but we dead can do nothing about our regrets."

Lily wished she could find some way of bringing her father out of the Shadow Library, not just to help her but also to share her life, see what she was up to. See how Gehenna was changing.

"Which reminds me. I have something for you." Iblis glided over to a nearby shelf.

The library wasn't all books and scrolls. It was a junkyard of magical objects, some real, most fake, collected by the Shadows over many centuries. Swords and armor, crowns and wands, and hundreds of other items lay scattered over tables and stacked in corners, blanketed with dust.

Iblis summoned a black lacquered box from one of the shelves. It floated, led by his fingers, to rest on the table. "Look inside."

Lily wiped the lid with her sleeve, then slid it open.

She found some letters, wrinkled and yellowed, wrapped in a black ribbon. A few small trinkets cluttered the bottom, including an old quill and some coins from other kingdoms.

"There's a ring in there," said Iblis. "You can't miss it."

Lily rummaged around until she spotted a large, chunky ring made of obsidian, bearing the twin crescent moon seal of their house. She held it up to examine it. "Is it magical?"

"No, not at all. It's just a small thing. I carved it for your mother when I first met her. Once we were married, it was replaced by finer jewelry. It ended up in here, with other forgotten things. I came across the box yesterday and thought the ring would suit you."

"What are these letters?" She recognized her father's handwriting, but some were written by others, their strokes unfamiliar.

"Just personal correspondence. They must have meant something to me once. I don't remember now." He took the box and put it back on the shelf.

Lily slipped the ring onto her left forefinger, turning her hand this way and that to see how it caught the light. The symbol was crude, but she liked that. "Thank you."

"Now let us begin. The baron delayed you long enough."

"He tried to stop me from coming. Sable knows, Father. They all do," she said. "Why are they all so afraid of women using magic?"

"Legend has it that the Six Princes laid a curse on women sorcerers," said Iblis. "There have been many stories of women using magic through the ages, and a terrible doom swiftly following. The Poison Sea was caused by the granddaughter of Prince Coral."

"In her war against her brother," added Lily. "Anyway, how could a curse last this long, even if it were true? The Six Princes existed thousands of years ago."

"They were the greatest sorcerers the world has ever known, Lily. No one knows the full extent of their powers. So much of their history is now just legend, much of it contradictory." Iblis looked around the crowded shelves.

"And what do you think, Father?"

"What do I think? I think the trouble could stem from the simplest thing: lack of education."

Lily cocked an eyebrow. "On whose part?"

"Consider that women sorcerers have rarely had anyone to teach them because of the penalty if caught doing so."

"Death by burning," said Lily.

"Yes. So women have had to learn magic in a haphazard fashion.

Which leads to the greater likelihood of something going wrong, wouldn't you agree?"

"That does make sense."

"You have relied on raw emotion and desire to fuel your magic. Those are very powerful, but they are uncontrolled." Iblis spread out his hands. "You summoned Custard. You entered the Twilight; you defeated Pan. And all without a single lesson. But that is the danger, too. No one has taught you to temper it. If you don't learn how to moderate your powers, disaster will strike, sooner or later."

Lily winced slightly. "And people will say it was because of the Princes' curse."

Iblis nodded. "Most likely. So, before we get to Lucifer's spells, let us do a control exercise." Iblis waved the moon orbs closer to him, to illuminate an object on the table. "Look at this."

"It's a dead mouse."

"The *skeleton* of a dead mouse," he corrected.

The pile of bones could fit in her palm. The ribs were no thicker than grass blades, and the skull was smaller than her thumb. It was curled up, skull resting on its folded forepaws and tail wrapped all the way around.

"Beautiful, don't you think?" said Iblis.

"In its own way, yes." But perhaps it was a beauty only someone brought up in Castle Gloom could appreciate.

"Make it move."

"I don't know how. I haven't studied that spell."

The ghost gestured at the endless rows of books. "These writings will help you become a necromancer, but they are nothing without the ability to create with your mind. Imagination is the fuel of magic." He caressed the bones with a fingernail. "Magic is an art, like music, or dancing. Sometimes the best way to learn is just by doing it."

"But *how?*"

"Use your imagination. Think about how a mouse moves. Think about how its joints are assembled. How the claws clink upon stone. How the tail twitches. Then give it a little push, just a small breath to remind it of what it was like to be alive and able to do such things. The bones will remember."

Lily sat down and placed her palms flat on the table, on either side of the skeleton.

Right. How do you start up a mouse?

What about cheese? Great big yellow wheels of cheese stacked on top of each other, towering high in their stinking, odorous glory?

Or perhaps she could awaken it with a dose of fear. With a stalking, hungry cat, moving paw by silent paw toward it.

Lily hunched over it, squeezing her shoulder blades into each other. She tensed herself, like a mouse preparing to flee. A trickle of excitement, or power, passed down her spine to an imaginary tail. Lily concentrated on moving each joint, right to the tip.

The mouse's tail twitched.

FIVE

The skull raised itself off its forepaws and looked about.

Custard stared. He edged closer and lowered his head to sniff the skeleton.

The mouse tested its legs. Lily felt its uncertainty. True enough, it wobbled and collapsed into a trembling pile of bones.

"Give it another try," urged her father.

Lily's brow creased as she focused. The mouse untangled itself, first its tail and then one foot after another. It stumbled, then grew more confident and soon darted across the table, Custard yapping and chasing after it. The mouse wove between the piles of books until it leaped onto a stack and looked at Lily, tail flicking back and forth.

Could she make it stand up, like a person? Do a little dance? Its body was hers to control any way she liked.

The mouse jerked. Its body arched back, quivering. If she could just make it wave its paw . . .

"Enough, Lily . . ."

Just a little wave . . .

The skeleton exploded. The bones flew in all directions, obliterated to minute splinters.

"I'm sorry," said Lily. "I broke it."

"The lesson was meant to be about *control*, Lily." Iblis wound his finger in a circle over the table, gathering up the shards. His expression was pleased, not angry. "You know, it took me two months to get the mouse just to scratch its nose."

Lily glowed inside. "Can I try something bigger?" she asked. "How about a dog?"

Custard barked.

"I mean another animal that's not a dog."

"In good time, daughter. There are dangers involved with overextending yourself. Didn't you read that diary I gave you? The one by Mephistopheles Shadow?"

"I did. The magic changed him."

"That is putting it mildly. Sensitivity to light. Premature aging. His skin sloughed off, and he had no appetite for anything but blood. All the great houses are similarly cursed. Overusing magic can turn the lords of light into glass—first their eyes, then their bones, and finally their flesh. The sorcerers of House Djinn can end up as beings of fire, which, as you can imagine, is highly awkward. And half the druids of Herne's Forest have leaves for hair and bark skin." Her father smiled at her. "So take it easy. We have time." He reached for a scroll.

But before he could open it, Custard growled. He faced the door, his four small legs braced wide and his tail low. The short bristles on his shoulders rose.

"What's wrong, Custard?" asked Lily.

He barked loudly and ran out.

"He's sensed something," Lily said. "I have to go."

"All right, then. You know where to find me."

"Wait for me!" Lily yelled.

Gathering up her skirts, Lily raced off after her dog. She caught up with him as they ascended the stairs leading into the courtyard of Dead Man's Gate. Lily heard shouting.

The first thing she saw were the wagons, three of them. Gaudy and festooned with ribbons, bunting, and flags. Across each was a painted banner: MERRICK'S WORLD-FAMOUS TRAVELING PLAYERS.

Luggage lay abandoned on the slush. About a score of performers stood gathered in a semicircle.

Watching a fight.

A pair of her soldiers wrestled in the muddy snow with two others. One was a skinny old man with a jingling three-belled jester's cap planted unevenly on a bald head. He was thwacking one of the soldiers with an inflated pig's bladder. "Unhand my master, you brute! Unhand him, I say!"

The second figure wore an outfit of pure white and lay face deep in the snow, struggling helplessly while a soldier knelt on his back. He spat out some dirty snow. "Get *off* me! Do you know who I am?"

Oh no. Not him.

Custard ran up and tried to bite the struggling boy, but his ghost teeth went straight through his leg. That only made the dog angrier.

"Get off me! I am Gabriel Sol—*mmmrpgh!*" yelled the boy before his face was pushed back down for another mouthful.

"Let him go!" commanded Lily.

The kneeling guard reluctantly stood and straightened his armor. The other guard helped the boy up, also reluctantly.

The boy glared, face red with fury, at the guard who had pinned him. "I'll have your head for this, peasant!" He brushed the dirt from his now-not-so-white fur coat. "How dare you! How *dare* you!"

The guard met Lily's gaze. "Do you know this person, m'lady?" he asked through gritted teeth.

"Yes, unfortunately." Lily sighed. "He's my fiancé."

SIX

I'll go see Tyburn. He'll know what to do.

The thought went around and around in Thorn's head as Hades carried him through the night sky.

The executioner had gone off on one of his missions, but Thorn expected him to be back by now. Tyburn hadn't asked Thorn to come with him, even though Thorn was supposed to be his squire.

Tyburn had saved him from a life as a slave working down in a mine. But that didn't mean that he liked Tyburn, or what he did for a living.

Executioner. The title said it all.

The wind, icy and sharp, cut deeper against Thorn's exposed face as Hades began to pick up the pace. That meant only one thing.

They were nearing home.

Torches shone brightly along the battlements of Castle Gloom.

Home.

It was now. Thorn shared a room with Wade, but back in Stour, he'd shared a similar-size room with his whole family and, in winter, the goats, too.

Thorn smiled. Wade and the rest were a day or two behind him, so he'd have the room to himself, free of Wade's snoring, smelly feet and stupid dancing.

Tonight was going to be a two-mango night.

Hades twisted suddenly, diving down through a break in the clouds.

A host of bats flew up to greet them, hundreds of lesser creatures that gathered thickly around their returning king. Hades snapped at them, and they shrieked and swarmed behind him as they all swooped over the castle.

On they flew, between the towers and along the top of Ghoul Gate to circle over Old Keep.

"Easy, boy. No need to rush." Thorn wanted a look at the ruins.

Castle Gloom wasn't a mere castle; it was a city, thousands of years old, sprawling for miles. Gehenna had once been a great kingdom, controlling lands and seas in all directions. Rising out of the legendary age of the Six Princes, countless Shadows had added to it, stretching it east to west, north to south, with buildings somber, macabre, and just plain spooky. Those days were long gone, but the grandeur of past glories remained in its crumbling halls, abandoned towers, ruined old mansions, overgrown parks, and endless corridors that included catacombs deep underground.

But one area stood separate from the chaotic expanse.

Moonlight shone on the iced-up moat surrounding Old Keep. There was snow sparkling on the gatehouse and its broken drawbridge. Old Keep was small, especially compared to the Needle, the Great Hall, and other later constructions. Even the stables were bigger.

But Old Keep was where the zombies lived. Or unlived. Or whatever it was they did.

There they were, snow-covered figures among the tumbledown stone. Not one moved. Had they frozen solid?

There—one turned his head.

Then another. Up they looked as Hades flapped fifty feet and more above them. Moonlight shone in their rheumy silvery eyes. Thorn shivered. They gave him the creeps. What was Lily going to do with them?

"Let's go, Hades."

The bat didn't need to be told twice. He twitched his left wing, and they glided toward another roofless ruin. Murk Hall.

Hades settled on the stub of a broken column. Thorn slid off and inspected his bandaged arm. He flexed his fingers. "Ow."

Old Colm had coated the wounds with a healing salve, but Thorn needed to see Dr. Byle. Bites carried diseases.

Hades hunched his shoulders and hissed as someone came toward them.

Ying, the Eagle Knight, raised his hand in greeting. "May I approach?"

Thorn smoothed down Hades's chin bristles. "Of course, m'lord."

Ying stood a few yards back but stared at Hades with awe. "House Typhoon had giant war hawks once. What a wonder it would have been to ride one into battle. You are very fortunate, young Thorn."

Thorn smiled. "There ain't no one in the world like Hades."

Hades raised his head proudly.

"Nor as pigheaded," Thorn added.

Ying walked slowly around the giant bat, admiring Hades from all directions. The young man's flowing robes were the blue of House Typhoon but decorated with a white feather symbol. Three eagle feathers rose out of his topknot of silky black hair. He was a few years older than Thorn, and his boyish physique had given way to a man's muscular litheness. He moved with an easy, fluid warrior's grace.

Ying wanted to marry Lily. He'd brought her a mechanical aviary as a gift, all the way from Lu Feng, the Land of Endless Winds, thousands of miles to the east. He was a prince, the sort of prince whom minstrels sang about and young girls dreamed of. Thorn shifted uneasily, painfully aware of his own weather-stained coat, his torn sleeves, and his smell of bat. He roughly brushed his hair from his eyes. Not that it did any good; it remained the color and texture of straw.

Ying belonged to the Feathered Council. The council had overthrown

House Typhoon, despite the fact that the council had no sorcerers. What sort of man could overthrow an ancient house of magic?

"May I do something for you, m'lord?" asked Thorn. "It's just I've got to be at the stables to prepare the horses for the Black Guard. Baron Sable's taking 'em north at first light."

"You're not going to tonight's feast?"

"There'll be dancing, right?" asked Thorn.

"Plenty."

"I'd rather spend the night shoveling horse dung."

Ying hooked his thumbs into his sash and looked at Thorn. "All warriors should know how to dance."

"Why? It ain't like it'll help you lop heads off."

"Speed. Grace. Nimbleness. All vital to warriors, yes?"

Thorn frowned. "Suppose."

Ying performed a neat, sinuous bow. "All acquired through dancing."

"I still ain't going." Thorn had his bow and arrows; he had Hades. He didn't need speed, grace, or nimbleness.

"Truth be told, the feast's been spoiled already." Ying adjusted an eagle feather. "Lady Shadow has a new guest." He looked meaningfully at Thorn. "One you know well, so I've been told."

"Who?"

"Gabriel Solar."

Thorn felt as if he'd been smacked with a tree trunk. "*Gabriel's* here? Why?"

"You're not a fan of his?"

This was grim news. Gabriel was trouble, and even though Thorn wasn't so great at spelling, he knew that his kind was spelled with a capital *T*.

Last time he'd been here, Gehenna had almost been destroyed. And it was a feast that had kicked it off. . . .

"Stay clear of him, m'lord. He's an idiot but a dangerous idiot. You don't want nothing to do with him."

"Alas, there are rules, among nobles."

"Stupid ones, I bet." Thorn shook his head. Nothing nobles did made any sense.

Ying moved on. "We leave tomorrow, and I could not go without seeing the famous Hades." His gaze did not leave the giant bat. Hades purred, enjoying the attention. Ying laughed.

Even his laugh is handsome.

Ying glanced at Thorn. "And meeting you, Thorn."

"Me? I ain't famous."

"No? The boy who saved Gehenna? You do yourself a disservice." Ying folded his arms and appraised Thorn. "We're not so different, you and I."

"Oh?" *We're as different as different can be.*

Ying arched an elegant, slim eyebrow. "A generation ago, my family were peasants. But we had talent. And talent can make a man rise very high." He looked back at Hades. "In many ways."

"Reckon I've gotten as high as I'll ever get."

Ying shrugged. "How went the patrol?"

"There's been attacks on several farms. Pitch Farm's just the latest. The reports are coming from down from Raven's Wood and the Troll-Teeth Mountains."

"How long has this been going on?"

"A month. Since the winter wind brought in the snow." Thorn scowled; he didn't understand it all. "There could've been more attacks we don't know about. Gehenna's got plenty of outta-the-way places. The baron's fretting."

"I don't blame him," said Ying. "Who do you think is behind it?" He seemed genuinely interested.

"People reckon it's trolls."

"But you don't. Why?"

"I ain't denying there have been troll attacks up north, but it weren't them at Pitch Farm. No tracks, for one thing. Trolls ain't light on their feet, and the snow's perfect for taking footprints. Then there's all the livestock they left behind. Raiders grab everything they can. They ignored fat sheep and goats and chickens, but stole two scrawny boys. Why?"

"Who understands trolls?"

"I understand being hungry, and that's what trolls are." Thorn shook his head. "No, it ain't trolls."

"Then what?"

That's where he was stuck. No tracks. No signs at all.

"Gonna ask Tyburn," said Thorn.

"Yes, your legendary executioner. You're his squire, aren't you?"

"I suppose. Don't do much for him but look after his horse. Tyburn's a loner."

"He treats you well, though?"

"Well enough. He's firm but fierce, as my grandpa would say." Thorn stood back and inspected Hades. The bat was clean and tidy. "I'd better go find him and give him the news."

"He's not here," said Ying.

Strange. What's delaying him?

Ying must have seen the look on his face. "Do you think something's happened to him?"

"Lily . . . er, *Lady Shadow*," Thorn corrected, "once told me that bad things never happen *to* Tyburn. Bad things happen *because* of Tyburn."

"Tyburn has his rivals, believe me."

Thorn's eyes narrowed. This sort of talk felt disloyal. "There ain't no better fighter than Tyburn."

"There's always someone better, somewhere."

"Is that how you defeated House Typhoon? You had better fighters? Better than sorcerers?" asked Thorn. "I heard that House Typhoon flew on clouds. Carried great big armies across the sky on them."

Ying wore a wry smile. "The legendary cloud ships. That's all anyone seems to know about House Typhoon. Alas, the ships are all gone. The magic required to keep even one aloft was immense. Toward the end, House Typhoon needed a dozen sorcerers to fly even the smallest."

That was a shame. Thorn would have loved to see one. Though nothing could be better than taking to the skies on Hades, of course. He pressed on. "I hear you know secret fighting skills where you come from. Punches that break through armor, and kicks that can knock down trees and such."

"Do you want to know how we beat House Typhoon?" Ying's eyes sparkled.

"Yeah." Maybe he'd teach Thorn one of those kicks.

Ying pulled a small leather tube from his waist sash. There was a cap at either end—one silver, the other black—and both were sealed with wax. Then he pointed at the wall. "Grab me that helmet."

Like most halls, Murk Hall was decorated with arms and armor; in this case, they were old and rusty. Thorn took down a heavy iron helmet and held it out.

The Eagle Knight tapped the iron. "What do you think? Do you believe you could put an ax blade through this?"

"Nope."

Ying uncapped one end of the tube and tipped a small pile of black powder onto a large broken piece of stone. He brushed the edges so it was a neat mound, less than an inch wide. "We knew the magic was fading, so we took precautions. House Typhoon was not interested. Despite the signs, they still thought they could regain their sorcerous powers, if not in one generation, then the next. But the sorcerers they did produce were pitiful. They began recruiting spellcasters from other kingdoms. Buying their magic, and loyalty, with gold."

"That sort of loyalty don't last long," said Thorn.

Ying laughed. "Very true. Only as long as the coffers are full, and House Typhoon was no longer rich. So when the Feathered Council seized control, most of the hired sorcerers abandoned House Typhoon, taking whatever treasures they could get their hands on as they fled. Great arti-facts of magic, many of them heirlooms from the days of the Six Princes, vanished that night."

"That still don't explain how you beat House Typhoon."

"With this." He resealed the black end and then, opening the other end, sprinkled silver powder onto the black, very carefully. He spun the hel-met nimbly and put it over the pile of powder. "Get behind that column."

"Why?"

"Get behind the column."

The powder hissed and sparked.

Ying jumped behind a slab. "Five parts black to one part silver. That's the secret."

"What secret?"

Ying winked, then cupped his ears.

A thunderous explosion knocked Thorn off his feet. The hall shook as it was filled with a flash of stark white light.

Hades roared. He jumped twenty feet into the air and, with a single, hurricane sweep of his wings, vanished into the night, taking his host of bats with him.

The noise echoed between the heavy walls, rumbling deep into Thorn's shaken bones. "What was that?"

Ying helped him up. The Eagle Knight collected the now-smoking helmet. "Look."

The helmet was shattered; the iron twisted, ragged, and hot to the touch.

"We call the black powder Thunderdust," said Ying. "A small pile will punch a big hole through armor. A small barrel will destroy a house. A big barrel will bring down a castle wall. You can make it explode by applying a flame, but then it might blow up in your face. The silver powder reacts with the Thunderdust but in a more controlled way. It's safer. Mostly." He tossed the tube over to Thorn. "A present. Be careful with it."

Thorn stared at the gift, half-afraid it was going to explode then and there. "Magic?"

Ying shook his head. "Better than magic. Science."

SEVEN

"I don't like it, not one little bit." The stable master, Ongar, held open the feedbag as Thorn poured in a fresh supply of oats. "Them zombies have got to go."

A few of the other stable boys nodded.

"Crawling out of their graves, stealing our jobs," continued Ongar. "Soon there won't be a breathing soul in the castle, and then you know what'll happen?"

"What?" said Thorn.

"Brains. They'll be wanting brains. Yours, mine, anyone's who's got the pink-and-mushies."

One bag filled, Thorn started on another. "But I thought you Gehennish loved your undead."

Ongar shrugged his shoulders. "I know that's what Lady Shadow wants, but she doesn't live downwind of Old Keep, does she? Oh, now, it's all well and good for her, telling us to be nice, to make friends with them. And it suits her. Cheap labor. Save on the servants, more coin for her statues."

"Lily's not like that."

The stable master gave him a mocking bow. "Oh, yes, I forgot. *Lily*, isn't it? Well, *m'lord*, I'm sure you know what's good for Gehenna better than I, whose family has been here since Prince Shadow laid the first stone of this here castle. You, who hasn't a drop of black in your blood."

There was no point arguing; Ongar was always grumbling about something. Thorn slung the feedbag over his shoulder and headed off to the stables. It was going to be a long night of hard, heavy work.

But it beat dancing.

Soldiers, the famed Black Guard of Gehenna, were already assembling in the icy courtyard along with the older squires. A few queued outside the blacksmith's shed. He worked at his wheel, grinding the edges of sword blades to a razor's keenness. Troll bones were hard and their skins had the toughness of old leather, so every man wanted his weapon perfect.

Each Black Guard wore a sculpted visor, a mark of his membership in the elite band. Captain Waylander owned a horned demon, passed down from his father, who'd inherited it from his father. The four Wicked brothers had grinning skulls. There were fanged vampires, bearded devils, and more than a few decaying zombies.

One day, he'd have a mask like that. Thorn fancied one with large bat wings and fangs. The bigger the better. But he wouldn't ride into battle on top of a warhorse.

A couple of the warriors waved to him, then got on with their business, helped by the older squires. Dawn would come soon enough, and they needed to be off on the road to the Troll-Teeth Mountains.

Someone put a hand on Thorn's arm.

"Excuse me, young master, but we're lost."

A woman stood facing him. She smiled, but she was weary. She carried a swaddled baby, and there were two young children with her, both bundled in layers of winter clothing, so they were as wide as they were high.

Thorn lowered the heavy feedbag. "Where are you heading?"

"We're looking for the . . . zombies?"

"Why?"

"We've lost our dad," said one of the children, the girl. "We've come here to find him."

They're shivering and look ready to drop.

"Come a long way?" Thorn asked.

"Skeletown," said the mother.

"You walked?"

She nodded. "We've never been more than five miles from home. Didn't realize how long the road was."

Thorn stopped one of the other stable boys. "This goes to feed the foal."

The stable boy stared at the feedbag. "Do I look like your servant?"

"You look like someone who's about to get his backside kicked if he don't hurry up."

The stable boy took the oat-filled sack, muttering as he left.

"Come with me, Mrs. . . . ?" said Thorn.

"Kath, just call me Kath." She patted the boy's head. "This is Hammel, and that's Janet." She hugged the baby. "This is Tomas."

"I'm Thorn." He pointed at the nearby steps. "There's a fire and some food left over at the squires' dorms."

"The grave was empty. His, and three others," said Kath. "First we thought it was grave robbers; then we heard what happened at Castle Gloom, about the dead rising."

It was just them in the dining room—the squires were all out on errands. Thorn threw a log into the fireplace to raise a bit of extra heat, and the family sat on stools, circling the flames as closely as they could. The only food available was leftovers, but they attacked it like famished wolves.

"So you think your husband's turned into a zombie?" he asked.

"We're from a poor village, Master Thorn. Not the sort to attract thieves looking for buried treasure." Kath smoothed her baby's hair as she rocked gently on the stool. "And the snow was fresh enough for us to see the footprints."

"You sure you want to go through with this?" asked Thorn.

"What do you mean?"

"If you do find him, he may not be the same as you remember." Was there a delicate way of putting this? Probably not. "He'll be a corpse."

"He's still our dad," said Janet, spitting out crumbs.

"He may not know that, though," replied Thorn.

Back in Herne's Forest, the druids said that death was just a means of making way for new life. He'd seen fallen tree trunks, which had once towered above all else, laid low and covered with mushrooms and ferns, slowly crumbling and enriching the earth for new saplings.

The dead should stay dead. The end should be the end. He didn't like this zombie business, but he hadn't been brought up in Gehenna. Now he had a giant vampire bat to tend, a ghost puppy nipping at his heels, and a castle steadily filling with all sorts of undead.

Maybe the stable master had a point after all.

Still, family was family. Kath and her children had struggled a long, cold way to find theirs.

"C'mon," he said. "Let's go look for your dad."

EIGHT

T horn knew there were many ways through Castle Gloom: long ways, quick ways, easy ways.

And hard ways.

The route from Murk Hall to the stables in Skeleton Gate was one of the hard ones. Lots of abandoned halls and empty corridors. You needed to stay clear of Weeping Alley; a pack of ghouls lurked within, and more than one servant had taken a shortcut down there and ended up as dinner.

"They're being housed in Old Keep." Thorn collected a burning torch from its wall socket. The family followed close behind, hand in hand in one long chain.

There wasn't a single window throughout the ancient castle. No matter what changes had been made in its long life, not one window had been installed. For Thorn, who'd grown up navigating by breeze, sun, and stars, it wasn't easy finding his way around the place.

So he made his way by smell.

They used olive oil for the lamps along Dead Man's Road. They filled the corridor with the scent of summer: greasy and sweet. Thorn crossed Tumbledown Town—nothing but a collection of buried hovels—lit by reed torches, which turned the air dry and arid; it coated your throat. Then it was along Lucifer's Path, lit with huge candelabras bearing ten-foot-tall tallow candles, and finally left into Hell's Hall. The steward used animal fat for the lamps here, giving off a smoky golden flame and a taste in the air that made Thorn's stomach growl.

"Why are we going down here?" asked Hammel.

"It's a shortcut. Don't worry, there ain't nothing down here to hurt you."

Thorn turned the door handle and led them out of the corridor.

No one knew how long Castle Gloom had stood here—thousands of years, most reckoned—and it was immense, having grown and grown over all those dusty centuries.

But once, at the beginning, it had been a mere keep. A single, stubby tower surrounded by a wall and a shallow moat.

Today, ice covered the moat. The walls had long since tumbled down, but the building remained, black, wreathed in sprawling ivy, and forlorn. Old Keep.

And there, across the moat, the zombies waited.

The weak light from Thorn's torch shimmered on their frost-flaked skin and the icicles that dangled from their hair and beards. Others hid within the broken walls and dense, shambolic foliage.

Thorn swallowed. "Are you sure about this?"

"Why don't they move?" asked the boy.

"Some have frozen," said Thorn. "They don't have inner warmth, like us. We tried putting fires along the walls to keep them from going stiff, but zombies fear fire and they catch easy; it's one of the few things that can destroy them."

Sally looked along the moat's edge. The drawbridge had long since rotted away. "How do we cross? Is there a boat?"

"It's stuck in the ice. We'll have to cross on foot." Thorn held up the torch. "I'll go first. Watch your step."

How had he gotten himself into this?

Old Keep had been built low and squat. The other, later buildings towered over it, casting it in perpetual darkness, no matter the time of day. It was a good place for abandoned things.

Thorn stepped slowly and carefully, checking for any breaks in the ice and listening for cracking. It was a mere fifteen feet across, but the far bank was steep and lined with reeds. A sad-looking willow tree clung to the bank, its roots creeping over tumbled-down stone slabs, its fronds locked in the frozen water.

Thorn gulped. He'd met zombies before, even fought one back when he'd first arrived in Gehenna, and his skin crawled as he saw them up close.

The zombies looked bad enough during daylight hours, but now, in this moonlight-tinged darkness, they were on the far side of grotesque. With swollen bellies, broken limbs, caved-in chests, or just bodies corrupted by age and illness, each zombie wore his or her death differently. They were dressed in the clothes they'd been buried in, thin shifts and tattered rags. A few, from the wealthier tombs, wore tunics or dresses and shoes, but most were barefoot, and their white feet were encrusted with dirty snow.

Thorn stopped at the edge of the bank while Kath waited a few paces behind. "I'm looking for Tom of Skeletown."

The zombies just stared, their mindless, glassy eyes reflecting only the amber torchlight.

"Tom of Skeletown!" Thorn shouted. "Your wife is here!"

He'd wait here for a minute, nothing would happen, and then he'd take Kath and her children back. At least he would have tried.

"Tom! It's me, Kath!" She shuffled forward, searching the faces of the undead. "Tom!"

"Watch yourself, Kath." He didn't like the way the ice was creaking.

And he didn't like the way the zombies were shuffling toward them. They moved with awkward, jagged steps, and Thorn realized it was because of the cold. He could see some covered in snow, completely immobile, like the statues they'd recently passed.

Thorn recognized a pair of undead.

First was Fairweather Fred, a farmer from Sepulchre. Fred's grandson visited him every Sunday. Boy and zombie would head up to the City of Silence and stay there till nightfall. When Thorn had once asked the grandson what they did, he had said, "We just sit there and watch the clouds go by."

Next to Fred, with half a jaw, was Eddie the Eel, from a village along River Styx. He'd wanted to be a pirate. He'd even gotten a pair of big gold earrings because he'd heard that's what they wore. But he'd died without ever having seen the sea. He had a seashell dangling around his neck, and Thorn had seen him put it to his ear, listening to the sound of the waves within.

The zombies slowly parted. Someone was coming through.

Kath gasped. "Tom?"

The zombie wasn't very broken up; there was just a dent in his skull, which was purple compared to the rest of his bloodless skin. But that dent had been enough. He'd been buried in a nice tunic and breeches, and he wore socks, one red and the other a faded blue. Around his neck was a string of dried flowers.

"Tom, it's me—Kath." She smiled though tears fell. "Your wife."

How much did he remember? Tom the zombie turned his head achingly slowly. He didn't blink his eyes, which had faded to a cloudy silver during his time in the grave.

Kath walked to the edge of the moat. "I've brought someone to see you, Tom."

The ice creaked noisily. Thorn reached for Kath. He needed her to step back a bit. He didn't know how Tom or the other zombies would react to her. There were a lot of them, and Thorn only had his torch.

"Tom?"

The zombie looked down at them.

"Forget it, Kath," said Thorn. "He doesn't know you."

Tom held out his hand.

Kath smiled and took it. "Thank you, husband."

Then, not letting go of her, Tom turned and marched stiffly up the slope of the bank. The baby started crying as Tom led his wife and children into Old Keep.

Now what? This wasn't what Thorn had planned. He'd thought they'd find Tom a mindless creature, then leave. Thorn didn't want to stay, but he could hardly abandon the family. It might not be safe, and they didn't know their way back.

He looked around him, at the undead and the ancient stones. He'd never been inside Old Keep.

"Wait for me!" Thorn shouted.

NINE

Lily had some serious questions for Gabriel Solar.

First, *Why are you back, ruining my life?*

Second, *When are you leaving?*

She still needed to get ready for tonight's feast. That dress Ying had given her needed wearing. The dove feathers were softer than silk, and she'd had no idea black doves even existed.

Instead she was here, dealing with uninvited—and unwanted—guests.

Custard scurried along at her heels, darting in and out through the walls and doors. It was still . . . strange, the puppy being just as he'd always been but a ghost. He still liked to wrestle with her clothes, but he couldn't understand why his teeth now went straight through the cloth and his small claws couldn't grab hold of anything. Then he'd forget about it and spend the rest of the morning chasing his tail.

Gabriel was up in the Moon chambers. Far away from Ying and the rest of her eastern visitors. The last thing she wanted was trouble between two rival houses.

And Gabriel was trouble all the way through.

So Lily continued to climb the spiral stairs, winding around toward the top of the tower.

What would Mother do?

Lily had seen her smile at rivals, dine with enemies, and laugh at the jokes of men she'd wanted to kill, all without ever betraying her true feelings. Salome Shadow had been the perfect hostess.

And fixer.

Like with Count Helborn.

He'd been behind raids on neighboring farms. Nothing was ever proved, but everyone knew. He'd dined and danced and then . . . disappeared. No one had ever mentioned him again. There'd been some strange sounds coming out of the well for the next few days, until her mother had ordered it bricked up.

Lily stopped at the top of the stairs. She took a deep breath and put on a smile.

"Let's get this over with," she said.

The door ahead was a perfect circle of black obsidian decorated with the phases of the moon, inlaid in mother-of-pearl. It was quite beautiful.

Not so beautiful was the man lying asleep in front of it.

Lily bent down and touched his shoulder. "Sir?"

It was the fool, the stick-thin man with the knobbly knees. He was the one who'd attacked her soldiers with the inflated pig's bladder, which he now clutched against his thin chest.

Pig's bladder. How pathetic. That hadn't been funny in five hundred years.

He lay under a patchy blanket and shivered as he snored. The stone floor was freezing.

"You poor man." How dare Gabriel leave his servant sleeping out here! "Wake up."

The man twitched and murmured in his sleep. "No . . . not the gerbils . . ."

Lily had no idea what that meant and decided she didn't want to know. She nudged him again. "Wake up."

The fool blinked and looked up at her, bewildered. "M . . . M'lady Shadow?" His eyes widened in terror. "M'lady Shadow!"

Lily helped him up, which wasn't easy, as he was shaking like a leaf in a hurricane. He started crying. "Please . . . please don't turn me into a zombie. . . . I have uses. . . ."

"I'm sure you have. And you've done nothing wrong." Lily took out the Skeleton Key and tapped the lock. "Gabriel!"

He screamed as she marched in. He was in a pair of white silken undergarments and was in the middle of knotting the waist ribbon. He grabbed a dressing gown. "Do you mind? I'm not decent!"

Lily pulled the fool in beside her. "No, you're not decent at all! Why do you have this man sleeping outside the door?"

"He was blocking the draft!"

Lily groaned. Gabriel was worse than ever, and she hadn't thought that possible.

"Mr. Funny"—Gabriel waved at the fool—"leave!"

Cringing and with knees knocking together, Mr. Funny rushed back out, slamming the door behind him.

"*Mr. Funny?* That's his name?" She couldn't imagine anyone less funny than that miserable wretch.

Gabriel snorted. "I assume you're here to move me out of this flea pit and into superior accommodations?"

"No. It seems to me you've made yourself perfectly at home."

"And where's the rest of my luggage? It had better not be stolen!"

"Dott's bringing it up."

"Dott? What happened to that fat old woman, Mary? I thought she was in charge of guests."

"She left," said Lily. "Abruptly."

Even now, Lily felt the loss. Mary, once a huge part of her life, was gone and wasn't coming back. Mary had betrayed Lily, not meaning to hurt her ward, but it had come between them. Then, one day, Lily had woken to learn that Mary had packed in the night and left.

But Lily wasn't going to discuss Mary with anyone.

Gabriel didn't travel light. Lily counted five big chests already in the room, each stuffed to overflowing with clothing. There were coats, all white fur, piled on top of the table, and across the bed were row upon row of neatly folded silken underwear. A fresh pair for every day of the year, apparently.

Lily picked one up. "It's very soft."

Gabriel snatched it from her. "I have sensitive skin. It's a sign of good breeding, not anything you'd know about."

"Why are you here, Gabriel?"

"Hardly out of choice." He refolded the underwear and added them back to the pile. "I . . . I needed to leave Lumina. In a hurry."

"Why? You're heir apparent. Aren't you?"

He was everything you'd expect of a noble. Tall and muscular, with elegant long limbs and a head crowned with fine platinum-blond hair; flawless, unblemished skin; and eyes the color and brightness of sapphires. A hero straight out of a fairy tale.

But he was a Solar.

And just as the sorcerers of House Shadow were masters of necromancy and the magic of darkness, so the scions of House Solar were masters of light and illusion. And everything about Gabriel was an illusion.

Lily knew the real Gabriel. She'd seen him last Halloween. For once, and perhaps the only time in his life, Gabriel had told—or shown—the truth. The lanky hair. The pockmarked skin. The yellowed teeth in a jaw that rested on a scrawny, spindly neck.

But it must have been too painful for him to bear. So now he was back to his usual false self.

And to think she'd once been destined to marry him.

"I burned the marriage contract, you know," she said, just in case he had any ideas.

"Good for you." He opened up a small trinket box on the dressing table and drew out a string of diamond-studded buttons. "The war's going badly, if you must know. Lumina's losing, and the sultan's army has besieged the Prism Palace. Father needed me somewhere safe. So I smuggled myself into this band of traveling players, disguising myself as one of *them*. It's been awful, a month traveling with"—he shivered—"commoners."

"You fled Lumina with just your fool?"

"I needed entertaining."

"Most people settle for a book."

"Books are boring."

Gabriel's father had started the war against Sultan Djinn. He'd captured one of the sultan's sons, K'leef, and held him hostage, all the while raiding the sultan's lands, robbing his caravans, and destroying his towns, the sultan unable to retaliate because of his imprisoned son. That was until Lily and Thorn had freed K'leef and sent him back home.

And now the sultan, the lord of fire, was burning Lumina's towns and cities.

Which reminded her, she needed to write a thank-you letter to K'leef for the beautiful fire horses he had sent her.

"I'm throwing a farewell feast for Prince Ying," said Lily. "The steward says I have to invite you."

"The Eagle Knight? I wondered who those blue banners belonged to."

"I need you ready in an hour."

"An hour?" Gabriel cried. "How can I be ready in an hour? I need at least three servants! I can't be expected to do up my own buttons!"

There was a knock at the door.

Actually, it was more like a hammerblow, hard enough to shake the door on its hinges.

"Prin'ess?" boomed a voice from the other side.

"Come in, Dott."

Dott entered.

Gabriel screamed and dove under the bed.

Dott stared around her, then grinned at Lily. "Prin'ess?"

Lily pointed to a clear patch of floor. "Put the trunks there."

"'Kay."

Dott had a boat-sized trunk on each shoulder. Chests made out of dense oak, bound by iron, and shut with a padlock the size of a brick. Each needed two grown men to lift.

Gabriel's head poked out from under the bed. "Run for your life! And get help!"

Dott dropped the trunks with a *slam*.

"Be careful with those!" screamed Gabriel.

Dott turned and peered under the bed. "Don't be scared. Dott'll look after little boy." Then, with one hand, she turned the four-poster bed onto its side. "Ooh, pretty boy."

Gabriel was now pressed against the wall, face stark white. "Get away from me, you . . . you troll!" He pointed. "She's a troll! She's going to eat me!" Then, as Dott reached out, he scurried off on his hands and knees to hide behind Lily. "Do something! Something violent!"

Lily grabbed Gabriel's ear. "Stop it. Dott's perfectly harmless. And trolls only eat important people, great enemies and the like. They believe that by doing so they gain some of their adversary's power. It's a sign of respect."

"Are you saying I'm not important?" Gabriel declared indignantly. "I bet they'd eat me before they'd eat you!"

"Why are we even having this conversation?" Lily snapped. "Just hurry up and get dressed."

Dott lowered the bed and smiled at Gabriel. "Be friends?"

Mr. Funny groaned as he leaned against the doorframe. He seemed to be coming out of a faint. He waved his inflated pig's bladder. "I'll save you, Master. . . ."

"You've got a troll . . . *working* for you?" whispered Gabriel, still keeping Lily between him and Dott. "How?"

"She was found in Spindlewood a month ago, unconscious and badly injured. The Black Guard didn't know what to do with her, so she was brought here."

That was only a small part of the story. No one could figure out how she'd gotten there, and Dott herself couldn't remember—the injuries had scrambled her memory. All she knew was the name Dott. The Black Guard had wanted to kill her—that was the way between Gehenna and the trolls—but Lily had realized that, despite her size, Dott was just a child, maybe not much older than Lily. And the Gehennish did not murder children. Not while Lily ruled.

And now, somehow, Dott was Lily's maid.

"Friends?" asked Dott, looking a little dejectedly at Gabriel.

"With you?" asked Gabriel. His face contorted with disgust. "Yuck. How utterly hideous."

Lily rested her hand on Dott's huge arm. "Let's go and get ready for the feast, Dott. There'll be music and dancing. It'll be fun."

Dott clapped. "Dancin' an' stompin'!"

Lily guided the troll girl out, then paused at the door and looked back at Gabriel. "You've got one hour."

TEN

The Shadows had abandoned Old Keep a thousand years ago, and nature now ruled. Seeds, drifting in from beyond the walls of Castle Gloom, had found fertile soil, and grown, undisturbed by mortals. Ivy crept over the battlements, thick, black, and shimmering with ice. Scarlet roses bloomed despite the snow, their heads hanging from worn statues like blood drops. Oak trees rose from the broken flagstones, their branches having brought down the walls and now spread out high and wide over the keep. Crooked hedges wound through the hall, draped with star-shaped nicotiana, their perfume thick in the still, crisp air.

The zombies had become part of this wild garden. They had remained still for too long and become beds for new life. One was covered in drooping bluebells, and another had a cluster of dark purple irises sprouting from his chest. The same magic that had given the undead life also fed the flowers, making them bloom in all seasons, larger and more glorious than Thorn had ever seen in mere soil.

Tom brushed the snow off a stone plinth and motioned for his wife to sit down with the baby. Their two older children watched warily.

Thorn stayed at the entrance, torch in hand. Its flame was weak and smoky. He needed to get back before it burned out, but a macabre curiosity held him. He wanted to see this.

"He's named Tomas," said Kath, tickling the baby's chin. "Your mom says he looks just like you did, and now and then, I can see it. When he's smiling, especially. Tom"—she looked up at her undead husband—"he's our beautiful boy."

The zombie gazed down. Each movement was work, the tilting of his head, how he raised his hand, unfurled each finger, one after the other. He reached, ever so slowly, and brushed his forefinger against his son's cheek.

The baby started crying.

Kath laughed. "Your hand's cold, Tom."

Thorn spoke. "We need to get going, Kath." The torch was little more than a flickering candle now. He nodded to Hammel and Janet. "Say your good-byes to your . . . dad."

Kath stood up and took Tom's hand. "Let's go."

"Wait. You can't take him with you."

Kath's expression hardened, and Thorn got a bad feeling about this. "He's my husband, Master Thorn. I know his . . . condition may be a little odd, but he's coming with me."

"It's more than a condition, Kath."

"I'll look after him."

"It's not that. They . . . deteriorate the farther they get from here." What he meant was the farther they got from Lily. "You take him back to Skeletown, you've no idea how long he'll last."

"Then I'll stay here. I'll work in Castle Gloom." She peered at Thorn, worried. "Could you put in a good word for me with Lady Shadow? I'm a hard worker, and all we need is room and board. There must be a thousand empty rooms in the castle. Hammel's young but strong. He can help out, and my daughter's got a keen eye and sews. Please, you have to help us."

Thorn looked helplessly from zombie to wife and back. Why was he the one having to sort this out?

"Okay, I'll speak to Lady Shadow, but in the meantime, you have to leave Tom here. Agreed?"

Kath stared hard, no doubt wondering if it was worth arguing. But Thorn spent half his time arguing with Lily, so he'd had plenty of practice in standing up to stubborn Gehennish folk. He folded his arms and waited.

Kath sighed and nodded. "Agreed. When can—"

"Wait a minute." Thorn sniffed. "Can you smell that?"

"Maybe it's the zombies? The flowers can't mask their, er, body odor?"

"No. That's smoke." Thorn climbed up the side of a wall to get a better idea of where the smell was coming from.

There was a flickering orange glow coming from a corner of Old Keep. Through the uneven shadows, he saw zombies stumbling, wailing, and clawing at one another, trying to escape. "Fire!" He jumped down. "A fire's broken out."

"A fire? But the zombies—" Kath cried.

Thorn looked around. "Take your children and Tom back to the moat. Cross over the ice, but *be careful.*"

"What about the others?" She glanced around at the figures watching from the nooks and crannies. "We can't just leave them."

"By the Six . . ." Since when was saving zombies part of his job? He ran into the center of the hall and cupped his mouth. "Listen up! You need to cross the moat! Got it? Follow Kath across the moat!"

Then Thorn ran toward the flames.

ELEVEN

"Remember to behave," said Lily.

"I shall behave like a true scion of House Solar," said Gabriel, taking her hand.

"That's what I'm afraid of," she whispered to herself.

They entered the Great Hall.

It heaved with people. Mostly nobles but also local merchants hoping to arrange trade with the Feathered Council, some village headmen and guildswomen who'd dressed up in their very best clothes to make an impression. Later they would tell their village all about the wonders of Castle Gloom.

Dott stood in front of the musicians, clapping and stomping her feet hard enough that the tables nearby juddered. She'd added decoration to her hair: red radishes, a few golden turnips, and strings of bright green runner beans. She glanced over, and when she saw Gabriel, she sighed, like any lovelorn maid.

The emissaries of the Feathered Council did not look happy. Why should they? Here they were, trying to arrange a marriage, and suddenly

Lily's old fiancé turns up. Was it mere coincidence, or a Solar plot to spoil their plans?

Lily and Gabriel made their way up to the high table, where the Eagle Knight, Ying, sat watching, his face as sour as month-old milk.

Ignoring him, Lily took her seat and asked brightly, "Is everyone hungry? I've been told the soup's something special. Ah, here it comes."

The servants shuffled up, being watchful of the plates and goblets, and two carried the huge brass tureen of soup. The smell made Lily's mouth water. Lamb with onions and dumplings, heady with spices. Her favorite.

Gabriel tapped his spoon on the table. "Can't they move a bit faster? I'm starving."

"It's their first feast. They're trying to be careful."

The Eagle Knight leaned across the table. "New servants? They look . . . are they zombies?"

Gabriel gulped. "Z-zombies? You have zombies working here?"

"Of course we have them; this is Gehenna. It's just we've gotten a sudden surplus. I felt it best we give them something to do. It's better than having them roam around the countryside, moaning and eating people's brains when they get peckish."

Now Gabriel turned whiter than his tunic. "Eating their brains?"

"Don't worry, Gabriel," said Lily. "I can't imagine they'd get much of a meal out of yours."

Feet dragging, the pair carried the bowl slowly, and then, ever so gently, lowered it onto the table. One of the zombies began grinning. Or at least, his black lips parted and a strange, horrific grimace broke over his pallid, torn skin. Lily could see the sinews tugging through the gaps.

"Well done," she said. Her mother had taught her it was always good to praise new servants. "Now, how about dishing it out? It smells absolutely love—"

Something splashed into the soup.

"Er . . ." said Lily, staring.

"Hurr . . . rorry," said the zombie.

A nose bobbed within the meaty broth.

Lily scooped the nose out and handed it back. "Never mind. These things happen." She sat down. "Maybe we'll pass on the soup. Have a bread roll, Gabriel."

The Great Hall echoed with a *clang*. A metal tray, a pair of hands still clinging to it, bounced across the flagstones. A now-handless zombie stumbled after it as carrots, potatoes, and peas rolled across the floor.

Lily groaned.

Ying cleared his throat. "May I say, Lady Shadow, how beautiful you look in your dress?"

Lily brushed her fingers over the bodice. "It was a very generous gift."

"A dress made entirely of black dove feathers," the knight continued. "Softer than any silk."

"Looks more like dyed chicken feathers to me," muttered Gabriel, just loud enough for everyone to hear. "*Cluck, cluck, cluck.* That's your war cry, isn't it?"

Lily kicked Gabriel under the table. "Now, Gabriel, remember that you're my guest, too. Play nice. And this is a lovely dress, sir."

Ying smiled and shuffled his chair closer. "And the portraits do not do you justice, m'lady. You have the neck of a swan, and your hair, it is as black as a raven's."

"You are too kind. See, Gabriel?" said Lily as she faced the Solar boy. "That's a compliment. Not so hard to give, if you try."

Gabriel shrugged.

The Eagle Knight continued. "Certainly I have never seen so elegant a profile. Your nose, it is so perfect. Like a beak."

"Er . . . thanks. I think."

Gabriel laughed.

Lily kicked him again.

Ying spoke. "I am sorry to hear about the attacks on your farms. If you need any help, it would be my honor to leave some of my men behind."

"You are generous to offer, but my Black Guard are more than capable of dealing with a few trolls." Lily might be new to politics, but she was savvy enough to know that allowing foreign soldiers into her country was foolish, as was admitting the weakness of her own troops.

"Have you any news about Tyburn?" asked Ying.

Gabriel sat up straight. "What of him?"

"Hunting trolls," interrupted Baron Sable, two seats farther down. "Tyburn made his reputation fighting them."

Ying nodded. "Yes. They say there are three great killers in the New Kingdoms: Tyburn, of House Shadow; Kali, of House Djinn; and Golgoth"—Ying looked over at Gabriel—"of House Solar."

Gabriel smiled. "Golgoth's the very best. Only my father knows who he is and what he's up to."

A troupe of clowns pranced in among the audience—the same troupe that Gabriel had stowed away with.

They should have named themselves the Unwanted.

That was what they were. Dwarves, and those born deformed, and others who'd been in accidents and lost a limb. They had gathered together and were earning a living the only way they could, from the laughter of other people.

But despite their disabilities, or perhaps because of them, they were talented. One dwarf balanced on the head of another and juggled with whatever the audience tossed him. A crippled man performed clever tricks with his one good hand; he was easily the best magician Lily had seen in a long time. Coins disappeared and reappeared at the bottom of goblets. He guessed names and birthdays and the contents of pockets. He made one of Sir Malcontent's big mastiffs shrink to the size of a puppy; it was then chased around the hall by a mouser cat. A young boy ran behind the magician, collecting coins from the guests.

When the conjuror limped toward the high table, he met Lily's gaze, no doubt expecting silver crowns instead of bronze pennies.

He bowed. "M'lady Shadow, may I entertain you and your noble companions with a few simple tricks?"

Gabriel bit on a chicken leg. "You are in the company of true sorcerers now, Weaver. These tricks had better be good."

"Weaver?" asked Lily. "That's an interesting name."

Gabriel interrupted before the conjuror could reply. "You know what these charlatans are like. A Weaver of Fate, he calls himself." Gabriel pointed at the man's deformed left hand. "Though with that he can't even thread a needle."

The man bowed again, shaking under Gabriel's abuse. He held his left hand tight against his chest. It was heavily scarred, burned, and was little more than wrinkled skin over bone. Patches of drab hair hung long, especially on his left side, where it had been combed to best cover his molten, waxy face. A cloak, embroidered with magical symbols—or what commoners thought might be magical symbols—partially hid his ruined body. Even the man's boots didn't match, the right a shoe, the left a sandal over a withered foot.

Another unwanted, earning a living the only way he can.

He spread his good hand over an array of knives and spoons. They stood up, and he made them dance as if marionettes. Sable clapped.

"Boring," declared Gabriel.

The conjuror let the cutlery fall. He took out a pack of cards and shuffled them with one hand. Not easy.

"Even more boring," said Gabriel, louder and emphasized with a yawn.

Weaver dropped the cards, his face flushed red with embarrassment. "Apologies, m'lady."

Lily felt sorry for him. She gestured to the baron. It wasn't like she ever carried money. She didn't need to—she already owned everything.

The baron handed her a crown, and Lily put it in the conjuror's right hand. "A most excellent trick. Thank you."

Weaver stared at the silver coin, a week's wage. "You are too generous, m'lady."

Gabriel slapped the table and laughed. "I think I've spotted a relative of yours, Ying." He pointed across the hall. "There she is. My lady! Come here! Come here!"

Lily's heart sank.

The woman wore a costume of ragged old feathers. Her nose was, unfortunately, exceedingly beaklike, and even worse, the sagging skin under her chin did resemble a turkey's wattle. She jumped along the table, arms folded against her body, clucking and pecking at dishes.

Gabriel tapped his chin. "Why, Ying, the family resemblance is uncanny. Your sister, perhaps?"

Ying stood up. "M'lady Shadow, I must protest at the presence of this . . . intruder!"

Gabriel threw his bread roll at Ying. "Here, have one of these, as I'm out of birdseed!"

Baron Sable jumped forward. "Please, sit down! You're of noble houses! You must show respect!"

Gabriel sneered. "He's not noble! The Feathered Council are a bunch of usurpers! Everyone knows they overthrew the *real* great house, House Typhoon! This lot aren't even sorcerers! The only wind he commands comes out of his bottom!"

Ying drew his blade. "How dare you!"

Gabriel waved wildly. "What are you going to do? *Pluck* me to death?"

"Take up your sword!"

The poor conjuror stood trapped between the pair of them, not knowing which way to turn. The Eagle Knight shoved him aside, knocking him into Lily. With only one strong leg, Weaver fell, taking Lily down with him.

Lily tried to get up, but Weaver couldn't raise himself with only one good arm. "Apologies, m'lady!" he said, panicking and only entangling himself further.

"Sable!" Lily shouted. Weaver cried out in pain as she pushed against his chest. "I'm sorry!"

Sable dragged the man off.

"I've had enough," Lily snarled as she stood.

The Eagle Knight waved his sword at Gabriel. "I said draw your weapon!"

Gabriel stood there defiantly. "I wouldn't dirty my sword on you. You should fight my fool. Mr. Funny, come here!"

"Coming, Master!" Gabriel's old fool started clambering over the tables to reach them, knocking over plates and goblets and smearing himself with food and wine. "Coming, Master!"

Lily tried to grab Ying but only ended up bumping into Weaver again. The man was turning in circles on his good, right leg, trapped between three great houses.

Gabriel was not stopping. "House Typhoon were true sorcerers! They had a fleet of cloud ships, and you've lost them all! Even worse, I hear the last one was stolen, not a year ago! Ha! It was the only true magic you had, and you couldn't even hang on to that!"

"I'll kill you for this insult!"

"*Shut up!* Both of you!" Lily yelled.

Then the hall doors crashed open. The stable master barged in, pushing aside nobles and squires. He was waving frantically, but Lily couldn't hear him over the challenges and insults flying between Ying and Gabriel.

She grabbed the heavy iron candelabra in front of her and slammed it down on the table. "SHUT UP!"

The iron's *clang* beat back and forth between the walls, and the hall fell silent long enough for the stable master to shout one word:

"Fire!"

TWELVE

Flames leaped high in the northeast corner of Old Keep, spewing black clouds over the whole building.

Thorn stared at the destruction before him. How could it have happened? And grown so big so quickly?

The vines crackled, and the tall birch tree nearby was a fiery spear now. Bats flew in turmoil from the blazing tower. A man stood at the foot of the structure, waving his hands. Who was he? One of the Black Guard? Thorn shielded his face against the intense heat. "Hey, you! You've got to run!"

The man turned, and Thorn saw that he was dark-skinned and dressed in flowing red-and-orange robes. The man swept his arm over the blaze, and a thick tongue of flame snaked out, straight at Thorn.

For a second, Thorn was blinded by the flames; then he leaped. The fire singed his back, and he rolled across the snow, extinguishing the sparks on his clothes. By the time Thorn had gathered himself, the man was gone.

Thorn had seen fire magic before, created by his friend K'leef. His family, House Djinn, were sorcerers of fire the same way the Shadows were sorcerers of darkness.

So was this man a sorcerer from the Sultanate of Fire? He had to be. But what was he doing here?

Thorn didn't have time to mull over that mystery right now.

Zombies stumbled, bodies burning. One collapsed, his mouth open in a desperate, soundless scream. Thorn dashed over and buried him with snow. The flames died, and the zombie lay there, a blackened husk, but still "alive."

Fire was one of the few things zombies feared, because it destroyed everything. You could hack them, smash them, and bash them, and as long as the body remained mostly intact, the zombie would keep going. But there wasn't much one could do when it was a pile of ash.

More barged out of the doorway; others tried to clamber over the tumbled walls or one another.

He had to get them out. Thorn spotted the old drawbridge through the gatehouse.

But the portcullis was down. Zombies piled up against it, desperate to escape the wall of fire closing in on them.

He needed to get the portcullis *up*.

Thorn climbed a pile of rubble and from there launched himself onto the low branch of an oak tree. The trunk smoldered and hissed with boiling sap; the heat penetrated his boots. Thorn ran along the bough and jumped. He cried out as he flung himself the last foot, to land sprawling on the hard, icy stone, every bone inside him reverberating.

What am I doing, risking my life for zombies?

Thorn stood and stole a quick look back to see Kath leading the undead across the ice. Her children were already on the other side, helping the zombies up the bank.

Thorn swiftly climbed the ivy clinging to the gatehouse. The smoke blew over him, stinging his eyes and burning his throat. The heat increased the higher he got.

The zombies barged up against the portcullis. Those at the back were already burning, but that didn't stop them from pushing, and spreading the fire to others.

Thorn reached the top of the gatehouse. The winch was a big iron wheel with a rusty handle. The chains disappeared through a slot in the floor.

Thorn put his shoulder against the wheel. "Come on, move." It creaked; rust flaked off the axle. "Come on!"

Smoke clogged his throat, and each breath burned. The wheel wasn't moving. He couldn't save them; he should run and save himself.

But Thorn never gave up. He was stupid that way.

He groped around the floor and found a long pike, four inches thick, with an upper shaft made of steel. Thorn stuck the metal end into the mechanism and leaned his full weight on the other end, using it as a lever. "Come on!"

The axle moaned. The wheel turned.

The portcullis rose an inch. Then another.

Each turn got easier until Thorn could abandon the pike and twist the wheel by hand. The gatehouse shook as the undead horde beat against it, consumed by the terror of the fire.

The portcullis rose a foot, and the zombies began crawling under it. Thorn worked harder to get it higher, and soon they were spilling along the drawbridge. It didn't reach all the way across the moat, so they fell off the end and crashed through the ice. They sank, but that wouldn't bother them, having long given up the burden of breathing.

People from the castle had gathered at the moat's edge and were yelling and waving and shouting. Some waded in to help drag the zombies out of the water.

The doors to the Great Hall swung open, and out poured more people, the rich nobles and visitors from the Feathered Council. Thorn even spotted one drop of white among all the Gehennish black. That had to be Gabriel.

Then he saw Lily.

She ran toward the bank edge. She was screaming at him. What was she trying to say?

A mighty rumble behind Thorn made him turn.

Flames engulfed the gatehouse. They reached a hundred feet high, and the clouds of smoke swelled and spread up and up, blacker than the night sky, smothering the stars and moonlight. Thorn stared as the upper level of the gatehouse trembled, then began to fall.

A brick hit him, blinding him with pain. Thorn wiped his face but only managed to smear blood over his eyes. Heart pounding, he tried to get up. He had to get off this bridge right now, escape the rubble raining down all around him.

A deep, ominous groan rose from the keep. It was the sound of thousands of tons of stone grinding against itself.

He had nowhere to run. It was too late.

THIRTEEN

Lily gazed at the burning gatehouse and the small figure of Thorn. He'd saved the zombies. They were crawling out of the moat, bedraggled, dripping wet, and covered in weeds.

He'd risked his life for the undead.

The gatehouse swayed. The flames had destroyed what little mortar was holding it together. "Run, Thorn!" she screamed, but Thorn wouldn't be able to hear her, not from here.

"He's dead," muttered Baron Sable. "It's coming down."

Dott bellowed. She and Thorn were friends.

The uppermost stones, those along the battlements, fell. It would only take one to flatten Thorn into a bloody paste, and there were thousands. No one could save him.

Except her.

Lily closed her eyes and forced all the darkness around her into . . . life.

The shadows between the wavering torches rushed toward her. The lightless patches in the empty doorways obeyed her summons. Long, rippling ribbons of darkness thrashed and flickered violently.

The Mantle of Sorrows pulsed as the spirits sewn within its uncanny cloth worked like fishermen to gather in the darkness.

Lily opened her eyes and cast the dark at the gatehouse.

People screamed in terror. Some fled as a huge, arching wave of oily blackness stretched out across the moat. Would it be strong enough to deflect the inestimable weight of stone falling on Thorn?

She had to believe it would. This was Shadow magic, and Lily was a Shadow. Her blood was blackest of all.

She cried out when the stone smashed against the shield of shadows. She felt as if she was being pummeled from all directions. As the crushing load bore down on her body and spirit, the weight pushed her to her knees.

Through tears of pain, she saw Thorn crawl toward the edge of the trembling bridge. He was bloody but alive. Unable to stand, he toppled over, and there was a splash as he disappeared into the moat.

"Get him," Lily whispered. "I can't hold it. . . ."

Baron Sable dove in. Ying ran across the broken ice and threw himself down near the hole where Thorn had gone in.

The stones were bearing down. Her shadow shield was cracking.

Dott yelled. "T'orn! T'orn!"

Lily glimpsed a soggy, shivering Thorn emerge from the moat, held up by Sable and Ying.

She dropped her magic.

The gatehouse finally collapsed completely, falling with a deafening roar, and shaking the ground so violently that people fell. Dust filled the air, stinging the eyes and obscuring everything. Eventually, the dust settled, and Lily got her first glimpse of the devastation.

The gatehouse was gone, and the keep still burning. The fire wouldn't go out until there was nothing left to burn. Tomorrow morning, there would just be a pile of blackened stone.

While Lily stared at the ruins, the others stared at her.

Villagers from afar. Her guests from the Feathered Council. Nobles she'd known her entire life.

"Did you see ..."

"I knew they were hiding something...."

"Not even her father could have done that...."

Thorn was alive. She'd saved him with her magic.

Magic she was supposed to keep secret.

She'd protected her best friend, used magic more powerful than anyone had ever seen, but no one was speaking with gratitude or admiration, only with fear.

Lily groped at the dirty, trampled snow. A savage pain ripped through her chest. She fought to breathe as her lungs tightened. Her bones ached.

What's happening to me?

She stared at her hands. The skin was wrinkled and becoming marked by ugly dark brown patches.

Too much. I used too much magic.

"Look at her...."

People backed away. Even Dott couldn't hide her bewilderment. "Prin'ess?"

A hand reached out, and Lily grabbed it. "Thank you."

She looked up to the dead gaze of a zombie. He was cold and dripping from the fall into the moat, and tangled with weeds and sprinkled with flowers. The other zombies gathered around her, reaching out to . . . help.

Lily's spine stiffened; she couldn't stand up straight. Each step was agony.

She stumbled on, slowing making her way back to the castle, and no one stopped her. She barely managed to turn the door handle, dragged herself over the threshold . . .

"Lily!"

It was Thorn, but she didn't turn around.

He mustn't see me like this.

"Lily! Wait!"

She got through the door, leaving the living and undead behind, and slammed it shut.

Why was it so bright? The candlelight burned her eyes.

She needed to get away from everyone. She needed to find out what was happening, and if she could stop it.

I need Father.

Lily faced the door of the Shadow Library.

It had taken her ages to reach it. She'd almost had to crawl at one point, when the pain had become crippling. But now she was upright, thank the Six. She could flex her fingers, and the wrinkles were fading. The effects hadn't been permanent.

This time.

But she felt weak, drained of all her energy.

There was still some pain when she looked at the lamps shining on the walls.

Iblis had warned her not to push past her limits. But he would understand why she had done it this time. He knew how much Thorn meant to her.

Lily reached into her pocket for the Skeleton Key. It wasn't there.

She checked her other pocket, then the first again. Both empty.

Maybe she'd dropped it? Maybe it had fallen out somewhere near Old Keep? Yes, that had to be it.

Just as she turned to head back, Lily heard the library door grinding apart.

It was a demon door. The first Lord Shadow had built it and bound a hundred and one demons into the strange metal. Only the bearer of the Skeleton Key could open it. Breaking in was impossible. Anyone else who even touched the door would awaken the hellish beasts trapped within its panels; not even bloody smears would be left. The demons took their task very seriously.

And yet now, unaided, the door was opening. . . .

The interior was lit by a pearly moonlight. It softly illuminated the statues and furniture within.

And the man standing there, waiting to flee. His crippled left hand was curled up against his chest, the Skeleton Key dangling from his clawlike fingers. In his right he carried a small black box.

It was Weaver, the conjuror from the feast.

"Ah, this is awkward," he said.

FOURTEEN

Weaver held her father's box. Why was he stealing that? There were far greater treasures in the library.

Not that it mattered.

"That does not belong to you," said Lily. "Put it back."

The man tightened his hold. "And if I don't?"

He covered himself with a tattered patchwork cloak, but there was no way for him to hide the hideously burned skin and the withered limbs, even in this dim light.

Lily stepped forward. "Put it back or I'll make you."

The conjuror tensed. "I made myself a promise, a long time ago. The Shadows hurt me once. But never again."

There was no mistaking the rage in that reply. "Who are you?"

"My first name was burned away. I am Weaver now."

"Then, Weaver, I'll tell you this just once more: put the key and the box down."

"No. I am owed both, at least."

What did he mean?

Lily edged a step closer. "The fire in Old Keep. That was deliberate, wasn't it?"

"My companion Firestarter." There was a hint of a smile. "A distraction to keep you all busy while I searched. But I had no idea how truly vast the library was, and it took me longer than expected to find what I was looking for."

"Why that box? It's just got a bunch of my father's letters in it, not magical scrolls, if that's what you're thinking. They're worthless to you."

"You have no idea."

His eyes were stony pale and bitter. This man was her enemy, but she couldn't understand why. "What is it that you want, Weaver?"

That bitterness deepened. "Oh, just everything."

Lily's magic was strongest down here in the buried heart of Castle Gloom. Normally she would just tie him up with black strands of shadow, or steal enough life from him to make him collapse. But right now it was Lily who felt on the verge of collapsing; she wasn't sure what would happen to her if she cast even the simplest magic. Her head still swam with exhaustion, and she struggled to remain standing.

And this Weaver looked so fragile, so broken. "I don't want to hurt you," she said.

"Hurt? As if you could." He took a step forward. Was he going to attack her? How? That rage he was trying to suppress, it was spilling out; his hate was almost overwhelming him. "I owe you so much pain . . . but not yet. Isn't there a saying here in Gehenna that revenge is a dish best served from the grave?"

"You're not dead."

"Oh, but I have been. For a long, long time." He took another step forward. "Now get out of my way."

"No."

Lily extended her hand and tried to tear a shadow off the wall, in that dull space between the spread of the torchlight. Just enough to trap him . . .

"Magic? This I'd like to see," mocked Weaver.

Lily pulled, but the strands just turned to smoke between her fingers. Her heart pounded as she tried to hold on to them. Every part of her ached.

Senses spinning, Lily gazed at Weaver; then her vision darkened and she fell. . . .

FIFTEEN

Thorn longed to check on Lily.

He didn't want to be here, in the Night chambers with Baron Sable and Gabriel, listening to the Solar boy's opinion on how to run Castle Gloom.

"A torturer is what's needed," declared Gabriel. "I cannot believe Lilith doesn't have one. We have three back at home, don't we, Mr. Funny?"

Mr. Funny jingle-jangled his head up and down on his scrawny neck. "Yes, Master. Three men with quick blades and hot pokers."

"Thank you for your suggestion," said Baron Sable. "But as you've said, Castle Gloom does not have a torturer, and hasn't for over three hundred years."

Gabriel scoffed. "It's amazing you've not been overthrown, then."

"Like you?" snapped Thorn.

Gabriel turned to look at him, a sneer cutting his face. "Baron Sable, is it really necessary to have this . . . *peasant* here?"

Baron Sable brushed his mustache. Thorn wasn't sure if it was because he was angry or smiling. "Young Thorn's one of us, m'lord. He has as much right to be here as you."

Gabriel stood up and brushed his white jacket. "It's an insult to compare a noble to a mere commoner, Baron." He snapped his fingers, and his jester jumped up. "Let us be on our way, Mr. Funny. I have letters to write. My father will be very interested to hear of tonight's events."

Thorn stepped aside, pausing only to swap scowls with Gabriel. They hated each other, and five minutes together was five minutes too long.

Mr. Funny giggled nervously as they left.

Thorn's head ached badly. Dr. Byle had coated the cut on his scalp and bandaged it tightly, promising that he'd stop any brains from spilling out. Then he'd offered to swap Thorn's brain for one in a jar he had on his desk. Thorn hadn't laughed, and he'd gotten out of the infirmary before the doctor could grab his saw.

Baron Sable filled a tall tankard with ale from a jug, then poured it back and drank from the jug instead. He glugged the whole contents down, not spilling a single drop. He gazed into the empty vessel and sighed. "What a mess."

"She saved my life," said Thorn, propped up at the door. "Lily's not to blame."

"You're right. This is *your* fault. What in the name of the Six were you doing at Old Keep, boy?" He gestured irritatedly at a chair. "And sit down before you fall down. Your swaying is making me seasick."

"I'm perfectly fine—"

Baron Sable growled, and Thorn sat down. And let his weariness seep out.

I should be in bed. I should be under the covers with a hot chocolate in my belly and the warming pan for my toes.

Or I should be dead.

The baron stomped over to the door and bellowed, "Will someone get me more ale?"

Thorn tried to find a position that didn't hurt. Bruises covered every inch of him. His bruises had bruises.

But he couldn't rest. The castle was in chaos.

Lily had used magic. She'd broken the first and greatest law of the New Kingdoms.

All to save him.

Word was that Ying and the rest of the Feathered Council had already left.

So much for that marriage proposal.

Thorn couldn't help but be a *little* glad.

He reached over to a glass of aqua vitae and let the cool, refreshing liquid run down his throat, warming as it went until he felt a happy glow in the pit of his stomach. "How much trouble is she in?"

"As much as anyone can be. I warned her," said the baron. "Everyone knew, of course, but as long as no one *knew*, then it didn't matter."

"I get it, I think. So what? Lily rules Gehenna. She's a Shadow. She can do what she likes."

"And that is where you are entirely wrong. The devil's at the door, boy, and there'll be hell to pay. You mark my words. Hell to pay."

As if they didn't have enough to worry about already. "What about them zombies?" asked Thorn. "Where are we gonna put them now?"

"The catacombs. Those we can find, that is. Half of them have roamed off. They could be anywhere by now." He shouted again from the doorway. "More ale!"

Something else was wrong, Thorn could tell. Baron Sable paced back and forth in the antechamber, pulling savagely at the ends of his mustache. It was more than Lily's magic. He must have known she'd do something public, sooner or later.

There was a nest of thin paper strips on the desk. The castle used the papers for sending coded messages via their bats. Thorn had worked with Tyburn long enough to learn the system. The executioner sent him up to collect the tiny scrolls from the belfry twice a day.

"Bad news, m'lord?" Thorn asked.

Baron Sable's fist tightened, and he tensed, as if searching for something to lash out at. Then his shoulders sank. "Word from Baal's legion."

Word from *his legion*. Not Baal himself.

Baron Sable picked up a strip of paper. He rubbed his eyes. "They came across a party of trolls. Baal was leading a patrol along the west of the Troll-Teeth, by Grendel's Gorge."

"Your son's dealt with troll raiders before."

"It wasn't a raiding party, Thorn. It was an army." He waved the paper. "The Stonehammers, the Rockheads, and the Flintfists. Three clans' worth of troll warriors."

Thorn knew what that meant. It meant hard times ahead. "So it's true, the trolls have a king."

"My son needs me," said the baron, looking weary and even a bit afraid.

"What happened to Baal?"

The baron shook his head. "No one knows. Half the patrol never made it back to camp."

"If the trolls break through and head south, we ain't got the men to defend Castle Gloom. It'll—"

"Don't you think I know that, boy?" snapped Sable. "What we need are allies, something we'll be sorely lacking once word gets out regarding . . . Lady Shadow's antics."

"She could use her magic to protect Gloom. Just like her father did."

Sable scoffed. "Look what happened to her when she tried to protect you."

The door opened, and a servant came in, carrying a jug. He shuffled, achingly slowly, being careful not to spill a drop. The zombie stopped at the table and steadied himself with an arm that was barely attached with poor stitches. Then he began the process of lowering the jug onto the table. Sable snatched it from him. "Why does she bother? These zombies are useless."

Thorn shrugged. The zombies seemed to work well enough when Lily was around. Probably because she treated them nicely, he supposed. Wasn't it the same for all servants? Treat them well, and they'll do well in return.

The baron gulped from the jug.

Then spat it out. "This is vinegar! You . . . you . . ."

"Uurh rurr rurh?"

Slowly, despairingly, the baron sank down into a chair. He waved. "Leave. Just . . . leave."

"I should go and see her." Thorn still hadn't thanked Lily for saving him, and then there was the break-in at the Shadow Library. "I should check to make sure she's all right."

"Lady Shadow does not need a smelly squire as a nursemaid. This matter will be picked up in the morning, and hopefully, we'll have our executioner back by then. Whatever Tyburn's up to, it's taking too long. I've sent bats out to summon him because I can't stay here. Those trolls aren't going to kill themselves; they'll be needing me to do it." He turned to Thorn. "Get yourself back to the infirmary. Now."

There was no point arguing with the baron. Thorn stood and bowed. "Good night, m'lord."

"'Night, Thorn." He put his hand on Thorn's shoulder. "And for what it's worth, I'm glad Lady Shadow saved you."

"Me too."

Thorn left and walked around the corner, then stopped. He waited and listened. The door closed, and he heard the chair creak as Sable sat down in it.

The infirmary could wait. He needed to go to the dungeons first. To have a word with an old friend.

All right, not exactly an old friend, but someone he'd spent a month chained to when he'd been a slave.

That counted for something, didn't it?

∽

"Hello, Merrick," said Thorn, leaning through the cell bars. "Why is it that every time we meet you're in chains?"

Beyond the bars, lying on a pallet, was a man dressed in a purple tunic with gold trim and a pair of boots with excessively turned-up toes. They twitched as the man rolled over and blinked, focusing his eyes on Thorn. "I recognize that voice. . . ."

"It's me, Thorn."

"Thorn!" Merrick leaped up and dashed to the bars. He grabbed Thorn's hands. "I am saved!"

"What happened?" Thorn asked, trying to wriggle his hands free as Merrick kissed them.

"Saved. *Saved!* I knew the Six wouldn't abandon me."

"Yeah, thank the Six, and can I have my hands back?" Thorn finally pulled them free.

"Who is it, Erik?" asked another voice.

Thorn realized there was someone else in the cell. A woman. She unwrapped herself from a blanket and adjusted her hair. "Who is it?"

Merrick clapped his hands. "My dear! This is the young boy I told you about!"

The woman looked at Thorn and didn't seem impressed. "The one you said abandoned you to slavers?"

"Yes, well . . ."

"The one whose life you saved when he fell overboard into a shark-infested sea?"

"Yes, well . . ."

"The one you said had an outlaw for a father and would no doubt come to an unfortunate, violent, but entirely predictable early death?"

"Er . . . did I say that?" Merrick looked at Thorn and twisted what could have been a smile onto his lips. "Ah, that was an entirely *different* Thorn. Common name. Terribly common."

"What are you doing here?" Thorn asked. "*Why* are you here?"

Merrick took the woman's hand. "Thorn, allow me to introduce you to my muse, my little viper of joy, my sweet cockroach of delight, Mrs. Esmeralda Merrick. My wife."

"Your wife? You're married? That's . . . er, strange. And surprising."

"Very recently married. Still in the honeymoon phase, as it were." Merrick smiled at his new bride. Thorn had seen happier expressions on zombies. "It's complicated and involves a game of cards that got out of hand."

She continued to look down at Thorn, and sniffed. "He smells, Erik."

"Boys do, my dear."

Thorn arched an eyebrow. "Erik Merrick?"

"Erik Merrick the *Third*. Son of Erik Merrick the Second, grandson of Erik Merrick the Original." He sighed. "A family entirely lacking in imagination."

"And musical talent?"

"How very droll, young Thorn. You're growing into a wit. There'll be no stopping you soon."

"You still ain't said why you're here."

Merrick puffed up his skinny chest. "Did you see those wagons out in the south courtyard? By Dead Man's Gate? They're mine. All of them. You are no longer looking at a mere minstrel, Thorn, but the *manager* of a troupe of traveling players. Not just manager, but director and star. Soon to be famous throughout the New Kingdoms."

"And starting in the dungeons of Castle Gloom?"

"A tragic misunderstanding. Most tragic." He sniffed loudly. "It is an artist's lot to suffer. It feeds the soul."

"Thought this might feed the stomach." Thorn pushed a wrapped-up packet of cold chicken into Merrick's grateful grasp. "What happened?"

Merrick and his wife tore the packet open, and three chicken legs disappeared in as many seconds. "Not my fault, Thorn," declared Merrick between mouthfuls. "Not my fault at all. How was I to know the three conjurors I'd hired were such criminals?"

Merrick sat and told Thorn a tale. Between them, they filled in many gaps for each other.

Merrick had recruited the three conjurors a week ago, one being Weaver. The other was a fire-eater from the far south, who called himself Firestarter. The third, an easterner from the same country as Ying. Merrick had thought such an exotic mix would surely add gold to his coffers.

It had been Weaver who'd suggested the journey to Castle Gloom.

What did Merrick know about Weaver? Not much. He'd had his hands full dealing with the jugglers and acrobats and clowns, and the trio of conjurors kept themselves to themselves and caused no trouble.

But Thorn had seen Firestarter use real magic, sorcery. Just to cause a distraction so Weaver could break into the Shadow Library.

Now they'd vanished. The guard at Skeleton Gate had seen them leave but hadn't stopped them; they'd left before any alarm had been raised. Baron Sable was planning a search party at dawn, but Thorn knew it would be too late by then.

"Is Lady Shadow unharmed?" asked Merrick. "Weaver didn't hurt her, did he? I heard—"

"She's fine. She tried to stop him but fainted. By the time she regained consciousness, he was gone." Baron Sable had told him as much. The baron had acted swiftly once Lily had appeared, imprisoning Merrick's entire troupe and shutting all the gates out of Gloom.

"What did he steal?" asked Merrick.

"Nothing important."

That was what Thorn didn't understand. The Shadow Library contained treasures from the earliest days, yet all Weaver had taken was a box of old letters.

Had Weaver, in a rush, mistaken them for something else?

That was the only thing that made sense, yet, as with the riddle of Pitch Farm, Thorn felt something wasn't right. . . .

"So here I am, Thorn," said Merrick morosely. He nibbled the last of the meat off his chicken leg. "Doomed. My life a constant tragedy."

"But you've got a lovely wife."

"Have I? Where?" He glanced over his shoulder at the woman devouring the remainder of the food. "Oh, her." He leaned closer to the bars and whispered, "You have to help me, Thorn."

"Don't worry. Once Lily knows what happened, I'm sure she'll let you go. It's that Weaver—"

Merrick shook his head. "I was not made for matrimony, Thorn."

"Oh?"

"It was a game of cards. One I was, surprisingly, winning." He went a sickly yellow. "I should have checked the small print. Before I knew it, I'd laid down the queen of hearts and won myself this band of players. Performers, wagons, livestock, and an amusing parrot. And . . . er, a wife."

"You *won* your wife?"

"Stranger things happen at cards." He leaned closer, reaching within an inch or two of Thorn's ear. "Is Tyburn here?"

"Why?"

Merrick bit his lip. "I . . . need to arrange a divorce."

"Why would you need an executioner to arrange . . . oh. *That* sort of divorce." Thorn tried to turn his smirk into a disapproving frown. "Shame on you, Merrick."

"It was never meant to be, Thorn. The troupe is a bunch of misfits who've taken to the road because they're too lazy and incompetent to do real work. They're the dross of the world, boy. The jugglers hate the acrobats, the dwarves argue with the stilt man, and the only ones who are any good are the conjurors, and they turned out to be the worst of the lot, stealing from Lady Shadow! I'll be lucky not to find my head up on Lamentation Hill!"

"It can't be that bad."

Tears filled Merrick's eyes. "I was born to be free, Thorn. Free!"

"Good-bye, Merrick. I'll see what I can do." Thorn stopped, then added, "About getting you freed, not the . . . other thing."

SIXTEEN

Lily knew it was dawn. She knew it from the smell of freshly baked bread drifting out of the kitchens. She knew it from the sound of footsteps as the maids scurried to light the fires and the stomp of boots as the night guards swapped duty with the day guards. It was dawn and she had a few more hours before she had to do *anything*.

Yet someone was knocking at her door. And she knew exactly who.

"Go away!" she shouted. The knocking continued.

"Go away!"

"Lily, it's me—Thorn."

"I don't want to see you."

"But we should talk!"

"I'm busy," Lily answered as she lay on her bed, staring up at the folds of the canopy.

"No, you're not. Dott says you're in there sulking."

"Dott should keep her big mouth shut."

There was a pause. Was he finally leaving?

"I have something for you," said Thorn. "A present. A beautiful golden gift. Very rare."

Lily sighed. "Is it a mango?"

Another pause.

"It is, isn't it?"

"You're no fun at all, Lily," said Thorn. "Now let me in."

He wasn't going to leave. And she loved mangoes. "The door's not locked."

Thorn entered, a fruit in his hand and a bandage around his head. "I just wanted to see how you were doing."

"Me? I'm not the one who had a building dropped on him." *I should have gone to check on him.* "Does it hurt?"

"It's a bit sore. Dr. Byle said he'd give me a new brain if mine weren't working properly no more."

"I'm sure he was joking," said Lily. Then she remembered Dr. Byle wasn't like other physicians. "No, he probably wasn't."

Thorn peered at Lily critically. "And how about you? All back to normal?"

"This time."

"What's that supposed to mean?"

Lily held up her hands. The skin was smooth and clear, her nails neat and straight. "Father warned me about overextending myself. Magic uses up a lot of energy. It can eat you up, change you."

Thorn frowned. "I didn't know that. Is magic worth it? I've overheard some of the squires, and some of the other servants. They're frightened."

"Of me?"

"In some ways, maybe." Thorn shrugged. He raised his golden fruit. "You want it?"

"Of course. How many of K'leef's mangoes do you have left?" Lily asked.

"Five." Thorn rubbed it against his sleeve. "Trying to make them last till spring."

After Thorn and Lily had helped K'leef escape and get back to his father, the sultan had been grateful. Thorn had received a crate of mangoes, and Lily had been sent twelve of the finest horses in the world. One might have thought the gifts were a bit uneven, depending on how much you liked mangoes.

Thorn took out a knife and started slicing. "What happened to your flowers?" he asked casually.

Lily's mother had always decorated with fresh-cut flowers, the only splash of color in the room, and Lily continued the practice. They perfumed her chambers with haunting smells. Ying had brought her rare orchids, and she'd put them in a crystal vase on the table. Two lava blooms had, until yesterday, glowed softly on either side of her bed.

Now they were all withered and dead, their petals discarded on the floor.

"It just . . . happened." She wasn't sure how. After she had regained consciousness last night, she'd been so angry at Weaver that she'd stormed into her room and screamed, and the flowers had died.

"You've got to control yourself," warned Thorn.

"Maybe I don't want to anymore."

Thorn's face hardened. "That's scary talk, Lily."

Lily sat up. "Is that what you want, Thorn? For me to be a good little girl? Mind my manners? Do what I'm told and sit quietly and say nothing? Do nothing?" She shoved the dead flowers off the side table. "I can do whatever I want, and you can't stop me."

"Of course I can't. No one can. You're too powerful."

That didn't sound like a compliment.

"If you hadn't been, I'd be dead under a thousand tons of gatehouse," he continued.

That did.

"Is that a thank-you?" she asked.

"Yeah. What do you want, a proclamation? I can arrange one, but I need to get the trumpeters first. They're having breakfast right now."

Lily sank back down. "It's all a disaster. Ying left without even saying good-bye, it was that bad. Baron Sable thinks one of the other lords might try and overthrow me for breaking the law. He's also worried about the other houses sending someone."

"Someone like who?"

"Assassins. Executioners. People of questionable morality," said Lily. "Father had three attempted assassinations in his first year as ruler. One from Lumina—but they always sent one. Then another from the Coral king, and one from his grandfather."

"Iblis's own grandfather tried to kill him?"

"We're a complicated family, Thorn."

"Then why are you leaving your door unlocked? You should have guards out there! C'mon, Lily! Think about it!" He was up and at the door immediately. He locked it, and put the key on the table.

"It'll be all right as soon as Tyburn gets back. No one will try anything with him around," Lily said. "And I've got you, haven't I?"

Thorn blushed. "Suppose." He handed her a slice.

"Delicious," Lily declared. Maybe Thorn had gotten a fair enough deal. Few in Gehenna had ever tasted mangoes.

"Lying on the bed with your boots on," said Thorn. "What would Mary say?"

"Are you here to be useful or annoying?"

"I had questions, is all. Like, what happened at the library? Sable says there was a break-in. I thought that was impossible. Anyone who tried it would be dinner for them door demons."

"Weaver stole the Skeleton Key off me during the feast. Still has it."

"So what else did he take, besides some letters?"

It had been on Lily's mind all night. "I don't know. But the letters are worthless."

"Maybe they are, maybe they ain't. Have you asked your dad about them?"

That was the worst of it. "I can't. Father only exists within the library, and without the key, I can't get in." Lily checked her pocket, as if the Skeleton Key might have magicked itself there. It hadn't. "It's not just the Shadow Library it opens, but any lock, anywhere. And it's one of a kind, made of the finger bones of the Scarlet Trickster, the greatest thief who ever lived."

Thorn nodded. "My grandpa had this great story about him. How he stole Prince Herne's magical chestnuts and trapped the world in ten years of winter. Then—"

"This is going to be one of those ponderous grandpa tales, isn't it?" Lily put up a hand. "Please, Thorn, not today."

"All right, just because you've had a tough night. But my grandpa always said—"

"Thorn!"

He laughed and took a second wedge of mango.

Lily felt miserable. "I can't believe I lost it."

"You didn't lose it; the key was stolen. Anyway, you don't need those books to do magic. You'll be all right."

"The books can go burn, Thorn. My *father* is in there. It's the only place he can manifest himself," said Lily, despairing. "I need him."

"We'll get the key back," said Thorn. "This Weaver and his mates can't get out of Gehenna. Sooner or later we'll find them." His gaze roamed over the desk as he put the slice of fruit in his mouth. "What are these?" He walked his fingers over a pile of paper.

"You really *are* full of questions today, aren't you? Those are letters from K'leef. A merchant brought them."

"Are these meant to be words? They look like ripples in the sand."

"That's Djinnic, the writing of the Sultanate. Their letters are very different from ours, all swoops and curves. It's very beautiful. K'leef's got an elegant hand."

"There's more than one type of writing?" Thorn's face crumpled. "And I suppose you can read this, too. What's he say?"

"A bit about the war with Lumina. Asks how the horses were coping with our winter," said Lily. "Asks when I'm coming to see him." There was more in those letters, but Lily didn't think Thorn would want to hear about it all.

"Oh. That's nice." He pushed the letters away from him.

They were friends, Thorn and K'leef. Thorn had risked his life to save the sultan's son, but K'leef was everything Thorn wasn't and, maybe, wished to be. Even friends could be jealous of each other.

Thorn licked the gold juice off his fingers. "Anyway, I hope the talk about last night settles down. It was just one little spell. . . ."

"People don't understand magic. And what they don't understand frightens them. They believe the Six Princes themselves laid a curse on women to stop them from attempting sorcery."

"Yeah, the druids back in Herne's Forest say the same thing. They say women's magic is to blame when the crops fail. Or when there's a drought. Or a flood. They say it upsets nature."

"Is that what you think?" Lily asked.

"I think I'd be dead if it weren't for your magic."

"Lady Shadow?" A fist banged on the door. "It's me, Sable!"

Thorn jumped up and unlocked the door. Baron Sable burst in, fully armored. He glowered at Thorn. "I thought I told you to leave Lady Shadow to rest?"

Lily put up her hand. "It's all right, Baron. Thorn was bringing me some breakfast. What is it?"

"It's Tyburn," said the baron.

Lily felt the weight rise off her shoulders. "Send him up. We have a lot to discuss before you leave."

The baron twisted his mustache. "M'lady . . ."

"What is it?"

The baron gestured at the door. "Old Colm's back with the squires. They've been searching Bone-Tree for the last couple of days. They found . . . they found . . ."

Lily grabbed Sable's arm, suddenly frightened. "Tell me."

"They found his body," said Sable. "Tyburn's dead."

SEVENTEEN

*T**his can't be real.*

Lily couldn't accept it. She had to be drifting in some awful dream.

Eight months ago, her world had been torn apart when her parents and brother were murdered. Black despair had planted itself in her heart, weighing her down, bleeding out any happiness she'd ever had. She'd *almost* given in to it. The temptation to sit silently in the dark forever had been nearly overwhelming.

Thorn had dragged her out of her misery. He, K'leef, and other people had cared for her, and eventually she'd cared for herself.

Now this.

Tyburn couldn't be dead. The world didn't work like that.

Grim news traveled fast. By the time Lily and Thorn reached Skeleton Gate, half of Castle Gloom had already collected to view the return of Tyburn's body. Some of the servants, Black Guard, and squires, still nervous about Lily's sorcery at Old Keep last night, watched from a wary distance. Dott stood at the door of the kitchens, with Cook and the rest of the staff. She had the baker's boy on her shoulders so he could see. The soldiers were pale-faced. Most had been through the wars with Lumina and knew death well, but this was different.

This was Tyburn.

He was a killer. An executioner who coldly meted out justice. But he was loyal to the Shadows and had never failed them. Lily's father had trusted him above all others, even old nobles like Baron Sable. He was as much part of Castle Gloom as the ghosts and the gargoyles. An ever-present mystery: no one had even learned his first name after all these years. What could she do, without her father to guide her and Tyburn to protect her? The executioner's reputation had been worth an entire army.

Lily felt truly defenseless. Truly afraid.

And she wasn't the only one. Her servants backed away as she passed by. Some, people she'd known her whole life, lowered their gaze so as not to meet hers.

How can they fear me? I'm the same Lily. Why should me being a necromancer make such a difference? They never looked at my father like that. They adored him.

Thorn drifted away from Lily and joined the returning squires. He lowered his head to whisper to Wade. The boy was leading Thunder, Tyburn's great ebony warhorse. The stallion had cuts on his legs and flank; he'd been fighting.

Old Colm looked like he'd aged ten years, and he didn't have the years to spare. He bowed awkwardly as Lily approached. "I must warn you, m'lady, it's not a pretty sight."

"Death rarely is," Lily replied. She reached a covered wagon. "Tyburn's in here?"

"What's left of him. Trolls smashed him up, not two whole bones in his body. Then dropped him to be picked at by whatever beast was passing."

Lily swallowed. They'd brought the remains of her parents and Dante back on a wagon just like this, each covered by a sheet. They'd looked so much smaller than she'd expected. But this . . . *thing* under the sheet wasn't even a human shape anymore.

Lily set her mouth into a hard line. She was House Shadow. Death couldn't frighten her.

She pulled back the sheet and wished she hadn't.

Lily closed her eyes to steady herself. *I'm weak from last night's magic, that's all. It's just a body. I've seen worse.*

But only once before.

"Send everyone back to work, Baron," she whispered.

Baron turned around, and the anger in his eyes had people scurrying off before he'd even taken a breath. When he did shout, the bats sprang awake in their hidden nests and flew, petrified, out and over them like a massive, swirling, shrieking cloud.

"Who are they?" Lily asked, pointing at the two other covered bodies.

"Pitch and his wife, Milly," said Old Colm. "We'd been patrolling the edge of Bone-Tree and saw their farm. Been attacked by trolls. Young Thorn found them but not their two sons. So I decided to spend another day searching, in case the boys had hidden themselves deeper in the forest. No luck with them, but we came across Thunder. He'd been attacked. Nothing broken, thank the Six. He's a tough beast."

"Where did you find Tyburn?"

"Nearby."

"Why did they smash him up so much?" They must have continued beating the body well after he was dead.

Old Colm sighed. "Revenge. The trolls hated Tyburn."

Lily scanned the crowd for Dott. There she was. The young troll met Lily's gaze, and it was obvious that she was frightened. Dott had had nothing to do with this, but Gehennish prejudices against trolls ran deep and long. Lily saw how some of the Black Guard and kitchen staff glared at Dott now.

What do I know about trolls?

The body lay under the shroud. It had been dead awhile, frozen in the snow.

The trolls feared Tyburn. Dott had told her that Tyburn was their bogeyman. Troll parents used him to frighten their children. *You misbehave and Tyburn will get you.*

Trolls feared and respected Tyburn.

Wait a minute. . . .

Lily stared at the covered body.

A *body.*

Her heart leaped in her chest, but on the outside she remained emotionless.

She couldn't let them know, not yet, but she had to tell someone. Who?

She searched for Thorn and found him, grim-faced, among the squires.

Baron Sable stood a few yards away, his hand squeezing his sword hilt so tightly it trembled. "No way for a man like Tyburn to die."

"No way for *any* man to die," said Lily.

He's thinking about his son Baal. By the Six, has the same thing happened to him?

Lily shook the hideous thought away. She needed to act. Everyone was standing around, too stunned to think. She needed to be Lady Shadow. "Gather your men, Baron. I want you at the Troll-Teeth."

"M'lady, this changes everything. Without Tyburn here, who'll keep you safe?"

"And without you at our borders, who will keep all of us safe?"

She could see that the baron was conflicted, torn between his love for his son and his sense of duty to her.

"Go, Baron. I need you up north."

"The Six guard you, m'lady." The baron snapped a half bow, then gestured to his captains. They marched off, their armored steps clanging on the cobblestones.

She could speak to the dead. She'd done it before, poorly, but she knew she could do it. Not with this body, though. It was so mangled that any spirit she'd summon would be in turmoil, consumed by madness and pain.

"Take the body to the chapel, Colm." Lily touched the old man's arm. "Have him prepared as best you can."

"And these two?" he asked.

Lily took a deep breath. "Pitch and Milly go to the mortuary."

EIGHTEEN

"Why are we going to the mortuary?" asked Thorn. "Why am *I* going?" He hated the place.

Lily put her finger to her lips.

Thorn followed, but slowly. Lily was up to something and that made him ... wary.

Tyburn's dead.

That made as much sense as ... fish flying.

He owed so much to Tyburn. His place here in Castle Gloom, his friendship with Lily, his very life, even. The executioner had rescued him from slavery and brought him to Gehenna.

He'd never really liked Tyburn—Thorn reckoned nobody did—but he'd respected the man. Thorn was more shocked than anything. How could Tyburn, of all people, be dead, just like that?

As for Lily, she seemed completely unmoved. Her coldness seemed cruel. But she was a Shadow; maybe the rules about life and death were a bit different to someone who could summon ghosts.

I'll never understand her.

"I should be helping the other squires," he said. "They'll be needing everyone at the stables."

Lily glanced back at him. "If I didn't know better, I'd think you were scared."

"That I ain't."

"Then hurry up."

The mortuary was busier than usual.

A line of zombies waited patiently for the surgeon. Zombies were good at waiting patiently. Each had a body part missing. A trio of squires shifted through a pile of limbs, searching, comparing, and fitting arms to sockets, legs to hips, heads to necks, looking for the piece that matched.

Thorn stepped carefully over a pile of left legs. He'd swapped double stable duty to avoid having to work down here. Sweeping up horse dung was way better than sweeping up bits of people.

"M'lady!" The surgeon dropped the arm he was working on and rushed over. "How good of you to visit!"

Lily greeted him. "I should have come earlier, Dr. Byle. How goes your work?"

"Overflowing with patients. Not that I'm complaining, but I could do with some extra hands? Preferably attached?"

"I thought I'd sent two of my serving girls down?"

"Lisbeth fainted the moment I asked her to push the intestines back into Mr. Gareth so I could sew up his belly. Such a mess she made, getting tangled up in all that tubing."

"Do zombies need intestines?" asked Thorn, trying to hold down his breakfast. The air was practically green with decomposition.

Dr. Byle stiffened. "They come in with guts; they leave with guts. It's called professionalism."

"What do you need, Dr. Byle?"

"A butcher's boy, handy with offal. I'll teach him to sew. To be honest, it's thick needles and twine for this lot." He gestured to the queue. "And not a few nails."

"I'll see what I can do," Lily replied. "Now, I need to see the two cadavers Old Colm brought in."

"In the cold room. You asked me not to work on them."

"That's right. I'll deal with them."

Dr. Byle bowed. "As you wish, m'lady."

"Is that it, Lily?" snapped Thorn. "Tyburn's dead, and you've not said anything."

How could she be so heartless?

He should have known she'd be like this. That was the trouble with nobles. They kept everything under wraps. Or maybe Tyburn was just another servant. They came, they went, no big deal.

"Or are you gonna bring him back? Make him one of your zombies? Get him to carry drinks at dinnertime?"

"The body's too badly damaged, Thorn. He'd be of no use."

Thorn grabbed her arm. "Tyburn's dead!"

Lily looked down at his hand, gripping her.

Still angry, Thorn let go.

"I know you're upset," said Lily. "I was, too."

"But now you're not? Wow, you got over it very quickly," Thorn replied bitterly.

"That's not Tyburn."

Thorn's breath stopped in his chest. He stared at her. Was this some bad joke? "But the body . . ."

"Some poor man's been killed, and the person responsible will pay for that, I promise you, but it's not Tyburn, and it wasn't trolls."

"What and ... *what*?" He rubbed his head. "I think you'd better explain. Assume I know nothing, it'll be easier."

"Old Colm should have realized, but he's so caught up in his hate that he can't see what's right in front of him: a body."

"A dead one. A very dead one."

Lily faced him, those gray eyes of hers shimmering like quicksilver. "Trolls ate Old Colm's leg. You know that?"

"Yeah, everyone knows that."

"Then why didn't they eat Tyburn?" said Lily. "That's what trolls do. It's a sign of respect for their enemies."

"So you think ...?"

Lily smiled. "No troll would abandon Tyburn. He'd be part of a feast, a big one. The trolls would hope to gain his courage, his skill, by eating his flesh. They'd decorate their armor and weapons with his bones, believing his spirit would lend them greater power. No, a body was left for us to find so we'd think that Tyburn's dead. That the trolls did it. But whoever's done this doesn't know about trolls like I do."

"All right, suppose you're right and it ain't trolls. It could still be brigands, or someone else with a grudge against Tyburn. The man must have had hundreds of enemies. Thousands."

Lily shook her head. "What does your gut tell you, Thorn? Do you honestly think a bunch of outlaws could take down Tyburn?"

Thorn could recall at least one occasion when Tyburn had wiped out a band of outlaws single-handedly. He nodded. "True, no bandit could. But as Ying said, there's always someone better out there."

"Ying said the same thing to me," added Lily. "But there are only two others who might have a *chance* against Tyburn. They are executioners, too. There's Lady Kali, who serves House Djinn. But they're our allies. The Solars have Golgoth, but the only Solars within a thousand miles of here are Gabriel and poor Mr. Funny."

"Then who—"

"It's a mystery," Lily said, looking at the two corpses. "A mystery I hope to solve—with them."

Thorn scowled. "So you're gonna talk to the dead? You sure about this?"

"I don't know. I feel like I'm looking at a jigsaw puzzle and there's a big piece in the middle missing. I need that piece if I'm to understand the picture." She pointed at a small vase. "Light those incense sticks, will you?"

"Is that to appease the spirits of the dead?"

"No, to appease their smell. This pair have a bit of a pong now that they're defrosting."

Death had locked their limbs, and the mixture of mud and blood on their skin had dried almost black. Their clothes, in the candlelight, seemed too thin for winter.

"They had hard lives," said Thorn.

Lily peered at the slash in the man's belly. She dipped her fingers into the gap and gently pulled the tear wider. "Their deaths were harder. Look at this."

"No." He didn't like being down here. Why did she need him, anyway? This was Shadow magic.

Necromancy.

Thorn gazed around the room, looking everywhere but at Lily and the two corpses. He took a candle and lit the incense sticks and watched the thin smoke spiral up from their glowing tips. "Don't you think it's weird? How easy you are with them?"

"Them?" Lily had her hand on the cheek of the woman. "They are my people, living or dead."

"And anything in between, right?"

"I was raised by a zombie, Thorn. Dante and I played with One-Eyed Ron since we could walk. He let me practice my sewing on him and never minded if I didn't get his ears exactly level."

"You're a strange, *strange* girl, Lily."

Lily collected a basin from a side table. "Let's get to work."

Black rose petals floated in the water, and they smelled of the perfume of soft dreams. Thorn took a cloth and washed the faces clean while Lily wiped down their hands. They cut the rags off their bodies and cleaned the dirt from the worn, pale flesh. Finally Lily spread black linen sheets over them, folding the edges neatly so it looked as if they were only sleeping, hands folded on top.

Lily moved to the head of the table. She looked up at Thorn. "Ready?"

"Not really."

Lily didn't bother to reply. She put one hand on the forehead of each corpse and closed her eyes.

"What are you doing?" Thorn asked. Was it his imagination, or was it getting colder?

"*Shh.*"

The hairs prickled up along the back of his neck. What was going to happen? Would a spirit enter Lily and she start talking in the voice of one of the dead? Or would their ghosts appear, hovering above their torn bodies? Maybe they'd sit up, blink, and shuffle off to join the ranks of zombies already occupying Castle Gloom. . . .

He really wished he hadn't come along.

How could she be so calm about this? Did Lily have nightmares? What scared her? Certainly not ghosts, ghouls, or vampires. They were her relatives. Maybe she was scared of fluffy cats and prancing ponies.

Custard jumped up on the table. He stood on the chest of the dead man, growling at his face.

The man's mouth moved.

Lips slowly parted into a loose sneer.

The body juddered, shaking and thrashing on the black marble slab.

Thorn's hand went to his belt; then he realized he hadn't brought his dagger.

The woman began to tremble. Her head twitched. Her neck stiffened as she arched her head back. Her jaw creaked.

"Lily, what are you doing?" He picked up a hefty candlestick.

Lily's eyes snapped open, and she stepped back. "It's not me."

"You sure?"

"Of course I'm sure!"

He'd had enough. "Time to go."

"No, I need to see."

"Lily . . ."

Both bodies were shaking. Under the black sheets their bellies began to swell, pushing the cloth up until the sheets were sitting over them like tents. Custard leaped off and scurried out through a wall.

That's not good. . . .

Much more and they could explode, which would mean he'd be having his weekly bath early.

A hideous, leathery sound interrupted the horror of the thrashing bodies. Thorn watched as the swollen bellies quivered under the cloth, then sagged.

"Get behind me," Thorn ordered.

"I will do what I—"

"Do it!"

She did. Thorn didn't need to see Lily to know she was scowling at him, her lips thin with anger. He held up the candlestick.

Something crawled out of the man's mouth. A needle-sized pair of crystal stalks. They twitched and tapped the man's lip.

Not stalks. Legs.

The man's mouth widened, and the legs were followed by another pair. The throat swelled as an object forced itself along, a body attached to the legs seeking freedom.

"Thorn!" Lily screamed.

The cloth *bubbled*.

Thorn used his candlestick to flick off the cloth.

Spiders covered the corpse. They were crawling out of a gash in his belly. Greasy with blood, they spread across him, their bodies all nervous and angular. Spiders and other insects sometimes planted eggs in other animals. But not like this. . . .

They were different sizes. Most not even an inch long, some almost the size of his fist. But they weren't anything like spiders he'd ever seen.

These were made of crystal.

Though still covered in gore, their limbs and bodies shone in the candlelight. They glistened like diamonds, or prisms. They reflected the light around them, breaking the glow into multicolors like sunlight on a raindrop.

The man's jaw cracked as another spider finally heaved itself out. Others followed until the man was lost under a sparkling shroud of crystal.

"What are they?" Thorn asked.

"I don't know." The spiders climbed down the slab and scuttled across the floor.

Thorn smashed his boot down. The spiders shattered. But more came forward. He took her wrist. "We're leaving. Right now."

More and more spun their webs. They scurried off the bodies, leaving them cocooned in silver webbing. The larger ones turned toward Lily and Thorn.

Lily retreated. "I think you're right."

Thorn stepped on another. He brushed off a few climbing up his boot.

A chink of glass tapping glass made him look up.

The large spider, the one from the man's mouth, tensed.

"Lily!"

Thorn jumped forward as it sprang at her. He swiped the candlestick across it, and two legs snapped off. But it still had six, and it landed on Thorn. It ran up his arm, digging into his flesh. Thorn stared at the jewel-like eyes and the needle-sharp fangs.

When it reached his shoulder, he smashed it.

Its shell cracked; he hit it again and again until it shattered. The pieces tinkled on the stony ground, which was now infested by these crystalline creatures.

Lily swung the door open and dragged him across the threshold. She slammed the door behind her, and he could see she was doing some kind of magic. Shadows from the corners of the corridor were gathering around the door, sealing the gaps.

She's trapping them inside.

She was talking to him.

What was she saying?

Thorn saw the fear in her eyes. He shook his head, trying to understand why she was afraid.

He felt heavy and slow. Why was it so hard to walk?

He dropped the candlestick. His fingers were numb, and his arm felt strange.

Thorn collapsed to his knees as the numbness spread. He gazed up at Lily as she shouted.

"It bit you, Thorn! It bit you!" She was trying to get him up. "We need help! Stay with me!"

The spider bit me?

That was his last thought.

NINETEEN

Thorn drew the arrow until the fletching brushed his chin. He let his gaze drift along the shaft, past the arrowhead, and through the curtain of green.

A gentle wind pushed the leaves, and bright summer sunlight danced on the silvery brook that gurgled between moss-patched boulders.

The deer—a three-year-old, judging by its height—tugged at a bush. Its hide was a soft, tawny brown, spotted with white along its shoulders.

Easy. So easy.

He sat, legs crossed, chewing the cooked deer meat. The sun had left the sky, and the moon now crowned the forest. Thorn ate alone at his camp with only moths for company. They flitted in their fatal dance around the waving flames of his fire.

Did anything taste better than meat hunted by your own hand? He didn't think so.

What a perfect day.

Thorn sipped some stream water, cold and delicious, then rubbed an apple against his sleeve. Look at that. He'd never seen an apple so red. Or tasted one so juicy!

He leaned back on his bed. The leaves were softer than any mattress he'd slept on back . . . back . . .

Where?

He shook his head. Something nibbled at him, a flea trapped in his head that he couldn't reach. What was it?

Homesickness?

No, impossible. Herne's Forest was his home. He was never going to leave it.

The branches creaked, and a man appeared through the trees. He paused at the edge of the campfire's glow.

"Mind if I join you?" His gray eyes sparkled with starlight, and his pale face wore an easy, friendly smile.

"Do I know you?" asked Thorn.

"My name is Iblis. You're friends with my daughter."

"Am I?" Thorn sat up and passed Iblis an apple.

"Thank you, Thorn." The firelight shone on the fine silk clothes and the black jewels he wore. He sliced the apple neatly with his fingernail. "Most fine."

"What brings you to Herne's Forest, m'lord?" Always best to be polite to nobles, just in case.

"Is that where you are?" Iblis looked around him. "Of course. We make our own heaven."

"This ain't Herne's Forest?" Thorn suppressed a shiver. Suddenly he wanted this man gone.

"No, Thorn. We're in Castle Gloom."

Thorn's heart fluttered with panic. "Lord Shadow?"

"That's right."

Thorn didn't understand. "But you're dead."

"Right again."

"Oh no." Thorn stood up. The trees were fading and the light around him turning pale. "I'm dead, too, aren't I?"

He remembered. He'd been running with Lily, and the spider bit him. And killed him?

"Is that why you're here?" he asked. "Am I in the lands of the dead?"

"No, it's nothing like that."

Thorn swallowed. "Lily's not going to make . . . to make me into a zombie or anything, is she?"

"No, she's not."

"I don't think Dad'll be happy about me being a zombie. Or any such undead thing." He grimaced. "No offense."

"None taken." Lord Shadow finished his apple and tossed the core into the flames. "You are not dead. Just sleeping."

"Sleeping? This is a dream?" He put his hand toward the fire. It felt hot. "If it's a dream, what are you doing here?"

"This is the Dreamtime. It lies beside, and overlaps, the realm of the dead. It is the way we spirits are sometimes able to visit the living." He flexed his fingers. "In the living world, I am a mere ghost. Here, I am more myself. More real. I've come to see if I can wake you."

"If I'm asleep, why don't you just throw a bucket of cold water over me?"

"You think we haven't tried that? No, you refuse to wake up. Lily's getting worried."

"What happened? I remember being bitten by this weird spider. . . ."

Lord Shadow opened up his hand. "Like this one?" There sat one of the horrid things.

Thorn stepped back. "Yeah."

Lord Shadow tickled the creature's head. It danced on its eight spindly legs. "It's a jewel spider. Its venom sends you to sleep, but it also sustains you; it's full of nutrients. Given the right circumstances, you could sleep for years, decades. Kept alive and happy in your personal dream world."

"*Happy?* Why would you be happy?"

"You were."

"I didn't know it was a dream."

"Who does, when they're dreaming?" Lord Shadow closed his hand, and the spider vanished. "The spiders feed off the host's dreams, but once the dreams go stale, they lay eggs within the hosts, to breed new jewel spiders. I believe that's what happened at Pitch Farm."

"How can dreams go stale?"

"Children have the most vivid imaginations and hence the richest dreams. Adults less so. The jewel spiders probably stole the two sons but implanted the parents with eggs. The spiders hatch within the body, and that's always fatal."

Thorn shuddered and looked about him. "How do I get out of here?"

Iblis smiled. "How do you think?"

Thorn's heart leaped as he heard the beat of massive leathery wings. A vast shape swooped overhead; moonlight caught on the beast's fangs and hooklike claws.

Hades circled, then folded his wings to half their full breadth and fluttered down to the camp.

Thorn grinned as he shook the bat's furry cheeks. "You'd follow me anywhere, wouldn't you?"

Iblis was up beside him, gazing at the monster with admiration. "The bond you have with Hades is quite unusual, Thorn."

"I'm just good with animals, m'lord. Ain't so special."

"Really? You are trapped within the Dreamtime, and when you wish to be saved, your heart summons Hades." He smiled. "Best you not mention that to Lily. She feels she's your protector."

Hades rolled his shoulders, the way he did when he was planning a long, hard flight. Thorn stroked the stiff fur. *If this is a dream, how come it feels so real?*

Iblis took Thorn's arm. "The spiders are building a web, to trap people in the Dreamtime. All those villagers who have gone missing are here, asleep in the waking world and lost in the Dreamtime."

"It ain't trolls taking them?"

"The trolls are a very real threat, but they're not behind the disappearances and attacks in Bone-Tree Forest." Iblis pondered. "Whoever's doing it is trying to create a war between us and the trolls."

"Then they've succeeded. Baron Sable just rode north."

"This is no accident, Thorn. Jewel spiders are constructs, devices, not creatures with instinct and purpose. They need a will to control them."

"Whose?"

"I don't know yet. But I feel his rage, hanging over all Dreamtime. War's coming, Thorn, a war that will cross worlds. Tell Lily."

"Why don't you tell her yourself?"

Iblis grimaced. "I could, if she could get back into the Shadow Library. And it's taken all my power to reach you here. I will try to contact her when she sleeps, but there is something stopping me from walking the path to Lily's own dreams, something I don't yet understand. You must locate the source of these jewel spiders. Find them, and you'll find our missing villagers."

"Where do I begin?"

"There was an infestation of these creatures in Malice, a town in the center of Bone-Tree Forest. That was about twenty years ago. My father, Charon Shadow, was ruler then and dealt with it. Perhaps a new nest has hatched?"

Was that it? Was there some hidden cave or den in Malice containing all the kidnapped villagers asleep and cocooned in webs like so many flies?

Thorn climbed up on Hades. The bat stretched out his wings and shivered, just to get the blood pumping to the very tips. This dream version of Hades was perfect in every way, even down to the stinky breath, full of the odor of half-digested cow.

"Tell Lily," said Iblis. "Tell her not to be afraid. No matter what."

Thorn gazed down at the man. He'd only seen him as a ghost, ethereal and little more than woven mist. Here, he was as real as any man. There was a light in his eyes that ghosts lacked. "I will, m'lord." Thorn gripped the thick fur between Hades's shoulders.

And then he flew up and out of the Dreamtime.

"Thorn?"

He groaned as he woke, feeling as stiff as a zombie. He blinked slowly, easing the pain out of his eyes.

Blurred shapes and muted colors filled his vision at first. Then the two spots of orange became sharper, and slowly he made out a pair of candles on a small table.

The ceiling above him had skeletons cavorting with one another and a devil beating a drum. Imps with colored hats and ribbons made up the rest of the orchestra.

"Where am I?" he whispered hoarsely.

Silk and linen rustled, and Lily leaned over with a glass of water. "The Bone Mile. It's part of the infirmary. You've been here two days."

"Infirmary? Why can I hear hammering, then? Or is it just in my head?"

"That's Dr. Byle's new apprentice, Eddie. He's putting Wobbly Winston back together. He froze into the snow last night, and his legs came off when they tried to pull him out."

Thorn's head felt full of fog as well as hammering. He tilted it side to side, hoping to pour some of it out. "Two days?"

"You slept so deeply, Thorn." Lily took the empty glass and refilled it. "I was . . . worried. Only a little, obviously."

"*Obviously.*"

She looked exhausted. Her clothes were all wrinkled, and her hair needed a serious combing. Her gray eyes were sunken, and a little wild. Lily's skin had always been pale but clear; now it was sallow, thin, and worn. A plate of nibbled-at food rested on the table, and there was a blanket at her feet.

She'd been here all this time.

"If I looked half as bad as you, it's a miracle you didn't bury me," said Thorn. "What happened to the spiders?"

"I had the blacksmith seal the room up with lead. They're not going anywhere, but you can still hear them scratching at the door." Lily shivered. "Horrible things."

"They're called jewel spiders," said Thorn. "Your dad told me all about them."

Her eyes widened. "You saw my father?"

His shoulder still felt sore from the bite. And a little numb. "Yeah. He told me to tell you not to be afraid."

"Anything else?"

"He thinks he knows where the spiders are coming from." Thorn dragged his legs out from under the covers. The feel of cold stone under his bare soles was refreshing. He wanted to get up and get going; he'd slept long enough. "A town called Malice."

MALICE

TWENTY

"Dirty troll!"

"We don't want your kind here!"

"Why don't you go back to your filthy country?"

Thorn had been heading back from the stables, when he heard the shouts coming from the alleyway. What was going on?

A mob of squires was throwing stones at Dott. The troll girl was backed into a corner, waving her hands and sobbing. "Leave me 'lone! You all bad!"

There were plenty of them: a mix of the older boys, and a few Thorn called friends. Some laughed, mocking Dott's clumsy attempts to deflect the stones.

"What in the Six are you doing?" He barged through the pack and planted himself in front of her. "Stop it!"

Lynch Tenebrae led the mob. He stood a good foot taller than Thorn and carried a blunt sword, one of the training tools the older squires used. "You here to save your girlfriend?"

Thorn had been warned about Lynch. He came from a clan that were rivals to the Shadows and always causing trouble among the other noble families. Lynch was a thug. But as a noble thug, no one could touch him.

Maybe it was time to change that.

A few of the other squires shifted uneasily. The fun of beating up a defenseless girl seemed to have dissipated now that Thorn was standing there.

Lynch prodded Thorn with his sword. "Out of the way."

"Make me."

Squires fought all the time. They fought in the courtyard, they fought in the dorms, they fought in the fields. They were a bunch of boys being trained for war, and fighting was part of the deal. Thorn had traded punches and black eyes and then shared breakfast with his opponents. It was a game, and there were rules.

But Lynch wasn't playing by the rules. Thorn ducked below a swing that would have shattered his skull.

A few of the squires gasped, shocked at the ferocity of Lynch's attack. One took hold of the big squire's arm. "Come on, Lynch. . . ."

Lynch shrugged him off. "The poacher's son wants a fight. I'm going to give him one." He edged forward, blocking any chance of escape. "No Lady Shadow here to save you now."

Thorn caught sight of the worried looks of the other squires. They didn't know what to do. No one was willing to stop Lynch, even though there were more than twenty of them. They just watched, afraid.

Thorn attacked, but Lynch laughed it off, dodging his punch with ease and slapping Thorn's ribs with a flick of his sword. He blocked Thorn's kick with one of his own, almost cracking Thorn's kneecap.

I can't beat him.

So Thorn picked up a rock and threw it hard.

Lynch ducked, and the rock smacked one of the squires behind him. There was a cry and a thud.

Lynch laughed. "You're nothing without a bow, aren't you?"

He swung his sword into the back of Thorn's knee, bringing him down.

Thorn was able to block the first kick to his ribs but not the second. He lay there, gasping.

"Make sure no one's coming," ordered Lynch.

"What are you going to do?" asked one of the boys.

"Never you mind." Lynch gripped the sword with both hands. He looked down at Thorn. "Training accident. It happens."

It was over . . . except for one thing.

The troll called Dott.

She roared and rose to her full height, towering over them all. Half the squires fled right then and there. The others stood, transfixed by fear.

She snatched the sword from Lynch and bent the blade in half with little effort. Her eyes blazed. "Don't hurt little T'orn. My friend." She lifted Thorn up by the collar. "You 'kay?"

"Yeah." Thorn straightened his tunic. "Can you count to three?"

Dott nodded. "Easy. Prin'ess teach me up to ten."

"Good, start at one. Then go to two, and when you hit three, tear Lynch's arms off. We'll call it an arm-wrestling accident." He winked at her. "It happens."

Dott flicked the broken sword aside. "One . . ."

No squire, including Lynch, waited for her to reach *two*.

"You've been fighting again," said Wade the moment Thorn entered the room. "Who was it this time?"

"Lynch Tenebrae." Thorn sat down on his bed. *Ow*, his side ached, and he had a day's worth of riding ahead.

"I'm impressed. If you're going to make enemies, you might as well make big ones. Why?"

"He was picking on Dott. They all were."

Wade shook his head. "Only you would fight for a troll."

"Someone had to do something." Thorn lifted up his shirt. That bruise was going to be there awhile. "Get packing. We're off to Malice."

"Are we?"

"Better grab your gear." Thorn glanced over. "Now, Wade."

His friend stood there in his armor. It wasn't the hard steel of the Black Guard but stiffened leather, well sculpted, if a size too big. Wade also carried a sword, a real blade. Then Thorn noticed Wade's rucksack, packed and waiting beside the door. "What's going on?"

"I'm going with Baron Sable."

"What? Why?"

"It's a squire's job to support the knights, remember?"

"Older squires, yeah. You need to be sixteen, and you ain't." Thorn didn't get it. "Are you in a rush for fame and glory? Want the minstrels to write a ballad for you, is that it? I'll tell you what, I'll have a word with Merrick, and he'll make you the hero of a play. Have you defeat the troll king, if that'll make you happy."

"You're an idiot, Thorn."

"The only idiot in this room is the one heading off to fight trolls for no good reason." Thorn scowled. "You'll end up on the spit, like Baal."

Wade slammed Thorn against the wall, right off his feet. His words came out hard through his gritted teeth. "You say that about Baal again, and I'll cut your heart out."

Thorn stared at Wade, shocked. He'd never seen him so wild with rage. Wade was the most easygoing person he knew.

Wade trembled with fury, and Thorn didn't doubt his threat. He looked ready to kill.

Old Colm taught the squires until they were sixteen. He'd finish their training with real experience by handing them over to one of the Black Guard. They'd take them into their first battle, and if they did well and earned a few scars, they'd become one of the Black Guard themselves. But that was still three years away for Wade.

Thorn often joined the debates about who would serve whom, when their time came. No one wanted to squire for Earl Grave, or Early Grave, as the boys called him. Three of his squires had died in as many years, the last having been eaten by an ogre. A couple had their eye on Sir Tartarus, a proper old-fashioned knight who rode a big warhorse and wielded a twenty-foot lance.

But everyone knew Wade was going to serve Baron Sable, or one of Sable's sons. Sable always tipped Wade for doing even the smallest chores. His horses were always tended by Wade. His sons gave him extra lessons when they were around, and Wade did all the carrying and fetching for Sable when he stayed at Castle Gloom. That armor he was wearing right now was probably one of Sable's hand-me-downs. It had been like that since Thorn had arrived, and he'd never really thought about it. Until now.

"Put me down, Wade," said Thorn. "Tell me what's going on."

Wade freed him. "I'm going to the Troll-Teeth, and that's all there is to know."

"I need you at Malice," Thorn urged. "That's where the problem really is."

"And how do you know?"

"Lord Shadow told me."

Wade stopped. "Lord Shadow? I thought he was trapped in the library."

"He came to me in a dream. He told me that we needed to go to Malice."

Wade tried not to laugh. "I should follow you because you had a *dream?*"

"It wasn't like that. It was Lord Shadow, for real. In a dream."

"Riiight." Wade unsheathed his sword. He flipped his whetstone from his bedside table and set to work sharpening the edge. "This is all about Lady Shadow. You'll do anything to impress her."

"It's nothing like that." Thorn sat down on his bed and drew one of his arrows from his quiver to check the fletching. "Lily believes me."

"I'm sure *Lily* does. That's the problem. Your blood isn't black, and yet you're the one meeting Lord Shadow. Nobody else is. Why's that?" Wade spun the sword, about to start on the opposite edge. "I'll tell you why: so you can seem important to *Lily*. This trip to Malice, now that's a fool's errand."

"And how big a difference are you going to make to Baron Sable's army? One thirteen-year-old squire?"

"It's not about making a difference. It's just . . . I need to go, Thorn."

"I knew you Gehennish were loyal, but this is something more." Thorn paused. "What is it?"

"What it is is none of your business."

Thorn looked hard at the boy across the room. Wade was a Castle Gloom squire, but he wasn't a fool, anything but. Yet he was willing to go fight a troll army, just because of Baron Sable and Baal. Thorn came from a small village. Life was dangerous enough without risking it needlessly. There were only a few souls Thorn was willing to die for.

His sisters, his brothers. Mom and Dad.

Thorn paused. That was it. His list wasn't so long.

Always family. They always came first. That was how he'd been brought up.

And that was how he'd ended up in Gehenna. He'd gone looking for his dad and eventually found him. His family would be here in the spring, when his dad became the new huntsman at Castle Gloom.

Family first, last, and always. Lily was the same—being a Shadow meant everything to her.

"What's the baron to you, Wade?" asked Thorn. "What's Baal to you? It ain't about the tips, that's for sure."

Wade shifted uneasily. "I said it's none of your business."

"Who is the baron to you?" Thorn asked, not willing to let it go now that he had scented a mystery. They'd swapped plenty of stories since they'd shared a room. But Wade had never mentioned his dad. Thorn had assumed he was dead.

"You've a lot to learn about nobility, Thorn."

"Why don't you tell me?"

Wade glanced at the door, as if he was expecting the baron to come in. "The baron looks after me because we're . . . related."

"*Related?* How?"

Wade lightly tapped Thorn on the forehead. "Sometimes you just can't see what's right in front of you. He's my father."

Suddenly a whole lot of little things now made a whole lot of sense. Thorn should have seen it earlier, but he hadn't been looking.

"Hold on. If he's your dad, then what are you doing here? Shouldn't you be back at Sable Manor?"

Wade swiped down his upper lip awkwardly. "The thing is, the baron's my father, but his wife, Baroness Suriya, she isn't my mother."

"Ah, right." He remembered now. Wade's mother was a fisherwoman.

"My mom lives down on the coast. The baron used to visit her village to go sailing and fishing. One thing led to another . . ." Wade patted his purse. "He's been good to us. Mom gets a yearly stipend, and when I was old enough, he got me a position here. Work hard, join the Black Guard, maybe become a captain one day. It's better than a life spent gutting fish."

"And the baron? And his other sons?"

"They look out for me. It's good to have brothers like them." Wade smiled. "I'm not the only natural son, or daughter, serving around Castle Gloom. Most of us have black blood. Or at least blood that's dark gray. For peasants like me, this is the best chance, probably the only chance, of bettering myself."

"Does anyone else know?"

Wade shrugged as he slid his sword back into the scabbard. "Lord Shadow did. Maybe a few others suspect, but no one says anything."

"But why are you just serving as a squire? Couldn't the baron get you a better position? The steward's a cushy job, and he runs the whole castle. Work for him. Warm, indoors, plenty of food."

Wade's eyes narrowed. "I want to make a name for myself, Thorn. Not borrow someone else's."

"A name written in troll blood, right?"

"You're not from around here, Thorn. You don't know. The trolls have kept to themselves for years, but that was when Lord Iblis was alive. Now that he's gone, they're becoming bolder. People are disappearing, and the trolls need to be taught a lesson."

"It ain't trolls."

"You don't know everything, Thorn."

Thorn looked at the small writing box beside his bed, a gift from Lily. Black-lacquered and inlaid with onyx, it had a small silver inkpot and a fistful of hardly used quills. He sighed. "That's true enough."

Wade strapped on his sword belt. He had a certain way of doing it, pulling the belt up, wriggling it around his hips, then tightening it another notch before looping the end through. Just like Baron Sable.

There was no way Thorn was going to change his friend's mind. He handed Wade his rucksack. "At least do one thing for me."

Wade raised a questioning eyebrow.

"If there's any real fighting, run away."

"When did you ever run from a fight?" Wade said, hefting the rucksack over his shoulder. "I have a favor to ask of you, too."

"Yeah?"

"Don't steal any of my stuff." Wade grinned.

Then he left.

Things were going from bad to worse. Thorn looked around the room. Wade's remaining stuff was neat and tidy. On his pillow rested his book, *The Adventures of Sir Blackheart*. Wade read it to him most nights.

He'll be back.

He'd better be back.

Thorn wiped his eyes. He needed Wade to tell him how the story ended.

Grandpa always said it wasn't the bear at your front you should worry about, but the wolf behind you. He'd been counting on Wade to watch out for him.

Now what was he going to do?

TWENTY-ONE

Saddlebags slung over one shoulder, his bow and quiver on the other, Thorn headed to the stables. He ignored the dark looks from the older squires practicing their sword drill in the courtyard. Thorn couldn't be trusted; he was a "troll friend."

Thorn just wanted to leave with no fuss, no trouble. If he traveled quickly, he'd be in Malice late tomorrow. Cook had given him two pies, each stuffed with onion, lamb, and turnips. She treated him well; they had a small business going. Thorn trapped rabbit and the occasional bird for her, and she gave him extra helpings and first pick of her belly-bursting tarts, one of which he had carefully wrapped and stowed at the top of the saddlebag.

It would be good to get out of the castle for a few days. He opened the stable doors.

And found Lily and Dott waiting.

"You took your time," said Lily. Zephyr was saddled already. Dott sat on a pile of kitchenware, and there was a wardrobe-sized rucksack leaning against a post. She clapped as Thorn entered. "My mate T'orn!"

"Going somewhere, Princess?" Thorn walked over to Thunder and checked the stitches on the horse's flanks. The odor of the healing salve was as foul as ever, but the stitches were as neat as any dressmaker's.

"Malice," said Lily.

"No, you ain't," said Thorn.

"Wait." Lily cleaned out her ear. "I must have heard that wrong. That sounded like an order, but it *couldn't* be. Thorn doesn't give orders, because someone else is in charge. Hmm . . . who could that be?" She looked up at Dott. "Who do you think?"

Dott frowned.

Lily coughed and pointed at herself.

Dott grinned. "Prin'ess! Prin'ess is in charge, T'orn!"

"It could be dangerous." Thorn led Thunder out of the pen.

"Good thing we'll be there to protect you, then."

Why, oh why did she have to be so stubborn about everything? Thorn never won these arguments, but that didn't mean he wasn't going to try. "Haven't you got work to be doing here? Servants needing ordering around and stuff?"

"The steward and Old Colm can manage just fine without me for a few days." Lily took a deep breath. "I feel so useless here, Thorn. I can't get into the library, can't use it for research or to contact my father. I need to get out of Gloom if I'm to sort out our troubles."

"You've left Old Colm in charge? Things must be bad."

Lily looked uneasy. "I've arranged some . . . reinforcements to replace the soldiers Baron Sable took to the Teeth. Old Colm's going to train them."

"Reinforcements from where?"

"Never you mind."

Thorn hauled the saddle over. "You really need to wear all that jewelry? We're going to investigate these magical spiders, not attend a royal wedding."

"I'm hardly wearing any jewelry," said Lily. "Just a few rings. A couple of necklaces. One or two, maybe three bracelets. And these armbands are just to hold my sleeves up. They don't count."

"What are those things in your hair?"

"Hairpins."

"With diamonds in them?"

"Very small diamonds."

"You really do have an answer for everything, don't you?"

"My mother said a lady should have three things, Thorn: grace, wit, and a hero willing to die for her."

"Two out of three ain't bad, I suppose." Thorn faced her. "And it ain't just that. I'm not sure I'm right about Malice."

"What do you mean? My father told you to go there."

"Did he really? It was a dream, Lily. Maybe that's all it was," he said, thinking of what Wade had said.

Lily shook her head. "No, it *was* my father. Had you ever heard about the jewel spiders before?"

"No. . . . Was that story true? About an infestation, long ago?"

Lily nodded. "I asked a few of the servants. They remembered trouble in Malice about twenty years past. I've also checked some of our records. You were right—there *had* been a plague of jewel spiders back then."

Just like he'd been told in his dream. Maybe it *had* been Iblis Shadow after all.

Lily continued. "Did you even know there was a town called Malice?"

"I don't think so, but maybe I heard someone talk about it and forgot. Maybe I just plucked it out of my sleeping head at random."

"Well, I believe you," said Lily. "And that's all that matters."

"And what if I'm wrong? What if we go there and there ain't nothing to find?"

Lily waved her hand, dismissing his doubt. "We will find something. My father isn't wrong about such things."

Thorn gave up. Lily would have it her way, as usual.

Despite the horse's wounds, it didn't take them long to saddle up Thunder. The stallion shook his head with impatience. He'd been cooped up too long. Thorn steadied him with strokes and pats and went through the whole routine, checking him down to his hooves. "We're taking a nice, easy walk. Nothing too rough, all right? I don't want them stitches opening up."

Thunder snapped at him.

"Watch it, or you ain't going nowhere."

Thunder's eyes narrowed, but he settled down.

"You're not taking Hades?" asked Lily.

Thorn slipped the bit in place and flipped the reins over Thunder's head. "That bat's useless these days. Now that it's getting a little cold, all he wants to do is eat and sleep. It's too hard to wake him."

Dott slung on a pair of shoulder bags and put a heavy belt around her huge waist. Then she tied on pouches and more bags and a hatchet, a saucepan, a pot, a bundle of skewers, a frying pan, a kettle, and a small cauldron.

"Let me help with your rucksack." Thorn went over to it and tried to pick it up.

It didn't budge. Not even an inch.

Thorn gritted his teeth and urged every ounce of strength through his legs and arms.

Nothing. Not. An. Inch.

Dott reached over, grabbed a strap with one hand, and swung the rucksack cleanly over her shoulder. She patted Thorn on the back. She tied a wool bobble hat to her head. Bells dangled from the twine she used as straps.

Lily settled herself on Zephyr. "Can we get a move on?"

They went out of the stables.

There was Gabriel.

"Oh no," said Thorn. He looked imploringly at Lily. "He's coming, too?"

"No, he most certainly is not."

Gabriel sat upon Lightning, the horse Thorn had "borrowed" from him several months back. "I've been waiting for ages. Mr. Funny, hurry up!"

"Coming, m'lord!"

Mr. Funny hauled at a stubborn donkey. He pulled its reins, and when it didn't move, he raced around the rear and pushed, his long, spindly legs trembling with the effort. "Just . . . a . . . moment . . ."

Gabriel was dressed in an ivory tunic with breeches, high white leather riding boots, and an ermine cloak. A thin platinum band encircled his brow and the golden shoulder-length hair shone only as hair that's been brushed a thousand times a night could shine.

If he put that much effort into sword fighting, he'd be better than Tyburn.

Opposite him was Lily, black from brow to boot. Those boots were studded with small black onyx buttons, and the only color on her was the dark red of her lips. Zephyr's coat shimmered with oily blackness, and his tail and mane rippled in the low breeze.

How could anyone have believed that Lily and Gabriel would ever be friends? They were born enemies.

The only person happy with this reunion was Dott. She did a joyous twirl. "Bootiful boy! Bootiful boy an' me!"

Lily straightened her spine and stuck her chin out. Thorn knew what was coming. Lily was in queen mode.

"Go back to your rooms, Gabriel," said Lily.

"I think not. I don't trust any of your servants, especially with you gone."

"It's too dangerous for you to be seen in these parts. You're a Solar."

"I have my faithful servant to protect me. And, of course, you are honor-bound to do the same, aren't you?"

"I could get my guards to drag you off your horse and lock you up in the Needle." Lily glanced over to four of her Black Guard. "I think they might enjoy it."

"I'm sure those vulgar thugs would. It would be the highlight of their boring, miserable lives. Something they may one day tell their children about—if such creatures breed children, rather than goblins."

"We might be roughing it. Camping out. You may not bathe for a few days."

"I never realized quite how uncivilized Gehenna was. Don't you have inns every twenty miles? We do, in Lumina."

"We have hedges and ditches and smelly caves."

Gabriel bit his lip and glanced back toward the Great Hall. "And I doubt your . . . *maid* can cook anything that resembles actual food?"

"Trolls haven't invented cooking yet." She smiled. "We'll be dining on raw hedgehog, most likely."

"No doubt a local delicacy?" Gabriel paled, then set his jaw as firmly as Lily's. "I shall suffer alongside you. After all, what sort of noble would I be if I let you venture forth into the wild without my sword to defend you?"

Thorn butted in. "The last time you were in danger, it was Lily who saved your white backside. From being devoured by specters, if I remember right."

Gabriel cleared his throat. "The ballads tell a different tale."

They did. The minstrels sang of the heroic Gabriel, the simpering Lily, and the peasant buffoon Thorn, who was always losing his pants.

Mr. Funny leaped onto the back of the donkey and clapped. "I'm ready, m'lord!"

Gabriel trotted through the gate. "Shall we?"

"Wait for me, m'lord!" yelled Mr. Funny.

TWENTY-TWO

Gabriel complained. Mr. Funny cried. Lily sulked. Dott sang, and Thorn . . . he wished he were somewhere else. Anywhere else.

Thunder shared his annoyance. The big warhorse snapped his teeth at the other mounts and wouldn't let anyone else take the lead.

"Will you control that beast? He's worse than that flying rat of yours," snarled Gabriel when Thunder buffeted his horse, Lightning, off the path.

"Control him? I don't control nothing about Thunder," replied Thorn. "I just sit here and try not to rile him."

"My father says servants and beasts need whipping. That's the only way they learn."

"Anyone who tries to whip Thunder best prepare to spend the rest of their life with a hoof-shaped dent in their face."

And so it went on, mile after mile, as snow fell gently over Gehenna.

"What's Malice like?" he asked Lily.

"Just a town. Quite a few ghosts, too, so I'm told." She fished a couple of pears from her saddlebag and tossed one to him. "The mayor sent a letter of complaint about them. A few were causing trouble, and he wanted them removed. Or, if that didn't work, he wanted to charge them rent."

"How can you charge a ghost rent?"

"Find the family they belong to. It's easier for some than others. They're affecting house prices, too. People don't like strangers floating through their bedrooms."

"I'm never going to get used to this place." He nudged Thunder over. "What's that up ahead?"

Long spindles of white rose out of the frosty earth. They were trees, but unlike any Thorn had ever seen. Their branches spread crookedly in all directions, and their trunks were twisted like the backs of old men, gnarly and bulging with knots.

Dott whimpered. "Bad place. Bad place."

Lily gazed up and around her. "Did you never wonder why it's called Bone-Tree Forest?"

Thorn dismounted and let Thunder go dig for some grass. He put a bare palm against a tree. It was smooth, not patterned with wrinkled bark. The main trunk looked like several thin trees melded together, moss and dead leaves wedged into the ruts between them.

"They do look like bones," declared Thorn. "Giant bones."

The boughs could have been arms, and the branches resembled fingers, ancient and bent and calcified.

Dott wailed. "Go now, Prin'ess! Me want to go *now*!"

Thorn was spooked, but Lily looked about in wonder, not fear.

She was a strange girl.

Lily brushed her fingers along a low branch. She turned away from Dott and said in a low voice, "This is why trolls don't come this far south, not unless they're desperate. These trees are made of the skeletons of the last troll army that dared to attack Gehenna."

"And which of your ancestors did that?"

Lily smiled. "Tormentus. He led a conclave of dark sorcerers who all shared Shadow blood, back when it was still thick with magic."

"You have the scariest family ever."

"Thank you."

Thorn stopped and sniffed. "Smoke." He turned left and right, trying to figure out where the smell was coming from. He pointed west. "Over there. A village?"

Lily nodded. "Must be Three Barrows. We've made better time than I thought. We could sleep there tonight and be in Malice by tomorrow."

"Sounds good to me."

They passed by three mounds with moss-covered stone entrances. Tombs? Thorn thought he heard tapping from within one.

Ten small, single-story thatched cottages made up Three Barrows, circling a central common where sheep nibbled at stalks through the snow. A pair of guard dogs barked as they approached, and within a minute, a small crowd of villagers had gathered to greet them.

"You honor us, Lady Shadow," said the headman, bowing. "How can we help?"

"Somewhere warm by the fire would be fine." Lily dismounted and handed the headman the reins. "Stable the animals and feed them well."

"Of course." He pointed toward the biggest of the cottages. "Please, be welcome in my home. I'll have one of the sheep slaughtered for dinner."

"Only if it's convenient."

Thorn scowled. A whole sheep? He nudged Lily as the villagers took care of the horses. "You'll pay them, right?"

"Why?"

"They can't afford a sheep."

Lily shook her head. "I am their ruler, and it's their honor to host me. If I offer to pay them, it's saying that there's a price on honor, when there isn't. It would shame them."

"You nobles have it all figured out, haven't you?"

"I think I know my people better than you do, Thorn."

How could she be so arrogant?

Nobles and commoners. They lived by different rules. When was he going to remember that?

"Please, have some more, m'lady." The headman, Jared, pushed the chunk of mutton across the table.

Lily leaned back in her chair, the only one with a cushion, and patted her stomach. "Honestly, you've been more than generous."

Generous didn't begin to describe it. The villagers had laid out a feast that would have filled their bellies a dozen times over. Everyone had brought something: breads, cakes, vegetables and fruit, plates of salted fish. Thorn knew they were part of their winter stores and couldn't be spared.

And Lily had hardly eaten a plateful. She'd nibbled this, broken a piece off that, dipped in one bowl, and spooned cream from another.

What a waste.

He would've rather dined in the stables, but his renown had preceded him. The villagers wanted to meet the famous Thorn Bat-Rider, so there was no escape. He'd eaten quickly, trying to ignore the faces peering in through the windows. He'd offered a chop to one of the children and seen her hand reach for it before her mother shook her head.

"The food's for our noble guests," the mother had warned.

Now a cat prowled under the table, and Thorn dropped it a strip of meat. At least he could feed the pet.

"More an' more, puhlease!" roared Dott. She belched, and the cat scampered off. Some of the smaller children, daring one another, crept closer, eyes and mouths wide open. Dott glared at one. "You for my dessert?"

They ran off screaming.

Gabriel meticulously trimmed off all the fat as he ate and fussed about how he didn't have a seat cushion. He'd grimaced when he was offered the apple pie, but Thorn noticed that he didn't hold back on the cream, pouring half a pot over it. Mr. Funny was missing from the feast. He'd dragged his aching bones off his donkey, accepted a bowl of soup, then headed off to the barn, moaning with each painful step.

Poor fool. He deserved a night away from Gabriel, even if it was sleeping with the animals.

"My, what a handsome child," said Lily as one of the village women showed her a baby.

Jared beamed. "My first grandchild. We named him Iblis, after your noble father."

"A proud name. Here . . ." Lily took off a ring and placed it in the baby's chubby fist. "You wear it when you're older, in honor of my father."

The baby put it in his mouth.

Lily winked at Thorn. He blushed; he should have known. Lily didn't pay, but she *did* give presents. That ring would buy them a whole flock to replace the one sheep they'd cooked tonight.

Talk moved on to farming, families, and the undead. In the last three months, the village had gained a zombie; it was him they had heard tapping inside one of the mounds.

Jared bounced his grandchild on his knee, took the ring out of its mouth, and put it into his pocket. "We reckon it's one of the old lords, from way back. More of a dusty skeleton, really, flesh long rotted away. We open up the tomb every week or two to let him stretch his legs."

One of the village women joined in. "Over at the next village, they've just got a couple of chattering skulls, not a proper crypt dweller like we have," she said proudly.

Thorn really didn't want to spend tonight listening about Gehenna's undead. He got up. "I'll go check on the horses."

A chilly mist covered the short distance between the headman's house and the barn, with just enough moonlight to mark the way. The guard dogs lurked within their kennels, but Thorn glimpsed their wary eyes in the dark. The ground, frosty already, broke and crunched under his heavy boots.

He'd better go in quietly. Mr. Funny would be asleep by now, and there was still a day's journey ahead; best let him rest his bones as long as possible.

Thorn crept in. He pushed the door shut behind him. He paused to let his eyes grow accustomed to the dimness within.

And saw Mr. Funny, wide-awake and unwrapping his traveling bundle.

Thorn stilled himself. Something wasn't right. Mr. Funny's movements were quick, sharp, methodical. Nimble fingers undid knots and rolled open the bundle. The dimming torchlight caught the edge of metal.

Mr. Funny stood up and buckled on a thick leather belt. He flipped a dagger from one hand to the other and slid it into a sheath. He attached a scabbard with a short sword to his left and then slid two hand axes into hoops dangling on either hip. He blew softly onto his hands and then wiped them on his threadbare trousers. He stretched, reaching his fists slowly toward the ceiling, as if he was unlocking his body from the twisted, bowlegged, and knock-kneed version. Whatever was going on, it wasn't good.

"I can hear you breathing," said Mr. Funny, his voice calm, steady, and deep. He turned around. "I'm surprised a poacher like you wouldn't be stealthier."

Thorn spoke. "Who are you?"

Mr. Funny cracked his knuckles, one after the other. His smile didn't shift, and his eyes were hard and pitiless.

Thorn threw the best punch he had. Hard and fast and straight, with shoulders and hips powering it. Enough to take a man off his feet and shake out a few teeth.

Mr. Funny brushed it aside and delivered a punch of his own.

Thorn was unconscious before he hit the ground.

TWENTY-THREE

"**T**horn, are you in here?" Lily entered the barn and looked around. Where was that boy? He'd gone to check on the horses ages ago!

She found him, asleep under a blanket, in the corner of the stables.

Typical. He had a comfortable pallet waiting back in the warm house, yet he'd decided to bed down with the animals.

She should wake him. Tell him it was rude to sleep out here when Jared had offered them his hospitality. That was the trouble with Thorn: he always did what he thought was right. Sometimes you had to do what *other* people thought was right.

And that's why I've got this stomachache.

Lily sat down on a hay bale. She'd had to try every single dish at dinner, so as not to offend anyone. She hadn't thought they would have laid out quite so many. At least she wouldn't have to eat for the next few days.

A heavy mist covered Three Barrows. She'd barely been able to see the stables from the cottage door. Ice was already glazing the puddles; it was going to be a cold night.

Maybe I'll let him sleep here. But he'll need another blanket.

She got up and turned to find Mr. Funny standing in the doorway.

"Oh," said Lily.

"Please do not move, Lady Shadow," said Mr. Funny. "If you scream or attempt any magic, I shall kill you immediately."

Lily stared, too stunned to speak. Mr. Funny had . . . threatened her? Was this some joke? Some very poor, very bad joke?

Then Lily saw his eyes and knew he wasn't joking at all.

She looked at the ax in each hand. "But you're going to kill me anyway, aren't you?"

"Yes. But there is no need for us to be uncivil. It's not every day I kill a ruler of a Great House." He pointed his weapon at a hay bale. "Please, sit."

"Since you asked so politely, I shall."

Think! Think!

She needed a plan, some way to get out of here, get help. But first she needed to know who she was up against.

Lily's mind raced. "Duke Solar sent you to kill me?"

"He did. You revealed your magical powers to Gabriel, remember? Back at Halloween."

"I save Gabriel's life, and this is how the duke rewards me? By sending an assassin?"

"Better a single man than an army. You have broken the most sacred law of the New Kingdoms, Lady Shadow. Death should be no surprise."

Duke Solar was no fool, even if Gabriel was. He'd send his very best. He'd send . . .

"You're the Solar executioner," said Lily. "Golgoth."

A smile flickered across Mr. Funny's lips. "Very good."

Lily would have collapsed if she hadn't already been sitting. Her strength abandoned her, leaving cold dread.

Golgoth. She'd heard the stories. An executioner who'd never failed. The perfect killer.

Better even than Tyburn.

Golgoth put the edge of his ax against her neck. Lily stiffened as the icy blade nicked her throat.

"My people will know," she said. "Then war will come, whether you like it or not."

"They'll never find the body. Believe me when I tell you I've done this before."

"I'll return as a ghost. I'll tell them what happened."

"Who'll bring you back? There are no other necromancers. You are the last Shadow."

She needed to play for time. Surely someone in the cottage would wonder why she wasn't back yet? But then again, Dott lay snoring by the fire, and Jared and his family had retreated to their beds. The only one still up was Gabriel. No help would be coming from him.

Lily glanced over at Thorn. "And what about him?"

"He'll die, too. People will think you ran off together."

It was dark. The lantern light was low, casting plenty of shadows. She needed to make her move.

But the edge of the ax was against her throat. She couldn't disappear into the darkness quickly enough.

She had to try. For her and for Thorn.

Then she heard something . . . odd.

A chiming.

She looked up.

"Hailstones?" asked Golgoth, also gazing at the ceiling.

Something was falling onto the wooden tiles above them. Pattering down.

Lily saw movement among the rafters. Light reflected off shiny glass legs and crystalline bodies.

She swallowed. "We need to run."

Dozens of jewel spiders glided down on silvery threads of silk. Others tumbled off or scurried down the wooden posts and walls. They formed shimmering, sparkling streams, their narrow stalklike legs prodding and testing ahead of them.

Everything depended on Golgoth. He was here to kill her, but now there was another threat. What would he do? He could finish her off, but then would he survive the spiders? This was magic—Lily's world, not his.

He needs me. But does he realize that?

He did. Golgoth flipped the ax away. "Get up. Go for the cottage. Warn them." He lifted up a bale and threw it between them and the creeping creatures. A few spiders shattered; the rest merely climbed over the obstacle.

Lily ran to Thorn.

"Leave him!" shouted Golgoth, smashing his axes down on the spiders. "You don't have time!"

"Get up, Thorn!"

Thorn tried opening his eyes. He groaned.

"For the Princes' sake, get up!"

"Watch out . . . for Mr. Funny . . ." he mumbled.

"Tell me something I don't know." Lily took his arm and tried to haul him up. When did he get so heavy?

"Behind you!" yelled Golgoth.

"All right!" Lily swept around and reached out. She tore a sheet of darkness off the far wall and threw it over the hundreds of glistening creatures.

The blackness lay there for a moment, then sank away, and the spiders were gone.

Golgoth looked about him. The walls sparkled with more jewel spiders. "A hundred down, only another thousand to go."

"Just help me with Thorn."

Golgoth grimaced, then handed her his dagger.

"What am I supposed to do with this?" she asked.

"Fight with it?" He lifted Thorn.

"I don't fight," said Lily. "That's why I have executioners."

"I am not *your* executioner, Lady Shadow."

Thorn shook Golgoth away. "Leave me!" He waggled his jaw. "I'm . . . I'm all right."

The horses were panicking, even Thunder. He slammed his front hooves against the pen door as the jewel spiders clambered over him. He tossed his head savagely, desperate to throw them off.

Each horse bled from dozens of tiny bites, but it seemed the jewel spider venom wasn't strong enough to take out such big animals. Lily patted Zephyr until the horse calmed down. "You get ready," she warned him.

Lily then checked outside.

The trees glistened. The jewel spiders coated every branch and trunk, and thousands of threads dangled down out of the mist.

Where were the spiders coming from?

Most were minute, some the size of her open hand, but she spotted larger creatures, as big as cats, with bodies lumpy with diamond warts and legs growing out at odd angles.

"Everyone get up!" Lily yelled. "We're being attacked!"

She flung the barn door open, and the horses bolted. Thunder stampeded over the spiders, crushing dozens with each hoof. Zephyr, the donkey, and Gabriel's white steed followed, neighing wildly and trampling the jewel spiders as they fled into the surrounding woods.

Golgoth pointed to the cottage. A mass of spiders blocked their way. "And how are we going to get across to there?"

"Leave that to me," said Thorn.

Lily stared at him. "With one arrow?"

He'd collected his bow and a single shaft. Even though he could barely stand, Thorn brought the bowstring to his chin using that weird thumb draw of his. "One's all I need."

He pointed into the sky and loosed.

Dozens of bigger jewel spiders swung from their threads above them. One was the size of a pony, an easy, ridiculously easy, shot for Thorn.

The arrow sailed over it.

"You missed," said Lily.

Thorn's gaze stayed upward. "I weren't aiming at the spider."

There was a sharp *snap* as the arrow cut through the silk the big spider was suspended from. The spider flailed frantically as it fell, tearing down through others that dangled in its way.

What followed was a waterfall of crystal. One spider brought down five. Those five knocked down twenty, and so on until they were all tumbling crazily over one another. They smashed on the ground, crushing the spiders beneath them. Shards of glass flew everywhere as legs snapped and bodies shattered.

The wave of spiders that had blocked their path was now just a twitching mass of broken glass. All with one arrow.

Thorn smirked. "Well?"

Sometimes Lily didn't know whether to slap Thorn or kiss him. This was one of those times.

"Run!" ordered Golgoth.

They ran. The remaining spiders raced after them. More fell from tree boughs. Others, larger and twisted in shape and cluttered with legs—ten, twelve, or more—glided down out of the mist on their spider silk.

Jared stood at the door, shouting at them. Lily ran, covering herself with her riding cloak yet feeling the *thump* of spiders landing on it. As she came within a few steps of the cottage, she tossed it away; dozens of creatures crawled all over it.

Dott tugged her inside. Golgoth was a step behind, Thorn last.

Jared slammed the door shut. His wife dashed forward and wedged a rolled-up blanket against the gap at the bottom.

Lily jumped up and down and shook her head. "Are there any on me? Check!"

"No, m'lady." Jared turned her about. "None at all."

Lily shivered. "Yuck. I hate spiders." She brushed her shoulders, just in case. She could still feel their spiky legs. . . .

"Not nice! Not nice a' all!" thundered Dott. "Prin'ess good now." She clasped Lily and gave her a lung-crushing squeeze.

Golgoth readied his axes and Thorn grabbed a log from beside the fireplace.

"What's . . . what's going on?" said Gabriel, cowering in the corner. "Mr. Funny? Why are you dressed like that? Is this some joke?"

Lily wriggled free of Dott. "You mean he doesn't know?"

"Know what?" asked Gabriel.

The window shattered, and a jewel spider burst in. Legs over a foot long, and a bloated body the size of a pig. Silver venom dripped from its fangs. It pounced.

Golgoth leaped between them. He swept both axes, one left, the other right. Glass splintered all around him and the spider crashed, all eight legs severed. It thrashed uselessly until Dott brought her saucepan down on it, crushing it into powder.

"Mr. . . . Funny?" asked Gabriel.

"His name's Golgoth," said Lily.

"No, he's Mr. Funny. He's always been Mr. Funny." Tears dribbled down Gabriel's cheeks. "Aren't you?"

Golgoth winked. "Take this, m'lord." He held an ax out to him.

More spiders tumbled through the now-shattered window.

"Into the next room," said Jared. His wife and their two children were already moving. "It has a thicker door and no windows."

"What about the rest of the villagers?" Lily asked.

Jared's face was grim. "They'll have to look after themselves."

Lily didn't like it. She could hear screams coming from the other cottages. But Jared was right—they had no choice.

They moved rooms, and Jared shut the door. There was just a single candle, sitting in a nook in the wall.

They heard a scratching at the door. The type of noise you might hear if hundreds of glass needlelike legs were trying to get in.

Lily looked around at the others. The candlelight turned their faces into almost primitive masks. From the grim determination of Golgoth to the fear worn by Gabriel. The keenness of Thorn to the simple faith of Dott.

A pair of legs reached under the gap. Thorn snapped them with a stamp of his foot.

"Where are they coming from?" asked Thorn.

"They were falling out of the sky." Lily shook her head. "I don't understand it."

Thorn frowned. "Some spiders drift in the wind. Small ones carry themselves along on threads of spider silk. But only very small ones."

"You stand beside me, boy, on my left," said Golgoth. "M'lord, I'll need you on my right."

"Me help good!" said Dott.

"Yes, you hit anything with more than two legs that gets past us." Golgoth shrugged his shoulders. "M'lord?"

Gabriel whimpered. "I can't."

"There's nothing to it."

Gabriel stumbled backward until he was right up against the fireplace. "No, I can't."

The pattering was all around. The cries coming from the other cottages rose in stark contrast to the relentless chimes of the spiders' bodies hitting one another.

The door cracked as slivers of wood were sliced off from the opposite side.

"Get ready," said Golgoth.

Lily turned the dagger in her hand. She'd played with toy swords when she was younger, but her parents had felt it wasn't ladylike to use weapons. The sharpest thing she'd wielded in the last few years was a needle.

Thorn bit his lip. "Hold on," he said. There was a loud scratching coming from behind them. "Did anyone block the flue?"

Gabriel screamed.

Curled up as he was, he didn't move quickly enough as the jewel spiders fell down upon him from the chimney. He thrashed as they scurried down his collar and up his sleeves and pant legs. "Help me!"

The door crumbled under the weight of jewel spiders piled against it.

Lily leaped at Gabriel, swatting the spiders as she saw them.

"Careful with that!" Gabriel yelled as she smashed a spider with the flat of the blade.

"Just shut up!"

Gabriel fell as webbing entangled his right leg and began dragging him back toward the fireplace.

"Someone help me!" Lily cried. She grabbed Gabriel's arm and fought, trying to hold him. Instead, she was slipping closer to the hearth.

Jared joined her, taking Gabriel's other arm. Small scratches and bites covered Jared's arms. He huffed and puffed, but he was sagging. He couldn't stay awake.

His fingers slipped. The jolt made Lily lose hold herself. Gabriel slid faster toward the chimney, and up into it.

"Come back here!" Lily grabbed hold of his hair.

"OW!"

Gabriel clung to her arm even as it disappeared up the flue. But his grip was weakening. He'd been bitten, too.

"Help . . . me . . ." he muttered. One finger after another lost hold of her. "Mind . . . the hair. . . ."

A sudden, final jerk ripped him from her. Soot fell as the boy disappeared up the chimney shaft.

"M'lord!" roared Golgoth. He flung off a larger spider, smashing it under his boot. His eyes were red with despair. "I've got to save him!"

"How?" Lily slumped. Her arms wobbled and she saw a pair of red bite marks on her hand. It must have happened while she was trying to save Gabriel.

I will not give in.

She gritted her teeth and stood up.

I will not.

Sleep was the brother of death, so they said. And she was House Shadow, a necromancer. She was the mistress of death. The only difference between a creature sleeping and a creature dead was the breathing.

Swaying where she stood, Lily breathed in.

Whatever little life those spiders had, she wanted it.

She continued to breathe in.

The spiders nearest her simply collapsed.

Still she drew breath.

Like a ripple spreading outward, the creatures fell. Those farthest away sensed the danger and fled, but many more expired where they were, their lives taken instantly.

The chiming stopped.

Someone took her hand. Warm fingers locked around her own.

She opened her eyes and saw Thorn.

"They're gone, Lily," he said.

Lily sighed, and sank to the ground.

TWENTY-FOUR

Thorn joined the cleanup the next morning. The mist was gone, revealing a village transformed by last night's attack.

Webs covered Three Barrows. From the roofs to the tree and everything in between. Great sheets of silver, dew-sprinkled webbing hung off the long boughs and between the cottages.

Dead jewel spiders lay scattered everywhere. The villagers were busy sweeping them up. Children prodded them with sticks, and one or two of the locals gathered them, carefully, into boxes.

Thorn picked one up. Utterly dead.

A lot of things were starting to make sense to him now. Jewel spiders, not trolls, had been responsible for the devastation he'd seen at Pitch Farm. As Lord Shadow had said, Pitch and Milly had been impregnated by the spiders, and their two sons must have been taken. Just like Gabriel was taken.

And had they taken Tyburn, too? He'd been at Pitch Farm. . . .

Thorn searched the sky. The sun had cleared away the clouds, driving them to form a thin gray haze to the north, revealing all, and nothing.

The spiders came from on high. But how?

Lily emerged from the cottage, with Dott helping her. She shuffled along like a witch from some old fairy tale, the hem of her dress dragging in the mushy snow.

"You look awful," said Thorn.

"Thanks," said Lily. "I'm just . . . tired."

It was more than that. Her eyes looked hollow and her cheeks sunken. She'd lost weight; her dress hung loose over her bony frame, and her wrists could barely stop her bracelets from sliding off.

She saw him staring. "It's the magic. Like I told you, it takes a toll. The more I use it, the more I'll . . . change."

"Then don't use it," said Thorn.

"What choice did I have?" she snapped. She touched her bony cheek. "The effects should wear off, given time. But if I overdo it, they'll become permanent."

"There's no hiding what you are, is there?"

Lily smiled weakly. "It could be worse. Sorcerers of House Djinn turn into beings of living fire. One apparently combusted at his wedding."

Dott picked up a snapped-off branch. "Not flyin', not flyin' at all." She looked up at the trees. "I got no wings."

Thorn gave Lily a querying look. Did she know what Dott was talking about? But Lily just shrugged.

Who understands trolls?

The three of them came upon Jared, gathering the thatch that had been torn off his roof last night. He bowed. "M'lady."

"What's the count?" Lily asked.

"Fifteen asleep. Ten gone," he replied grimly. "Seven of those stolen were children. Their families are beside themselves." Then, as though he'd just remembered who Lily was, he did his best to put on a brave face. "But it could have been much worse. No doubt those spiders would have taken all of us, including me, if it hadn't been for you, m'lady. You have all our thanks."

Did she? Thorn wasn't so sure. Yesterday it had all been bows and curt-seys; now he noticed a wariness. The villagers were keeping clear of Lily. He couldn't hear what they were whispering, but he bet it was about her using magic.

Jared must have guessed how Lily was feeling. "It shames me, Lady Shadow, that they don't see what's right in front of them; that it would have been so much worse if you hadn't, er, done what you did."

"We'll find everyone, Jared, I promise. And we'll bring them back, if we possibly can." She picked up a straw. "In the meantime, I'll send my thatcher to repair the roofs. You'll have dry homes, at least."

He bowed again and went back to dealing with the damage.

Thorn waited until the headman was out of earshot. "You got a plan?"

"I'm open to suggestions."

Thorn peered down the road. "We're not far from Malice. The town was the source of the last infestation. Keep going?"

"I agree—for some of us, at least. But there's something I don't get. Look at the trees." She pointed to the highest point of a nearby oak. Webs fluttered among the uppermost branches. "The jewel spiders came from up high. How?"

"I've been wondering the same thing."

"They were carried, somehow. There's more to this than a random infestation, Thorn. The answer's there," she said, pointing toward the sky. "And you need to go look."

"On Hades? He won't like being woken up."

"You have to, and then you must find our missing people." She smiled the smile that always meant trouble. For him. "And Gabriel."

"You want me to rescue Gabriel? Seriously?" Thorn shook his head. "I'd rather kiss a troll."

"Smoochies?" said Dott, lips puckered and waiting.

"Uh, later, maybe," said Thorn. "All right. I'll go look for the missing villagers and if—and that's a big if—I *happen* to stumble on Gabriel, I'll bring him back to Castle Gloom. Probably."

"Thank you. And one more thing: you'd better take his fool with you."

"You mean Golgoth, the Solar executioner?" Thorn crossed his arms. "That'll be a no. I'm squire to one executioner already, thank you very much."

"I spoke to him. We've decided to forget about the incident in the barn."

"How can you? Last night he was going to chop your head off, and now we're joining forces with him? That's insane, that is."

"That's politics, Thorn."

Golgoth stood at the open door of the barn, his equipment spread out on a table. A pair of curved swords. His axes. A cluster of daggers, narrow-bladed for sliding between ribs. A lot for a skinny man to carry. He was no longer wearing his fool's motley but a tunic of stiff leather covered with strips of steel. A crowd of children watched him, fascinated, and a little bit frightened. Golgoth glared at them as he strapped the swords to his back. Then he picked up three of his daggers and started juggling. The children cheered.

"Now that's plain weird," said Thorn.

"See? Both murderous and entertaining," said Lily. "I'm sure the two of you will get on just fine."

"I still think you and I should stick together."

"I'll have Dott. We'll keep going to Malice. Jared warned me that the town's deep within House Tenebrae lands, and I may not get as warm a welcome there as I did here. So I'll be traveling more discreetly."

"Ain't they loyal to the Shadows?"

"Until they see a weakness." Lily sighed. "I won't stay long—a day, at most. There's a place called the Baker's Inn; that's where I'll be."

"The Baker's Inn? Sounds almost quaint." Thorn hesitated. "I still don't like it, though. I'll come with you, just in case."

"I can look after myself," said Lily with a wry smile. "But it's good to know you care, Thorn."

Thorn blushed. "Well, y'know, you do pay my wages."

From one of the many mysterious folds in her skirt, Lily pulled an envelope closed with her seal, the twin crescent moon of House Shadow. "This will explain it all to Old Colm. He's to send bats to every village and town in Gehenna warning them about the jewel spiders." She handed the letter to Thorn. "Now get going."

"All right. You look after yourself, Princess." He turned toward the barn.

"Wait, Thorn."

"What?"

She pouted. "Smoochies?"

Thorn's blush deepened. Lily laughed and waved him off.

TWENTY-FIVE

"Tyburn will kill you the moment he's back," said Thorn to his companion.

Golgoth raised an eyebrow. "Will he now?"

Lily had told Golgoth the truth, that Tyburn was still alive, somewhere. Maybe she'd thought it would scare him to know that if he tried anything he'd face her executioner sooner or later.

The trouble was, Golgoth was an executioner himself. They didn't scare easily.

Thorn continued. "He's the greatest executioner there's ever been. Better than you, that's for sure."

"If you say so."

"I've seen him kill seven men with nothing but a branch."

"Why'd he use a branch?"

"Er . . ." Thorn decided that telling the truth—that Tyburn had fought with a branch because Thorn had stolen his sword at the time—wasn't such a good idea. "Because he's amazing."

"Clearly," replied Golgoth, sounding anything but amazed.

"So if you want to run off and hide in a cave somewhere for the rest of your life, I won't stop you."

"Thank you for your concern, but for now, until Gabriel is safe, I'll be sticking around."

"He thought you were his fool."

"I am. Is that so bad? The boy's been raised with the burden of being the only son of Duke Solar, the first boy after twelve daughters. He's spoiled, foolish, arrogant, and a sharp pain in the backside, but I was there when he first laughed. When his eyes lit up with something other than fear and worry. And I aim to get him back."

"I ain't heard no one speak about Gabriel like that before."

"I doubt his own father knows him half as well as I do."

No wonder Gabriel was so messed up. His only friend was an executioner.

Webs hung from the trees, and Thorn thought he'd heard the fateful chiming of jewel spiders moving, sometimes nearby, sometimes not. And Bone-Tree was too quiet. No birdsong. No animals moving through the foliage. No calls of deer, no foxes barking.

Thunder shifted uneasily, sensing the unnatural atmosphere as keenly as Thorn. Golgoth's right hand rested on his ax, and his left kept tight hold of the reins of the skittish Lightning. The sun, weak as it was, glowed above the treetops and was on its way west. Thorn wanted to be back within the walls of Castle Gloom before the shadows grew much longer.

But if the spiders did attack and Golgoth happened to get caught . . .

Thorn smiled.

"Lady Shadow's days are numbered anyway." Golgoth offered him a slice of cheese. "Now that everyone in the New Kingdoms knows she's a witch."

"Let's hope the other houses send better assassins than you."

Golgoth laughed. "Oh, it won't be the executioners you need to worry about." He drew his fingers through stands of spiderweb dangling off a branch. "It'll be armies."

"We'll beat whatever anyone sends." He hoped he sounded more confident than he felt. Gehenna was in dire straits. Lily played it down, but she was desperate. No Skeleton Key meant no help from her father. With trolls marching down from the north and these jewel spiders falling out of the sky, Thorn feared it wouldn't take much more to bring House Shadow crashing down.

"You haven't the men. Everyone knows that."

"Yes, we have. Lily's come up with reinforcements. Old Colm's probably training them right now."

"Reinforcements, eh?" Golgoth scratched his stringy beard. "I wonder where she found them."

The road began to widen and the trees were thinning out. "We're back." He nudged Thunder into a trot.

There were still a few miles between the edge of Bone-Tree and the walls of Castle Gloom, but as soon as Devil's Knoll came into view, you knew you were there. Thunder picked up the pace as he sensed the end of the journey. Golgoth rode beside them, and eight hooves kicked through the snow.

Castle Gloom rose steadily from the horizon. First to be seen was, of course, the Needle. The tower was twice the height of the next tallest. Smoke still lingered over the remains of Old Keep. Closer were the dark walls upon which layers of black ivy, painted with frost, sparkled with the light of the fading sun.

Something wasn't right. There should be twenty men at the gate; Thorn spotted only two.

The portcullis rose as they drew nearer. They were on the drawbridge when the inner gates swung open.

Slowly, cautiously, they entered the courtyard.

Old Colm hobbled over to meet them.

"What's going on? Where are the reinforcements?" Thorn jumped off Thunder and searched around him. The place was empty except for a few workhorses, a bunch of squires, and some odd-looking soldiers.

Old Colm pointed at them. "Right there."

"Oh no," muttered Thorn. No wonder they looked odd. They were zombies dressed in armor. So that's why Lily had been so secretive about them.

Golgoth laughed.

Old Colm stared at him. "Why is this fool wearing armor?"

"Master Colm, meet Golgoth. Golgoth, meet Master Colm."

Old Colm scowled. "More mischief?"

A zombie had a helmet on and a spear sticking out of his chest. It didn't seem to be bothering him. A squire was trying to pull it out.

"They're supposed to defend Gloom?" Thorn asked.

Old Colm looked as if he was going to cry with despair. "Meet the new Immortals."

The Immortals. That was the name the Shadows had given their undead regiment, back in the days of the great necromancers.

"More like the Incompetents," Old Colm continued. "We can't get them to do anything useful. We've been trying to get them to line up along the battlements, but they keep wandering off. Either that or they stumble over the edge into the moat. We've fished two out this morning already."

Golgoth dismounted, wiping tears from his eyes. "This is the finest jest I've heard in years. Wait till Duke Solar hears it."

Thorn handed the letter over. "Is this all we've got to defend Castle Gloom?"

Old Colm grimaced. "Defending the castle is meant to be the executioner's job."

"But we ain't got no executioner at the moment," said Thorn.

Old Colm's eyes narrowed as he looked over at Golgoth. "Seems to me we do."

TWENTY-SIX

Thorn stirred the honey into his porridge while the old men argued over breakfast the next morning.

There was Old Colm. He banged his peg leg on the flagstones of the kitchen. "What about the trolls?" He waved a slip of paper at the others. "This came by bat this morning, from Baron Sable. He's facing a horde, and there's no knowing which way it'll go. We need to deal with the trolls first!"

There was Sir Grimsoul, leader of the few Black Guard who had remained behind at the castle. He was older than Old Colm, and some of the squires believed Grimsoul was actually a zombie. He'd always been so dull and doddering that nobody could tell whether he was alive or dead. Grimsoul waved his spoon at Old Colm, flicking watery porridge over the weapons master's face. "Listen here, sonny. Listen here. Listen. Are you listening?"

"Get on with it, you old git!" snapped Old Colm, snatching the spoon out of his hand.

Grimsoul screwed up his eyes to stare hard at Old Colm. "We've been given a job to do, and that's what we must do. Guard Castle Gloom. And that's the front and back of it."

And then there was Golgoth.

Considering that he was their sworn enemy and had recently tried to kill their ruler, he was making himself quite at home. He picked a bun and sliced it into quarters with two swift strokes of his knife. "The trolls are not behind the kidnapped villagers; we know that now. That is the work of these magical spiders. While Lady Shadow investigates them, we need to prepare ourselves against further attacks. And"—he looked meaningfully at Thorn—"find a way to rescue our loved ones."

The trouble was, all of them were right. But each thought he was more right than the others, so they couldn't agree on anything.

Thorn didn't know what to do. So he grabbed the milk jug.

As he poured himself a second—or it could have been a third— mug, he noticed someone waving at him from the doorway. The air wasn't clear in here; it was a mix of floating flour dust and steam, but it looked like . . .

One of the Shade brothers.

What did they want? They usually haunted the maids' changing rooms.

Thorn wiped his bowl clean with a piece of bread and shoved as much of it as he could in his mouth, then went to see the spirit.

It was hard to think of Mal Shade as a ghost. Aside from the pale, semitransparent form, he looked and acted just like a squire. But ghost he was, and so was his brother. Gart hung farther back, in the corridor, playing with Custard.

"What's up?" Thorn asked.

"You want to tell him?" Mal asked his brother.

Gart tickled the pup's nose. "We've spoken to Lord Shadow."

"You?" Thorn exclaimed. "Why hasn't he contacted Lily?"

"He's tried, but something—or someone—is stopping him," said Gart. "He wants to know how she is."

"She's fine, last I saw of her." That wasn't entirely true, but there wasn't much anyone could do about it, even if Lily let them. "Iblis is worried about something?"

Mal gestured at the kitchen. "They're talking. The servants and soldiers and the squires. We hear it all."

"When you're lurking in the changing rooms, right?"

If a ghost could blush, then Mal would have. "We don't do that anymore. You tell him, Gart."

"We don't," said Gart. "We're good little ghosts."

Mal continued. "They're blaming Lily for their troubles. They think her using magic has brought the curse of the Six Princes upon the country. They think that's why the trolls are attacking. That's why the villagers are disappearing and we have these spiders plaguing us. All because of Lily."

"That's stupid," Thorn declared. "She's only trying to help."

"The Gehennish are a superstitious bunch, Thorn."

He was never going to get used to this place.

"The number of sleepers are growing, Thorn. Those villagers taken from Pitch Farm and Three Barrows? They're not the only ones, just the latest."

Thorn thought back to when he was in a spider-induced sleep. "The sleepers will wake up soon, I reckon. Meantime, they can't do nothing to no one."

"They can dream," Mal said.

"What difference does dreaming make?"

Mal shrugged. "We're dead. We don't sleep, and we don't dream. But Lord Shadow believes dreams can give power. Those spiders live off them, don't they?"

Thorn agreed.

"What if they're not the only things that feed off dreams? What if there is something else, greater than the jewel spiders? Growing fatter and more powerful all the time? That's what Lord Shadow's afraid of—not the enemy we face, but the one hidden. He told us to tell you: *Dreams are pure imagination, and imagination is the fuel of magic.*"

"Why tell me? Why not Old Colm? Or anyone else?"

They all turned at the shout. Old Colm was standing, his chair knocked back, glaring at Sir Grimsoul.

"That's why," said Mal. "They'll be bickering till Doomsday."

"Come on," Thorn said to the two ghosts. He was fed up with hanging around. "I've got to make two stops, and you can tell me everything along the way."

First it was back to his room for weapons—bow, a quiver full of arrows, and a long knife—and the warmest coat he had. The twins repeated what they'd already told him, but the second time around, it felt clearer.

"The jewel spider's bite sent you to sleep. The dreams were being gathered for some reason."

But by whom? And for what?

Thorn searched the dull gray sky as they crossed the courtyard to Murk Hall. The answer was up there, somewhere.

It seemed that there was no escaping the mist. It filled the roofless hall so much that Thorn could hardly see anything. He peered hard, and only then did he recognize a vast, snow-covered mass perched on a broken column. "Hades?"

The bat replied with a deep, rumbling snore.

Mal gestured back over his shoulder. "I could go get a sheep. Once Hades smells it, he'll be licking his chops. Might wake him up."

"He'll just gobble it down and then be out for another three days," said Thorn. "All he's interested in when it's cold is eating and sleeping. Lazier than a cat."

Thorn stroked Hades's chin, brushing off dangling icicles. "What are you dreaming about, boy?"

Hades's ears twitched. His eyes remained closed.

Thorn rested his head against the giant creature's chest. The bat was so warm, and he felt his massive heart beating like a drum. *Boom, boom, boom.* The bat smelled, but Thorn loved the strange odor of moist, warm fur.

It seemed a shame to wake him.

The other bats flittered overhead.

"I need your help, Hades, and I need it now."

Thorn tugged an ear. Hades twitched, and the snore became a snarl.

"I know you don't like it, so why don't you just wake up?"

Lily was waiting on him, and Thorn *needed* Hades. He tugged harder—

Hades rammed his head into Thorn's chest. Thorn fell back and crashed to the floor. Before he could blink, Hades was on top of him, pinning his arms with his claws, his snarling face inches above his.

"Get off me, you hairy bag of wind!"

Hades hissed.

"And when did you last clean your teeth?"

Hades flapped his wings and rose a few feet. Snow and mist swirled around him, creating ministorms within the hall. Thorn rolled over and stood. "Good. You're finally awake. We've got work to do."

"One day you're going to push that beast too far," said Mal. "Where are you headed?"

"Up."

The quiver of arrows he buckled to his belt; the bow he slung across his back. Then Thorn climbed up between Hades's shoulders, tucking his heels well in. He scratched the monster at his favorite spot between the ears. "Lily's counting on us, boy."

Each wing sweep lurched boy and bat another ten feet higher. Within seconds, they were out between the broken roof timbers of Murk Hall.

What a miserable gray day.

It didn't look like the mist was going to clear anytime soon. They'd be flying blind.

Luckily, that wasn't a problem for bats.

TWENTY-SEVEN

They rose higher, losing sight of the ground, the castle, the world beneath them. Thorn wrapped the scarf over his ears. It was cold enough on the ground, but up here the icy winds howled and cut his skin like razors. His fingers froze even inside the thick, fur-lined gloves.

Hades sailed northeast, across Spindlewood and toward Three Barrows. What had taken them all day by horse would only take him an hour or so.

Thorn settled himself and let Hades take charge of business. With his heels locked under Hades's shoulders and seated neatly back, he hardly needed to hold on, so he tucked his hands under his armpits to keep them warm.

Where did the jewel spiders come from? Gabriel had been pulled up the chimney. The webs had covered the treetops, and there was the lack of footprints back at Pitch Farm.

The answer's up here, somewhere.

But how would he find it? The clouds surrounded him. Gehenna spent all of winter cloaked in fog, and even riding high on Hades, he only fleetingly glimpsed the sun.

Then, after an hour of gliding through the brooding gray curtains, Thorn glimpsed something.

What was it? The freezing wind bit his eyes, making it hard to see. He blinked away the tears as best he could.

Small flashes of rainbow-hued light sparkled up ahead. They swooped closer toward—

Hades shrieked and swerved sharply; Thorn grabbed his fur before he fell off.

"What was that? Just go through the cloud!"

But Hades snarled and dove through a break in the clouds.

Brushing along the edge of the dense mist, Thorn discovered what was creating the rainbows.

Jewel spiders.

The sun pierced through gaps above him and struck the creatures, which refracted the light like a prism.

Up Hades flew, alongside columns made of cloud, hundreds of feet high. Wispy tendrils twisted and bent in the wind, ripped apart, and then re-formed farther along. They spread out like branches of some immense tree, their limbs supporting the upper sections of the cloud. At the top, Thorn swore he could see different levels, with floors and walls and platforms, all crawling with glass spiders, great and small.

The cloud's solid.

Thorn tentatively touched a column; it resisted a little, as if he was pressing through wet sand, then thickened to stony hardness.

Hades spun sideways.

Thorn grabbed on. "Hey! You almost dropped me!"

Then Thorn realized Hades had just *saved* them both.

Hanging between the columns were webs. Hundreds of feet wide, their strands pulsed with hundreds of colors. And trapped within them, some cocooned and others dangling like puppets, were people. Men, women, and children.

"By the Six . . ." Thorn whispered, horrified.

The jewel spiders climbed from one victim to another. One man still moved, and his eyes met Thorn's as he circled above him.

"Help me!" he shouted. "Please!"

Thorn grabbed his bow. His frozen fingers fumbled on the arrow, and he drew slower than he wanted, his arms and shoulders stiff with cold. He aimed—

The spider crept over the villager's neck, and bit.

Thorn cursed, and loosed, knowing he was too late. The spider broke apart as the arrow pierced it straight through.

"Help . . ." The man sagged and was asleep.

More spiders slid along the web, and Thorn backed away. He couldn't risk getting bitten all the way up here.

A castle in the clouds. How is that even possible?

This was how the jewel spiders were being transported across Gehenna; this was why the attacks had been impossible to trace.

It wasn't a castle in the sky.

It was one of House Typhoon's fabled cloud ships.

TWENTY-EIGHT

Hades rose higher, up into the shallow domes above the field of webs. He dug his claws into a smoky beam, and folded his wings.

Thorn remembered his talk with Ying, about how the cloud ships needed huge amounts of magical energy to fly, let alone sail all the way here from Lu Feng.

So how was this still up in the sky?

It's because of the dreamers.

Dreams were a sort of magical energy.

Yes, it had to be. The people trapped in the webs were powering the ship. Their dreams were keeping it aloft.

Thorn watched in surprise as men slid down the spider silk. They wore strange blue armor with cloud symbols engraved upon the breastplates. Their hair was up in topknots, the same style Ying wore.

Thorn felt as if he'd been stuck wandering through fog for days, hardly understanding what was happening around him. Now that fog was lifting.

Lily used her learning to solve a puzzle. She would search through her books about the history of the New Kingdoms. Thorn couldn't do that, but he could track and hunt. He solved mysteries by looking at what was in front of him and trying to match it with what he knew.

Ying and the Feathered Council had overthrown House Typhoon, defeating the ancient sorcerous family with new science. The few sorcerers serving House Typhoon had fled, taking whatever treasures they could lay their hands on. One of these sorcerers had managed to lay his hands on this, a whole cloud ship.

Normally it would take the power of dozens of sorcerers to fly even the smallest ship, or so Ying had told him.

But how many sorcerers would you need if you could harvest all this . . . dream magic?

A handful? Maybe even just one?

The cloud ship was a living thing. The dreamers produced the energy, and the webs took that energy and spread it throughout the body of the ship, holding it together, and holding it up. But there would need to be someone directing it, a will, a mind, to control it and keep it from just . . . drifting off. And there was one obvious suspect for the ship's captain.

A renegade sorcerer of House Typhoon.

He rubbed Hades's left ear as he pondered. It all fit, didn't it? He'd guessed how the cloud ship had gotten here, and that a sorcerer was controlling both the vessel and the jewel spiders. What he didn't know was *why.*

Why attack Gehenna? This sorcerer didn't need to kidnap its people; he or she must've had plenty of dreamers already in order to sail the ship all the way from Lu Feng, across the Eagle Mountains, the Centaur Grasslands, and a few seas.

Unless their power ran out over time, when their dreams grew stale . . .

Thorn felt a chill as he watched one of the soldiers check an old woman who was suspended from the webs. Whether she was asleep or dead, Thorn couldn't tell.

Then, to his horror, the soldier sliced her open.

Out tumbled thousands of sparkling newborn jewel spiders.

Thorn retched.

The man cut the body from the web and dragged it away, letting the new spiders creep off to find their first meal of dreams.

There was Thorn's answer: the sorcerer was using up his dreamers, including those from Gehenna.

He had to do something.

Thorn patted Hades's furry cheek. "You wait here, all right?"

Hades snarled.

"Oh, you've got a better plan?"

Thorn checked to make sure his bow, arrows, and knife were all in place. He grabbed a strand of spider silk and tested it with a good pull. It was secure.

Hades snapped his teeth.

"I'm just going to have a look around," said Thorn. "I'll be back soon."

And with that he slid down into the heart of the jewel spiders' nest.

TWENTY-NINE

Malice. A bad name for a bad town.

Nobody chose to live in Malice. You ended up there when there was nowhere else to go. It was a place for exiles.

"Not nice. Not nice at all . . ." whispered a frightened Dott.

Crows haunted the bare branches, and they flocked in cawing packs above the town gates, where a gallows hung on either side. Thankfully, they were empty.

Lily was glad she'd swapped her dress for a plain one from Jared's daughter and had left Zephyr back at Three Barrows. Instead, she rode on a mule. Even though she was still within the boundary of her own realm, Lily felt unsafe.

A gang of ragged children barged past, bumping into her mule, yelling at Dott.

"Watch it!" Lily shouted as one tugged the mule's tail.

A boy threw a slushy snowball. A few more followed, aimed at Dott. Then the troll stamped her foot. "Not nice!" she bellowed. The children fled.

More crows watched from the rusty bars of the portcullis. They were big, ugly, and . . . feathery. Nowhere as handsome as the bats of Castle Gloom.

"Not nice at all," repeated Dott.

Where to begin?

Lily nudged her mule toward a couple of guards. They wore the uniform of her Black Guard but without pride. One of them poked his spear at Dott. "You're an ugly one, aren't you?"

"Leave her alone." Lily pushed the spear aside.

"Lord Tenebrae doesn't want trolls here, terrorizing decent folk."

"There are decent folk in Malice?"

The second guard laughed as his companion scowled. "That's true enough. A girl like you will need a troll, in case that sharp tongue of yours gets you in trouble. Now what is it that you want?"

"I'm looking for the cave of jewel spiders," she said.

The guard scratched his nose. "Is that right? Hmm . . . where is it?"

The other guard made an extravagant shrug. "Y'know what? Slipped right out of my head." He grinned at her and rubbed his fingers together. "A crown or two might prompt my memory."

Lily reached for her purse.

It wasn't there. Had she dropped it? She looked at the muddy ground. She checked her belt again. She was sure she'd tied it on. . . .

"Lost something?" asked a guard.

Lily patted her clothing. Where was it?

Then she saw the children at the end of the street, laughing and waving a small silk purse. Her purse. A moment later, they vanished down an alleyway.

"You're not from around here, are you?" asked the other guard.

"Just visiting," Lily hissed through her gritted teeth. Robbed, right at the gates. "Aren't you going to chase after them?"

The guards looked at each other, then at her. "No. We guard the gate; we don't catch thieves."

"Look, where are the jewel spider caves?"

"You got any money?"

"No."

"Then we can't help you."

Lily sighed and looked over to Dott. "I asked these two men for help, but they won't give it."

"Not 'elp?"

"If they don't help me, we'll never find Gabriel."

"Bootiful boy?"

"Yes, the beautiful boy."

"I like bootiful boy."

"We all do," Lily lied. "But if these men won't help, we won't find him."

Dott thought. Then her small eyes grew red and her teeth ground together as she faced the two guardsmen. "Not 'elp?"

Lily smiled. "Oh, dear. She's upset. You ever dealt with an upset troll?"

The two guardsmen backed away, their spears shaking in their hands. "Keep her away. We're warning you."

Dott grabbed a spear and snapped it in half. "Not 'elp?"

"Now tell us where the caves are before my friend rearranges your limbs in strange and unusual ways," Lily said sincerely.

The guard who'd lost his spear turned tail and ran off. The remaining one gulped. "The caves are east of Malice," he said. "People used to live there but not in a long while."

"Because of the jewel spiders?"

"Yeah. That, and the burning."

Now that was interesting. "Tell me more."

The guard spoke. "It was before my time, but some of the old boys talk about it. Everyone knows the jewel spiders came from Malice, but not everyone knows how they were destroyed."

"You found the nest and set fire to it."

"The nest wasn't the only thing that went to the flames, m'lady." The guard touched an amulet at his neck. "There was a woman who lived near the caves. She kept herself to herself, and people said she had airs and graces. Rumors spread, like they do. People said she was a witch and claimed it was her who summoned the jewel spiders in the first place. You know how it is with witches. Women shouldn't practice magic. It's not natural."

"So they say," Lily replied coolly.

"I hear stories that the folk at Castle Gloom were behind it, Lord Charon himself." He looked around him, checking to make sure no one else was listening. "He wanted rid of this woman and didn't care how. Anyway, he bribed a few of the locals, who then took it upon themselves to deal with her. If you know what I mean . . ."

She did. Her father had banned execution by fire on the first day of his rule, and Lily knew, proudly, that there hadn't been a single one in the last fifteen years. But her grandfather, Iblis's own sire, Charon, had been a fanatic about burnings. Hundreds had gone up in flames during his time. The ballads and tales referred to him as Charon the Baker. A silly nickname for so evil a man. Lily shook her head. "These things used to happen, sadly."

"Oh, the story's not finished. They say she's back."

"The woman who died?"

"Her ghost. Back for revenge. A couple of houses have burned down. Suspicious, if you ask me."

"That happens when you've got thatched roofs and open fires. Doesn't mean it's a ghost."

"Maybe you're right. Maybe you're not." He turned along the dirt road. "I'll show you the caves, but that's it, agreed?"

The town sprawled. The outer walls had either crumbled or the stones had been stolen to build houses. Rickety hovels crowded the crooked alleyways, and mangy dogs barked from the doorways. Lily saw zombies and beggars, and sometimes it was hard to tell which was which.

Children picked through garbage, searching for morsels and fighting off the crows.

Lily felt shame. These were her people. They shouldn't be living like this, coffin-measured already.

Eventually they reached an abandoned hill. The houses were wrecks and hadn't been occupied in years; now they were home only to mice and pigeons.

The guard pointed to a ruined structure. "That's where she lived. The witch, I mean."

Caves indented the hillside another hundred yards along from the witch's house. Icicles hung over the entrance of the largest. It looked as if a giant mouth was waiting to swallow them up.

"Me not go," said Dott, putting her arm protectively around the mule. "Bob scared."

"You want to stay and look after him?"

Dott nodded vigorously.

"I've shown you the caves," said the guard, shifting uneasily. "You can find your own way back, right? I need to return to the gate."

Lily waved the guard away.

So this was where the jewel spider nest had been found twenty years ago. Lily inspected the cave mouth. Nothing moved.

She lit a candle. The entrance wasn't very high, and she had to crouch to enter. Webs caught in her fingertips and hair, but these were the webs of common spiders, not the crystal-covered silk threads of the jewel spiders. The air was stale and the ground littered with more than a decade's worth of dried leaves and other rubbish.

Fifteen or so feet in, the cave opened up and Lily could straighten. Ice coated the walls and a thin mist chilled her ankles. There were thousands of crevasses and narrow cracks within the walls. Any one of them could have hidden a hundred spiders, big and small.

"Hello?"

Only her echo answered.

Lily straightened her collar. There was no escape from the cold.

What had she expected? To find all her lost villagers neatly tied up in cobwebs for her to rescue?

All she'd gotten was a story about a poor innocent woman, burned alive for something she knew nothing about.

She turned and saw Dott approaching.

"Go back, Dott. There's nothing—"

It wasn't her troll friend.

The candlelight flickered as the figure, a woman, entered the cavern.

"Hello," said Lily. "Who are . . . ?"

She was young, beautiful, sad, and very dead. Her pale, delicate features were not of flesh and bone but the ethereal mist of a phantom.

The ghost looked around her. She clutched at her neck with long, thin fingers.

"Who are you?" Lily reached forward. If she could touch her, she might be able to learn something. "I'm Lily Shadow."

The woman paused, then slowly rotated toward Lily. Her eyes widened.

She recognizes me. But how?

"Do I know you?"

The woman's eyes narrowed, and she pulled at her hair, or so it seemed. She shook her head. Her face twisted into a mask of agony and rage.

"Let me help you."

The ice began to melt and crack. The woman's clothing blackened and flames, white and the faintest blue, licked along her arms. The flesh began to bubble and peel.

Lily backed away. The heat was singeing her own skin.

The woman reached toward her.

"Stay back . . ." Lily choked out.

Now the ghost's hair caught alight. The flames burned silently but with ferocious intensity.

Smoke began to fill the cavern, carrying with it the stench of cooking flesh.

Lily darted to the left, but the ghost clutched her arm. The sleeve burst into flame, and Lily tore it off even as she screamed from the pain. The ghost tried to grab her by her hair, but Lily stumbled away.

"What do you want?" Lily cried. "Who are you?"

"Prin'ess!"

Dott barged straight through the ghost. Flames hit the troll, but they didn't stop her. She tucked Lily under one arm and, protecting her with her own body, charged back out. They were blasted by fire and Lily screamed, but a second later she was outside, flat on the ground. Dott groaned, steam rolling off her burned back and smoldering clothes.

Lily lay in the snow, stunned.

And the ghost was gone.

THIRTY

"**S**he's a revenant," said Lily as she scooped more snow over her injured arm.

"Rev'nant?" asked Dott.

They sat outside the caves, a safe distance away. The mule, Bob, pawed at the ground, looking for some green grass.

"A vengeful spirit." Her skin was red but unbroken, and the snow was already cooling it off. But if Dott hadn't come along . . .

Revenants were bad news. Unjustly murdered, the spirit would never rest until it had had its revenge. There were plenty of tragic tales of revenants harming the descendants of those responsible for their deaths because they'd been unable to avenge themselves on their original enemies. To make matters worse, their powers grew over time. Right now, Lily reckoned the revenant was limited to the cave and areas nearby, but the longer the ghost waited for revenge, the farther she'd be able to reach.

It seemed the guard had spoken true about Charon Shadow being behind the burning. The revenant couldn't get him, so it had attacked Lily, his granddaughter.

But why had Charon arranged this woman's death in the first place?

And why the secrecy? If she had been the one responsible for the jewel spiders, then he would have attended the burning and condemned the victim personally. Something wasn't right.

"Who are you?" Lily asked the empty air.

The woman's former house was just a few hundred yards back up the road. Maybe she'd find out there?

As long as the revenant doesn't reappear to cook me up . . .

Lily brushed the snow off. Her arm felt better now. "Let's go have a look, shall we?"

Dott gathered Bob's reins.

The place was desolate. Tall grass covered the ground, and the thistles were chest high. Thick bands of ivy choked the trees. The house, overgrown, was a decaying ruin, though with a little imagination Lily could picture what it had once been: a two-story town house with strong walls and thick thatch.

"Not nice," complained Dott. "Go home now."

"I just want to look around."

"Home . . ."

"I'll be quick. Promise." Lily waded through the grass and stepped over the threshold.

Rats scurried back into their holes as Lily entered the main room. There were the remnants of a staircase, and a few timbers framed what had once been a roof.

Hands on hips, Lily turned slowly. Snow covered the flagstones, but the coating of white failed to cover the pall of deep sadness that lingered here.

"What do you want?" Lily asked. Was the ghost nearby? If only she could speak with it . . .

The furniture remained, rotten due to years of exposure, and laced with cobwebs. The fireplace, built of good, close-fitting stone, looked like it could still be used. The iron frame around it was twisted, but a blacksmith could beat it back into shape.

"Now, this is strange. . . ."

The table had a vase on it, one filled with fresh flowers.

Black roses.

The only place black roses grew was in the Night Garden at Castle Gloom. Lily bent over to smell them.

Hmm, the scent was weak. Someone must have taken a clipping from her own bushes and replanted it here. But without the . . . *unique* soil of the Night Garden to nourish it, the roses had lost most of their perfume.

The flowers were an offering to the unquiet spirit. Giving gifts to the dead, and undead, was a common practice in Gehenna. But who was the giver?

Whoever the woman had been in life, she'd been better off than most of the locals. A few battered pewter plates lay in the corner, and there was a jug just like the ones she'd find on her table back in Castle Gloom. Pewter wasn't cheap.

Not cheap at all.

Lily picked up the jug and looked at its base. She wiped off the twenty years' worth of soot and dirt.

And saw the hammer and crescent symbol.

This *was* from Castle Gloom.

She found a plate and inspected it. It bore the same maker's mark. So did the goblet.

"Who are you?" Lily asked. "Tell me."

Where would you keep secrets?

Lily's gaze landed on the stairs. The bottom few steps had survived because they were made of stone. That was unusual. She tapped them—they were solid—then she looked behind them.

Under the collapsed, rotten timbers, she spotted a chest. The wooden lid had warped and was held together by rusty iron bands.

"I've found something!" she shouted, pulling the chest into the center of the room.

Dott came in and joined her. "Nice stuff?"

"Let's see." Lily tried to lift the lid. She couldn't; the hinges had rusted through.

Dott dug her fingers into the lid and tore it off, wood, hinges, and bindings.

"Thanks."

Damp and moths had destroyed the dresses, but from the patches of silk Lily could tell they'd once been fine and beautiful. And black. The stitching was small and neat, not the coarse sewing used on servants' clothing.

Under the clothing were pieces of jewelry: a necklace and two bracelets. The silver had fused; still, Lily saw that it had been fine, delicate work, similar to the pieces she'd inherited from her mother. Black pearls dotted the bottom of the chest.

And finally, letters, most reduced to mulch. Lily carefully lifted out a tissue-thin sheet. The ink had faded to brown and could barely be read. The handwriting was neat, long, and elegant.

"This writing . . ." said Lily, checking the achingly familiar style, the narrow *l*, the small loop that made the *e* and the *a* look nearly identical. She could just make out the last line. She read it aloud.

"You will always have my love, now and forever . . ."

Lily's heart skipped a beat as she saw the signature, one she recognized almost as well as her own.

"Iblis Shadow."

THIRTY-ONE

Thorn crept through the cloud ship. The walls, floor, and columns felt like marble, but he noticed some of them unravel and sway in the breeze. Stairs linked the many levels and platforms, and he walked over rainclouds and through chambers where the air was filled with a static buzz and lightning flashed high above him.

Webs draped across the columns and walls. Others dangled from the roof like flags. Jewel spiders busied themselves upon the poor victims.

There were people from all over. Gehennish for sure, with their sallow skin and gaunt features, but also folk from Lu Feng and even green-tinted natives of the Coral Isles. The cloud ship had traveled far and wide, kidnapping along the way.

How many were trapped here? Hundreds for sure, and he'd only explored a fraction of the cloud. Maybe thousands. A few were swollen, their bodies hosts for baby jewel spiders, but most looked merely, but deeply, asleep.

Some were completely cocooned in webbing. What if one of those was Gabriel? How he would find the Solar boy among this crowd?

Then Thorn found something stranger still.

Trolls.

And he'd thought Dott was big.

Dozens dangled from the webs, their limbs bound by the thickest silk. Not one was under ten feet in height; most were double that. They had wide, broad bodies and long arms, especially compared to the legs, which were thick and short. Their skin was as gnarly as old bark and their hair the texture of wet rope. Some had moss growing in the folds of their chins or within the wrinkles of their eyes. Others had horns and tusks.

The men wore bone jewelry; the women, when he could tell the difference, decorated themselves with necklaces of stones and shells and carved figurines. Both had tattoos, and Thorn had heard that each clan had unique designs. Lily would know all about them, but to Thorn, a troll was a troll.

The webs pulsed with multicolored lights. These colors rippled along the glassy threads, and the strings hummed, releasing a deep, continuous sound that resonated within Thorn's chest.

The webs pulse with their dreams.

Some webs were wider than the Great Hall at Castle Gloom and covered with sleepers; others would have accommodated a bed bearing a couple of victims. The size of each web corresponded with the size of the spinners. Thorn could see how the individual webs were all linked, like a patchwork quilt, steadily growing larger and attracting more jewel spiders.

There's a pattern to them. It tells when the victims were captured.

The natives of Lu Feng had been caught first. That made sense; that's where the cloud ship had come from. The Lu Fengese filled the biggest, most complex webs. The ones that had been woven first.

Thorn grinned. He'd seen enough cobwebs in his life to know how they worked, and now he knew how to find—

Bootsteps beat the floor, interrupting his thoughts. Thorn ducked behind a column as a trio of soldiers marched past. He peeked.

Their armor was horizontal strips, laced in place. The helmets they carried were plumed with different colored feathers. One was more elaborate than the others; maybe he was a captain? Instead of belts, their swords were tucked into blue silk sashes wrapped around their waists. Each wore his hair in a topknot, again decorated with feathers.

Renegades from House Typhoon? Were they the crew of the cloud ship?

Thorn waited until they were long gone before he came out of hiding. He scanned the chamber, searching for the smaller, and thus most recent, webs. The ones containing Gehennish sleepers.

He found one maybe a dozen feet wide, with three or four jewel spiders working on it. A handful of victims, all dressed in local black, dangled from the strands.

"Boy . . ."

Thorn stopped in his tracks.

"Boy . . ." Someone was calling from the web.

One of the trapped men moved. He pulled his head free of the webbing. "Boy . . ."

"Tyburn?"

He was alive! Lily had been right!

The executioner snarled as he struggled, and the activity drew the attention of one of the jewel spiders. It scuttled over the threads.

Thorn put an arrow through it.

He re-slung his bow and pulled out his dagger. "Just give me a minute."

"I'm . . . not going anywhere."

Hope surged through Thorn. With Tyburn back, the odds had suddenly changed in their favor.

Thorn sawed through the threads as quickly as he could. They weren't thick but surprisingly tough. The vibrations were alerting the other spiders. "How come you're not asleep like the rest?"

"You have any idea how many times someone's tried to poison me?" Tyburn leaned forward, stretching the bindings. "You build up a resistance, or you don't last long as an executioner."

Thorn began hacking. "Come on . . ."

Tyburn's arm broke free. He ripped at the bindings on his other arm while Thorn set to work cutting free his legs. Eventually the threads parted, and he helped Tyburn away from the web. The old man was sluggish and didn't have the strength to hold himself up.

"You took your time getting here," muttered Tyburn.

"How was I supposed to know the spiders were coming from a cloud ship?"

"I'd have thought it was obvious." Tyburn rubbed his legs to get the blood flowing. "How else do you think Dott ended up in Gehenna? Don't you remember where she was found?"

"Spindlewood. All beaten up and unconscious."

Tyburn nodded. "I wondered how a lone troll child could be so far from the Troll-Teeth Mountains. Then I noticed the broken branches. She'd fallen out of the sky. Simple, and obvious."

"Oh, yes. *Very* simple and obvious," said Thorn. "I'm being sarcastic."

"Didn't know you knew how."

"Lily's been teaching me."

"Using your spare time fruitfully, then?" replied Tyburn. He shook his head and moved on. "They've been kidnapping trolls. That's why all the clans are on the march. The trolls think *we're* behind the disappearances of their kin."

"And half of Gehenna thinks trolls are stealing our villagers." Thorn groaned as he saw the pieces falling into place. "What a mess. There's war coming, Tyburn. All because we don't trust trolls."

Tyburn released himself from Thorn's support, filled his chest, and let out a long, steady breath. "I followed the weather, the drift of the clouds, and that led me to Pitch Farm. I was too late and ended up getting caught myself. Left you a clue, though. Only thing I could think of. Threw it off me as I was being hauled on board, drugged by those spiders."

Thorn slapped his forehead. "Your sword! It was stuck in the roof. It was there at the very beginning, and I didn't recognize it."

Tyburn grunted. He limped back to the web. "Help me with this one."

It was a young boy. Thorn cleared some webbing from his face. "Alfie Pitch."

Together they dragged the sleeping boy out of the cobwebs and laid him down. Tyburn patted the boy's cheek. "I don't know where they took his brother, but at least we can get Alfie out."

The boy blinked. He was bewildered, his eyes glazed. "I . . . I was dreaming."

Thorn smiled. "About what?"

"We had the biggest farm with the fattest pigs ever."

Thorn helped the boy up. Alfie looked around. "Where's Sam? Where's my mom? And Dad?"

Thorn frowned. Now was not the time to tell him that his parents were dead. "Do you trust me, Alfie?"

"I suppose."

"Then do as I say for now, and we'll sort it all out. I promise."

"Stick with me, child." Tyburn held Alfie's hand. "You take the lead, Thorn."

They headed toward a staircase. Thorn reckoned that if he went this route he'd end up near Hades. They'd find somewhere to hide and he'd take Alfie down first, then come back for Tyburn. Easy. And *then* he could search for Gabriel.

Probably . . .

But it all looked the same. He couldn't figure out where he'd left Hades.

"Give me the dagger, boy," muttered Tyburn. "I'll be needing it."

"Why are you stopping? We just need to get a bit farther. . . ."

Thorn looked up as he heard the whisper of swords being drawn.

The three soldiers stood at the top of the stairs, waiting.

"You're in no condition to fight, Tyburn," said Thorn.

"Just give me the blade."

Thorn handed it to him and stepped back down. He nocked an arrow. Their armor looked good, but there were gaps he could aim at.

Except he'd never shot at a man before. He wasn't sure he could.

Tyburn's legs wobbled as he took a step.

The soldiers grinned. Three of them versus an old, sleepy man with a mere dagger.

Tyburn flicked the dagger into the throat of the first man and snatched the sword from him as he tumbled past.

Thorn put an arrow through the hand of the second. The soldier cried out, and now Tyburn had two swords.

The third ran down the stairs and jabbed, scoring a red wound across Tyburn's ribs. Tyburn brought both blades across.

The soldier's head sprang off his shoulders.

Tyburn groaned as he put his hand against his bleeding side. "Move. Keep going down."

Cries rose across the cloud ship. Bolts whizzed through the air, their steel tips rattling against the walls. Soldiers ran toward them, packs of them coming from all directions. Jewel spiders of all sizes swung down from their webs.

Thorn tried supporting Tyburn, but their progress was painfully slow. After a dozen steps, Tyburn let go.

"Get back to Gloom. Warn them of what's coming," he said.

Thorn didn't want to leave him. "We need you!"

Thorn despaired. They couldn't win without Tyburn. But it wasn't just that. Thorn felt . . . Tyburn had brought him to Gehenna. He'd given him this life.

The executioner glanced sideways at him. "You're not getting all sentimental on me, are you?"

Thorn blushed. "No, of course not. It's just . . . Lily will blame me if you get yourself killed."

"I'm not in my tomb yet," said Tyburn.

If they were out of time, Thorn needed to know something. "Who's behind this, Tyburn? There's a sorcerer, isn't there?"

Tyburn smiled, clearly impressed. "You work that out yourself?"

"Only way to make the cloud ship fly, ain't it?"

"There's hope for you yet, Thorn. Yes, there's a sorcerer behind this, one trained by House Typhoon but returned here, for revenge."

"Revenge? For what?"

Tyburn grimaced. "Does it matter? Whatever else happened in the past, he is our enemy now."

"How do we stop him?"

"You'll find a way, boy. Now get going." Tyburn pushed him off. He tightened his grip on the sword and stood up, facing a gang of soldiers.

"Stick with me, Alfie!" Thorn ran, bow and arrow in hand. He needed to get back to Hades.

But which way?

The cloud ship's form changed with the currents. He wasn't sure where he'd come from and had no idea where he was headed.

A sudden blast of wind blew him and Alfie off their feet. Alfie grabbed a column, but Thorn slid across the smooth floor. His arrows skittered over the edge. Thorn dropped his bow to grab hold of the floor before he was tossed over into empty sky. He halted mere inches from the lip.

The wind howled around him, but he managed to get to his feet.

The air crackled with lightning. The clouds darkened with rage, and the hairs on his neck rose. Sparks bounced across the walls. Lightning flashed overhead, and Alfie screamed in terror.

High above him stood a man looking down from one of the platforms.

His robes of midnight silk flapped in the wind, and he held out a claw-curled hand.

He threw himself off the ledge, in Thorn's direction. It was a hundred-foot drop.

Shadows enveloped him and carried him down on smoky black wings.

The sorcerer landed gently, facing Thorn. The wind dwindled to a faint breeze, and the thunder quieted. The man was wearing a hood, but it couldn't hide the hideously burned face or the feverish eyes.

"Weaver . . ." Thorn said.

The man who had robbed Lily of the Skeleton Key and broken into the Shadow Library. Thorn might have laughed. This fearsome sorcerer had pretended to be a mere conjuror.

Jewel spiders scuttled over him, and his robes glistened with their silvery spider silk. Thorn glimpsed dancing skeletons among the embroidery. Weaver limped closer, dragging his left foot behind the other. "We don't appreciate stowaways on the *Baofengyu.*"

Was that the name of the ship? "Who are you? What do you want?" Thorn asked.

Weaver's body jerked, and a feeble hiss came shaking out of his lips. He lowered his hood. "I want . . . justice."

Thorn grimaced. Lily had told him about the injuries, but up close . . . His skin was blackened and wrinkled. The lips were gone, and the ears were wax lumps clinging to either side of his head, which was bald except for a few dull black patches. The body was as broken as a body could be. The power lay in the eyes, storm-gray with suppressed rage. A red tongue rolled over the edges of his mouth, constantly wetting them so he could speak. "Your attempt to save the executioner has failed. It would have saddened me to lose so important a . . . guest."

So Weaver knows who Tyburn is, and wants him alive for a reason.

"And who are you, boy?"

"Thorn. Of Herne's Forest."

"You are far from home, young Thorn."

"You are, too." Thorn pointed eastward. "Yours is a long way off in that direction."

"And there you are so very wrong. Though you'll never know why."

The jewel spiders crept forward. They were less than ten feet away. Thorn gripped Alfie as they backed away.

Weaver smiled. "You're running out of floor, young Thorn."

Thorn glanced over the edge. All he saw was a lot of sky. He tightened his hold on Alfie and asked him once again, "Do you trust me?"

Alfie looked petrified, but he forced a nod.

Weaver scowled. "You're trapped. Surrender."

"And what?" snapped Thorn. "Become spider food? Forget it."

"You won't survive the fall."

Thorn grinned. "I dunno. The snow's pretty deep."

He hurled himself and Alfie over the edge of the cloud ship and into free sky, a thousand feet above the earth.

THIRTY-TWO

"Hades!" yelled Thorn. "Hades!"

Where is that bat?

"Hades! I need you RIGHT NOW!"

Thorn tumbled. Over and over he turned—the world was up, down, all around—with Alfie locked in his arms. The small boy had his eyes squeezed shut.

"Hades!"

The rushing air stole his cries from his lips and threw them into the clouds.

That stupid bat. What was the point of him having those big ears if he didn't use them?

"HADEEES!"

The clouds parted, revealing the ground, far below. The patches of snow in the clearings between closely packed trees. The bare rock. He even glimpsed a cluster of cottages, and the square white fields surrounding them.

Would he feel anything when he hit?

His fear of death only came second. What he was really afraid of was that Lily wouldn't know. She wouldn't know that Weaver was behind this attack. That the jewel spiders could come and go on their cloud ship. That this war with the trolls had been a setup from the beginning.

She wouldn't know, and that would be that.

He couldn't let it end like this! "Hades!"

He bet the greedy bat was off hunting some poor sheep. Swooping over an unfortunate farmer's fields with no thought of anything except filling his belly.

If Thorn ever got his hands on that monster, he'd tweak his ears until they fell off.

Stupid bat!

Thorn faced the ground. It was zooming toward him. He gritted his teeth. The wind roared and stung his eyes. He was crying and wasn't sure if it was because of the cold wind or . . . the end?

Should have made me a whistle. Hades would have heard that.

Why hadn't he?

Because Hades weren't no pet.

He'd never again run his hands through the monster's spiky black fur. Never feel the heart beating against his when he lay down on the bat's back. Nor the roll of Hades's shoulders or the thrum of the wind through his sail-sized wings.

Thorn gazed at the ground. He could make out the individual trees now. He hugged Alfie, preparing . . .

A shriek shook the snow off the trees.

Hades!

The bat tucked in his wings and dove.

Thorn cried, "Come on, boy!"

Hades gritted his own teeth, and his eyes blazed. He hunched his shoulders to tighten his body. No falcon had ever swooped so fast.

But would he be fast enough?

Thorn didn't look down. He stared at Hades, willing him to become a lightning bolt.

"Come on . . ."

Thorn held Alfie with one arm, and reached out with the other.

"Will you hurry up? I thought you were fast!"

Hades twisted. His claws spread and plucked Thorn and Alfie out of the air. He threw out his wings and jerked them downward.

The snow blurred beneath them. Thorn grabbed on to Hades's legs.

Hades cried and stretched every muscle in his body to rise.

But it wasn't enough.

Flying too fast to change direction, Hades plowed into a snowdrift. Thorn flipped head over heels, dropping Alfie as he went, before collapsing, face-first, into a heap.

Snow stuffed his eyes, nose, and ears. It was up his sleeves and down his neck. Every part of him was one huge ache. But he was alive.

Thorn rolled onto his back and lay there, staring up at the clouds. He wiggled his toes and fingers, checking, bit by bit, that he was all there, unbroken.

He sighed with huge relief.

"The things I do for you, Lily . . ."

Over the last few days, he'd been bitten by a rabid dog, poisoned, and attacked by one of the head squires. He'd nearly been murdered by an executioner. He'd had to beat off a horde of jewel spiders, and just now, dive off a cloud. Oh, and he'd almost been crushed to death by a collapsing gatehouse.

He deserved a raise.

Thorn pushed himself to his feet. He wobbled but only a bit.

"Next time, don't wait so long," he chastised the bat. He stumbled over to Alfie and dragged the boy out of a drift. "Are you all right?"

The boy brushed the snow off his grinning face. "I wanna do that again! Can we? Can we?"

Hades shook the snow off himself. He lowered his head so that he and Thorn were eye to eye, and he growled.

"Oh, like it's my fault you crashed?" Thorn replied. Then he grabbed hold of the big monster's hairy cheeks and hugged him with all his might.

THIRTY-THREE

There was no flying after that. Hades needed food and a sleep, so off he went. Thorn watched him disappear south, heading home to Castle Gloom.

"We need to get moving ourselves," Thorn said to Alfie. He gestured to a muddy track nearby. "That'll take us to Malice, right?"

Alfie sat glumly upon a boulder. "We should have gotten Sam, too."

Thorn pitied the young boy. Alfie had stopped asking about his parents. He must've guessed they were dead. But that made his longing for his brother even greater.

Thorn sat next to him. "What do you remember about the attack on your home?"

"I was asleep, till Devil started barking at something on the roof. We didn't know what was going on . . . then them spiders started creeping down the chimney. Dad grabbed his ax, and we ran for the forest. We'd just reached the edge of the trees when Tyburn appeared. Webs fell out of the sky, and Sam got caught. Spiders climbed all over Tyburn; he kept on fighting, but you could tell he was getting weak. Mom and Dad, they tried, but one of the big spiders . . . I saw . . . blood. Then one bit me, and that was all till you woke me up."

"We'll do our best to get Sam back, I promise." Thorn took the boy's hand. "It's getting dark."

Alfie hesitated. "You think Lady Shadow could do something? Bring Mom and Dad to life if they're . . . ? People say she's got magic."

Thorn tried to smile, but he could see the overwhelming desire in Alfie's gaze, and he hated being the one to disappoint him. "I don't think it works like that."

"Just for a little while? Maybe only a minute. Why couldn't she bring them back for just a minute?"

Thorn remained silent, not wanting to create any false hope. They walked through Bone-Tree Forest as the shadows grew longer. Thunder rumbled in the distance, and the pair of them quickened their pace. It was dusk when they saw the lights of a town ahead.

"Malice," said Alfie.

Thorn found the Baker's Inn. It was the most famous landmark in Malice, and not for a good reason.

It looked out over the stakes where people had once been burned alive.

Lily pointed to the three posts that still stood in the center of a square. Ten-foot stone columns, each with an iron ring at the top.

"They'd manacle the guilty to those. Then a pile of wood would be stacked all around, and the condemned would be brushed with tar so they'd catch fire more quickly. My grandfather Charon used to watch from here while he had his dinner. That's why it's called the Baker's Inn."

"I had a hunch it wasn't to do with cupcakes," said Thorn. Just when he thought Lily's family couldn't get any stranger, here was another gruesome story about her ancestors. "But your dad stopped the burnings, didn't he?"

Lily nodded. "He'd been forced to watch them as a child. He hated it, but Charon wanted him to . . . I don't know, learn cruelty?"

Thorn and Lily had met up just after nightfall, Dott greeting him in the courtyard with a bone-crunching hug. Alfie, barely awake by that point, had been fed and put to bed. Lily had then proceeded to bombard Thorn with her news, and Thorn had hit her with his. Now, several courses later and an apple pie split between them, it was time to decide what to do next.

"Sleep," said Thorn. "My belly feels like it's gonna burst." Then he sat up, sniffing the air. "Is that toffee tart I smell?"

"Seriously, Thorn? You want more?"

"Just a thin slice. C'mon, you're Lady Shadow. Make the most of it."

"I was trying to be discreet."

"Then what happened?"

"They recognized me." Lily gestured at a table at the far end. Three well-dressed merchants were dining, but their eyes were on Lily and Thorn. All stood and bowed.

Thorn peered at them. "Gehenna's a small place. Everyone knows everyone." He patted his taut belly. "Anyway, about that toffee tart?"

Lily gave a slight nod to the ever-waiting innkeeper, and the tart was hurried over. It was much more than a thin slice. Thorn smacked his lips.

"Yeah, traveling with the country's ruler has its perks," he declared.

"You're going to eat all that?" said Lily.

"It would be rude not to," said Thorn. "My grandpa said an empty plate is the best compliment you can give a cook."

"When you were up in that cloud ship, did you have a good look for Gabriel? A *real* look?"

"I was busy saving Tyburn!" Thorn complained. "And I was lucky to find him. The ship's huge. Weaver called it, er, *Baofengyu* or something."

"*Baofengyu*? That means 'tempest,'" said Lily. "I wish I'd asked Ying more about the cloud ship theft when I'd had the chance."

Thorn turned to Lily, feeling a mix of admiration and stupidity. "You know Lu Fengese?"

Lily shrugged, as if knowing all the languages of the New Kingdoms was no big deal. "We need to find out who this Weaver is."

"*Mmhf,*" Thorn replied. The toffee had glued his jaw together.

"You eat like a pig, Thorn."

Thorn worked his mouth open. "If you don't know when your next meal's gonna be, you eat as much as you can, when you can."

"Was that what it was like in Stour?"

Thorn didn't want to talk about it. He'd been hungry plenty of times, but why dwell on it when you had a dessert like this sitting in front of you? "Any idea about Weaver, who he might be?"

"House Typhoon hired foreign sorcerers to strengthen their numbers. Plenty of lesser sons ended up working for them. Men who'd been born second or third or fourth to one of the Great Houses, all with magic in their blood but little else. They wouldn't inherit any lands or castles, so they took their talents elsewhere, to serve as sorcerers in other realms. House Typhoon paid well, and with so many sorcerers in one place, it was a great opportunity to study magic. My father considered going to Lu Feng, too, once."

Thorn picked the toffee out of his teeth with his fingernail. "That's right. Iblis was the second son himself, wasn't he? Gehenna should have gone to your uncle."

Lily's eyes darkened.

"I'm sorry, Lily. Wasn't thinking." Thorn moved his attention back to the tart.

Pandemonium Shadow should have ruled Gehenna but for one flaw: he couldn't cast a spell. Not one. And to rule Gehenna, you had to be a sorcerer. So the kingdom had gone to Lily's dad.

They'd thought Earl Pan had accepted his lot, but they'd been wrong. He'd murdered Lily's family in a bid to become ruler. He would have killed her, too, if it hadn't been for Thorn. That, more than anything, was why he called her Lily and everyone else called her Lady Shadow.

Secretly, Thorn agreed with Baron Sable and pretty much everyone else in Castle Gloom. Lily should have had Tyburn execute her uncle. Instead, she'd merely banished Pan.

He could be anywhere by now.

"You think Pan might be involved in this? That he might have recruited this Weaver?" said Lily.

"Nope. Tyburn seemed sure this Weaver bloke was in it for himself. He wants revenge, Lily. Though I don't know why."

"Yes, I think you're right. When I met him outside the Shadow Library, I felt his hatred." Lily shook her head. "He's no mercenary of my uncle's. And then there are the trolls," Lily said, moving on. "We should send word to the troll king, tell him that his people have been kidnapped by Weaver, and we had nothing to do with it."

"I ain't no troll expert, but unless you've got proof, I can't see how he'll believe you."

"We need to find a way to free them, then. Rescue the trolls, and there'll be no need for war."

"Even if I could get back up into that cloud ship, Hades couldn't carry a troll—way too heavy."

Lily frowned. She idly rolled a black rose petal between her thumb and index finger. She laid the rest of the flower on the table. "Where do you think these came from? They're like the ones in the Night Garden, but not quite."

"*Mmph?*" asked Thorn, cheeks packed with tart. Again. It was really, *really* good and he was determined to finish it.

"Someone put them in the revenant woman's house in the last day or two. And they did it more than once; I spotted some older petals under the table."

"Why, d'you think?"

"To appease the dead. Tell them they've not been forgotten. It could've been an attempt to mollify the revenant, but it won't work. Revenants won't settle for a bunch of roses, black or otherwise."

The innkeeper came over. "Is everything to your satisfaction, m'lady?"

Lily smiled. "It's all absolutely delicious. Isn't it, Thorn?"

"Mmrph!" Thorn gave him a double thumbs-up.

The innkeeper began collecting the empty plates, then paused. "I can have more roses brought to your room, if you wish?"

Thorn stopped chewing.

"You grow them here?" Lily asked, sitting up and interested.

"Not personally, but I know who does. She only moved here recently, got a house at the end of Cadaver Street. I don't have much to do with her, but if you like, I'll ask her for a bunch. If she knows they're for you, I'm sure she'll be more than happy to hand them over."

Lily tugged her collar looser. "What's this woman's name?"

The innkeeper pondered. "Hmm, hardly said more than 'good morning' to her. . . . What was it again?"

Thorn decided to give the innkeeper some help. "Might it be . . . Mary?"

THIRTY-FOUR

"You should go," said Lily. "By yourself."

"Nope. It's the both of us," said Thorn.

"I should have brought Dott."

"Again, nope. Somehow I don't think Mary would be happy about a troll knocking on her door this time of night." Thorn stopped at a crossroad and held up the borrowed lantern. "Which way did the innkeeper say?"

"Left here."

Thorn nodded and started along the road. "I don't know why you kicked her out of Gloom in the first place."

"I did not 'kick her out,'" said Lily. "She . . . left."

"Why? Mary had been there longer than anyone. She brought you up."

Why?

Because she'd tried to poison Gabriel but inadvertently killed Custard instead. She'd almost started a war to avenge the death of her two sons, slain in one of the battles between Gehenna, the kingdom of darkness, and Lumina, the kingdom of light.

She betrayed me.

Lily had loved Mary deeply. Mary had raised her and Dante, and Lily had shared secrets with her old nanny that she'd not shared with her own mother. After having lost her own family, Lily understood Mary's pain.

Still, that didn't make Mary's actions right. Lily hadn't banished her from Gehenna the way she'd done with Pan, but she'd banished Mary from her heart, which was far worse.

One night soon after Halloween, Mary had quietly departed, leaving behind the castle keys, her infamous red ledger, and Lily.

"So what happened between the two of you?"

"It's not your concern, Thorn."

He frowned and met her gaze. "You're a pain in the backside, Lily. And right now you need all the friends you can get."

They fell into a grumpy silence, and Lily dragged her feet through the mud.

What would she say to Mary when she opened the door?

What would Mary do?

They reached a small stone bridge that crossed over an iced-up stream. Thorn stopped. "Should I check underneath for trolls?"

"I'm glad Dott isn't here; otherwise she might pop that empty head of yours right off."

Smoke drifted out of the chimney of the cottage.

"She's home," said Lily. She still didn't cross the bridge.

I could turn back now.

Did she really need to know the revenant's connection with her father? What difference could it possibly make? They were both dead.

But not gone. Their ghosts lingered, and that meant there was unfinished business. She put one foot in front of the other.

When they got close to the house, Lily saw that Mary had been busy, as usual. The thatch was new, and so was the wood on the shutters and door. The hinges had recently been replaced, and someone had dug the moss out of the joints between the stonework and filled it in with limestone. The low wall around the vegetable patch seemed newly built. And on either side of the door was a bush of black roses, flowering despite the cold.

Thorn banged on the door. "Mary!"

She's cooking chicken-and-onion pie. Lily could smell it. Mary had overdone it with the basil, as always.

But Lily's mouth watered. Her stomach gurgled as if it hadn't been fed in months. In a way, it hadn't. When Mary had left, she'd taken her recipes with her, and her great rival, Cook, had her own ways of preparing Lily's meals.

Life just hadn't been the same without Mary.

Lily stood farther back. She blew into her fingers. It was colder here than around Castle Gloom, and it had started snowing.

What was keeping Mary? Maybe she wasn't home. Maybe they should just go, leave a letter instead. Yes, a letter. That would be—

The door opened, and there she stood.

Lily's heart surged.

Mary hadn't changed one single bit. Her hair was under a cap, and threads of silver hung over her plump red cheeks. Her apron was white, but Lily didn't mind because her dress was pure Shadow black. Mary beat her palms on her apron to rid herself of flour.

"Thorn?" She looked confused, then smiled. "Thorn! What are you doing here?"

He kicked his heels and looked back to Lily. "I've brought someone to see you."

"Hello, Mary," said Lily. She stepped forward and leaned in to kiss her former nanny.

Mary lowered her head, and curtseyed. "M'lady."

Lily stopped short. She hadn't expected that. She was angry, with Mary, and herself. At all the things that had changed. "May we come in?"

"As you command, Lady Shadow."

Thorn stood at the door, arms folded. "You two are as bad as each other." He snapped his fingers. "Lily, go kiss Mary. Mary, give Lily a hug. And hurry up. That pie ain't gonna eat itself."

Mary raised her head and looked Lily up and down. Then, with tears in her eyes, she extended her arms. "Come here, child."

Maybe some things hadn't changed after all.

THIRTY-FIVE

"I hear you replaced me with a troll. Very nice." Mary lifted the kettle off the fire and poured the tea.

"I did not *replace* you with anyone," said Lily. "You left." She took the cup and added three sugars. "And what are you doing *here*?"

"Trying to get some peace and quiet. People mind their own business in Malice." She shook her head as she collected the pie from her oven. "Trolls in Castle Gloom. What would your grandfather say?"

Thorn sniffed the chicken-and-onion pie. "Mmm. *My* grandpa would say the only good troll is—"

"A dead one?" interrupted Mary.

"—is the one guarding your village from other trolls," finished Thorn.

How could Thorn have room for more pie? How could *she*? Yet her mouth watered. Lily kicked him under the table. "Is your grandfather coming here with the rest of your family? I'd like to have a few words with him about his stupid sayings."

"Nope, he ain't. You can't replant an old oak." Thorn grinned slowly. "As my grandpa would say."

The cottage was small but comfortable. The fire burned brightly, and the herbs added a soft, country scent to the main room. A cat lounged at the top of the stairs, watching them with mild interest. The pots and pans and plates were shiny from hard scrubbing, and a broom stood up against the door. Lily guessed Mary washed the floor daily; it practically shone.

Mary sliced the pie. "Who's hungry?"

Thorn put up his hand.

Lily answered nonchalantly. "I might have a slice. Just to be polite."

Mary bit her lip, and Lily could tell there was some cutting remark lurking just on the tip of her tongue. Mary put a slice down in front of her, then paused to look her over. "*Tsk.* What do you comb your hair with, a hedgehog?" She sniffed disapprovingly. "Dressing yourself, I see."

"Most people dress themselves."

"Most people dress badly."

Lily and Mary sat facing each other over the pie.

I miss you.

Lily wanted to say it, but something stopped her. She examined Mary. She saw the wrinkles around her eyes, the brown irises fading with time. The silvery hair drawn back into a tight bun and locked in place with a pair of bone hairpins. Mary still wore the pair of black pearl stud earrings that Lily had given her two birthdays ago.

"What happened to your arm?" asked Mary.

"I got burned."

Mary's lips set into a firm line as she examined the crude bandage. "I suppose you wrapped that yourself, too?"

"I did."

Mary took a box down off the shelf. Tutting loudly to demonstrate her disapproval of Lily doing anything without her, she removed the bandage and chucked it on the fire. She pulled a jar from the box. "Healing salve. It'll cool your burn, and hopefully you won't have a scar. The ruler of Gehenna can't be looking like some clumsy kitchen maid." She turned Lily's arm toward the candlelight. "These burns. They're spaced like . . .

fingers." She began rubbing the salve over Lily's forearm. Instantly, Lily's skin cooled. "What is your business, Lily? It wasn't to visit your dear destitute nanny, I'm sure."

"You know about the ghost, Mary. I'm sure you do; I've seen the black roses."

Mary hesitated, and Lily could read the worry in the old woman's creased brow. "Child, no good can come from digging up the past."

"Who was she?" asked Lily.

Mary's shoulders sank. "Is that why you're here? To find out about her?"

That was an odd question. "No. I came to search the jewel spider cave. They're back."

"Back? How?"

"A sorcerer's behind it—a renegade from House Typhoon, we think. They've been raiding villages all over Gehenna, and beyond. They're using the jewel spiders to capture people and put them to sleep. We lost Gabriel to them."

Mary stared in shock. "Gabriel Solar? What was he doing back here in Gehenna? Don't tell me the wedding's back on?"

Lily laughed. "No. He was fleeing the war between Lumina and the Sultanate. It's going badly for his father, so he sought refuge in Castle Gloom."

Lily drew out the letter she'd found at the abandoned house and carefully opened it. She also took out the jewelry that had been in the chest with it. The silver and black pearls shone in the candlelight. "Tell me about the ghost."

Mary plucked nervously at the edge of her apron. She sat and poured herself a cup. "You might as well hear it from me." She tilted her head toward the door. "The ghost you met was a revenant. You know that, don't you?"

"Yes. A spirit driven by revenge. Something terrible happened to her, didn't it? Something terrible and unjust?"

Mary nodded. "There *was* a jewel spider infestation in Gehenna, twenty years ago. They were tracked here, to a cave. Someone got it in his head that this woman, a newcomer, was responsible. You know what people are like. Ready to blame their misfortune on strangers. Called her a witch. Put her on trial."

Lily stopped her. "They say Charon was responsible."

Mary replied angrily, "They were right. He made sure she was found guilty and she was burned."

"That's horrible."

Mary gulped down the tea. "Then, about three months ago, things started happening. It's the ghost. She's set alight a few houses already. One was owned by the judge at her sham of a trial. The other two, the families of those who served in the jury."

"And she attacked me because of Charon."

Mary looked at her with pity in her eyes. "Lily, I wish things were different. I tried to appease her with roses, but her rage is too great."

Lily felt a chill spread through her body. "And so she'll come after me." There were ways to stop revenants with magic, but the instructions were back on the shelves of the Shadow Library. She did know this much, however: "She suffered an injustice, one terrible enough to bring her back from the Twilight. If I can somehow rectify that, she'll find peace, and go."

"You're not going to let this matter rest; I can see it in your eyes," Mary said, then sighed. "You're so like your father." She gathered the fragile letter in her palm. "All right. Let me tell you about Iblis and Branwen."

THIRTY-SIX

"She was beautiful, was Branwen, beautiful and clever and generous and all things a man could wish for, except one: she was poor. Her father was a tenant farmer, no land of his own, merely a worker in the field. Like his father before him, and so on. Times I wish she'd never left that farm, but she wanted better for herself and came, like so many ambitious folk, to Castle Gloom. And I gave her a job."

"When was this?" asked Thorn.

"About twenty-five years ago. Iblis was a young man, not quite twenty, and Charon Shadow, Lily's grandfather, ruled Gehenna." Mary cleared her throat. "Anyway, Iblis and Branwen saw each other. As young folk do. They became close."

Lily's mouth hardened. "Father never spoke of her."

Mary smiled. "And why should he have? He loved your mother. But this was before he'd even met Salome." She brushed her fingertips over the letter. "He taught Branwen to read and write. To count and to dance and to ride. They would picnic in Spindlewood on any warm day. Gone from breakfast to dusk. I didn't mind. Iblis was happy, and if you'd known his father, you'd have known that was a rare thing indeed."

Lily bristled. No one should make her father happy but her mother. "So he gave her this jewelry, I suppose?"

"Yes. Among many other gifts. He was the young lord of Gehenna and already a masterful sorcerer. People had high hopes. Things . . . moved swiftly."

Thorn waved his knife as he ate. "This is real good. Better than what—"

"Will you shut up, Thorn?" Lily demanded. Thorn glowered, then added more pie to his ever-ready mouth. She turned back to Mary. "Moved swiftly between my father and . . . this woman?"

"You never knew her, Lily. They say women shouldn't have magic, but they don't understand—we all have it. Oh, maybe not in ways that men count, but it's magic nonetheless. Branwen, she could beguile a man. Her eyes were as dark as the devil's promise, and when she smiled, it made you dream of wonderful things."

"I get it, Mary. You're saying my father lost his heart to her."

"Yes, I guess I am."

They sat in silence. Lily shifted on her chair, staring at the flames. "What happened then?"

"War. The trolls had been troubling our northern domains, so Charon sent Iblis. He was gone a year, and when he came back, Branwen had vanished. He searched, but then soon after met your mother and . . . well, you know the rest."

"Why did she leave?" asked Lily. "Maybe my father had got bored with her."

Mary's gaze darkened. "She had to leave. She was afraid of Charon and what he might do to her."

"Why would Charon care about a servant?" Lily asked.

"Charon had plans for your father. By then he knew there was no magic in your uncle Pan, so Iblis would inherit Gehenna. He would not want the fate of his country to be . . . upset over a serving girl." Mary frowned, unwilling to explain further. She gave a little shrug. "But your father met Salome. Life moved on."

Thorn tapped his plate with a fork. "End of story."

"Not quite, unfortunately." Mary wiped her face. "Branwen had been gone a few years; I'd almost forgotten all about her. Then I heard that a woman had been burned at the stake in Malice. There'd been a plague of jewel spiders, and Branwen had been condemned for causing it. Your grandfather was behind the investigation; I know that now, but at the time, he used others to carry out his dirty work."

"Was my father aware?"

"No. Charon had sent him far away, on another one of his missions. His timing was deliberate, I suspect."

Lily stood up. She knew all she needed to know. "And now this ghost blames us, the Shadows, for her death." It was getting late, and she wanted to get back. She didn't need to hear any more.

"Lily . . ." started Mary.

Lily's heart was beating fast and she felt dizzy, but why? Her father had . . . known another woman before her mother. So what? It was normal.

Mary eased Lily back down into her chair. "I've started this tale and you must—you will—hear me out."

Despite her dread, Lily nodded.

Mary sat and folded the remnants of the necklace back into its cloth. "They said she'd been seen with the jewel spiders, and that was true. A few had been found at her home. Not live ones, just broken pieces, something a child might collect to play with."

Lily's eyes widened. "A child?"

Mary nodded, her face a grim mask. She took Lily's hand. "Yes. Branwen had a young son. That's why she left Castle Gloom in the first place. Charon wasn't after her; he was after the boy."

Lily stared at her old nanny, her own blood growing colder by the moment. "What happened to him?"

"Charon's men found him," said Mary, her voice trembling. "They threw him on the fire."

"By Herne, that's the most horrible thing I've ever heard," said Thorn. "So he died, too?"

Lily couldn't speak. She felt sick, and ashamed. How could she share the same blood with someone so evil?

"The boy was burned, and burned badly," said Mary. "But he survived, somehow. The townsfolk reckoned it was due to damp wood not burning properly, but the pyre consumed his mother sure enough. He was a poor, broken thing, skin black and peeling, half his body wrecked beyond repair. I stayed by his side, tending to him, thinking any day would be his last, yet he hung on. Despite everything, he would not give in. You could see it in his eyes, the will to live."

Thorn spoke hesitantly. "What color were his eyes?"

"Gray. Gray like storm clouds in winter. Gray like his father's," said Mary. "Gray like yours, Lily."

Lily pulled free. "No. That's impossible." She needed to leave before Mary said anything else. She needed to leave *now*. She stumbled to the door, but she couldn't get it to open. Why wouldn't it open?

Mary turned her around. "Branwen and Iblis had a child, Lily. That's why she left. Iblis never knew, but I'm telling you. You have a brother."

THIRTY-SEVEN

I have a brother.

A *half* brother, to be exact, but that didn't seem remotely important right now.

The thought circled around and around in Lily's mind as she sat silently in Mary's cottage, listening to the rest of her tale.

"It wasn't damp wood that saved the child," said Mary. "It was magic. And I suspect he was the one who had awoken the jewel spiders. Just a little child playing with some shiny toys, not realizing what they were. Even though he was just four, his magical powers were already manifesting—he was Iblis's son after all."

Lily forced herself to look into Mary's eyes. How many other secrets was her old nanny keeping? "How long did you take care of him?"

"A few weeks. He started moving again but didn't speak. I feared the fire and smoke had destroyed his voice. Then, one morning, I found him drawing. He'd taken some charcoal from the fireplace and covered the floor and walls with cobweb patterns. When I asked him what he was doing, he looked at me with an intensity no child should have." Mary shivered. "'I am weaving.' That's what he said, in a broken, croaking voice. I didn't know what name his mother had given him, so I called him Weaver. He responded to it, so it seemed good enough."

Thorn had stopped eating, enthralled by Mary's tale. "What happened when he got better?"

"I managed to find Branwen's parents," said Mary. "Told them the news of her death. They couldn't look after the boy themselves; they were afraid if Charon found out he was still alive, he'd come after them, and they were right to be afraid. But there was another relative, a sailor or merchant or something, I can't remember which. He took Weaver on his ship, bound for Lu Feng, which is as far away from Gehenna as is possible."

The rest was easy to guess. There was no hiding Weaver's magical potential, so he was recruited by House Typhoon and taught the magic that suited him best, which was all things of darkness. Then they gave him a position within their bureaucracy.

When House Typhoon was overthrown by the Feathered Council, all their sorcerers had abandoned them, stealing what they could. In Weaver's case, that had meant a cloud ship.

How long had it taken him to sail back to Gehenna? Kidnapping people all the way, binding them to his webs?

It should have been obvious, from early on, who they faced. Sleep was the brother of death, and the Shadows were the masters of death.

I have a brother.

And he wants to destroy me.

That was the truth of it. After all these years, he'd come back for his revenge. For the death of his mother, for his own mutilation, for his birthright.

In another world, at another time, perhaps in a better, more just world, *he* would be ruler of Gehenna.

And I would never have existed.

What would have it been like if her father had married his first love instead of his true love?

Lord Iblis and Lady Branwen Shadow.

Lily squeezed her eyes shut as tightly as she could, but she couldn't block out the image of Weaver. His burned body, his twisted limbs, and the fierce desire in his eyes, those familiar gray eyes.

Why hadn't she realized, the moment she'd first seen him? It was obvious, despite the deformities, that he was her father's son.

My father has another son, and I have a brother.

Pie unfinished, Thorn pushed the plate away. "Now we know about Weaver, what are we gonna do?"

Thorn on one side, Mary on the other, just like the old days. Lily was glad to have them both. They were very different from each other, but they both provided her with balance and perspective. They stood up for what they knew was right. True, it got them in plenty of trouble—Mary had almost started a war, and Thorn seemed to attract enemies like a dog did fleas—but Lily admired them all the same. They didn't shy away from a challenge, and neither would she.

Lily stood up. "We're going to set things right. And start by speaking to Branwen."

"Branwen? Can you hear me?" Lily stood at the mouth of the cave of jewel spiders, just an hour later, clutching a bunch of black roses. "I've come to talk."

The others, Mary, Dott, and Thorn, stood a way back, all looking on anxiously. Thorn held two buckets of water, just in case.

Lily made her way back into the cavern. It was dark, misty, and cold.

"Branwen?"

No answer.

Lily carefully unwrapped the twisted silver bracelet and put it down on the ground. "I have something for you. A gift from my father. Do you remember it?"

Lily gasped as fire flickered in the corner. The flame swelled into an unsteady shape, but Lily recognized her. The revenant. The temperature began to rise, and Lily glanced toward the exit.

She steadied herself. She couldn't run away.

The revenant approached the piece of jewelry and crouched down. Her fiery fingers brushed the metal, ever so slightly, and the silver bubbled and melted into a puddle.

If she can do that to metal, what could she do to me?

"I know what happened, Branwen," said Lily, her voice trembling. "I am sorry, so sorry. I want to make it right."

The revenant looked up at her with burning eyes. The flames thickened, and the heat intensified.

"Your son is here in Gehenna." There was no way to retreat; the revenant was between her and the exit now. The smoke was already thick above her head. "I want to help him. He deserves justice. I know he does."

"Lily! Get out of there!" yelled Thorn. He had crept halfway in and held one of the buckets ready.

"Stay back! I'm talking!" Lily faced the revenant even as the fire grew brighter and hotter. "Please, Branwen. I will make it right. Just give me time, that's all I ask. Do not harm anyone else, and your son will have what he deserves. I promise." Lily reached out. "He is my brother."

The fiery spirit held out her own hand, and Lily gritted her teeth, preparing for the pain. But she couldn't falter, couldn't let the spirit of Branwen think she was telling her anything but the truth. Their fingers were inches apart, and her skin tingled.

Lily trembled as her hand grew hotter. "He is a Shadow, and we look after our own."

"Lily . . ." Thorn edged closer.

The revenant vanished. All that remained was the molten lump of silver.

Thorn ran up to her, and Lily shoved her hand into the bucket. She sighed as the cold water began to reduce the pain. "I think she believed me, Thorn."

He looked over both shoulders. "That was a big promise to make, Lily."

They left the cave. Mary inspected her fingers, tutting loudly. "It's clear to me you can't look after yourself."

Despite the pain, Lily smiled. "You're probably right."

Mary huffed. "There's no 'probably' about it. I'm surprised Castle Gloom's still standing. I heard half of it collapsed not a week ago."

Lily and Thorn locked eyes. Thorn winked.

"I suppose I'd better come back, just to make sure the steward's doing a good job and Cook hasn't emptied the treasury by overpaying the farmers. And the zombies . . ." Mary put her fists on her hips. "They'll need managing, too."

Lily kissed her.

Thorn didn't. He was frowning. "You hear that?"

Lily paused. She couldn't hear much more than the sound of her beating heart. "What?"

"I heard it last night. I thought it was thunder, but it ain't."

There was a sound, echoing down from the northeast, from the slopes of the distant Troll-Teeth. Lily peered toward the black silhouette of the mountains. "Can you see lights?"

"Yeah, I can. Must be campfires."

Then Dott clapped. "I know the big noise. It not thunder, little T'orn! It feet stompin'!"

"She's right," said Lily. "The troll army is on the march."

THIRTY-EIGHT

They needed to get back to Castle Gloom fast. Lily put Mary on the mule led by Dott, and borrowed horses from the innkeeper for herself and Thorn. She pushed them hard back south through Bone-Tree Forest. Thorn took them off the main trail and, thanks to his uncanny knack for navigating the woods, had them through the forest within the day.

It was Lily who spotted the familiar black spike of the Needle first. "We're almost home."

"Hold on, Lily." Thorn reined in his mount. He pointed off to the southeast. "Who are they?"

A line of people trudged through the snow, a way off. They carried their belongings on their backs or on skinny donkeys. One or two had converted their plow horses into wagon pullers and were shouldering the wheels out of deep ruts. They moved in a thin, snaking line, all heading toward the castle.

What was going on? She needed to find out. "Come on."

"What about us?" asked Mary, shifting awkwardly on the mule.

"Catch up."

With that, the two of them spurred their horses into a canter, and then, when the trees had cleared, a gallop, eating up the last few miles between the boundary of Bone-Tree Forest and the walls of Castle Gloom.

"What in the name of the Six is happening here?" Lily pulled Zephyr up to a sharp stop as she entered through Skeleton Gate.

Custard appeared out of nowhere, literally, and barked and jumped around the horse's hooves.

The courtyard, normally used for weapons training and riding practice, was now a campsite.

Most had wandered in on foot, carrying bundles of blankets and food. Others had loaded furniture and older relatives on top of their wagons. Children herded in goats and sheep, and baskets of squawking chickens dangled off the backs of farmers.

Dozens of small fires smoldered among crude tents and hastily erected huts. A bunch of squires were chopping up logs for a queue of waiting villagers. Another group lined up in front of a stack of barrels. The baker was handing out flour, two scoops per family.

Those are our winter supplies.

Music rose over the din of people and livestock. Merrick conducted his musicians up on the steps. His jugglers and acrobats had a clear space in front of the stables and were busy performing tricks and feats for a ragged crowd. Children clapped and the parents laughed as Merrick's wife burst into song.

Thorn frowned. "She's singing 'The Old Duke's Longsword,' I think."

Merrick joined her, to the cheers of the audience. So did a few of the donkeys, in their own way.

"*Tsk,*" Mary said when she and Dott arrived. The troll lifted her off the mule. "Look at this mess. Thank the Six I'm back."

Mary stood in the center of Skeleton courtyard, hands resting on her wide hips, and rocked on her heels. She grabbed one of the stable boys by his collar. "Go find me the red ledger."

"But it's with the steward, Mary."

"Get it *off* him." She dropped him and clapped. "Gather round, you lot!"

"It's funny," said Thorn as he shoved the stable boys into a group to listen to Lily's maid, "but I think we've got a chance if Mary's back."

"I know what you mean," said Lily, smiling. "The castle hasn't felt right, till now."

The red ledger arrived, along with the steward. There was an audible sigh of relief when he handed Mary her precious book containing list after list of what the castle required to run properly. Mary tutted as she flicked through the pages. "We should have double this amount of flour. And what's this with the salted beef? Don't tell me Hades ate all the cows!" She slammed the book shut. "Any villager with an animal to slaughter—go tell them we'll pay double market rate, but only if they sell it to us right now. And that goes for eggs, too. Find out who's got milking cows. Put them in the pens along Bone Yard."

Thorn pointed toward a group of shambling figures by the entrance. "What are we going to do with them?"

People had brought more than just livestock; they'd brought their *entire* families.

Living and otherwise.

A zombie was hopping around, having dropped his leg somewhere. A small girl, his granddaughter or even great-granddaughter, was helping him search for it and lifting him back up whenever he fell, which was every few paces, or hops.

"I don't know whether to laugh or . . . really laugh," said Thorn. "Still, family is family."

A squire ran up to take care of Lily's horse. "M'lady Shadow! You're back!"

"Who are all these people, Marts?" asked Thorn.

Lily gave the squire a second glance. Yes, *Martin*, that was his name.

How was it that Thorn remembered everyone's name when he'd only been here three months? She'd lived here her whole life and could only put names to a dozen, maybe a score if pushed, of her servants.

Martin looked from her to Thorn and back, not sure whom he should direct his answer to. Which was irritating. It should be obvious. "Well?" she prompted.

"Local villagers. They're here because of the trolls," said Martin, answering the space between her and Thorn. "You must have heard the drums?"

"The trolls should never have gotten this close." Lily grabbed his arm. "But what's happened to Baron Sable? Where's his army?"

"There isn't one, not anymore," Martin answered, pale-faced. "The trolls destroyed it."

THIRTY-NINE

Wade had one arm in a sling. He was ashen, his eyes darkly ringed and wide with fear. Whatever had taken place, it now haunted his sleep.

"Go on, boy, tell us what happened," said Old Colm, more kindly than Lily had ever heard him speak.

Wade nodded. "We met the trolls just south of Ice Bridge. They'd already crossed, and they were lined up to face us—just a few hundred yards lay between our two forces. Baron Sable didn't waste any time. He had the archers fill the air with arrows for a few minutes, to get the trolls angry and stewed."

"No discipline; trolls don't know the meaning of the word," said Sir Grimsoul. "That would have prompted a charge, yes, sonny?"

"That it did, m'lord. Or so we thought. The trolls came on, a broken, ragged line. Easy pickings for our cavalry. Baron Sable gave the signal, and the whole of the Black Guard galloped in." Wade wiped his eyes. "Straight into a trap."

Lily stared. "A trap?"

"Trolls came out of hiding, on both our flanks. They'd buried half their army in the snow. The weather was so bad we hadn't spotted them, and . . . well, no one thought trolls could make such plans." Wade sank. "The Black Guard was cut off, and that just left the militia. Everyone knew it was hopeless, but no one backed down. We fought till our spears broke, then fought with rocks and our bare hands. It was . . . horrible. The snow fell harder and harder, and you couldn't see anything. All you heard was the screaming."

Lily's heart raced. She wanted to give Wade a reassuring hug; he looked so lost in it all, as if he was still on the battlefield. "What about the baron?"

"I don't know, m'lady. All I heard was the horn sounding the retreat, and that's what I did. We ran away as fast as we could. I hid in the mountains the first night. Then, by morning, I saw a line of Black Guard and others making their way back. I joined up, and they gave me new orders." He drew a line across the table. "This is Grendel's Gorge. We were to get across it with the squires and wounded and head back to Castle Gloom. Our fight was over. Whoever could still wield a sword was going to stay and make a last stand, to delay the trolls long enough for us to get back. That was three days ago."

She couldn't believe it. "Has anyone come back from the gorge?"

Old Colm's answer was grim. "No, m'lady. We have to assume the worst."

Thorn sat with Wade on a bench and put his arm around him. Wade seemed so . . . small.

They were in her study, her best men.

Correction: her best *remaining* men. She had Old Colm, Grimsoul, a few of the captains, and now Golgoth, who was determined to stay until they saved Gabriel. But there was no Baron Sable, and there was no Tyburn.

Lily thought back to when she'd arrived and walked through the Great Hall, unprepared for the shock, the scale, of the wounded soldiers lying there. The stench had been unbearable.

How could it have gone so wrong so quickly?

Golgoth leaned over the map of Gehenna. "Baron Sable—er, I mean the remaining Black Guard would have destroyed the bridge. That'll slow the trolls down, won't it?"

Lily joined him. "Only a little. There are too many other ways through the Troll-Teeth."

Old Colm spoke. "A big army moves slower than most. I estimate they're five days away, give or take."

"Reinforcements, that's the answer," said Sir Grimsoul.

Old Colm snarled. "And where are we to get them? Baron Sable took almost every fighting man north with him! And those zombies . . . they're a joke!"

"If we fight, we'll lose," said Lily.

Old Colm stared at her in horror. "We can't surrender. . . ."

Golgoth tapped the map. "We could raise the drawbridges and ration the supplies. Sit tight in Castle Gloom. Its walls are thick enough to withstand trolls. They're raiders. They lack the patience for a long fight. They'll give up and head home."

"The trolls aren't here looking for a fight," said Lily. "They're here looking for their kin." Lily nodded at Thorn. "Tell them what you saw up in the cloud ship."

Lily watched Old Colm, Sir Grimsoul, and Golgoth as they digested Thorn's tale. He went all the way up to what they had learned from Mary. When Thorn finished, the three men sat silently. It was Golgoth who hit upon the answer first, the same one Lily had reached.

"We give the trolls their people back, and the war's over."

"Exactly," said Lily. "And to do that, we need to meet with Weaver."

Sir Grimsoul only remembered Branwen vaguely. Old Colm would have been around, too, but he was adamant in saying that he recalled nothing about her father's early "dalliances."

Still, neither of them, nor Golgoth, seemed surprised. Natural-born children weren't uncommon.

Old Colm looked grim. "And a cloud ship. These walls won't be of much use then, will they? He'll drift right over them."

Lily glanced over at Wade, who was sitting with Thorn. She knew about Wade's parentage, though she pretended she didn't. She and Wade had played together when they were little, and she'd seen the way Baron Sable looked at Wade, like a loving father would look at his son. But Wade had never wanted to talk about it, so she hadn't asked. First it had felt like a big secret; now it didn't matter. Wade was Wade.

Golgoth spoke. "It's revenge Weaver wants. He's got the manpower—or the spider-power, we should say—to achieve it. We've only got beardless boys and old men to stop him."

"Old men, like old dogs, still bite," growled Old Colm.

"We're not all beardless," said Wade, scratching the pale downy tuft on his chin as if that might make it grow faster. "Not completely."

Golgoth turned his blade over and over, as if frustrated he had no target. "Why don't you have Thorn drop me into that cloud ship? I'll find Gabriel and finish off this sorcerer while I'm at it."

Lily put up her palm. "I am not in the habit of killing off my, er, relatives."

"Then, if you don't mind me saying, you won't be ruling for long."

Lily needed her father. Without his wisdom, and the resources of the Shadow Library, she was second-guessing everything. She didn't have Thorn's natural instincts. She'd been brought up to study, to approach problems from all angles, take advice, and then make a decision, as well informed as possible. Weaver's theft of the Skeleton Key had crippled her—not physically, but mentally. What would her father do? What would he want?

He'd want to meet his son.

"Thorn, go to the belfry. Tell the bat master I want twenty of his best flyers fed and ready to take a message within the hour."

"What's on your mind, m'lady?" asked Old Colm.

"I need to talk to this sorcerer. If we send the same message twenty times, one of them should find him, and he'll know that I'm coming in peace."

Old Colm shook his head. "It's too dangerous. What if he ambushes you?"

Lily patted her weapons master's gnarly hand. "I'll have you to protect me."

                    ✎

The moment they were out of the hall, Thorn stopped her. He didn't look happy. "Golgoth might have a point."

"Weaver has been dealt a great injustice, Thorn. I will not add another to it by killing him."

"I saw the webs, Lily. With hundreds, thousands, of people hanging from them. Whole families wrapped up like meat. Some already dead husks for those spiders. He doesn't care, Lily. Not for nobody."

"I've got to try, Thorn. His mother was burned to death, and he was mutilated. I have to find a way to fix that."

"There ain't no way to fix that. It's the past," said Thorn. "I get it; you want justice. But he wants revenge, pure and simple. He's here to destroy you."

"No, you *don't* get it, Thorn. I will not kill the son of my father. No matter what."

"Then you are going to lose, Lily."

"Go to the belfry and get twenty bats ready." Lily took out a box of parchment. She dipped her quill in the ink. She'd keep the message simple: a time and place.

"How do you know he'll come?" Thorn asked.

"He'll come."

"Weaver won't be satisfied until he has *everything*."

"I know, but if that's what it takes to save Gehenna, then I'll give him everything."

FORTY

Forlorn Bridge was the most desolate place in Gehenna. The mists hung there all year, and the ground was scarred with cracks that smoked, filling the still air with poisonous smells. Small, sickly-looking shrubs dotted the mismatch of bitter grass and exposed flint. A few mangy birds nested in the stunted, ugly trees, but otherwise no living creature inhabited the moors.

It was the perfect place for making secret deals.

Lily rode at the front, on Zephyr, who, along with Thunder, had accompanied the villagers of Three Barrows when they'd sought refuge at Castle Gloom. The stallion was usually calm, confident, and totally under her control, but throughout this journey, he'd been edgy, as skittish as a colt, and unwilling to obey her.

Thorn wasn't much better. "This is a stupid idea."

"No one asked you to come," Lily replied. "Why did you, anyway?"

"That's easy. So I can tell you 'I told you so' in about an hour."

There was a sun up there somewhere, but its light failed to penetrate the thick, opaque air.

Thorn edged closer. "And we should have brought Golgoth."

"I don't trust him."

Thorn shrugged. "Me neither. But right now an executioner's what you need."

"We'll get Tyburn back," said Lily, watching Thorn. She could tell he missed Tyburn more than most.

Lily thought about the taciturn, plain-speaking warrior, one of the most dangerous killers in the world. Or so everyone said. In all her life, she'd never seen him even raise a fist in anger. In fact, she'd never seen Tyburn angry. His silent, methodical nature was what made him so menacing.

As opposed to Thorn, who couldn't restrain his emotions if they were wrapped in iron chains.

What were Tyburn's plans for Thorn? Tyburn was well over forty, and executioners rarely made it to old age.

No one could shoot like Thorn. There was a gargoyle up on the outside of the Great Hall with an arrow down its throat, put there by this boy from Herne's Forest. The other squires still talked about it. Every one of them had tried to hit the same spot, and none had gotten anywhere close.

But Thorn couldn't be an executioner. He'd never kill on command, never slay rivals nor behead traitors on her, or anyone else's, orders. He'd never call her "m'lady." And that suited Lily just fine.

"What are you looking at?" Thorn asked suspiciously. "Have I got something hanging out of my nose?" He rubbed it hard. "Is it gone?"

Lily laughed, and it was good to fill her lungs with merriment instead of dread. "I was thinking, why do I need an executioner when I have the likes of you and Old Colm?"

They both looked back.

Old Colm struggled along the path, thirty or so yards away.

He wore his ancient battle armor and with it his ferocious skull-faced helmet. Old Colm had been one of Gehenna's fabled death knights, the best of the best. Waaay back in her grandfather's time. The sword on his side could take the head off an ox, but now he struggled even to lift it. He sat on his warhorse, huffing and red-faced but refusing any help. Thorn was keeping an eye on him. With only one real leg, Old Colm was at risk of simply tilting out of his saddle.

Thorn stopped. "Now that doesn't look good."

Thick, sparkling cobwebs covered the trees lining the riverbank. Barely a piece of bark could be seen under the heavy layers of crystalline spider silk. Nets stretched from branch to branch, and birds and bats hung trapped within them.

Of the jewel spiders themselves, there were thousands. The ground itself moved, made up as it was by a rolling sea of crystalline arachnids.

"We should turn back, m'lady," urged Old Colm.

"This is Gehenna," stated Lily, more bravely than she felt, "and I can go wherever I want."

It's so much worse than I'd imagined.

What if this spread across Gehenna? A kingdom of dreamers, all under the control of her half brother?

The mist remained, obscuring everything beyond twenty yards. The only sound, aside from the nervous whinnying of the horses, was the constant chiming of the jewel spiders.

Thorn reined in Thunder. "Look."

On the far side of the river waited three men, one of them Weaver.

"You were right," said Thorn. "He did come. What message did you send him?"

"The one he wanted."

"I should have brought Hades," Thorn complained. "And my bow. I don't feel right without my bow."

"We're not here to fight, Thorn." Fighting wasn't going to get them anything but more trouble, and right now she was drowning in it.

"I know that, and you know that. But do *they* know that?"

Lily felt cold and afraid. She was taking the biggest risk of her life.

Weaver was her enemy. But he was also her brother. Her older brother, and a powerful sorcerer. In a just, fair world, he would be sitting in Castle Gloom.

Lily wanted to be a just ruler. Otherwise, what was the point?

His shoulders sloped to one side, and his left arm was twisted, the fingers curled in on themselves like the legs of a dead spider. Half of his face was raw, red, and shriveled. Only the eyes remained whole and true. Gray and brooding and full of a storm's fury.

His robes were old-fashioned, theatrical. Black with silver spider-silk embroidery.

He thinks that's how a sorcerer should look. A Shadow sorcerer.

Nearby were two others, likewise dressed to impress. One man, dark-skinned and in a turban, wore long, flowing red-and-yellow robes, and beside him was an older man in blue and white, his cloak lined with feathers.

More sorcerers.

Weaver shuffled forward, leaning heavily on a stick made of pure crystal. It looked like every movement was painful; he gritted his teeth with each feeble step. Then he grinned. The clawlike hand rose and beckoned her.

He stepped onto the old, narrow bridge that crossed the River Forlorn.

"Wait here," said Lily as she dismounted.

Thorn scowled. "Cross that bridge, and you ain't coming back."

"I have to go, Thorn."

Lily stepped onto the cobblestone bridge. The webbing stuck to her hands and her clothing and tried to catch her boots, so by the time she'd crossed, she was tangled in a fine crystal cloth.

Halfway across, she faced the sorcerer. He bowed. "M'lady."

"Weaver," said Lily. "Is that what I should call you?"

His gray eyes darkened. "I did have another name, once. But it was burned away in a terrible fire."

"I am sorry for that, I truly am. But I had nothing to do with it."

"Isn't it strange, you and I both being here? It's as though two separate worlds have collided, thanks to our father."

"Strange? How?"

"Don't be naive. I am the rightful heir of Gehenna."

"It's not that simple."

He laughed—or it could have been a laugh. Instead, air rattled in his lungs and out from his ruined throat. "You are a talented witch but an amateur. I've been weaving spells since I was a small boy. I was taught in the best schools of House Typhoon. The spiders feed me dreams. Dreams strengthen me, and every living thing dreams."

"Dreams that you rob from the innocent. What have you done with my people?" said Lily. "What have you done with Gabriel?"

"He dreams, m'lady. And he is happy."

"How can he be happy trapped in a dream?"

"I've seen his visions." The sorcerer shrugged his narrow shoulders. "Gabriel is all that his father wishes him to be—clever, accomplished, handsome. All those things that in the waking world he is not."

"But they're only dreams. They're not real."

"Ah, but when do you know the difference between a dream and reality?"

"When you wake."

"And if you never wake?" he asked.

Lily tried to stifle a shiver. "What about Tyburn? You have him, too."

Weaver scowled. "His are nightmares. He cannot escape the people he's killed. His guilt consumes him, as well it should."

"And do you feel any guilt? For the people you stole out of their homes? For the ones you've killed by turning them into breeding bags for your spiders?"

"That is fine coming from a Shadow. Your ancestors often fed upon their own people, did they not?"

There was no point in arguing. She was here to save her people; nothing else mattered. Lily looked over at the other waiting sorcerers. "And who are they?"

"My brothers in magic," Weaver replied, without looking back at them. "The one in red is Firestarter, a *very* remote cousin to the Sultan of Fire."

Lily nodded. Weaver had mentioned him on the night of the Old Keep fire.

"You came for the letters, didn't you?" All those treasures in the library, and that was all he'd stolen. But Lily could guess who'd written them, and that perhaps made them the most valuable things in the world to Weaver. "Letters from your mother to . . . our father?"

"I wanted to find out what sort of person she was and how she felt about Iblis." He grimaced. "I don't remember anything about her. I was only four when she died." His gaze hardened. "When you Shadows killed her."

The rage filled him. Lily wondered if there was room for anything else. She hoped there was, or else all was lost. "And what about your other friend?"

"Hurricane. My wind sorcerer. He guides the cloud ship."

"A fire sorcerer, a wind sorcerer, and a sorcerer of darkness, working together. Think of the great things you could do," said Lily.

"We are already doing great things." Weaver smiled maliciously. "We're conquering your country."

"What if I gave you Gehenna?" said Lily. "What would you give me in return?"

Weaver paused. He'd not been expecting such an offer. How could he? Kingdoms weren't usually traded on bridges in the middle of lonely moors.

"You're lying," he whispered. "This is a trick."

Lily shook her head. "I cannot beat you, and there is a troll army descending from the north. A ruler's duty is to her or his people. I have to do my best to protect them, otherwise I'm no ruler."

"You'd give up your kingdom?"

"If that's what it takes," said Lily. Strangely, she felt lighter. Had ruling Gehenna weighed her down so much? "But on one condition, easily fulfilled."

"Ah. What is it? You want to keep the Shadow Library? Or leave with all your fabled treasures? The Mantle of Sorrows?"

"I want you to free everyone trapped in your webs. All of them. Human and troll. And you must make amends for those you've killed."

"*Amends?* How?"

"Seek their forgiveness. Make good their loss, as best you can."

"Why? They aren't important."

Lily stared at Weaver. "Is that what you think?"

His lips parted in a grotesque smile. "Surely it is their duty to serve their ruler in any way he demands? They sleep; they dream. The power of their dreams keeps the cloud ship aloft. The webs hold it together. And I venture into the Dreamtime and harvest dreams for myself. They give me strength. They are what makes me greater than you."

Lily bit her lip. She'd not expected such arrogance, or cruelty. He had suffered more than most, and she'd thought he'd have pity. Instead, Weaver was happy—no, *driven*—to spread suffering to any who crossed his path. That was not how rulers should be.

But perhaps he could change? If he could be diverted from this blind need for revenge, maybe he might do right by Gehenna. There *had* to be a chance. He was her brother.

"It is my only demand. Gehenna for the people you've stolen," said Lily. "You have the Skeleton Key. The library is yours. You could learn other ways to be great, without robbing the lives of innocent people."

Weaver looked at her, disappointed. "You are weak. It's a surprise you've survived this long."

"I have friends who'll stand by me," said Lily.

"Ha!" He pointed past her to Thorn and Old Colm. "Them?"

"Free my people, Weaver. You know it's the right thing to do. Do it, and I'll pack my bags tonight."

"I have another suggestion," said Weaver. "Give me Gehenna and everything within its boundaries, and in return, I'll give you . . . absolutely nothing."

Lily glared at him but held her mouth shut.

Weaver continued. "You come here to make a deal, but you have nothing to offer that I couldn't just take for myself. You see, sweet sister, the Shadows must be destroyed. As you did to my family, so I shall do to yours. I will take Gehenna from you and will not be gentle. Then I shall cast my jewel spiders across the whole land. Entire towns and villages will be wrapped in silvery webs. I'll have thousands upon thousands of dreamers, all feeding me. I shall reap *such* a harvest."

"You are insane," said Lily. That fire in his eyes was more than revenge; it was madness.

"I am what the Shadows made me."

Lily stepped forward, suddenly consumed by the urge to push Weaver into the River Forlorn and hold him under until that cruel smile was washed off. "Gehenna is not your home; you do not have any right to it," she said. "You've come, uninvited, on a cloud ship that you stole from your masters, with renegades and these parasites that feed on my people. What power you have is just thievery. You'll never have my country."

"How will you stop me? I know your castle is defended by boys and frightened servants. Every dreamer trapped in my webs strengthens me. I could crush you right now, sweep you away, but you are my sister, so I'll give you a chance. Pack your bags, take as much as you want, and go. I care not where."

"The other nobles won't accept you."

"Oh, and they accept *you*? They'll have no choice once they see what I can do. I am a truer heir to your father's kingdom than you are. I am his firstborn *son*."

"I came here to make peace with you. To find a way. You're my brother."

"You came because you were desperate." He turned to leave.

"Wait . . ."

The wind swelled around them. The sheets of spiderwebs fluttered. Weaver retreated into the mists, along with his companions. Their cloaks flapped, and the leaves swirled around them, spinning faster and faster.

The three men rose, lifted by the winds. Weaver's cloak of spider silk shone with scintillating colors, spinning him in a rainbow.

And then they were gone.

Thorn crossed the bridge. "Well?"

The mist evaporated, revealing a desolate wasteland of cobwebs.

"There was no bargaining with him," said Lily.

"I told you so," replied Thorn with a nonchalant shrug. "So what do you think of your brother?"

"He's a dream thief," said Lily.

A small jewel spider scuttled along the ground, probing ahead of it with its front legs. It crept up to Lily.

Lily slammed her boot on it.

"Just a thief." She plucked the remains off her heel. "And I know how to beat him."

THE
DREAMTIME

FORTY-ONE

Lily explained her plan to Thorn once they were back in Castle Gloom.

"Nope. You ain't gonna do it" was his reply.

"I thought you'd understand." Lily folded her arms as she faced him. "It's the only way to stop Weaver."

"It's the only way to stop him that you can think of *right now*. Give it time, and we'll come up with something way better."

"Time we don't have," said Lily. "The trolls are only a few days away."

Thorn kicked a stone. "Is this why you wanted to talk here? In the Night Garden?"

He wasn't stupid, that was for sure.

The Castle was heaving. Villagers fleeing both the advancing trolls and the creeping jewel spiders continued to arrive daily. Four villages in Bone-Tree had gone silent.

A trickle of her Black Guard had made it back, survivors of the battle at Grendel Gorge. No news of Baron Sable, though.

"This is the only quiet place left in Castle Gloom," she said. "This is where I can think."

"Yeah, I know what you mean. Have you heard what Merrick's got going at Skeleton Gate? A zombie chorus."

"Let me guess. He's teaching them 'The Old Duke's Longsword'?"

Thorn nodded. "They're not that bad, considering."

Custard howled, as if he wanted to audition for Merrick's undead musical group.

The pup followed her everywhere, always keen and excitable about everything. Being a ghost had not changed him one bit. In fact, he seemed more puppyish than ever. He was never going to grow up.

Twin opposing forces tugged inside Lily. The happiness of having Custard like this forever, and the regret—for his sake—that he'd never be different from what he was now.

His bones lay between two rosebushes not twenty yards from here. She'd caught the ghost pup sniffing around the grave once, but then he'd dashed off after a butterfly.

Lily picked up a branch and waved it at him until she had his attention. Then she tossed it over a wall. "Fetch, boy!"

Custard didn't hesitate to run straight through the brickwork.

"He's going to spend the next half hour trying to pick up that stick," said Lily, pleased to have some quiet at last. "Silly dog."

Thorn leaned over a well. "You got a penny?"

"Why?"

"So I can make a wish. They say fairies live down wells. Give them a penny, and they'll make your wish come true."

"Won't buy much of a wish with a penny." Lily joined him. "No fairies down there. This is Lady Gorgon's cursing well."

"Ah, I forgot. This is Gehenna, so . . ."

"So you write your curse on a sliver of lead, and here"—she pointed at a wedge of folded gray metal—"put it between the bricks."

"And do these curses work?"

Lily thought about what she knew about Great-Aunt Gorgon. "I know she cursed her husband to drown in a well." She pointed down the hole. "Which he did—after she had him tied up and thrown in by her two brothers."

"I've stopped being surprised by anything your family does." He looked down, as if he might spot a pile of old bones. "You all are sunk into this place. That's why I can't believe you'd ever give Gehenna up. You love it too much."

"I do, more than anything. So I'd do whatever it takes to save it, and that includes giving it up." Lily turned from the well. "But only to someone who loves it just as much."

"You really don't like ruling, do you?"

Startled, Lily stared at Thorn. He couldn't read or write, and he didn't know history beyond what he himself had lived. Most people dismissed him as a peasant who was good with a bow, and nothing more. Yet he clearly saw what was what, just like that.

No, she didn't like ruling. How could she ever know what was right, and what was wrong? Chop down trees for farmers, and the foresters lose their livelihoods. Build a dam here, cause a drought there. Decide in favor of one noble, create an enemy of the other. Every decision had its perils.

"It's an obligation; a duty," she said, "to do right by the people."

"You're a strange, strange girl, Lily Shadow." Thorn hooked his thumbs into his belt. "Look, we'll fight. Now that we've got a few more of the Black Guard here, we'll have enough to give Weaver a bloody nose. Make him think twice about taking us on."

"Weaver's never going to give up. All he's got is revenge. It's eaten him up for so long there's nothing left in his heart but bitterness and bile."

"Then we're back to Golgoth's plan, ain't we?"

"No, we're back to *my* plan." Lily reached carefully into her pocket. "We go with this."

A broken jewel spider lay in her palm. "The only way to win is to beat Weaver at his own game."

Thorn looked disturbed. "You'd better not be thinking—"

"There's enough venom still in it to carry me into the Dreamtime," she continued. "Weaver told me what I have to do to stop him. He gets his powers from dreams, so the answer is simple: I need to wake the dreamers."

Thorn wasn't convinced. "How you ever tried anything like this?"

"What? Sleeping and dreaming? Every night."

"You know what I mean, Lily."

She looked at the broken pieces. "The magic of darkness covers so many things. We sleep in the dark, don't we? I have to try."

Thorn frowned. "Even if you wake the captives, they'll all still be trapped in the webs. So what's going to stop them spiders from just biting 'em as they wake and sending them straight back to sleep? No, we need a better plan."

"There isn't one." Lily looked down at the broken spider. "And we're running out of time."

"No, Lily, don't!" Thorn leaped at her—

She closed her fist.

"You idiot!" snarled Thorn. "What have you done?"

Lily opened her hand. Tiny puncture wounds decorated her palm with bright red beads of blood. The spider itself was just silvery dust now.

She drooped. A warm, heavy feeling was spreading through her, weighing her down. "Get me a cushion, Thorn. . . ."

He shook her. "Stay awake, Lily. Fight it."

She couldn't. She didn't want to.

She smiled and touched his cheek. "I like it that you care about me."

"Lily . . ."

Then she slept.

FORTY-TWO

"This is a dream," Lily declared. "I am awake in a dream."

She mustn't forget that. If she did, she'd be lost.

"I am in the Dreamtime."

Yes, dream magic was in the sphere of darkness, but she hadn't been completely honest with Thorn. She had never studied it; her education had been focused on the undead for the past few months, mainly because there were so many of them to deal with.

Still, Lily knew that the Dreamtime, like any realm, could be mapped.

It was a single realm but made of a patchwork of all the dreams occurring at any given moment. Lily needed to see the stitches that held the quilt together. If she could detect the design, she should be able to move from one person's dream to another's.

What had she said to Thorn, just as she'd fallen asleep?

He'd looked so worried, she'd almost laughed.

She stood in a desert of white sand. The wind blew fiercely around her, forcing Lily to cover her eyes to keep out the stinging particles. Great waves of sand lapped over distant dunes, and spiraling dust devils danced, forming elaborate patterns across the ever-changing surface.

"Show me a path," Lily ordered.

The wind blew before her, and the sands shifted, revealing . . .

Footprints.

Lily smiled. This was going to be easier than she thought.

She followed the prints, her boots sinking into the sand as she marched. It was tiring, even though she knew she was dreaming and her body was lying flat out on the ground of the Night Garden. She should have arranged for a bed, or at least a couch.

The sand hissed as a stream began to wind its way through, widening and deepening as it spread. Tall grass formed around her, and Lily felt cold water against her ankles and then calves.

A riverbank rose, a willow tree appeared, and there were two black-clad figures sitting it its shade, boots off and fishing rods in hand.

"Wade?" asked Lily, now standing waist-deep in the middle of a river. A kingfisher darted by.

"M'lady Shadow?" Wade dropped his rod and jumped into the water. "Here, let me help you."

As the pair of them climbed out, the second figure stood up and bowed. Lily smiled. "Baron Sable. Having fun?"

Whose dream is this? Wade's or Sable's?

Here they were, father and son, enjoying a summer's day fishing, a long way from the cares and worries of Castle Gloom.

Sable's rod jerked. "I've got something, Son! Help me!"

This had to be Wade's dream. All his life he must have dreamed of being called "Son." Something the baron would not, could not, call him in the waking world.

Lily wrung out her skirt and walked off, leaving father and son to wrestle with whatever it was in the sparkling water.

It only took a few paces to return to the formless desert. The sand swirled all about her, and in that brewing chaos stood a figure, waiting.

Lily's heart quickened. Could it be . . . "Father?"

The laugh was a dry rasp. "Hello, Sister."

It was Weaver.

"I knew you'd come," he said.

"How?"

"We Shadows are ambitious, are we not? You needed to test yourself. To see if you could do it. Well done." He gave her a mocking bow. "You are very talented. But you're walking in *my* garden now."

"Please, Weaver. You don't need to do this. There's a home for you in Castle Gloom."

"And all I have to do is give up my dreaming prisoners?"

"Yes." If there was a way to make a bargain between the two of them, then all her problems would be solved. And she would have a brother again. Why couldn't he see this was best for both of them?

He sneered. "And be that miserable cripple at the end of the table during the great feasts? Hear all the nobles whisper as I limp past? No. Thank you for your offer, but I'd rather destroy you and conquer Gehenna."

"You'd prefer to rule with fear?"

"Better people fear me than pity me."

"I don't want to fight you, Brother."

Weaver responded with a malicious smile. "I know. Because you will lose."

Lily was loath to give up. "Is there no hope, then, between us?"

Weaver hesitated. As he looked at her, his eyes glimmered with a light. Maybe there was a chance for something good to come from all this. . . .

But he put that light out with a grimace. "There has been no hope since the day you Shadows burned my mother."

There was no getting through to him. Lily backed away.

Walls formed around her. The sand gave way to grass. Trees rose; boughs and branches and twigs and leaves burst from their expanding trunks.

Wake up. I need to wake up.

The dream thief waved a crooked finger. "No. You are asleep, Sister."

"Wake up!" Lily yelled. She slapped herself. "Wake up!"

Weaver took her hand. Lily couldn't resist.

Jewel spiders crawled along his arm. They crept out of every fold of his silken robe.

"No. . . ." Lily tried to pull herself free. "This is a dream. It's only a dream. . . ."

The spiders hopped from his hand onto hers. Her skin crawled just as they crawled over it.

"Wake up, Lily. Wake up."

How could they affect her? She was already asleep.

A spider bit the back of her hand. Lily cried out. The fangs burned.

The dream thief held her gently as she sank into the grass. "I do not want you to suffer, Sister. You are family, after all." He touched her eyelids. "Close them. Close them and be happy."

Lily closed them.

"Lily. Lily, darling."

"Ow."

"Wake up, Lily."

Lily blinked. She shifted onto her elbow as she awoke. "Ow."

She looked around, confused. What was she doing in the Night Garden?

"Ow," she repeated. She scratched the back of her hand. It itched as if she'd been . . . bitten?

The sun shone through the leaves overhead. The branches of the oak tree stretched above her like roof beams. A warm breeze brushed her skin.

Soft, firm hands scooped her from under her armpits. "Up you get. What will Mary say if she finds you asleep in the garden?"

Lily stood up. "Mary's a fusspot."

She heard laughter. Laughter that filled Lily's heart and also brought tears to her eyes.

"She may be, Lily, but don't let her hear you say that. Here, let me." Gentle fingers drew her hair from her face and tucked it neatly aside. "Much better."

Lily faced her mother. She gazed into the deep, dark eyes of love, then leaped forward and hugged her. She gave her a squeeze worth a hundred years of squeezes. "Mother . . ."

Her mother's laughter rocked them both. "Now, Lily, you'll crush me!"

Someone tugged Lily's hair from behind.

"Ow!"

"Playing hooky from lessons, I see?"

Lily's brother, Dante, gave her hair another sharp tug.

"Ow! Dante!" Lily slapped his hand. "That hurt!"

Lady Salome Shadow stretched out her arms. "Ah, it's too fine a day for lessons. I was thinking about a picnic. What do you think, Lily?"

Lily grinned. "A picnic."

Dante dropped his big arm over her shoulder. "An excellent idea."

"Mother hadn't invited you." Lily scowled. Dante could be so annoying. "But you can come, I suppose."

Dante bowed. "Why, thank you, Lady Shadow."

Lily frowned. She wasn't Lady Shadow. She didn't like him calling her that. Still, what was better than a picnic with her mother and brother? She'd missed them but couldn't understand why. They'd been here all along.

She recalled some . . . bad dream. She shook her head. Dreams weren't real. "Where shall we have it? By the pond?"

The *real* Lady Shadow, her mother, pointed to a gathering of dark stones on the horizon. "No. We want someplace quiet, where Mary won't find us. How about the City of Silence?"

FORTY-THREE

Thorn got Wade to help carry Lily up to her bedroom. Mary arranged the pillows and curtains as he and Wade laid her down.

"How long has she been like this?" asked Mary.

"Ten minutes? I tried to wake her." Thorn looked at Lily. He saw a slight wrinkle on her brow, as if she was worried in her dreams. That did not make him feel better.

There was a light tap at the door, and Dr. Byle came in, carrying a basket of small jars. "I've got these smelling salts. One of them should wake her up." He took the cork off one.

"Gross!" declared Wade. "Smells like zombie puke!"

"Funny you should say that . . ." Dr. Byle passed the jar under Lily's nose, to no effect. He tried four other jars, each more stomach-churningly foul than the last. Lily remained stubbornly asleep. The doctor frowned. "A jewel spider bite, you say?"

Thorn nodded.

Dr. Byle scratched his chin. "I could get one of those creatures, study it, and see if there's some way of concocting an antidote. But that will take time, assuming it's even possible."

"Then you'd better start right away." Mary bustled him out the door and then closed it. "Of all the stupid things . . ."

"Now what?" asked Thorn.

"We could kiss her," suggested Wade. "It works in the fairy tales."

Thorn didn't like that idea—for Wade, at least. "What are you going on about?"

"'The Sleeping Princess.' She pricks her thumb on a poisoned spindle because some evil witch—I think it was Eriynes Shadow—wasn't invited to her birthday party or something. Then she's asleep for a hundred years—"

"That can't happen. You'd be dead," said Thorn.

"Anyway . . ." continued Wade, "a prince comes along, kisses her, and she wakes up. True love and all that."

It sounded stupid to Thorn, but then, he didn't know much about magic. "So?"

"Better give it a try."

Thorn stopped him. "How come it's you?"

Wade smiled. "Look in a mirror. Look at me. Then look in the mirror again and ask yourself honestly, who's the *most* handsome, by far?"

Thorn shook his head. "Good to see you've got your spirit back." Wade had been morose ever since returning from battle. "If I know anything about . . . Baron Sable, I know he'll be home again soon, tugging on that mustache of his."

"I just dreamed about him. We were fishing, and Lady Shadow was there, too, standing in the water. Strange, but I feel that he's alive. He has to be." Wade wiped his lips. "So, back to the kissing—"

Mary cuffed him. "Neither of you are going anywhere near Lily. I've never heard anything so . . . wrong. And disgusting."

"But it's written in all the fairy tales, Mary," complained Wade.

"Written by men, no doubt," she scoffed. "You put those puckering lips away before I punch them."

Thorn laughed as Wade blushed. He shouldn't have, because that only brought Mary's attention back to him.

"And you, you young idiot, why didn't you stop her?" Mary got up and straightened Lily's pillow. "So quick at shoveling beans down that gaping maw of yours, yet when it really matters, you dawdle like a serving girl on her wedding night."

Wade grinned as Thorn's cheeks now reddened. "How was I to know that Lily would—"

"Do something rash and reckless? You only need to meet the girl for a minute to know that! Honestly," huffed Mary. "Why don't you two go off and bother someone else?"

"What shall I tell Dott?" Thorn asked. "She'll be beside herself when she finds out about Lily. Could I send her up?"

Mary said, "I'll not have that . . . big lummox clomping around in here."

"She's her *friend*, Mary." Thorn turned to Wade to back him up.

Wade responded with a shrug. "Don't ask me."

Thorn didn't like it. People were terrified of the approaching troll horde, and he didn't want anyone to take it out on Dott. She had nothing to do with it.

"Please, Mary."

Mary locked her arms across her chest. Then she nodded. "But she sits outside, understood?"

Thorn looked down at the sleeping Lily.

What's going on in your dreams?

"Now be off, the pair of you," snapped Mary.

Wade jerked his head to the door, and Thorn was there in a blink. They closed the door gently behind them.

Wade made a face. "I'd rather be back fighting trolls than be stuck with Mary. Why don't we send her out to face them? One tongue-lashing from her, and they'd probably surrender."

Thorn kicked the wall in frustration. Now that Lily had done something reckless, what choice did he have but to do something equally reckless? "I've got to go find that cloud ship."

"Er . . . why? And how?"

"The how's called Hades, and the why . . . I haven't worked it out yet."

Wade slapped his forehead. "None of this fills me with confidence."

"I've got to try, Wade. Lily hopes to wake the dreamers, but even if she does, Weaver's got other uses for his captives—" He shuddered, remembering what happened to the Pitch couple. "I need to bring the cloud ship down."

"But the ship and those webs are magic, serious magic. How are you intending to deal with that?"

Thorn thought of the gift from Ying he had hidden in his room. "With something better than magic: science."

"Sounds idiotic."

"Idiotic is taking on a troll army. This is just . . . desperate."

The tube went down his sock. That was the best way to keep it secure no matter what stunts Hades performed. Then Thorn grabbed his bow and a fistful of his best arrows.

"Only six arrows?" asked Wade.

"I'm not planning on fighting a war." Thorn slung the bow over his shoulder. He slid the long dagger in his sheath.

"Just be careful, Thorn. You've come a long way pretty quickly." Wade helped buckle the quiver on. "I remember the first day I saw you. Scrawny, head shaved, and stinking of horse dung. Now look at you."

"Jealous?"

"There's an old story about a boy who had wings made of wax and feathers. He flew too high, the sun melted the wax, and down he went. Just make sure that doesn't happen to you."

"It won't," replied Thorn. "When is it ever sunny in Gehenna?"

FORTY-FOUR

The brutally icy wind found every little gap in his clothing, biting viciously at his bare skin. So Thorn snuggled closer to Hades, to borrow some of the bat's warmth.

That's better.

He'd found Hades wide-awake and waiting for him in Murk Hall. The bat knew something was going on and had been impatient to get into the air.

Cap firmly down to his eyebrows, Thorn wondered what to do next. They'd been flying for hours and well into the night, yet they'd had no luck spotting the cloud ship.

His fingers were frozen stiff, and his knees felt like they'd locked into place.

How do you find a single cloud when the sky is full of them?

He was just thinking of heading back when Hades suddenly changed direction.

"What is it?" Thorn instinctively tightened his legs under the bat's shoulders as Hades dove sideways. "You spotted a sheep or something?"

Hades snarled, and then . . . and then Thorn saw it.

The cloud ship sparkled like frost in moonlight. It was bigger than before, towering high above all the other clouds. It glowed softly from within, the colors ever changing through the entire palette of a rainbow.

Thorn wondered how many dreamers were needed to keep such a thing aloft: like slaves in the galley of a ship, chained not with iron but with spider silk. He readied his bow. "This is it, Hades."

Hades swooped toward it, riding the storm current.

Countless jewel spiderwebs covered the ship, their strands trailing wildly in the high winds.

Thorn rubbed Hades between the ears. "Good boy."

Hades circled above, then glided under it to search for a way in. Every entrance now seemed curtained by webs.

But the wind was doing its work. A rip developed, revealing a long, clear wormhole that spiraled into the heart of the cloud ship.

Hades took it.

They flew through a tunnel that twisted and turned, expanded and contracted as though it were an artery in a living thing. Thorn brushed his fingers lightly against an arrow's fletching. He felt nervous. The time for action, for him to kill a living man, was rapidly approaching.

This is for Lily.

He couldn't fail her.

They approached an opening. They would find a perch and wait for a sorcerer to—

The tunnel darkened.

Thorn spotted the jewel spiders too late.

A net of spider silk dropped over the opening just as Hades reached it. He shrieked as Hades flew straight into it, entangling them both.

Jewel spiders dashed across the thread.

Thorn tried to tear the webbing, but it was too thick and sticky. Hades flapped his wings, which only served to trap him further. Now outside of the tunnel, they dropped, as Hades was unable to get enough air under his wings. He shook his head as the net stuck to his fur and ears.

Thorn grabbed his dagger and set to sawing the biggest strand apart. If he could just get Hades's wings free . . .

They slammed into an even bigger net. They bounced against it as Hades tumbled down along its pattern, tearing it into long, ragged strips. But the webbing cinched tighter and tighter around them as they fell and eventually held them fast, two flies trapped in a mesh large enough to roof one of the halls in Castle Gloom.

Stupid, stupid, stupid!

He cursed himself. It was an old hunter's ploy: cover all exit routes but one. That *guaranteed* the prey would pick it.

Steel flashed before his eyes. A sword hacked at the strands holding him, and then a pair of strong hands ripped him, only him, out of the web. He was dumped onto the floor.

A vicious kick knocked all the wind out of him and sent the dagger spinning out of his hand. Thorn gasped as a second kick slammed into his chest. Then he was hoisted to his feet by two blue-cloaked guards.

Weaver shuffled toward him. Thorn glared, clenching his teeth with rage. He tried to pull free of the guards so he could attack, but they didn't give an inch.

Weaver raised his staff and struck Thorn across the face. Blood oozed from the gash on Thorn's cheek.

"How good of you to drop in," said Weaver.

FORTY-FIVE

"**B**ring the boy," ordered Weaver.

Hades was totally trapped. More jewel spiders had set to work, weaving thicker ropes around the bat until he could barely move an ear. He shrieked at the silver cords that held him better than iron chains ever had.

Thorn took a step toward him, but the guard stopped him with a spear.

"I'll come back for you, Hades. You just wait."

Weaver smirked. Steps formed out of the cloud material as Thorn was led deeper into the heart of the ship. Walls and doors appeared and disappeared, one moment harder than rock, the next as insubstantial as fog.

Lightning flashed across the roof, thousands of feet above them. The cloud ship rumbled, and snow swirled in open pockets. Thorn wasn't a sorcerer, but even he could sense the power building.

Weaver followed his gaze. "Admiring my cloud ship, eh?"

"*Tempest*, right?" Thorn gazed upward. "Is that its original name or the one you gave it after you just stole it from House Typhoon?" He looked at Weaver. "House Typhoon housed you, trained you, made you the sorcerer you are. But when they needed you, you abandoned them. Am I missing anything?"

"House Typhoon made me a servant. Me, their greatest sorcerer. They had me bowing and scraping, and all the while they never saw how much I despised them. I was happy when they were defeated, old and pathetic as they were. I swore I'd never be anyone's servant again. Not when I could be their *master*. It is my birthright, my destiny, to be the ruler of men."

Thorn couldn't help but bark a laugh. Lily's puppy would make a better ruler.

Weaver scowled. "Careful, boy. You're treading on very dangerous ground."

A hole opened up in front of Thorn. He stopped walking just in time to avoid falling through it into open sky.

Through the gap he saw the snow-covered forest. And campfires—hundreds of them glinting in the night.

"Trolls," he muttered. "They've nearly made it through Spindlewood."

Weaver waved his hand, and the hole sealed up. "The troll army has moved swiftly. They'll be upon Castle Gloom tomorrow."

Thorn despaired. The army looked unstoppable.

Weaver was responsible for all this death and destruction, and it was just the beginning. For a moment, a brief moment, but one that filled him from top to bottom, Thorn agreed with Golgoth. Maybe some people did deserve to die.

Thorn needed to escape. But how? The guards were at his shoulder. In the meantime, he kept talking. "So you're all about overthrowing the masters, I get it. I'm the same—a lowly peasant, working for stuck-up nobles who think they're in charge, just because they were born with silver spoons in their fat faces."

"Oh? Is that true?"

"Yeah. I ain't even from Gehenna. I'm from Herne's Forest." He met Weaver's questioning look. "I had to run; I was an outlaw."

"What crime did you commit?"

"Poaching. To feed my family. Trouble was, the local lord didn't take kindly to people trying that sort of thing. My dad had already lost two fingers as punishment. I had to run, or it was the rope." It was close enough to the truth. "Then I was caught by slavers and brought here."

Weaver put his good hand on Thorn's arm. "What of Lilith? I understand you are friends."

"*Friends?* Maybe she does like me, as a pet. We ain't never gonna be equals, not like true friends." He paused, no longer knowing where he was with the lies and the truth. "I ain't important to her."

"I understand," said Weaver thoughtfully. "For all your talents, your heroism, you will never be allowed to sit at the high table. You will, like I did, take meals with the dogs. That is the world I hate, young Thorn. Where a man's worth is not measured by his deeds, but by his birth." He looked down through another hole in the cloud floor. "And that is the world I intend to destroy, beginning with Castle Gloom."

"Maybe you could get Lily to surrender? It's clear you're gonna win."

"You have so little faith in your mistress?"

"Lily's good at magic, but not that good." Thorn gazed around him. "Nowhere as good as you."

"Nor as powerful. I have these." Weaver plucked at a web. The whole thing thrummed, and pulses of light ran back and forth along the threads. "These webs absorb the dreams of those held within. It's not learning from spell books that makes a great sorcerer; it's one's imagination. That's what fuels magic, and there is no greater source of imagination than people's dreams."

"Look, I ain't stupid," said Thorn. "You'll win, and there's no point in me backing Lily or anyone in Castle Gloom. You and I are the same—you said so. Let me join you. I can help. I know the layout of Castle Gloom, its weaknesses."

"You would betray Lily?"

"She never earned my loyalty. She only bought it."

Was that enough to convince him? Thorn settled down. He couldn't risk slipping up.

"You would be a valuable ally, I'm not denying that. You could scout out the opposition, fly above it all on your bat. Count the enemy troops, see where they're positioned."

He'd give him Hades? It just got better and better with this maniac.

Thorn grinned inwardly. Lily had always called him a poor liar. She wouldn't say that after this. He'd be called Sir Thorn Charm-Tongue. He liked the sound of that.

Weaver stroked his chin. "Yes. You could use your bat. I could even send you to speak to Lilith. She would trust you after all. But to do that I would have to . . ." He looked up slowly.

So did Thorn. Into the mandibles of a dozen descending jewel spiders.

Weaver sighed. "I would have to be a total moron."

Thorn made a move to run, but the webs caught his shoulders. He fell as more trapped his legs. The jewel spiders began dragging him upward.

"Nice try, Thorn."

They began weaving webs over his limbs and torso. Thorn flinched as their needle-thin legs scratched his face and prodded at his mouth. He squirmed, keeping his lips firmly sealed. No way was one of them getting inside to lay its eggs.

They crawled all over him, minute, sharp, searching.

Weaver looked up at him as he dangled a few feet off the floor. "Don't worry, they're not going to bite you, not yet." Weaver instructed one of his guards. "Tell Hurricane to bring the cloud ship down to a hundred feet. We will release the jewel spiders at first light."

Thorn glared at him. "She'll beat you. Lily always finds a way."

"Lily's lost, boy. Lost deep in her dreams. She's not coming back." He jabbed Thorn with his staff. "You just stay here and watch me conquer Gehenna."

FORTY-SIX

"This is perfect," said Lily as she admired the view. "I don't want this day ever to end."

It was glorious, her home. The spires of Castle Gloom stood straight and proud. Their tips would have pierced the clouds if there'd been any to disturb the clear blue sky. The marble walls of the Great Hall shimmered like oil on water, and she could see the Black Guard training on the field outside Phantom Gate, their armor glossy black as they rode their majestic warhorses.

"I know what you mean," said Dante as he searched one of the baskets, no doubt trying to find the cakes.

Her mother joined them with blackberries she'd picked from around a tomb. She popped one in Lily's mouth.

Lily sucked the juice out. "Delicious."

The sun shone brightly on the City of Silence and its countless tombs. They'd walked up the hill and spent a good while looking for the perfect spot, in the shade of one of the huge family mausoleums. Lily sighed. "I should come up here more often."

"We're here all the time," said Dante.

"When was Phantom Gate rebuilt?" Lily asked. "It's been a ruin since—"

"What does it matter?" said Dante. He started on a muffin. "And thanks for helping, by the way."

Lily joined him in eating. Plums, tarts with the richest, darkest blackberry jam, and bottles of grape juice, ice-cold. She picked up a tart.

Her mother laughed. "That's for dessert, sweetheart."

"Too late," said Lily, and she pushed the whole tart into her mouth. It barely fit and crumbs spilled out as she munched.

"*Very* ladylike," muttered Dante.

Lily lay down on the cool grass and closed her eyes. "I could stay here forever."

She felt her mother lightly brush hair out of her face. She'd forgotten how soft her mother's skin was. "I'd like that, dear," said Salome.

This was all Lily wanted.

Then there was a yelp.

Lily opened her eyes.

Small, energetic legs scampered through the overgrown bushes, and a soft, silly growl rose up from behind a gravestone.

"Custard?" Lily rolled onto her elbows as her dog began sniffing at the basket.

Dante laughed and swept him up. He hugged Custard as the puppy licked his face. "No, don't eat me! Help! I'm being devoured by a savage beast! Help!"

Custard was wild with excitement; to him, having someone to wrestle with was the best thing in the world. Dante picked up a sausage and held one end between his teeth. He scampered around on all fours, and Custard chased after the sausage, yapping and jumping for all he was worth.

Lily watched, grinning. "Don't get him too excited, or he'll wet himself!"

Eventually Custard grabbed the sausage and bit it in half. Dog and boy both settled to enjoy their portion. Dante rubbed Custard under the chin. "I never thanked you, Lily. For giving him to me."

Lily faltered. "When? He's . . . mine."

Dante rolled over and growled at Custard, who wasn't the least bit interested in playing now that he had his prize. "You gave him to me," Dante went on. "You kissed him, told him to find me, and put him in the ground. Buried between two rosebushes."

"That's not funny, Dante." Lily got up. "Tell him, Mother."

Lady Shadow smiled. "But he's telling the truth, Lily. Don't you remember?"

Lily stood up. Her chest heaved, and she started crying. "No. Don't talk about such things."

Her mother took her hand. "Lily, it's for the best. Come now, it's only death."

"No!"

Lily wrenched away. She kicked over the basket and watched the plums roll away. The picnic was spoiled. She needed to get back to the castle. "I need to go. . . ."

Dante grabbed her. "Stay with us, Lily."

"I . . . can't."

Pulling free, she stumbled and landed on her knees in front of the tomb. A sharp pain suddenly shot through her hands. She stared at the thorns sticking out of her palms. Black rosebushes surrounded the large sarcophagus. More tears fell.

Dante scoffed. "It's just a thorn."

The pain sharpened her thoughts. She plucked it out and watched the blood swell. "No. Not just a thorn. Thorn."

She stared at the tomb and read its inscription:

LORD IBLIS SHADOW AND LADY SALOME SHADOW

RULERS OF GEHENNA AND DEVOTED PARENTS

TOGETHER IN DEATH, AS IN LIFE

The roses melded with the stonework, pure black marble and exquisitely done. She got up and saw, lying upon the tomb, two perfect effigies of her mother and father with rose petals sprinkled over them.

"No, no, no . . ." Lily sobbed, her tears mixing with the blood on her hands.

She faced her mother and brother.

"You're just shadows," she said. "Of my love."

Lady Shadow reached out to her. "We don't need to be, sweetheart. You can stay with us forever. You'll always be happy."

"Life's not like that, Mother. Happiness needs to be special; it needs to be fleeting. Otherwise, how can it be precious?" She plucked a rose, stem and all. She squeezed it, forcing the thorns into her palm. "I need to go."

Dante took his mother's hand. He smiled sadly at Lily, his head cocked to one side, his black hair hanging over one eye. Looking at her just like he used to. "Good-bye, Lily."

She almost ran to them. She almost broke her faith in the real world and embraced the Dreamtime. Her heart felt ready to burst from her chest.

Her mother nodded, accepting Lily's decision. "Remember us, Lily."

Lily couldn't speak. Tears were her answer.

The wind of Dreamtime blew them away. It tore up the tombs and gravestones, and then even the earth began to disintegrate. Castle Gloom vanished as if made of smoke and sadness.

FORTY-SEVEN

I am dreaming. I am in the Dreamtime.

    Lily repeated it over and over.

I am in the Dreamtime.

But it's not my dream anymore. . . . Whose is it?

Screams ripped the air. Lily spun around. She was trapped in a small, broken-down cottage. A table had been pushed up against the door, and it jumped each time someone, or some*thing*, beat against the door from outside. The windows were shuttered and barred, but through the gaps Lily glimpsed figures moving.

The screams turned into ferocious roars. The cottage shook from above and they, whatever *they* were, began tearing at the thatched roof, digging their way down and in.

A small, ragged boy was curled up in the corner, eyes squeezed shut and hands covering his ears.

Lily knelt down and put her hand softly on his. "Hello."

His face was pinched, his body scrawny due to lack of food. His dark eyes were hollow, ringed with terror. The dirt on his face was dug in deep, and his tears had done little to remove it. The boy shook from head to toe. He wore no shoes, and Lily wondered if he ever had.

"I'm scared," said the boy. He gripped her hand with terrible desperation.

Lily smiled and wiped his face. "You need to be brave."

"I don't know how."

The howls rose into a bloodcurdling frenzy. What horrors were out there? Why were they tormenting this little child?

"Are you a princess?" the boy asked.

"I am. And you know what all princesses need, don't you?"

He shook his head.

"We need three things, that's all: grace, wit, and brave knights to protect us. Will you be brave, for me?"

The boy's eyes widened; then he slowly nodded. "I'll try."

"Thank you. So I shall dub you"—she tapped one shoulder, then the other—"Sir . . . ?"

"My name's Bill. Bill Tyburn."

Lily faltered. Then she smiled. "Arise, Sir Bill Tyburn. The fearless."

The boy leaped forward and wrapped his arms around her. He buried his head into her neck. "Don't let them get me."

This was Tyburn's nightmare. Deep in his soul, Tyburn remained this terrified little boy. He'd never escaped this cottage nor faced the monsters outside: the guilt he carried for all the things he'd done.

Lily lifted Bill up. "We're leaving now," she told him.

"How? There's no way out!"

"Of course there is. I can see a door right in front of me."

He was frantic. "No! They'll get us!"

"No. I don't think they will. Hold on tight, though. If both of us go out together, well, I think we'll be fine."

Lily pushed the table aside and turned the door handle. The latch clicked. She pulled it open.

The monsters were gone. There was nothing outside but stillness and silence.

Lily met the boy's dark gaze. She brushed the last tears away. "Time to wake up, Bill."

FORTY-EIGHT

Tyburn's dream may have been a surprise, but Gabriel's was *entirely* predictable.

"All hail High King Gabriel Solar!"

Trumpets blasted. Thousands of flags, all white and gold, fluttered in the crisp morning breeze, and doves filled the skies.

Gabriel sat upon a giant throne. His silver armor sparkled with diamonds.

The herald stood on the steps of the palace, halfway between the high king and the sea of adoring subjects. "Conqueror of the east, south, north, and west! Master of the New Kingdoms! Peacemaker and justice-bringer! All hail the high king!"

Lily was at the foot of the steps. In chains. To her left was Ying; beyond him stood a man with scales and gills.

The Coral king?

To her right was the Sultan of Fire, with K'leef, and several druids from Herne's Forest, with Thorn. Thorn was in rags and wore a double helping of chains.

Nice fantasy, Gabriel.

"This is ridiculous." Lily tugged her chains apart and marched up the flight of stairs.

"Guards! Stop that prisoner!" ordered the herald.

Paladins, the Solars' elite warriors, rushed down to attack.

Lily ignored them, and their swords and spears passed harmlessly through her.

"Really, Gabriel? And I thought we were friends," said Lily, stopping at the throne.

Gabriel arched his eyebrows. "So, Lady Shadow, we meet again. You are no match for me in sorcery, and your womanly wiles will not sway me."

"*Womanly wiles?* Never mind." She looked at the endless pageantry. "So, 'high king'? What's that all about?"

Gabriel raised his chin. "I have conquered all the other kingdoms. With my magic and my sword. None could stand against me. I defeated, in single combat, twelve of the sultan's sons!"

"That's not so hard. Four of them are still in diapers."

High king. The only true high king was the father of the fabled Six Princes. After his death those six, all brothers, had torn the world apart through war. But all rulers had ambitions. She wondered if her father had once had similar dreams, to combine the kingdoms into a single empire.

An impossible dream.

And who would want to? She had enough trouble making sure Castle Gloom didn't run out of flour.

Lily pulled him off his throne. "Come on, we're going."

Gabriel flung up his hands. "Begone, foul seductress!"

"Who are you calling *seductress*?"

"I said . . . begone!"

Gabriel was used to getting his own way, in real life and even more so in the Dreamtime. But the dream was crumbling. The colors were draining, and the surroundings were blurring, no longer able to retain their sharp details.

"What's . . . what's happening?" Gabriel's hands dropped to his sides. His armor lost its sheen, and the diamonds turned to gray stones. Then he glared at Lily. "Whatever you're doing, stop it! Put it back! All of it!"

She'd had enough. Lily grabbed his collar and shook him. "There is nothing here! It's all a dream, and you need to wake up!"

"A dream?" He looked ready to cry. "It can't be."

Why did she feel sorry for him? Gabriel, of all people!

"It's a dream, Gabriel. A trap Weaver made for you."

He reached out, trying to hold on to his phantasmal surroundings. "I'm asleep?"

"Yes."

"Then let me sleep! I want to stay here!" He shouted to the disappearing crowds. "Don't go! Remain with me!"

"You can't sleep your life away. We . . . er, need you."

"I don't care! Just leave me! That's what I want!" He paused and looked worriedly at her. "Just don't shave off my eyebrows while I'm asleep. Or, you know, paint my face or anything."

Lily rubbed her temples, just like Mary did when she was getting one of her "special" headaches. How could Gabriel be such a pain even in his dreams? "What are you jabbering about?"

He covered his eyebrows as if Lily had a razor in her hand. "It's just that one of my sisters, Raphaela—she, well, this one time . . . oh, never mind."

Lily shook him violently. "I swear, by the Six . . ."

"Ow! Be careful! I bruise easily!"

"Just. Wake. Up."

They were back in the desert of pure, formless Dreamtime. The wind howled, and the sands trembled. Crevasses opened up. Out of the corner of her eye Lily glimpsed other dreams. Farmers with fat cows and fields full of tall crops. Plain men marrying the village beauty. Village beauties marrying princes. Old women dancing at fairs, young and nimble once more, and children being heroes, slaying monsters with magic swords in a world without grown-ups.

"The dreams are fading. They're waking up . . ." said Lily.

How many? Just a few? Or all of them?

Gabriel knelt in the sand, clawing at it in despair. "Please, I want it back. Just for a little while longer."

Lily helped him get to his feet. He looked miserable. "It's time to face reality," she said.

And then Lily woke up.

FORTY-NINE

Mary snoozed in the armchair, head down on her chest and hands neatly folded on her lap.

Just like old times. Whenever she or Dante had gotten sick, Mary would park herself there and look after them.

Some things never change. The best things.

Lily struggled to get her sluggish body moving. The bed creaked as she swung her feet over the side, toes searching for her slippers.

Custard barked and jumped onto her lap.

Mary jerked awake. She blinked, then saw Lily. She pounced across the room and hugged her. "You had me worried, girl."

"I'm all right. Help me up, Mary."

"You stay put. You need to rest. I'll have some food brought up."

"I've been doing nothing but resting." She stood up. *Wow.* Why was the floor tilting like that? "How long was I asleep?"

Mary steadied her. "A day."

A day. A lot could happen in a day.

As if sensing her question, Mary nodded grimly. "The cloud ship drifted over Devil's Knoll this morning, dropping those spiders. Never seen anything like it. The ground looks like it's covered in diamonds."

So the battle had begun. Lily straightened, fixing her resolve for what lay ahead. "Then?"

"Old Colm gathered every man and boy he could, as well as some of the older girls, and gave them each a weapon. Then the storm hit and . . . who knows. That was an hour ago."

"What about Golgoth?"

Mary shrugged. "He's out there, too, but people were flooding in through Barrow's Gate screaming that there was an army of trolls at their heels. Sir Grimsoul took what was left of the Black Guard and rode off to face them."

More bad news. She'd not thought the trolls would get through Spindlewood so quickly. "Summon Thorn. We need to talk."

"He's gone, Lily," said Mary worriedly.

"Gone? Where?" Then she realized. Thorn wouldn't have just sat around, waiting for her to wake. "He went looking for Weaver, didn't he?"

"You're both as bad as each other."

"I try to do the right thing, Mary. But each decision I make only seems to make matters worse. Thorn said I was too arrogant, and he was right. I walked straight into Weaver's trap, and I'm afraid I've sent Thorn straight into one as well."

Mary fidgeted with a hairbrush. "I wouldn't count him out just yet. He'll surprise us, you wait and see."

She cupped Mary's face. "You always know what to say. I've missed you."

Mary's cheeks warmed as she blushed.

Lily looked around. "The Mantle of Sorrows—where is it?"

"In the dressing room."

"I need it."

"Of course." Mary put the hairbrush in Lily's hand. "Now make yourself look presentable."

"Mary, there's a war going on. Why do I need to brush my hair?"

"*Because* there's a war going on. You need to show everyone that no matter what's happening, you are Lady Shadow and ruler of Castle Gloom."

Lily started brushing.

Even from deep inside the castle, with no windows, Lily heard the howling gale. In the distance, doors slammed and tiles rattled. She predicted that by tomorrow a few of the older, less robust towers would be leaning a bit more, if they didn't fall down.

If I'm still here tomorrow.

The thought hit her hard. Today would decide the future of Gehenna.

She missed her father desperately. She needed him to tell her what to do, what to say. He'd fought dozens of battles, hundreds. He knew about strategy and tactics, and he could lead a cavalry charge and fight with both sword and spell.

But a door guarded by demons separated her from him. No hammer, no battering ram could open it, only the Skeleton Key. What if she never got it back? What if he stayed trapped in the Shadow Library?

"What shall I do, Custard?" If she left Gloom, he'd have to stay behind, too. The ghost puppy couldn't leave the castle; none of the ghosts could, including her father. Weaver would have everything she loved.

No, she'd never let that happen. She would not let Weaver win. "I'll never leave you."

Mary returned with the Mantle of Sorrows, and Lily slipped it on. It was heavy, much heavier than she remembered.

Hobnailed boots beat on the stairs outside before the door burst open and, huffing and cheery, in stormed Dott. "Prin'ess is up!"

She hoisted Lily into her arms. Custard barked at their feet, caught up in the excitement.

"Put her down, you great big elephant! You'll crush her!" shouted Mary.

Dott stopped immediately and down Lily went. Dott looked sheepish. "Sorry 'bout swingin' prin'ess, Mary."

Mary bristled. "I was . . . concerned, that's all. Someone sensible has to look after Lily since she's surrounded by oafs and imbeciles. But you are a good friend to her, Dott."

The troll beamed.

Lily stood between them, swelling with happiness. With Mary on her right, Dott on her left, and Custard at her heels, she suddenly felt real hope.

They made their way out of her chambers and down toward the Great Hall.

"We've crammed everyone we could in there, and Merrick's entertaining them." Mary dusted off Lily's shoulders as they walked. "Who would have thought he'd be any use?"

Despite the thick walls, she heard the song.

Dott started clapping, joining in. "Old Duke Longsword!"

"You know," said Lily, "I don't think the song's actually about a—"

Mary cleared her throat. "Let's not worry about that right now." She reached for the door handle.

Lily stopped her. "Let's go by Oblivion stairs. I . . . I can't go through there."

"This is much quicker."

"But everyone's in there." Lily pulled Mary away. "Mary, it's all my fault."

"What is?"

"All this. It's the curse of me using magic. They were right. Ever since I cast a spell, it's been one disaster after another. That's why Weaver's come, and the trolls. I've destroyed Gehenna, Mary." She looked at the door, imagining all the people on the other side. People who'd lost family, their homes, everything. "They must hate me."

"You think this is because you used magic?" Mary held her hand.

"Isn't it?"

Mary scowled. "Listen here, Lilith Shadow. You have nothing to be ashamed of. If people can't see the good you've done, then they can go to the Pit for all I care. I'm proud of you. Your father's proud of you, and if I know anything about Thorn, we'll be seeing his smug dirty face before the day's out. The boy's as canny and as brave as they come." She held Lily's hand and wrapped her fingers firmly around hers. "Now we're going through this door and right down the middle of the Great Hall so everyone, and I mean everyone, can see you."

With that said, Mary gave a sharp nod, and Dott pushed the door open.

The singing stopped as Lily entered. Children were hushed, and all eyes turned toward her.

Gehenna was under attack. The enemy was at the gates of Castle Gloom. And it was her job to protect them. Not just their lives today, but their homes and livelihoods for all the days that followed.

Why her? They all stared at her as if she had the answers. She didn't. Not one.

The men were missing and some of the younger women. All that remained here were the old, the children, and the mothers.

"The Six Princes protect you, m'lady!" shouted someone.

"Long live House Shadow!" called another.

More joined the cry. Their shouts grew and grew within the hall, the echoes doubling their voices until it seemed as though the stones themselves called her name.

People reached out to touch her, and Lily passed through a gauntlet of soft hands and gentle fingers.

Mary guided Lily out into the main corridor. "You give them hope, Lily."

"Is that enough?"

Mary took her hand as they faced the main door. "There's only one way to find out."

Lily stepped out and faced her first battle.

THE CLOUD SHIP TEMPEST

FIFTY

Thorn dangled in the air, a marionette suspended over a hole. The cobwebs encased his wrists, and strands trapped his ankles. He swung in tempo with the movement of the cloud ship.

He shivered, and it wasn't just because of the freezing wind funneling up through the hole. Jewel spiders scrabbled over him, their horrible spiky legs poking his flesh, scratching his skin. One tiny creature had crept into his ear to have a look. Thorn had managed to shake it out, but the sensation was horrible. He hated spiders now.

The night gave way to a pale, feeble morning. The sun couldn't be seen through the walls of the cloud ship but filled it with a pearly glow.

The jewel spiders began leaving the webs. Thorn could guess why.

They were gathering for the final assault.

"Good, you're awake."

Neck stiff, Thorn still managed to twist it enough to see Weaver shuffle up with a few of his guards.

"Come to gloat?" asked Thorn.

"Do you not take pride in your accomplishments?"

"You ain't sitting in the Great Hall yet, Weaver," Thorn answered, and he was rewarded by a scowl from the dream thief.

"Can't you see victory is inevitable?"

"Nope, can't see nothing from here. You cut me free, and maybe the view'll be better."

Weaver laughed. He nodded to one of his soldiers. "Release his ankles."

Two slashes of the sword freed Thorn's legs, and Weaver gave him a push, swinging Thorn over the hole. "Enjoying the view now?"

Thorn gulped. Somehow heights felt so much higher without Hades.

"I don't want you to miss anything." Weaver tapped his crystal staff on the floor. "Shall we begin?"

Long, twisted tears formed in the cloud material below him. The jewel spiders piled on one another, and down through the gaps they tumbled, wave after wave, forming a sparkling waterfall of diamonds, rubies, sapphires, and amber, all the bright treasures of the jeweler's trade. Their bodies chimed as they collided, bouncing down through the air to vanish into the thick cloud, dangling from their threads.

Thorn pulled against his bonds. Somewhere down there were Lily, Wade, Mary, Old Colm, dozens of others he knew, and hundreds he didn't. There were the undead, like Tom, and the living, like Tom's wife, Kath, and their children, trying to make a better life for themselves.

He had to do something!

Weaver laughed his horrible, rasping, cruel laugh. "How very heroic. And futile."

The cloud ship trembled. A wall ripped open, and a powerful wind blasted through. A guard, sword drawn, stumbled as the hole in the floor grew wider, sending cracks running in three directions. He screamed when the ship tilted, as though hit by a giant wave, and he dropped his sword as he tried to grab hold of something. But the floor kept on slanting, and the tear expanded. With a wild cry he was gone, practically sucked through the crack.

"What's happening?" yelled Weaver.

The webs shook violently. Jewel spiders scuttled in all directions as the prisoners began to thrash and tear themselves free. Thorn saw a young woman dangling from the silver spider silk, shaking and moaning. She was blinking as she woke from a deep sleep.

Another wall crumbled, and a flurry of snow suddenly filled the chamber.

The cloud ship was breaking apart.

Weaver hooked his crippled arm through a loop in the nearest web and hung on for dear life. "She's waking them," he snarled. "She's waking them!" He stared as the webs trembled with awakening dreamers. "No . . ." He turned and scurried off with his guards.

Thorn smiled grimly. He should have known. Lily had come through. Like she always did.

Now it's my turn.

His gaze fell on the sword that had been dropped by the guard.

Thorn swung toward it. He stretched but didn't quite reach. If he were as tall as Wade, he'd have it!

Thorn put all his strength into the next swing. "Come on. . . ." He lurched forward and reached out. His foot touched the hilt. *Yeah!* One more time . . .

Chimes alerted Thorn to a fresh danger.

A jewel spider was coming. It must have picked up his movements.

One more big swing . . .

He hooked his right boot under the sword hilt, then carefully did the same with his left. Pressing them together, he slid the blade up. Thorn curled, raising his feet to his right hand. His felt the sword slipping between his feet. He snapped his legs upward, and the sword jumped the last few inches into his hand.

The jewel spider swung down, but with a flick of the blade Thorn snapped off its crystal head. Then he twisted as best he could and hooked the tip of the sword around the bindings on his left wrist. The razor-sharp edge sliced the webbing easily.

A moment later, he dropped onto the shaking floor.

Would Weaver be able to restore the magic? The spiders were already biting people, sending them back into the Dreamtime.

Thorn tightened his grip on his sword. There was only one way to win. He had to sink the cloud ship.

FIFTY-ONE

T horn ran up to one of the struggling wakers and slashed at the threads. The man grunted his thanks as he came free.

"Help the others," Thorn told him. "And tell the strongest to get hacking. Do it before they're bitten again."

The webs pulsed erratically. But Thorn guessed it wouldn't be long before Weaver regained control and the dream magic returned in full force. Was it his imagination, or was the cloud ship already beginning to level out?

"You, peasant! Help me!"

Oh no . . .

Thorn lowered his head and kept walking.

"I know you heard me! I'm up here, and I demand you free me! Now!"

Forty feet above him dangled Gabriel.

The boy was twisting savagely, but all he'd managed to do was get even more knotted. Thorn sighed and began climbing.

"About time," complained Gabriel. "Cut me free, and be quick about it. And watch out for the silk sleeves. You so much as tear a thread, you'll be paying for a new shirt."

Thorn gritted his teeth, resisting the urge to cut Gabriel's precious shirt into shreds.

"Can't you go any quicker?"

"Shut your mouth, Gabriel, or I'm leaving you here."

"You shall address me as 'm'lord,' peasant."

"Shut your mouth, *m'lord*."

Gabriel opened it to say something stupid; then that little brain of his overruled it. For once.

Thorn slashed the cords, and the two boys clambered down. "Now what?" asked Gabriel. "I assume you have a plan for getting us off?"

"Yeah. All you gotta do is jump. Just make sure you land on something soft. Like your head."

Thorn stared at the webs, glowing brightly with dream magic. The cloud ship was definitely repairing itself.

He had to destroy the webs themselves, but for that he needed Hades. Where was he?

"Hades!" Thorn yelled.

Gabriel grabbed his arm. "What are you doing?"

"Trying to find my—"

Then the wall before him shook so hard that it evaporated into thousands of puffs of mist, and the floor flipped so it was a wall, sending Thorn tumbling. He slid along the floor, saw a flash of silver, and grabbed it. The sudden jolt almost pulled his arm off, but he was glad he did it nevertheless; he realized he was now hanging over a thousand-foot drop.

"Help!" Gabriel yelled. The Solar boy was clinging onto the web with his arms and knees wrapped around the strands.

Thorn ignored him. Gabriel was fine for now.

From his current position, Thorn could see that the web was huge, spreading hundreds of feet in all directions. There were people everywhere, some struggling, others still fast asleep. The thread hummed loudly and great beads of light raced along them: red, gold, yellow, blue, and dozens of other colors and shades.

And to his left was a massive cocoon of spider silk.

A giant bat–sized cocoon.

The tip of a wing poked out. He saw the edge of an ear. The lump twisted; unlike most, this captive was wide-awake.

Thorn crawled carefully over the web, trying not to worry about the gaps and the long drop. The web shuddered, and his movements didn't help. Once or twice it trembled so violently he thought he'd be flipped off, but he hung on, sword tucked in his belt.

He put his hand against the lumpy cocoon, feeling the bristles that were sticking through it. "Don't fidget. I'm cutting you free."

He set to work.

Thankfully the sword sliced easily through spider thread. The trouble was, there was a *lot* of thread, much of it thicker than anchor rope.

"You, peasant!" shouted Gabriel.

Thorn ignored him.

"Peasant!"

"I'm busy!"

Hades's head was beginning to break free, but there was still so much webbing. How many spiders had it taken to trap Hades? Thousands?

Hades hissed angrily.

"I'm going as fast as I can." He pulled off another tangle of spiderweb, and Hades began working his right wing loose. Hades widened his jaws and shook off the last of the spider silk around his mouth. He twisted and tugged frantically.

"Peasant boy!" yelled Gabriel.

"All right! Calm down! Just give me another couple of minutes!"

Then the web vibrated again. Thorn heard the ominous music of jewel spiders.

Thorn searched around him. Where were they?

Then, through the unraveling mist, he saw and understood what had made this web.

"By the Six . . ."

It hadn't been thousands of jewel spiders after all. Quite the opposite.

It had been *one*.

Thorn sawed faster.

Each of its eight legs was twenty feet long and tipped with a sickle-curved talon. The body was bigger than a cart horse, and its head was encrusted with malformed *blinking* silvery lumps. The fangs clicked together, oily with yellowish venom and as long as Hades's own deadly canines.

"Forget the bat!" shouted Gabriel. "Save me first!"

"That ain't never gonna happen," swore Thorn.

He stopped sawing and started hacking.

Hades glared at the spider and hissed. He jerked, and there was a loud ripping noise as his left wing began to break free.

"This is so bad. . . ." The sword was going blunt, as it was now covered with sticky webbing. He swapped to his left hand to rest his aching right.

The spider, sensing that its prey was escaping, slid down its own line, turning itself elegantly and opening its mouth, revealing rows of needle-thin glass shards.

"Now that's just not fair. . . ."

The spider was less than ten feet away.

Hades screeched as Thorn finally sliced through. The bat flipped, tearing himself free of the few remaining strands.

The spider swung its front pair of legs at Thorn, but he simply let go and tumbled after his bat.

Hades flicked his wings half-open and caught Thorn neatly between

his shoulders. Thorn automatically locked his legs over the shoulder joints, his balance instinctively responding to the changes in direction. The wind howled in his ears as Hades arced wide around the web.

The spider, having lost them, turned to the nearest person still awake on the web.

Gabriel.

"Help me!" screamed Gabriel. He waved frantically at the gigantic monster. "Shoo! Shoo, I say, shoo!"

"You sure about this?" Thorn asked, wiping his sweaty hands before settling the sword back into his grip.

Hades growled, fanged and furious. He was so very sure.

"Let's go save Gabriel." Thorn grinned. "Now that's something I never thought I'd ever say."

They swooped down to battle the mother of all jewel spiders.

FIFTY-TWO

A howling blizzard raged, throwing gigantic waves of snow against the walls of Castle Gloom. Lily stumbled back from the onslaught, holding on to Dott to stop herself from being blown over. Everything beyond a few yards was white.

Her surviving Black Guard galloped out of the swirling snow, then just as swiftly vanished back into it. Fiery arrows arced overhead, to be extinguished before they even hit the ground.

And then, falling out of the sky, spinning and dancing in the wind, came the jewel spiders.

Lily had read about battles, of neatly lined cavalry, ranks of archers, and tight battalions of spearmen, all part of one orchestrated whole, controlled by a commander on a high horse, accompanied by flag bearers and trumpeters.

This was nothing like that. This was chaos; the soldiers had no more order than the falling snowflakes. How could they? It was hard to see the man next to you, much less one on the other side of the battlefield.

The jewel spiders needed no instructions. They leaped and scuttled, and

Lily watched as they piled over a squad of soldiers, biting and stabbing until the troops sank under a glistening mound of crystal.

Spiders were already climbing up the outer walls, having crossed the frozen surface of the moat. Archers along the battlements loosed arrows, but the winds blew them off course, and those that did strike bounced harmlessly off the hard, smooth carapace that protected each spider. Other fighters dropped rocks and pieces of slate to better effect.

"M'lady!"

Wade ran over to her, waving a large iron hammer. "You must go inside!"

"Look out!" Lily yelled.

Wade gripped the hammer with both hands and swung it as a jewel spider, as big as a wolf, leaped out of the blizzard. Legs snapped off with the first blow, and the spider fell. It sprang up onto its remaining limbs, but Wade slammed one foot on it, holding it steady as he smashed its skull.

"Better than a sword," said Wade. He flipped the hammer in the air.

"There's so many. We don't have enough men."

And just one bite would send each of them to sleep.

She had to stem the tide, even just for a little while. Lily reached up, opened her hands, and spread out her senses, searching for the minute sparks of energy within each spider, the small glow that enabled it to act.

She felt them, small candle flames of life. Then she closed her hands and snuffed them out.

Hundreds of spiders tumbled off their prey like rain. Yet many thousands remained.

Lily groaned. That magic . . . hurt.

"M'lady!"

"Prin'ess!"

She doubled over as her chest tightened and she struggled to breathe.

Wade put his arms around her shoulders. "Someone help! It's Lady Shadow!" But his cries were swept away in the wind.

Too much magic. She'd overdone it. By the Six, she couldn't stop shaking. Tears froze on her cheeks. She clenched her hands to try and control them, and gasped.

"No, no, no . . ."

Wade stared at her, horrified.

"What?"

Her hands were gnarled, and her black hair, whipping across her face in the wind, was now threaded with white.

It's temporary. It's temporary. It has to be.

There were risks for those who went too far.

But she'd had no other choice. She could only fight magic with magic. Even if it killed her.

No, her magic wouldn't kill her. Leaning on Wade, Lily got to her feet. She was House Shadow.

She'd live on as one of the undead.

In what form, though? A vampire? There were plenty of those in her family.

Maybe nothing so glamorous. Maybe she'd just become a ghost, or even a zombie. Spend her days being stitched together by Dr. Byle.

Zombies?

Everyone thought they were useless. Old Colm couldn't get them to march or to fight, and Sable had given up on them. Yet they served Lily. They were more . . . lively around her. Her father had told her as much the last time they'd spoken.

You are a necromancer. The dead are yours to command.

"Of course!" Lily grabbed Wade. "Gather the zombies. All of them."

Wade shook his head. "M'lady? The zombies?"

"Do as I say, Wade."

"But someone needs to guard you. It's too dangerous."

With her eyes closed, Lily dug deep. She felt the Mantle of Sorrows caressing her. It was no earthly material. Each Shadow who'd worn it before her had left something, an imprint or outline of their souls, upon it. She needed them now, to add their power to hers. A tremor rose from deep inside her heart.

She opened her eyes and let the darkness pour out.

Dott cried out in fright.

Lily trembled. She couldn't keep this up for long. "The zombies, Wade . . ."

Wade stared as the oily blackness spread around them. "The zombies?" He shook himself. "Yes, yes! The zombies!" He ran back into Castle Gloom.

FIFTY-THREE

Hades screamed as he dove at the giant spider. The eight-legged horror scuttled across the web, abandoning Gabriel to face them. The icy air bit Thorn's flesh, but he didn't feel it; he was too hot with the urge to fight. He leaned right as they tore along the surface of the web. The spider twisted, faster than Thorn thought possible for a beast so huge. It flicked out a net.

Hades jerked, and the strands passed overhead, missing them only by inches.

Thorn swung mightily as they shot by the spider, the same instant it thrust out his front leg. *CLANG!* The end, tipped with a wickedly sharp claw, would have parted Thorn's head from his neck if Thorn hadn't raised his sword in time.

"Help!" Gabriel cried as the spider scrabbled toward him.

"Turn!" ordered Thorn.

Hades arced back and readied for a second pass.

If only I had my bow!

But what good would an arrow be? A steel-like carapace covered the spider's body, and bristling spikes protected it in all directions.

Again they struck, but this time Hades slammed into the web, claws out. The whole net quivered as both monsters went at each other. Hades clamped his teeth around one of the legs, and with a sharp twist he broke it off.

That still left seven more.

Thorn slashed and jabbed, searching for gaps between the monster's armor plating. He wedged the sword tip into a space between the head and torso and thrust with all his might. But the spider flicked its head, and the sword snapped, leaving Thorn just a few inches of blade above the hilt. Thorn ducked as another leg swooped sideways, nicking him on the neck.

This isn't working.

Gabriel dropped through the web and grabbed hold of Hades's ear as he fell.

Hades screamed.

"Don't do that! He doesn't like it!" Thorn yelled.

"Help meee!" yelled Gabriel.

The long claws at the end of the spider's legs raked gashes into Hades's fur. Bright red blood splashed over the spider's crystal body. Hades grabbed another leg and wrenched it off.

"No you don't." Thorn jammed the broken blade into the spider's mouth as it tried to bite, locking it between the pair of fangs. Thorn gritted his teeth and twisted, pushing with all his strength.

The spider thrashed as the edge of the blade began to tear through the softer material in its mouth.

That's it! It's soft on the inside!

The spider venom fell over Thorn's arm as he sawed at the loosening fang. The spider jerked back, but Thorn grabbed hold of the fang and, grimacing ferociously, gave it an almighty *yank*.

The spider shrieked as the tooth tore out.

Hades's claws ripped the web, and it began to sag. It was strong but not that strong. Both bat and spider were shredding it.

The pulsing dream lights were dimming. This time there really was no more dream magic holding the cloud ship together.

The immense walls of cloud began to separate as they transformed back into their natural state of mist. Great crackling spears of lightning tore up the vaulted ceiling.

It won't hold together for long. . . .

Thorn's broken sword had fallen. He had nothing else. He dangled off Hades, his legs wrapped around the bat's shoulders.

He needed to attack the spider from the inside. . . .

Thorn unhooked one leg, grabbed a wing, and swung himself up.

Hades hissed loudly.

"I'm sorry!" shouted Thorn. "Just give me a lift!"

Thorn climbed up Hades, the bat twisting and snarling as Thorn accidently stood on the bat's nose. "Sorry!"

Thorn fumbled for the tube in his boot.

The spider's eight gemlike eyes glared at him, and it snapped its jaws. Venom, thick and sticky, hung off its remaining fang in long, bubbled strings.

Hades wasn't enjoying it. Blood was dripping from half a dozen gashes, and he was shaking his head, trying to fight the poison fouling his veins.

The spider scuttled onto Hades's back, hooking its legs around his body. It widened its mouth, aiming its one fang at the back of the bat's skull.

Thorn flung the tube—the tube of Thunderdust—straight into the monster's mouth.

The spider turned its head, focusing its attention on Thorn. It bore down on him, closer and closer, until its eyes were only inches away. They shone with fiery hate.

"By the Six," Thorn cursed, "you are real ugly."

He kicked its jaw hard.

The spider jerked. A flash of soft red light shone from within, and there was a muted *thud* from within its body. It juddered as more lights burst from inside: greens, yellows, and blues as well as reds, all visible through its semitransparent body. They multiplied, and cracks burst across the spider's abdomen.

Thorn grabbed the tuft of hair at Hades's shoulder and centered himself on the bat's back. "Go!"

Hades released his grip on the spider, and they fell away.

The spider's body glowed with multiple lights, and it trembled harder and harder as the cracks widened.

The final explosion shook the air, and the spider was obliterated into a million shards. They flew in all directions, and Hades roared in triumph.

Thorn sagged. Countless sparkling diamonds fell around him, some still glowing with the colored heat of the explosions.

"Done it again," said Thorn, rubbing Hades. "How many times have we saved the kingdom now, eh?"

Shame there was no one nearby to witness the epic battle.

Well, there was . . .

"Gabriel!" Thorn spun around. Where was the Solar boy? "Oh no . . ."

He looked down just in time to see Gabriel Solar, the only son of Duke Raphael Solar and heir apparent to the kingdom of Lumina, plummet into the clouds.

FIFTY-FOUR

"Protect Lady Shadow!" roared Old Colm. His voice carried over the gale. He wore his old, battered breastplate, and his skull-face mask was raised, revealing his even more terrifying real face. His eyes blazed as he snarled, "Form up!"

Soldiers ran out of the snow toward them, quickly setting out a wide circle with Lily and Old Colm in the center. They were a mix of squires and remnants of the Black Guard. Some weren't even properly armed, having come straight out with shovels, knobbly sticks, and pitchforks. Lacking the ferocious face masks of the Black Guard, the squires had painted their faces, so Lily was surrounded by skeletons, ghouls, and vampires.

Dott carried a huge spade and used it to flatten dozens of spiders with each blow. "Crunchy time!" she bellowed. But for every one she destroyed, there were a hundred more.

Lily was on her knees, exhausted. She'd swept a trench of darkness across them, a bottomless moat that had given her troops time to gather, but the gap was closing now, leaving them on an island of black surrounded by a sea of crawling, sparkling spiders. Too many even for her magic.

Lily pushed herself back onto her feet, moving like she was a hundred years old. Her beautiful black hair had bled color until it was pure white. She'd checked her teeth, worried that she might be growing fangs, but they felt normal. She peered into the blizzard, the vortex of white that seemed to have consumed the whole world. Her eyes hurt, as if pins were being poked into them.

The Shadow magic had changed her. And it wasn't over yet.

"I don't know about you all, but I'm having a lovely day!" Old Colm slapped the hilt of his sword against his armored chest. The loud *clang* raised an uneven cheer from the rest.

They stood there, weapons trembling, legs quaking. A few glanced back at the castle, no doubt wondering if they could make a run for it.

They're terrified.

And if Lily could see the fear, then so could Old Colm.

The weapons master limped over to one of the squires. "You're an ugly little one, aren't you?" He tapped the small boy's oversized helmet. "You'd be Oskar's son, am I right?"

"Grandson, Master Colm."

"Grandson?" Old Colm blinked in surprise. He turned to the ragtag circle of warriors. "Let me tell you about Oskar, a man so ugly that the devil wouldn't take him! Came back from the dead three times, and that's no lie! Spear in the chest, ax in the head, and, if I remember, a dagger in the guts?"

The boy nodded, grinning.

"Now you're at least twice as ugly as he was. I expect great things from you."

Lily watched the boy grow ten feet taller with pride.

Old Colm wasn't finished. "Your fathers were devils. Your grandfathers demons from the Pit. Your mothers were witches who raised you on the bitterest milk and the meat of the damned. Your blood is black, and each and every one of you is a nightmare born. Stand fast, and let your ancestors hear you in hell! Make them proud!"

The ragged band roared.

"I can't hear you!"

They roared again.

"Louder!"

They roared and roared. They beat their chests and banged their shields.

Old Colm joined Lily. "We'll clear a path for you, m'lady. You and your"—he glanced at Dott—"*maid* will make a run for the castle. We'll hold them off as long as we can."

"Did my father ever abandon a fight, Master Colm?"

"No, but you know that."

"Then neither shall I."

He laughed. "As you wish."

One of the squires yelled, "Look! It's Wade!"

Wade stumbled into the circle. He panted as he spoke. "Found you . . . at last."

Lily grabbed him. "Well?"

Wade grinned. "And I got some reinforcements."

The new arrivals shuffled out of the blizzard, moving awkwardly, but with some strange purpose. First came Tom, then Old Man Husk. Then a few more. Then *many* more.

"By the Six," muttered Old Colm. "I didn't know there were so many. . . ."

A soldier stepped back. "But they're just zombies."

"No," replied Lily. "They're the Immortals."

They parted as she stepped in among them. Lily took a deep breath. What should she say? Her father would have prepared a speech. He'd have known the names of his men and the stories of their families. Lily didn't. She hadn't been brought up to lead battles.

Lily didn't say anything at first. She just became part of the crowd. It was as if she were the center of a web, one formed of invisible threads linking her to each and every one of the zombies here. If she concentrated she could feel the strands and make them obey her wishes and needs.

This was true Shadow magic—necromancy—the magic of the undead.

"Please," she started, "I am the same as you. Living or dead, what difference is there between us but breath? We are one; we are Gehennish. I love my country, and I know you do, too." She turned to look at the endless multitude of jewel spiders before them. "Help me save it."

And then the spiders attacked.

FIFTY-FIVE

"**I**s that the fastest you can go?" Thorn was bent down against Hades, trying to reduce the wind resistance as much as he could. "Maybe I should get off and push?"

Hades was too busy flying to snap.

Thorn glanced back. Then wished he hadn't.

Colossal mountains of cloud sank earthward. The webs strained, stretched, and finally snapped, unable to hold the *Tempest* together as the dreamers woke and the magic failed. Violent vortexes of air clashed all around them, and Hades cried out as they threatened to tear off his wings in their fury.

"Over there!" yelled Thorn, pointing at a minute tumbling shape. They flew into the heart of a storm.

There Gabriel was, in his shining white suit, screaming and flapping his arms like he belonged to the Feathered Council.

"Want a lift?" Thorn shouted.

"Save me!" Gabriel yelled.

Hades swooped under Gabriel, slowing just enough to allow Thorn to grab the falling boy.

Gabriel landed on the bat, facing Thorn. He locked his arms around Thorn's waist and sobbed with relief.

Thorn patted him on the back. "There, there."

Hades twitched his shoulder.

"What?" Thorn didn't understand.

Then he did.

Hades threw out his wings to their widest span and angled them as they broke free of the clouds. They emerged only yards above the battle-field, and the giant bat pulled up short.

The sudden halt flung Thorn's stomach up into his throat.

Hades roared over the fighting, above the spear tips, and dipped to snatch a jewel spider in his claws. He ripped its head off and tossed it back into the fray, to the cheers of the Black Guard.

Fighting in a blizzard—was there anything worse?

Thorn shielded his eyes and tried to make sense of it.

The battle had degenerated into a desperate brawl. There were small groups of Black Guard fighting, scattered over the battlefield and with no discipline at all. Some rode horses, but most slogged away on foot, swinging their weapons at the jewel spiders. Villagers had joined, too, using their spades, tree axes, and whatever else they could use to bash the crystalline monsters. Thorn saw many, many sleeping figures, warriors who'd succumbed to the spiders.

Then there were others marching. Thorn had to shake his head to make sure he was really seeing what he thought he was seeing. Row upon row of zombies. Slowly, step by step, they plodded forward, armed no better than the villagers. Spiders crawled over them, but that didn't stop them. Their venom didn't work on undead.

Every few yards, the zombies halted, raised their weapons, and smashed everything before them. They beat down the spiders until they were nothing but sparkling dust.

And behind the zombies was Lily, along with a bunch of squires and

Old Colm. One of the squires blew a horn, a rally call. Thorn watched the Black Guard break off and run toward them, joining the fight alongside the undead.

"Put me down!" Thorn told Hades.

Hades landed on a small knoll near a cluster of squires. Thorn clambered off. "You all right?"

"A bit shaken, and I think I need to change my trousers," said Gabriel.

"I was asking the bat."

Hades gave Thorn what was probably a grin.

"Good. Now get back inside the castle."

The grin vanished, and an evil frown replaced it.

"No, I mean it. Go find Dr. Byle, and get yourself patched up." Thorn looked upward. "The rest of this fight's gonna be on the ground, Hades." Thorn gave the bat a gentle slap. "Go on."

Hades hesitated, then flapped his wings. He hovered over them for a moment and, with one mighty thrust, vanished into the roof of mist.

The cloud ship was now fifty or more falling fluffy rocks. Webs sparkled, and more jewel spiders fell. In another few minutes, everyone on it would hit the earth. Then what?

Thorn didn't have a weapon, only the sliced-off fang. He inspected it, being careful of the venom still coating it.

A squire ran up to him, his companions a few paces behind, all of them armed with bows. "We're glad to see you, Thorn. What should we do now?"

"Shaitan, isn't it?" Thorn tucked the tooth back into his belt. "Stay here and keep an eye on him." He gestured to Gabriel. "Whatever he tells you to do, don't do it."

Gabriel puffed up his chest. "I am a noble, and I am in command. I demand—"

A snowball flew out of the crowd and smacked Gabriel in his big open mouth.

Thorn took Shaitan's bow from him. "Thanks."

"Hey!"

Thorn held out his hand. "Arrows. Now."

Swearing quietly to himself, the squire reluctantly handed over his quiver.

Thorn felt his whole self relax. A bow. A fistful of arrows. Now he could take on *anything*.

He ran into the battle.

FIFTY-SIX

"Forward!" Lily shouted.

The Mantle of Sorrows shimmered with dark patterns. Faces appeared in the phantasmal cloth, ancient and long forgotten. It was alive and amplifying Lily's power so she could command her army of undead.

The ground shook as the zombies paced forward, their feet trampling the smaller jewel spiders. Some spiders scuttled between the zombies or through their legs only to find Old Colm and his squires waiting; they brought down their shovels and hammers until the snow was littered with broken crystal bodies and shattered glass legs.

"Stop!" commanded Lily.

The zombies did, all at once. They raised their weapons.

"Smash!"

The jewel spiders ran and scurried, but the zombies beat and beat until they caught them. Some of Lily's troops grabbed them with their bare hands and, immune to the spider bites, plucked off legs and tossed the spiders aside for the others—the living—to finish the job.

"Lily!"

Who was that? She shielded her eyes against the biting wind and searched the snow.

"Lily!"

A figure stumbled through the deep snow, waving at her.

Her heart burst with joy. "Thorn!"

She gave him the sort of hug Dott would have been proud of, one to crush the air out of him. Then she cupped his cold face and kissed him. A few of the squires cheered.

Thorn blushed as he pulled himself free. "Why'd you do that for? In front of everybody? And what have you done to your hair?"

Lily couldn't keep the grin off her face. "Did you find the cloud ship? Where is it?"

Thorn stuck his thumb up.

Lily looked. "Oh. I've never seen clouds falling before."

"I destroyed the webs," said Thorn. "Without them holding it together . . . well, you can see. We've got about a minute before your brother and his two sorcerer friends drop in."

"I'll make sure you're well rewarded for this, Thorn."

His blush deepened. "You know I didn't do it for no reward."

Snow flurries spun around them. The wind rose greater than before, and Lily saw some fire whirls, too, as fragments of the *Tempest* descended. Dott grabbed her. "Come, Prin'ess! Big storm comin'!"

Lily reached for Thorn. "We need to take shelter."

"You go, I'll follow." Thorn flicked out an arrow.

She knew that look on his face. The calm and focus that came over him when he had a bow in his hand and a target in his sights.

"Come on, Thorn. It's too dangerous."

He shook his head. "I've got one more thing to take care of, Lily. I won't be long." Within a few paces, he had disappeared into the whiteout.

"Thorn!"

FIFTY-SEVEN

The last of the cloud ship crumbled as it struck the ground, finally dissolving into wild, churning fog laced with the broken threads of webs. A blizzard swept over the battlefield, and Thorn curled up, clinging on to his weapons. He glimpsed zombies tumbling in the chaos, horses struggling vainly against gales that came from every direction.

Thorn had no idea how long it took, but eventually the wind weakened. Thorn pulled himself out of a drift and shook the snow off.

After this, he was going to move to the Sultanate of Fire and live with K'leef. He'd had enough of snow to last him a dozen long lifetimes.

All around him the world had turned into a featureless void.

The wind dropped, and people began to crawl out of the snow in ones and twos.

Nearby was a cocoon, and it was moving. A muffled voice called from inside, and Thorn tore it open to reveal a gasping woman underneath. She blinked and looked around. "I had this wonderful dream. . . ."

Are all the dreamers awake now?

Then, from behind him, he heard, "All your fault . . . all your fault . . ."

Thorn spun around, an arrow nocked and aimed in a heartbeat.

Weaver shuffled toward him, jerking forward on his right leg, dragging his left. His forehead was bruised and his clothes were torn, but otherwise he seemed unhurt. There was no sign of the other two sorcerers.

Thorn got up close to him. "It's over, Weaver. You lost."

Weaver snarled, and Thorn readied to shoot. At less than ten yards, he couldn't miss, and there'd be no time for any tricks from the sorcerer. They both knew it. Weaver raised his good right hand. "I surrender."

"Surrender?" Thorn kept the arrow drawn. "This is an act."

Weaver shook his head. "No. Take me to Lilith Shadow."

Thorn didn't move. The arrow stayed aimed at Weaver's heart.

Weaver took Thorn's silence as refusal. "I will surrender and swear an oath of undying loyalty," the sorcerer went on. "I shall be her faithful *servant*."

Thorn just needed to slip his thumb and the arrowhead would end it all. "Is this the same oath you swore to House Typhoon?"

"What?" Weaver's eyes narrowed.

"You swore to serve House Typhoon, didn't you? Then you abandoned your masters, stole the ship, and came here. Ain't that right?"

Weaver hesitated. "That was completely different. . . ."

Thorn had never killed a man before. But every instinct in him was screaming to do it this once. "And you said you'd never serve anyone ever again."

Weaver met his gaze. "So what are you planning to do? Shoot me? You think Lilith will be happy about you killing her brother? Her only remaining brother?"

"*Half* brother. And you'll betray her the first chance you get."

Weaver smiled but said nothing.

Thorn shot.

The arrow skimmed the side of Weaver's head and *thrummed* into a tree trunk a few yards behind him.

He clutched his bleeding ear and narrowed his eyes, those fierce gray eyes. "You'll pay for that."

Thorn threw the bow away. "You've got nothing but hate in you, Weaver. But Lily refuses to see it. She wants a family so badly."

Weaver shuffled up to him. "Oh, I shall play the dutiful brother, you'll see."

"Right up to the moment you stab her in the back, right?"

Weaver's cruel, cold gaze told Thorn all he needed to know.

The sorcerer stumbled in the deep snow and held out his hand. "Please help me up, Thorn. I'm just a poor cripple after all."

Thorn took it and pulled him closer. "I won't have you hurt Lily."

Weaver responded with his hissing laugh. "And how exactly do you intend to stop me, peasant?"

Thorn locked his grip. "Like this." He stabbed the sorcerer's hand with the spider fang.

Weaver's eyes widened. "What? No!" He broke free and stared at the thin red scratch along his palm. "No . . ."

Thorn watched Weaver sink to the ground.

The dream thief beat his chest even as his eyelids fluttered. "I . . . I must stay awake. . . . I must . . ."

His eyes closed. He sighed. Weaver lay in the snow and slept.

"Thorn!"

Lily ran toward him and stared at Weaver. "What have you done?"

Thorn tossed the fang away. "What I had to. I'm sorry, Lily. I did it because I knew you wouldn't."

FIFTY-EIGHT

Lily knelt down beside Weaver and put her hands against his face. "He's dropping into the Dreamtime." She didn't have long.

Thorn shook her. "What are you doing? You can't wake him!"

"Shhh." She closed her eyes. Weaver's breath was a trembling hiss, but she did her best to match it, pace her own breathing with his. She had to catch him before he was lost in the endless paths of sleep. "Into the Dreamtime . . ."

She felt lighter; she was starting to drift.

"Into the Dreamtime . . ."

"Into . . ."

Weaver moaned, and he snapped open his eyes.

"You're awake?" Lily exclaimed.

Weaver shoved her away from him. "Did you really think the dream weaver's venom could work on me? I've played with them since I was a small child; they cannot harm me!"

Lily let her shoulders slump. She bowed her head. "I cannot beat you. Your magic is greater than mine. I surrender." Her reply was heavy with a sense of defeat.

She watched him struggle up. He was so broken, the damage had gone far beyond his body into his heart and mind. His hate kept him going; the blaze was ever present in his eyes.

That's why I need to give him everything.

Lily took off her father's ring and handed it to Weaver. "You are firstborn, Brother. Gehenna is rightfully yours."

"Is this my father's?" He cradled it, and something briefly softened his eyes—a moment of calm and . . . happiness?

The zombies shuffled closer.

Lily raised her hands. "I surrender! All of you, kneel before your new ruler, Weaver of House Shadow!"

They hesitated. Thorn stared at her, then at Weaver, in utter disbelief. But he too knelt.

Old Colm, grim-faced, did the same. His squires, one after the other, followed his example.

"Kneel before your new ruler!" Lily repeated.

Weaver slid the ring onto the forefinger of his crooked left hand. "At last. At last—"

The ring began to glow.

Lily gasped.

It pulsed with a pale blue light, gaining brightness. Soon the light was blinding, and Lily stumbled back.

The light died, and what remained was a transformed Weaver.

"Of course," whispered Lily. She should have guessed this would be his deepest wish. Now his victory was complete.

He has it all.

His injures were gone. He stood whole. Weaver laughed as he flexed his left hand, the limb that had been withered and useless, for so many years. Now it swelled with powerful, sleek muscle. He touched his face, feeling the smooth skin, the ridge of his nose, the curve of his left ear. He drew his fingers through his dense black hair. "Am I . . . handsome?"

Lord Iblis appeared. Lily's heart jumped. Iblis was as he had been in life, not the pale phantom she knew in the Shadow Library. He marched through the snow, leaving footprints behind. Breath smoked in the cold air. His face bore fresh color.

"Father," said Lily.

He paused, nodded once at her, then joined Weaver. "You are handsome indeed, my son."

Lily fought down the shock of seeing her father like this. Why was she surprised? He would be more real *here*.

How would Weaver react? She watched silently as father and son met for the first time.

Deep, conflicting emotions fought for dominance on Weaver's now-unblemished face. Iblis bowed. "Lord Weaver Shadow."

Her brother, hand still against his face, looked about him as the snow stopped and the sky cleared. A pale, soft sun shone over the battlefield. "Weaver Shadow . . ."

The zombies knelt. The soldiers knelt. Farther away, the villagers began to slowly walk out of the gates, bewildered, relieved it was over. When they saw him, splendid in the sun, they too fell to their knees.

"Lord Weaver Shadow," said Lily as she, too, went down in the snow.

Weaver addressed her. "I shall be a generous ruler, Lilith. I shall let you live, but there can be only one Shadow in Castle Gloom. You are banished, forever."

Lily nodded. "And Thorn? Mary?"

Weaver waved his hand indifferently. "Take whatever servants you wish."

Iblis put his hand on Lily's shoulder. "Well done, Lily."

"Did I do right, Father? He has everything, and nothing."

Weaver spread out his arms, as if he wanted to embrace all of Gehenna. "This is perfect. It's everything I dreamed of. . . ."

"He dreams," said Lily, looking down at the sleeping figure. "He dreams his perfect dream."

Weaver lay twisted in the snow. The puncture wound was black in his palm, and she could see the tendrils of venom spreading out under his skin, trapping him in his dream forever.

"His perfect dream," she repeated.

The battle was over. With Weaver asleep, the jewel spiders had ceased functioning. They lay scattered across the snow, shining diamonds on a cold white carpet.

Zombies shuffled, a bit confused, like the soldiers. A few of the men poked at the jewel spiders, wary that they might still be alive and ready to spring at them suddenly.

Villagers escaped the webs and gathered in their groups, seeking out others from their homes.

So did the trolls.

They looked as bewildered as everyone else as they untangled themselves from the remains of the webs, rubbing sleep from their eyes and staring around in fright at all the soldiers surrounding them.

They needed to be dealt with, and soon.

Thorn looked down at the sleeping sorcerer. "Weird. He's smiling."

The Skeleton Key hung from his wrist by a black ribbon. Lily untied the bow and returned the key to her own pocket.

Thorn helped her up. "Must be good to get that back, eh? You can see your dad again."

"I've just seen him. He's with my brother in the Dreamtime. I surrendered to Weaver and handed over Gehenna. Now he has everything he ever wanted."

"Do . . . do you intend to wake him?"

She gazed down at her half brother. He looked peaceful; perhaps for the first time in his life, all the rage and hate had disappeared from his brow. "He is happy. Why should I deny him that?"

"I suppose we'd better take him back and—"

A mighty, branch-shaking roar cut Thorn short. The whole of Spindlewood seemed to tremble and thrash. The ground shook with the tread of huge feet.

"Now what?" Thorn complained.

Lily saw huge, lumbering shapes among the trees. "That'll be the troll army."

Trees fell, bent by bull-broad shoulders and splintered under iron-shod boots. The trolls lined up at the edge of the woods, beating drums and roaring, and waving banners and weapons. Some were as tall as birch trees and had bodies wider than the oldest oaks.

And at the head of the group was their king. He raised a hand, and the horde fell silent.

Lily looked around her. "Someone get the trolls who've just woken. We'll hand them over. He'll understand it wasn't our fault. That we've saved them."

Thorn frowned. "He don't look too understanding."

The king wore a necklace of helmets.

Wade snarled. "That's my father's!" He took a step forward, hammer raised to his shoulder. "If he's done anything to him, I'll—"

Thorn stopped him before he got any farther, but Wade was right. The battered horned-demon mask was definitely the baron's. Lily recognized a few of the others hanging from the troll king's neck.

Her zombies, sensing her fear, gathered into a mob. Old Colm stood with his squires. The boys were exhausted, but Lily saw the fire in their hearts shining out. They'd survived a battle and were swollen with courage. The spiders had been defeated; was a troll army so much harder?

Others joined them, all aware that *this* was the real fight. A few riders plodded up, their lances poised for a futile charge. There were crossbowmen and there were spearmen, led by Golgoth. He rushed up to the front. He barely glanced at the waiting trolls, turning instead to Thorn. "Gabriel?"

"Safe," replied Thorn.

Golgoth smiled, visibly relieved. Lily did not understand why Golgoth felt any fondness for the Solar boy. Still, there were many people in the world, so perhaps it was inevitable that *someone* would have warm feelings for Gabriel. How strange that it was an executioner.

"Any advice for us?" she asked him.

Golgoth turned his axes in slow loops, loosening himself up. "Fight well, and hope those trolls choke on our bones when they eat us."

Thorn nudged her. "Got any more magic up those baggy sleeves of yours? Bang out a spell, and we can all go home for supper."

"If I could, I would."

Dott joined them, a twisted, dented old shovel in her hand. She was grinning from ear to ear. "Big bash! Bash some more?"

Lily straightened her robes and faced the line of trolls. "I'll go and talk with the king."

Thorn took her arm. "No! He'll put you in a stew pot."

Dott frowned when she saw what Lily was looking at. She dropped the shovel and took a few steps forward. "Big kin?"

"*King,*" corrected Lily. She and Thorn exchanged glances, worried that she might set something off. If the king thought Dott had been kidnapped . . .

The troll king marched forward; his army waited behind, but stirred impatiently.

Dott moved closer. "Dada?"

Thorn looked at Lily. "You don't think . . . ?"

"Dada!"

The troll king stopped. "Dottir? Dottir here?"

Dott ran to him, laughing in delight.

"What's going on?" asked Wade as he watched Dott embrace the troll king. Big as she was, she barely came up to his waist.

Dott took the king's hand and pulled, saying, "Come meet friends!"

Lily smiled. "Any father would go to war to rescue his daughter, whether troll or human. I think Dott just saved Gehenna."

Thorn shook his head in amazement. "Now that's not something you see every day."

"Thank the Six," muttered Old Colm.

FIFTY-NINE

"Hail Lady Shadow!"

"Hail Lilith, friend to trolls!"

Castle Gloom had never held a feast like it, not in all its thousands of years.

"Hail the witch queen!"

The Great Hall boomed with voices, with cheers and oaths and singing.

There were hundreds of soldiers, both commoners and the Black Guard. They drank and wrestled with one another, the trolls scattered among them. The trolls were trying hard not to win too easily.

Zombies and ghosts mingled with the living. Many of the zombies were wearing armor from the depths of the catacombs, the armor of the Immortals. Most of it was rusty and clouded with cobwebs, but they didn't seem to mind.

And in among them were people who had been rescued from the cloud ship. Had the Great Hall ever seen clothing of such varied and vivid colors? The green of folk from the Coral Isles, the red of those stolen from the south, the Lu Fengese in their flowing blue robes, and the earthy browns and gray of villagers from Thorn's old home, Herne's Forest. Half of the people couldn't understand the other half, their babble of languages trampling over each other's. Yet they knew how to eat and drink and, somehow, join in the chorus of "The Old Duke's Longsword."

Thorn snatched another chicken drumstick from the pile on the table. He elbowed one of the squires aside for the jug of gravy. He poured it over his plate, soaking the bread and the potatoes and turnips until it was an inch deep.

"You're going to explode," commented Wade as he crashed down on the bench beside him.

Thorn burped. "Oh, come down to sit with us commoners, have you, m'lord?"

Wade pulled the drumstick out of Thorn's slippery grasp and bit off a strip. "I won't forget you, Thorn. After all, I'll still need someone to clean my boots."

"I'm honored." Thorn paused and looked up at the high table.

Lily sat in the middle, smiling and nodding at this person and that. On her left was the immense troll king. No chair could accommodate him, so he'd been seated on a tree trunk. Even then his knees were folded up near his chin. On her right were Baron Sable and other nobles, including Gabriel, looking sullenly at the chaos around him.

"Who would have believed it," said Thorn. "A feast even Gabriel can't spoil."

Dott climbed over the table and, to mighty, roof-shaking cheers from the trolls, lifted Gabriel out of his seat and dragged him toward the dance floor. Terrified out of his wits, Gabriel hung in her arms like a rag doll as she swung him around while hundreds stomped their feet and beat their mugs in unison.

"I've heard that Gabriel's father is considering a marriage between them." Wade handed back the now-bare chicken bone. "Makes sense. Dott is technically a princess, and the Solars could use trolls in their war with the Sultanate."

Thorn faced his friend. "So you're now part of the Gehennish Council?" Wade laughed.

Thorn had been there when Baron Sable had marched across the field, embraced Wade, and declared him his son. His legitimate son. Wade now wore the Sable coat of arms on his tunic, the fanged demon, and there was no one prouder in the hall tonight.

"They've reopened West Skull," said Wade.

"Where's that?"

Wade sighed. "Everyone knows West Skull. You know those big halls to the north of the Needle? Just beside Old Keep?"

"Yeah, I think." Thorn frowned. "Isn't it haunted?"

"What part of Castle Gloom isn't?" Wade picked up a sausage and dipped it in Thorn's gravy. "The ghosts there aren't happy about war refugees taking over their haunts. Some of them are even demanding rent."

"What can ghosts do with rent money? That's stupid."

"It's not always coin they ask for. You know Rattler?"

"The one with all those chains?"

"Now he wants a new bell added to his chains at the beginning of every month."

"I'm never gonna get used to this place."

So the population of Castle Gloom was growing. With the living as well as the undead. There would be plenty of work for his family when they arrived come spring.

The troll king laughed, which shook frightened bats out of their roosts. They swirled overhead before vanishing out through the doorways and vents. And they weren't the only ones. Thorn saw Lily rise and slip away.

Where was she off to? Maybe she'd gotten tired of everyone fawning all over her. Thorn refilled his goblet. Things had been bad enough before, with him hardly ever seeing her. Now? He'd be lucky to have two words with her before next winter. And Wade was heading off to Sable's manor up near the Troll-Teeth.

This wasn't how he thought things would turn out.

"Hey, Wade, you think your dad might need a stable boy to look—"

Someone slammed into Thorn's back, knocking him hard into the table, and sending his goblet skittering across the floor.

"Oh, sorry. I didn't see you there."

Lynch Tenebrae stood with two of the older squires. They were dressed in their noble finery—velvet tunics studded with black pearls, and belts embroidered with silver thread. Skulls decorated Lynch's cuffs, and the sword on his hip was a real slicer; the hilt was wrapped in leather and the pommel dotted with onyx. He held out his own cup. "Didn't mean to spill your drink. Have mine."

He tipped it over Thorn's head.

Thorn glared at him, and his hand went to the knife sheathed at his belt.

Lynch leaned over, half drawing his sword. "Try it."

"Don't," warned Wade, putting his hand on Thorn's wrist. Then he stood up. "Get lost, Tenebrae."

Lynch glared at Wade. "You fighting his battles? Now that you've got this"—he flicked at the symbol on Wade's chest—"stamp of approval?"

"What do you want?" Thorn snarled.

Lynch looked around the feast, lip curled in distaste. "Aren't you ashamed of what House Shadow has become? Dining with monsters?" He half drew his sword. "Trolls in Castle Gloom . . . Our ancestors are weeping."

Thorn pointed over at the high table. "Be my guest and kick them out."

Lynch slammed the sword back. "Their time will come, you just wait and see. You think the noble families will let that . . . that white-haired *freak* ruin Gehenna with her peace treaties and magic?"

Thorn grabbed Lynch and thrust him against the wall. "You dare touch Lily, and I'll put an arrow straight into your heart. Got it?"

Lynch shoved him off. He straightened his tunic and cuffs. "You're going to regret laying hands on me, peasant scum." Then he turned and stalked off with his allies.

Wade slapped his back. "Forget him. He's just bitter. And a coward, despite all his tough talk. Didn't see him at the battle." Wade picked a fresh drumstick off the tray and waved it in front of him. "Look, delicious food. Yummy."

Thorn pushed it aside. "You finish it."

Wade shrugged and took a bite.

Thorn headed for the door. His appetite was gone, and he wasn't in the mood for celebrating anymore.

Someone blocked his way.

Who is it now?

"Not like you to leave food behind, boy."

Tyburn leaned against the doorframe, completely at ease, puffing his pipe. Thorn examined him for signs that he had suffered on the cloud ship. Were the lines in his face a little deeper? Was his hair marked with more gray? And did he have a few fresh scars to add to the hundreds his body already wore? It was difficult to tell. His dark eyes remained as sharp and watchful as ever.

"We haven't spoken," said the executioner.

"No, we ain't. I expect you've been busy," said Thorn. "You caught them two other sorcerers?"

Tyburn nodded. "They didn't get far. Not with the whole country looking out for them. They were lucky I caught them before the villagers had their way. They were planning to hack them to pieces and feed them to their pigs."

"And you're just going to stick their heads up on Lamentation Hill?"

"You got a problem with that?"

He did, but he wasn't going to say. What was the point? "It's your job."

"It is indeed."

Thorn glanced back at the crowd. "Where's Golgoth? Thought I'd see him around. Have you . . . done something to him? Merrick will be beside himself if there's been a duel and he missed it."

"There's no quarrel between Golgoth and me," said Tyburn. "He's busy in the stables. He and the Solar boy are heading home tomorrow, first light."

"Or else, right?" suggested Thorn.

He couldn't be sure with Tyburn's mustache, but there may have been a wry smile under it. "Golgoth's no fool."

Thorn didn't understand Tyburn, but then, nobody did. The man trained him, occasionally, and kept an eye on him. Yet he made no demands or requests. It was as if he was just waiting. Waiting for Thorn to change? Was that it?

No executioner lived forever, not even ones serving House Shadow.

So what did Tyburn want from him?

Tyburn pointed off with the stem of his pipe. "You'll probably find her in the Night Garden."

"Thanks." He should hurry, in case Lily didn't hang around for long.

"Wait a moment."

Thorn turned and met Tyburn's gaze.

"You did well," the man said, to Thorn's surprise. "Better than anyone could have hoped or expected. They won't write stories about it, and they won't sing your praises. They don't, for the likes of us."

"I don't expect—"

"Thank you, Thorn." Tyburn held out his hand. "For saving us all."

Stunned, Thorn could only stare at the offered hand. Slowly he took it. "I . . . I did what I had to do."

Tyburn nodded. "Don't we all?"

Thorn did find Lily in the Night Garden.

She sat on a stone bench, half-hidden from the world, with a pile of letters beside her and a lost look on her face.

Thorn didn't move for a minute.

Her black dress shone in the moonlight, and she was daydreaming, swinging her feet back and forth while she pondered. . . .

Pondered what?

Thorn couldn't guess. How could he? How could anyone?

She was just thirteen, a year older than him. She ruled a country. She'd beaten her brother in a war of magic—his spiders against her zombies— and made peace with the troll king.

She'd saved Thorn's life.

Her hair was done up with a series of bone pins. Her long, pure white hair.

"Had enough of the feast?" she called.

Thorn stepped out from the doorway. "How did you know I was there?"

Lily motioned toward Custard. "He sniffs you out."

Thorn peered down the cursing well. "I brought a couple of pennies."

"You thinking of anyone in particular?"

Lynch sprang to mind, but he didn't want to worry Lily about the Tenebrae idiot. "The dancing master. Apparently I have to attend the classes. Old Colm insists."

Lily gazed up, up at the Needle. "Do you know the fairy tale about the evil witch who put a beautiful princess to sleep for a hundred years?"

"Yeah, Wade told me about it. Don't make no sense, though."

"There will be a new version of that tale now, won't there?" said Lily. "'The Prince in the Needle.' It'll be about how an evil witch imprisoned her own brother in a high tower and allowed it to be covered in spider-webs. How she put him into a sleep that will last the rest of his life."

"But he's happy. Happier than he ever was when awake."

Lily wasn't really listening. "They'll add things to the story. About how she's friends with trolls and has an army of zombies and her favorite pet is the ghost of her dog."

Custard barked from under a bush.

"Yes, Custard, I'm sure you'll be a big part of the story." Lily looked at her bare hand. "I gave Weaver my father's ring. At least he has something *real*."

The battle had been just a few days ago, and life was already returning to normal. As normal as a place like Castle Gloom could ever be.

"Did I do right, Thorn?" asked Lily. "He's my brother, and now he's my prisoner. Forever."

"It wasn't just you. We both did what needed to be done. And it could have been much worse for him." Thorn recalled how much he had wanted to kill the sorcerer.

Weaver slept in the very highest room of the Needle. Mary told Thorn they'd dressed him as a Shadow. The belt he wore had belonged to Iblis, his father, and was decorated with crescent moons made from the purest silver. The shoemaker had made him boots of fine calfskin, and there were three antique family necklaces around his neck. He'd been put to rest in the trappings of a ruler.

"Is there any chance he'll wake?" asked Thorn.

"He won't," Lily answered. "There are a dozen small dream weavers in his bedchamber, keeping him asleep. Most of the spiders ceased when he was defeated, but a few lurk nearby and tend him. I suspect they only work if they're close to him."

"The servants are already calling it Cobweb Tower."

"I know."

Sparkling webs covered the roof, and long threads of spider silk drifted in the breeze. Dr. Byle had tried to check on his patient, but he hadn't been able to get up the last flight of steps; the webs were already too thick. It wouldn't be long—a year or two at most—before the tower itself would be cocooned within a cloak of silvery spider silk.

"Lily, you saw how many people he had in his webs. Thousands, and he didn't care about any of them."

"And now Weaver is trapped in a web *I've* made."

"Trapped in a world he *rules*. There are worse prisons, Lily."

"At least he's not alone. My father enters the Dreamtime. To get to know . . . his son." Lily shook her head. "But he doesn't tell me what he finds there, and I don't ask." She drew out a bone pin from her hair and reset it, removing the white curls from her face.

"You gonna leave your hair like that?" asked Thorn.

"We thought it would return to black by itself, but it hasn't." Lily swept her hand over her white locks. "Now I quite like it."

"I thought Mary wanted you to dye it," said Thorn. Actually, she'd done more than ask. He'd heard the pair of them, Mary and Lily, shouting at each other all the way down to the stables. At least that hadn't changed.

"There is no more hiding, Thorn. I am a witch. And I'm proud of it."

"The witch queen," said Thorn. "They're proud of you, too, Lily."

"Not all of them." Lily sighed. "Gehenna's an ancient place, Thorn. It'll take people time to get used to the changes."

Thorn spotted a servant lurking by the doorway. "Looks like they need you back at the Great Hall." He turned to escort her.

"Wait, Thorn." She took his hand. "Let's not go in quite yet." She shooed the servant away.

"But . . ."

"But what, Thorn?" She stepped closer.

Thorn shrugged. He didn't know what to say. "Things get so busy. We don't have time to, y'know, see one another and stuff."

She tightened her grip. "You and I will *always* have time."

"What happens next?" asked Thorn, aware of her closeness.

"This happens." Lily held out her hand. "Are you ready?"

He hesitated. "You're not going to do something . . . magical to me, are you?"

"No, I'm going to do something much, much worse," she declared. "I'm going to teach you to dance."

"Oh. Uh . . ."

She grinned, hand still out, waiting.

Thorn took it, most reluctantly.

And they danced.

ACKNOWLEDGMENTS

So ends our second trip to Castle Gloom. It wasn't just me that brought you there, and I'd like to take a page or two to mention a few other members of House Shadow.

At the high table is my agent, the unstoppable Sarah Davies of the Greenhouse Literary Agency. She helped lay the first paths through the kingdom, and I'd be totally lost without her.

Alongside her is editor-in-awesome Stephanie Lurie, and her companions at Disney•Hyperion. Stephanie helped turn Lily into the darkest of princesses, and Thorn into the boldest of scoundrels.

As great as the Six Princes are my family. My wife, without whom Shadow Magic wouldn't even exist; my youngest, who named the series; and the eldest, who was my first reader and guide in what did and didn't work within Castle Gloom. Then there are Ruth and Alison, surely the greatest of nobles within this realm, and my father and sisters, dukes and duchesses all.

Finally, there's you, my great and wonderful readers. The feedback I've had to my little dark book has been most pleasant (and unexpected!). It seems there are more than a few who believe bats are the next BIG THING. It is your voices that fill the halls of Castle Gloom with cheer and life, and for that I am forever in your debt.

And on the subject of next big things, what do Thorn and Lily (and Hades) have left to do now that Gehenna is at peace?

Well, there is trouble brewing south, in the Sultanate of Fire.

Burning Magic takes our heroes to the vast desert kingdom, where they must aid an old friend to defeat a new enemy. . . .

Coming in Spring 2018

BURNING MAGIC